"Masterfully plotted. . . . *American Woman* is that rarest of creations, a political novel that gives equal weight to its characters' inner and outer lives."
—Laura Miller, Salon.com

"Brilliant. . . . Choi's insightful understanding, vivid description, lyrical use of language, and deft dialogue make it an overall reading pleasure."
—*Oregonian*

"An amazing sense of control . . . [and] a compelling exactness. . . . Fantasy confronts fantasy in the confusion that gives rise to love, to hatred, to politics. And to gunshots."
—*Los Angeles Times*

"What I find so genuinely exhilarating about Choi's project is her old-fashioned intrepidness, her desire to plunder history without apology in order to recover its heart."
—Minna Proctor, *Bookforum*

"Enthralling. . . . It is Choi's skill at getting inside the heads of her protagonists that gives the novel its particular, unsettling appeal [and] . . . grainy psychological depth and texture."
—*Publishers Weekly*

"Choi crafts complex, believable characters whose lives intersect with American politics over issues of loss and betrayal, economics and identity. How it all comes together in an engrossing and emotive story is testament to Choi's deft narration . . . [and] unwavering, original voice."
—*Library Journal*

"Intellectually provocative and vividly imagined."
—*Kirkus Reviews*

Praise for *American Woman*

"[*American Woman*] takes a hard-eyed look at American idealism, and yet its imaginative abundance, its fascination with self-invention, and its portrayal of the landscape as a living, breathing presence provide a quintessentially American sense of possibility." —*The New Yorker*

"A brilliant read. . . . Astonishing in its honesty and confidence. *American Woman* is a haunting book." —*Denver Post*

"With wit and empathy . . . *American Woman* first and foremost examines a young radical's eroding moral certainty. But it also mines the tragicomic elements inherent in good intentions gone murderously awry. Its great achievement is the tale of the shrill, the obnoxious, the armed and dangerous told in a wondrously beautiful voice."

—*Boston Globe*

"*American Woman* is a riveting, deeply affecting portrait of a young antiwar radical and her turbulent times. With uncompromising grace and mastery, Susan Choi renders the intimate moments that bring to life a tale of prodigious sweep. It is a beautifully wrought, exceptionally powerful novel."

—Jhumpa Lahiri, Pulitzer Prize–winning author of *Interpreter of Maladies* and *The Namesake*

"An artful, insightful meditation on the radical impulse. . . . Jenny's wrenching struggle to come to terms with what she's done makes the book resonate with compassion and regret." —Dan Cryer, *Newsday*

"Extraordinary generosity and grace. . . . The author, perhaps as successfully and as powerfully as anyone has, makes us understand how it felt, what it was like. . . . [An] assured, accomplished work."

—*San Diego Union-Tribune*

"A tightly plotted thriller that is also an imaginative thought experiment conducted with the past. . . . Brilliant and often hilarious. . . . Choi has a whole continent, as well as an epoch, in her sights."

—*Chicago Tribune*

"Prepare to be held hostage by Susan Choi's mesmerizing *American Woman*."

—*Vanity Fair*

"A hypnotic, winding route through the scorched emotional landscape of 1974. . . . Choi's prose radiates intelligence as she traces circles around Jenny and Pauline—near enough that you can feel their warmth, but not so close that you'd ever nail them down."

—*Village Voice*

"Susan Choi in this second novel proves herself a natural—a writer whose intelligence and historical awareness effortlessly serve a breathtaking narrative ability. I couldn't put *American Woman* down, and wanted when I finished it to do nothing but read it again."

—Joan Didion

"Choi is a gifted prose stylist and composer of lovely, lingering paragraphs. . . . But even more than that, *American Woman* is a thoughtful, meditative interrogation of . . . history and politics, of power and racism, and, finally, of radicalism."

—*San Francisco Chronicle*

"Riveting. . . . Choi has the rare gift of bringing such notorious moments of history back to life and making them altogether new."

—*Vogue*

"Few writers since Graham Greene have brought such tender, insightful, poetic, intelligent, darkly comic writing to the political thriller. I have to admit this novel made me frantic with suspense—all I wanted to do was jump in and save its unforgettable protagonist from her excruciating destiny."

—Francisco Goldman

About the Author

SUSAN CHOI was born in Indiana and grew up in Texas. Her first novel, *The Foreign Student*, won the Asian-American Literary Award for Fiction and was a finalist for the Discover Great New Writers Award at Barnes & Noble. With David Remnick, she edited an anthology of fiction entitled *Wonderful Town: New York Stories from "The New Yorker."* In 2004, Susan Choi was awarded a Guggenheim Fellowship. She lives in Brooklyn, New York.

ALSO BY SUSAN CHOI

The Foreign Student

American Woman

A Novel

SUSAN CHOI

Perennial
An Imprint of HarperCollins*Publishers*

A hardcover edition of this book was published in 2003 by HarperCollins Publishers.

HarperCollins books may be purchased for educational, business, or sales promotional use. For information please write: Special Markets Department, HarperCollins Publishers Inc., 10 East 53rd Street, New York, NY 10022.

FIRST PERENNIAL EDITION PUBLISHED 2004.

Designed by Sarah Maya Gubkin

The Library of Congress has catalogued the hardcover edition as follows:

Choi, Susan.
American woman : a novel / Susan Choi.—1st ed.
p. cm.
ISBN 0-06-054221-7
1. Hudson River Valley (N.Y. and N.J.)—Fiction. 2. Fugitives from justice—Fiction. 3. Women revolutionaries—Fiction. 4. Kidnapping victims—Fiction. 5. Women terrorists—Fiction. 6. Social isolation—Fiction. 7. Women radicals—Fiction. 8. Young women—Fiction. 9. California—Fiction. I. Title.

PS3553.H584A64 2003
813'.54—dc21

ISBN 0-06-054222-5 (pbk.)

2002191935

04 05 06 07 08 ❖/RRD 10 9 8 7 6 5 4 3 2 1

— For Pete Wells —

Acknowledgments

I am indebted to the Ucross Foundation, Ledig House, and the National Endowment for the Arts for having given me money and time while I was writing this book. I also owe great thanks to Francisco Goldman, Chris Harris, and Hilary Liftin for their enthusiastic support.

And for their indispensable and tireless assistance, which nothing, I fear, can repay, I am enormously grateful to Semi Chellas, Bill Clegg, Terry Karten, Jhumpa Lahiri, Kenna Lee-Ribas, Andrew Proctor, Adam Schnitzer, Steven Stern, and Pete Wells.

Part One

1.

Red Hook is little more than the junction of a couple of roads, with a farm store, a church and graveyard, a diner. And the post office, a small square cement building with RED HOOK NY 12571 spelled out in metal letters across the flat gray façade. He keeps flying through this sparse nexus of structures, first along the south-north road, then, when he finally manages to slow down and make the turn, along the east-west. He has the idea that the rest of the town must lie just farther on, and that the diner and farm store and church and post office are a far-flung outpost, but he keeps ending up twenty-odd miles away in front of a sign welcoming him to a new town, and so he keeps turning back and retracing his route. He doesn't even see houses in Red Hook, just fence lines along the roads, a dirt drive sometimes winding away. Some of the fences contain fields and some just grass and grazing animals, but everywhere there are smooth humps of hills and distant darknesses of untouched woodland, interesting vistas to the harried urban man. He's enjoying tearing up and down these roads, like swinging hard through the same arc again and again, and catching the same glimpse of the sorry little huddle at the center point, and he keeps at it for a while pointlessly, up down, zoom zoom, but finally he's forced to conclude that he's not missing anything. At the post office he parks and goes in to take a look at her box. If there were a tiny window in the little metal door he would stoop and peer in, but there isn't. At the diner he orders coffee and a jelly donut and tries to figure out where all the people live. A man in overalls asks another man at the counter how to get somewhere. "I'm from over-river," he explains. Back in his car Frazer studies the map. The Hudson lies west of here, about a ten-minute drive on these roads. Might be pretty. Frazer knows he is possessed of the skills to solve such problems as the one that lies before him. He can recognize, for example, that right now he is looking too hard at the wrong thing, and missing the point. He needs to do something else, maybe even give up for the day, find a bar and a motel, and start fresh in the morning. He should have realized that she wouldn't live here; she wouldn't want to be too near the post office. Yet she wouldn't want to travel too far. This is the sort of zero-sum compromise she makes all the time; Frazer knows this about her, having been subjected to the same flawed formulation. Trust Frazer or spurn him? A little of both? He notices, thinking of the man in overalls from over-river, that there aren't so many bridges: just four in the 150-mile stretch from the city to Albany. One lies due west of here, but Frazer's willing to bet that Jenny wouldn't cross the river for her mail. Too much traffic concentration, too confined; there's no good exit from a bridge. He puts an X on Red Hook, then estimates a half hour's driving distance and draws a circle around Red Hook with that radius. He does this mostly to amuse himself, but also because he believes in the inflexibility, predictability, knowability of people. They never stray far from their familiar realms of being. The most shocking act, closely examined, is just a louder version of some habitual gesture. No one is ever "out of character." That idea just makes Frazer laugh.

The next morning he rises early and nearly pulls the room down in the course of his exercise. He usually travels with a pair of very small, very heavy barbells, but when he finds himself without them he does other things. Five hundred jumping jacks. One-armed push-ups. He'll stand on his head for a while, and feel the pressure of the blood in his skull and the fumes of last night's alcohol steaming out of his pores. On this day he's well into the spirit of things when he grabs the bathroom door frame and pulls himself into the air, legs thrust forward a little because he's tall and the door frame is small. Then the molding around the frame—after holding him for a beat during which he does nothing but hang there, blinking confusedly, as if sensing what's coming—peels away with a terrible shriek of nails extracting from wood. Although the disaster is preceded by that beat, when it happens it happens all at once, before he can think or find his legs, and he lands heavily on his ass like a sack of grain. There is abrupt, alarming pain. He keels over sideways and lies there curled up, half of him on one side of the door and half of him on the other. He has the yellowish linoleum of the bathroom floor against his ear, and his face is contorted, partly an effort to keep the tears that have filled his eyes from streaming down his cheeks, but they do anyway.

He gives up and cries a little, quietly. In truth, sacrosanct as his exercise is, he is a little embarrassed by it—perhaps because it is so sacrosanct. He remembers being surprised once by Mike Sorsa, in the apartment they'd shared in North Berkeley. He'd always waited until Sorsa left for class, and he'd heard the door slam downstairs and Sorsa's footsteps cross the creaking wood porch and drop onto the sidewalk, but on this morning, almost an hour after Sorsa had left, he'd unexpectedly come home. Frazer had been so deeply enveloped in his routine and in the music he'd put on to accompany himself he hadn't heard anything until Sorsa was standing there in the doorway. Sorsa had just stared for a long minute before saying, "Hey, man," and continuing down the hall to his room, but Frazer had glimpsed the expression on his face, one that mingled slight embarrassment with incompletely concealed contempt, as if Frazer had been masturbating frantically into the couch cushions rather than simply standing with his feet apart and his head bowed, curling the barbell and counting off repetitions. Frazer's body had been silver, he imagined, with coursing sweat, and his smell—a sharp but sweet smell, not like the smell of unwashed socks or underwear—had probably filled the small room. And he had been humiliated, though he had not stopped, nor had the feeling of humiliation surprised him. He knows he is a person misperceived as a caricature. The contour of his impression on the world has always been dominated by an enlargement of his physicality, the way a hunchback is dominated by his hump, or a goitrous man by his goiter. And so Frazer, in the circles he moves in, is sometimes viewed as a clown.

But what has never occurred to these people, the ones who consider him "just a jock," or, better, "just a dumb jock," is that he doesn't hang out just with jocks. If he were "just a jock," that's just what he'd do, and he doesn't.

This thought makes him feel better. He gets to his feet and begins testing things. Head turns, knee bends. Everything basically works but it makes him sweat bullets. He's really landed on his coccyx, not his ass. The vestigial tail: a segmented pile of calcium, like something weird ants would construct. Now it's been dented or crushed, or maybe snapped clean off the rest of his skeleton. Well, there's nothing he can do about that. For him, this is as good as Problem Solved. He lumbers Frankenstein-style to his bag and eats a handful of pills so that he won't, scrunched up with pain, do anything to hurt himself further. Let the healing begin.

When he starts feeling better he tries to reattach the molding to the door frame, but the nails have bent too much, and the door frame is too splintered. He ends up using the piece of molding to knock down the big dangling slivers. Then he starts packing, but unhappy confusion has overtaken him. He's scooted right past feeling physically better into feeling good enough to notice he feels bad in some less tangible way. He is a little too upset about breaking the door frame, because he meant to keep this room, in the eventuality he found her today. They'll need a place to talk. He could put the DO NOT DISTURB sign on the door, but there doesn't seem to be such a sign. He could drop by the office and ask the woman not to clean, although this is just what he wants to avoid: seeming strange. The night before it had made him feel very good, very safe, to find this motel, an anonymous cinder-block box lying off to one side of the state highway that ran north out of Red Hook. The woman at the desk had been so gray-skinned and blank-eyed and vague, so obviously distracted by the demands of the small children screaming in the back room, so clearly unable to spare any amount of mental energy on her rare customers, that Frazer had known the motel was a true sanctuary; he'd paid her in cash for one night but had already decided, at that point, to stay for two. Now he feels skinless and broken. He wonders if all his efforts to think like Jenny are making him into a Jennylike person. But that isn't fair; she's not foolish or helpless. Far from it. Frazer thinks of her eyes. He used to answer that self-defining male question, What part of the woman most matters to you? (Tits, ass, hair; for some disturbing men, feet.) *Eyes*, without hesitation. Eyes, because the eyes are intelligence and because Frazer knows, now, that he is only a fairly intelligent man, intelligent enough for vast ambition, perhaps not intelligent enough to achieve it. He remembers the period of his life during which he recognized this, the period during which he was courting Carol, in the face of what you'd have to call resistance. No—rejection. You'd have to call it rejection. Against which he'd kept swimming, head down, fins paddling. Not free of the persistent question: Why? When there were other women—on the bus, in his classes, on the sidelines and waggling pom-poms. Other women who *liked* him. But he'd come to understand, perhaps landing on the sidewalk in front of Carol's building at the hands of her then-live-in-boyfriend, perhaps contracting pneumonia while hitchhiking cross-country one Christmas to surprise Carol at the home of her parents, that there was no *why*, there was no choice, there was only the body's nonnegotiable instinct for self-preservation. He'd needed Carol, because she was the smartest girl he'd met then, at the tender age of twenty. And he hadn't been wrong, then, although the subsequent decade has taught him and changed him.

It was a motel room like this that he and Jenny had stayed in. No, that's not true. He only wants the bridge to the thought, so he might seem to come upon it accidentally. Apart from both being motel rooms, the two places could not be less similar. Outside the window, past the roof of his car, he sees the same undulating, untouched pastureland and woodland he drove through for hours yesterday. The rare car passing by on the road seems no louder than his own exhalation. That other room had sat across the highway from Kennedy Airport, shaken by the thunder of planes, awash all night in orange light that had leaked around the edges of the curtains and streamed like fingers down the walls and on the bed. It had been so unendingly loud, like a war zone, that they could hardly hear each other, but they had argued uncontrollably anyway, as if they both had a death wish, and longed to be overheard by their neighbors. It would have taken a lot more than their fighting to attract someone's attention in that place; that was why he had chosen it. In the morning he had jerked awake with the gray dawn, only a few hours after going to sleep. He had watched her strange face. Not beautiful. But disabling. He had felt brand-new longing, as if they were back at the beginning, but with everything else sheared away, all other persons, objects, events.

Wake up, he'd said, closing his hand carefully on her shoulder. Then he'd shaken it, in a quick, utilitarian way, and her eyes had flown open. The mortification he'd seen there was like death.

He stands up, plowing straight through the pain in his back, and strides out of the room. In the office he pays the woman for a second night and hands her the molding. "It fell off," he begins, but she just shrugs and drops it into her wastebasket.

June 4, 1974. This does not turn out to be the day he sees her, but it is the day he finds her. The simplicity of it amazes him. For all her precautions, all her veils upon veils dropped over her acts, he can still see the shape of them perfectly. She's like a Boy Scout who thinks he's an Indian; he imagines her walking bac. sweeping out her footprints as she goes, leaving clear arcs in . dust. The same hieroglyphic again and again: I'M AFRAID.

He starts with the motel proprietress: He's an architecture buff. Any nice big old houses around here?

She looks at him blankly, or maybe it's searchingly. He can almost see her detaching the far-flung tentacles of her overtaxed brain from their many deep worries, slowly reeling them in, to assist him.

Maybe over-river? he adds, wanting to sound native.

Oh no, she says quickly. No, the rich folks, they all lived on this side.

Ah.

You could try in Rhinebeck, she offers hopefully.

Is that where the rich folks lived? Rhinebeck?

Um, no, she's shaking her head.

But I could try asking somebody there, he says, watching her nod.

Although he leaves the motel office sighing, he is suddenly full of the intimation that he could not go wrong now if he wanted to. He's looking for a Japanese girl, after all, in a lily-white corner of upstate New York. The course of events won't contain any more random padding. In Rhinebeck he is assaulted all at once by incredible hunger, and he stops short of going into the public library and instead enters the coffee shop and takes a booth by the window. He eats with his eyes on his watch, both impatient and reluctant. Yesterday, the errand felt like a game, with its pleasant outfield intervals of waiting. Today the outcome is clear, and he's stalling. He's surprised by the possibility that he doesn't want to see her. No: He's surprised by the fact she provokes any feeling at all. For years she's been marginal, right? Even before that, she was nothing important. She's like a job he once had that he's finished with. He's sometimes been vaguely offended by how far out of her way she went to show she'd never wanted his help, but beneath this affronted feeling he's very rarely wondered where she was. He's certainly never cared.

akes a walk around town before he visits the
, and even after sitting through the eager dis-
ocal librarian, small and gray and darting as a
ne for the ten-thirty tour. He sits awkwardly in a
nair on the narrow sun porch, hands between his
knees. is large and crude; though elaborate with colored trim, shutters, shingles, and finely wrought lengths of cast-iron lace, the house is neither huge nor grand but eccentric, delicate, badly deteriorating and slightly sunken in the overgrown grass, as if adrift on a pale yellow sea. It's called Wildmoor, which seems very appropriate, though he guesses it was named in better days. He had approached it with legs of rubber. Just his coccyx injury, he thinks angrily. Fists balled to conceal wet palms. Now that he's here, he can't believe this is it. He can't imagine her here. The librarian had told him about two other area mansions in addition to this that give tours, and countless more that are private, gated and guarded. He knows she's in one of these fortresses, gold-leafing the fireplace or restaining the sideboard or whatever it is that she does, but he can't believe it's this place, where anybody can pay to walk in. And yet he has a wrenched-up, anxious gut, growing worse every minute. In the off-chance he has to be ready. He knows that she'll know better than to scream and run off when she sees him. She's a wreck, but she's a tough wreck, and good at thinking on her feet. They'll improvise something, a stage play, and then they'll exit unobserved into the wings. They'll talk. In an artificial dusk of velvet drapes.

His only companions on the tour are an elderly retired couple from Kingston. They introduce themselves and smile brightly until he's forced to converse. "I'm a carpenter," he says, wondering whether he can get away with this. He used to go out on big house-painting jobs with Sorsa, and he learned fancy words: *oriel, pediment.* He can never remember what they mean.

"You build houses?" the woman asks.

"Yes."

"This is a fascinating house! It's almost one hundred years old."

"Sort of a busman's holiday for you, isn't it," her husband says heartily.

Frazer wonders what the hell the man means by this. He feels himself sweating. He keeps wanting to look around for Jenny, but he's aware that his eyes are darting like a freak's, and he wills them to stop. "Yes," he says, and the couple both laugh. He can't tell if they're laughing at him or "with him." He's always despised that expression.

The tour is led by an excited lady with a nimbus of reddish hair and a pair of cat's-eye glasses on a chain. She and the couple turn out to be kindred spirits, adept in the same obscure language—porte cochere, rococo. The situation worsens for Frazer, because the threesome, elated by their companionship, feel guilty and strive to include him. "Mr. Jones," the wife inquires, again and again, giving him a start the first time because he's forgotten saying this is his name. "What do you think of these gables? Would you do them this way? Do any persons these days still like fish-scale shingles? Where on earth have you found them available?" It turns out that the last surviving member of the family, a lady named Dolly, still lives in the house, "but in her wonderful generosity, because she has always been such a good friend to this community, has opened the house to the public, for tours twice a week." Frazer knows what this means. The woman ran out of money. The tour cost three dollars, "to contribute to upkeep," the guide had said, seeming faintly embarrassed as she took the bills from them. But it doesn't look as if there's much upkeep. Frazer would bet that the money buys groceries.

They come into a room at the back of the house, startlingly empty and bright, with two great windows and a paint-spattered cloth on the floor. Frazer's pulse accelerates before he knows why. Everything else in the room has been pushed to one side, away from the drop cloth, neatly arranged though cramped up. The guide has been breathlessly narrating the objects they encounter: "Nineteenth-century Mexican beggar's bowl. 925-sterling-silver filigree. Of course, a beggar in nineteenth-century Mexico couldn't afford such a thing; the term *beggar's bowl* is fanciful." Frazer stares at the drop cloth, and the dots of paint on it. "What's happening here?" he blurts out.

Although he's interrupted her, the guide is incandescent; she is delighted to have piqued his curiosity. "It must be clear to you, Mr. Jones, that the house is in need of attention. There's so much to be done, and we are tackling things one at a time. I was just about to draw your attention to these beautiful windows; notice the light, so much brighter here than in the rest of the house. This room, seventeen feet square with nearly sixteen-foot ceilings, was the painting studio of Mrs. Brinson Henley; here she strived to capture the light of the great Hudson Valley. Notice that the panes are not leaded; they are all in one piece, very rare for that time, and very heavy. In the course of the decades these panes have warped away from their frames, and we have had tragic water damage as a result." She stops for breath and looks at them solemnly. The retired couple seems stricken with horror. Frazer himself feels his lungs empty out. Slowly, calmly, he looks around the room. He fixes his gaze on each object, as if picking it up in his hands. A cushioned chair. A floor lamp. A huge, dark, oily cabinet. The beggar's bowl. Nothing here that is hers.

"But now," the guide resumes, clasping her hands at her breast, "we have an Oriental girl who's helping us with restoration." Her voice grows confiding. "It's just *beautiful*, watching her work."

IT HAD BEEN some years before, long enough ago for a full cycle of students to have matriculated and departed in the interval, that the Manhattan university near Frazer's current apartment, upon receipt of an endowment of undisclosed millions from a once-athletic, now nostalgic alumnus, announced plans for a huge new gymnasium. The gymnasium would be the university's first building project in a very long time, and great hopes and intents were attached to it. Its neo-Victorian style would serve as a reproach to the chill modernism then dominating architectural design. Its material, red sandstone, would echo the elegant yet whimsical Furness Palace of Fine Arts in Philadelphia. It would employ stonecutters, an endangered breed of craftsman. It would have the upward thrust and rich ornamentation of a cathedral, dedicated as it would be to the tabernacle that is the human body; and its great window frames would contain, instead of inspirational religious images, inspirational secular phrases painted onto the panes. It would take up a full city block, in the midst of the adjacent black ghetto, much of which the university owned.

To be fair, the university had not left the ghetto entirely out of its thinking. It had plans for relocating those families whose buildings would have to be razed. It had also declared that ghetto inhabitants would be allowed to benefit from the gym's facilities; that the gym was being placed in that spot not merely for lack of an alternative but to serve as a "bridge" to what the university called "its community." Informational meetings were held for community members; some time later, a scale model was unveiled. Despite its location in the lobby of the university's white-marble library, situated squarely on its green, fortressed quad, a sprinkling of curious community members ventured over to look, with ideas of enrolling their children in "kinderswim" classes, or themselves for the use of the weight room, all of which possibilities had first been suggested by university spokesmen. At first glance the scale model was impressive, even exciting. It did look like a beautiful church. On closer perusal the more design-minded of the observers noticed that the accompanying blueprints described a side entrance as a "community access point." This was just to "streamline traffic flow"; students also had an "access point"—a larger one, by chance at the front of the building. It additionally emerged that the university had decided, for reasons having to do with insurance, that community members would not be able to use the pool, or enroll their younger members in kinderswim class, after all, though they would probably be welcome to use the exercise machines for an annual membership fee, at particular hours.

Even these disappointments might have been absorbed in due

time if it hadn't been for the aphorisms on the windows. Judging from the model, the aphorisms faced out, like ads, or parental exhortations. No one was sure what TALKERS ARE NO GREAT DOERS was supposed to be saying, but all agreed it seemed somehow insulting, as if the neighborhood people were morons, or crooks.

There was, eventually, an act of vandalism. Somebody smashed the glass box enclosing the model, and then the model itself. It might have ended there, if the student community hadn't by then become aware of the project. The student community at that time was becoming aware of a lot of things: the university's role in the production of the weapons of mass destruction then raining down on certain parts of southeast Asia. The university's friendly accommodation of recruiters from the Central Intelligence Agency. The university's staggering whiteness. Because most of the students were themselves white, and from equally white places, they hadn't noticed this aspect at first, but upon venturing further and further afield from classrooms and dorms, perhaps drawn forth by nothing more than the desire for a snack in the middle of the night, they had discovered that a vast black neighborhood encircled their school, and this had made it easier, somehow, to notice the disproportion of whites on the campus. Global forces, bad ones, seemed everywhere suddenly. And it was all very hard to understand, but the gymnasium—because it was a thing, because it was nearby, because it just seemed really stupid—was easy to understand. And so the gym became a catalyst for action, though soon, with the seizures of buildings and hapless staff members and the paintings of banners and the smashings of windows, and the multiplication of incendiary students and the absence from the fray of "community members"—in spite of the students' claim and the university administrators' fear that the community comprised a sort of secret weapon awaiting deployment—the battle was about any number of things having nothing to do with the gym.

And it was at around this same time that Rob Frazer, on the other side of the country, was well into his first—hopefully not his last—bout of genuine celebrity. It was Frazer's theory that the vast majority of people live a decade behind the times, happily, and that a tragic few live ahead of the times, miserably, and are misunderstood and punished. And then there are the people on the leading edge, riding it forward, like surfers, and this was what Frazer was, in his own estimation. Since the dawn of his maturity he'd been seeing his own particular obsessions bloom into cultural obsession all around him—no more in response to his presence than his presence was in response to these developments. It was just sync, a wave traveling forward that he was inside of. Frazer had arrived as an undergraduate at Berkeley on the football ticket, another side of beef with the jock's guaranteed C-minus like a rubber floor that bounced him back no matter how much he fucked off. Double-portion privileges the first time through the chow line and that was the end of respect as he knew it. He'd ditched football at the end of his first year—Berkeley, like many high-minded schools, wasn't really permitted to base acceptance on football, and so they couldn't throw him out when he refused to play the game. He moved into bona fide student life, never quite got a toehold, moved toward nonpompommed women, fought for years for his toehold, moved leftward through politics—but here he had his toehold, capped to his toe and awaiting the rest. When it came, it would hold on to *him*.

Because Frazer had had an idea, and though the anticapitalists and the anti-imperialists and the antiracists and the antiexploitationists who should have been his natural allies thought him a boneheaded joke, an irrelevance, he knew that his moment would come, and it did. The moment came, surprisingly soon, when people saw he'd been right about the exploitation of athletes in professional sports, and the way it rhymed in so many respects with racism, and the way the exceptional status of black athletes proved the rule of American fear and loathing of the rest of black people. He'd been right about all of this—not being a black man, not being a great or even a consistently good athlete, not being some politico-sociotheorist, just being a hyperactive middle-class white kid with the scary muscularity of a blue-collar thug and a brain that, though flawed, was a lot better at thinking than most people thought. Stubbornly, he'd gotten himself into the sociology department, stubbornly started a mimeographed, smeary newsletter, at first just his own trademarked ranting and raving. Then he'd written his first book, a compendium, typos corrected, of the newsletter. Gotten it published by a very small press, sold it out of the back of his car in the stadium parking lot. Been abused by a number of sports fans, and, unsurprisingly to him, intensely supported by more and more athletes. Swung his way into the socio doctoral program and started getting submissions to the newsletter, and inquiries from like-minded writers who thought he could help them—and it turned out he could. And then, all of a sudden and almost too fast, had come Mexico City's raised fists and the threat of the boycott, his loud support, a pipe bomb through his window, a national news crew the same afternoon, and, crowningly, a denunciation from a Republican senator and former football star who called him, Frazer, a sour-grapes football failure turned Commie destroyer of the American way. Which meant, just like that, fame.

After Berkeley he'd gotten hired at a small East Coast college as athletic director, over the unanimous objection of the corps of individual team coaches. He was fired before he'd worked a single day, with a full year's salary as severance—a full year's pay without work! Carol had wanted to move to Manhattan, and he'd been able to take her there, set up an office for himself, get the newsletter going again—now with the senator's denunciation as part of the masthead—and start writing his next book. He found that he knew people—academic types drawn to his anti-intellectual ass-kicking hard-left persona, professional athletes he'd helped learn how to voice their critiques of the system while negotiating lucrative contracts, sportswriters who knew who he knew, and who amusingly abased themselves before him. The fracas over the gymnasium at the local university hadn't initially grabbed his allegiance—by this time it had dragged through three semesters and two student strikes—but he'd eventually gone over to find out about it, and one thing had led to another, and in the end the university, in its abject confusion, had hired him, as athletic director and as sop to the student insurgency, in the hopes that his reputation as a left-leaning white with black friends would be helpful to them in the course of a now-labyrinthine negotiation schedule. Frazer had reveled for a few weeks in his power, given about a hundred interviews to local media, and then, as all was threatening to cool, hired a known black Muslim and world-ranked 800-meter runner as his co-director, and been fired again, this time for almost twice his previous severance, as he made them buy out his whole contract. He gave the runner a chunk of the money, gave more interviews, and continued to settle with Carol into their university-owned apartment, which they'd decided to keep, by whatever legal or illegal means necessary.

It was a nice apartment, with high ceilings and creaking french doors and a claw-footed tub in the bathroom. Calling Carol that night from his Rhinebeck motel room, Frazer thought happily of its shambling extent. "Hi," he said when she finally answered. "Did you pick up milk yet?"

"Oh, my God." He could hear Carol dragging the phone across the room and down the hall, pictured the cord slithering over the rug, catching on a chair leg and going taut until Carol yanked it impatiently. On cue, something crashed in the background. "Fuck!" Carol said. Frazer had bought Carol the fifty-foot phone cord just after they'd gotten married. He'd come home and found her lying on their bed, fully dressed, sobbing at the ceiling. It was like Carol to cry flat on her back, arms and legs splayed, eyes open and angry. She wasn't the kind of woman to roll into a ball or hide under a blanket. "What is it, baby?" he'd asked her. She'd said, with difficulty, but vehemently, "What about my privacy? Goddammit! What if I want to be alone?"

She'd gotten the phone down the hall to the bathroom. Carol had turned the bathroom into a sort of private office; it was full of water-warped feminist books and all manner of atmospheric scenting equipment. Frazer liked to go in there when she wasn't home, finger her little incense bowls and read the labels on her candles. That sort of stuff generally got lost or broken in the rest of their apartment. He heard her push the bathroom door firmly shut. "Goddammit, Robbie! Where are you?"

"I said, did you pick up milk yet?"

"Oh, Rob. It's pouring out."

"Will you go get milk, please?"

There was a long pause, during which Frazer waited for Carol to accept that the rain wasn't his fault, that the milk was in her interest, too, and that for all these reasons, she couldn't yell at him. "Okay," she said finally. "Fifteen minutes. But don't blame me if—"

"Later, Carol," he said. She sighed and hung up.

Frazer looked at his watch, bounced onto the bed, bounced back to his feet. Fifteen long minutes. As usual, given a very brief, exact amount of time to kill, he found idleness unbearable. He opened the door to his room and stood watching the fading light darken the fields on the far side of the road. Out here the air cooled so quickly at sundown; he felt it seeping through his shirt, raising the small hairs on his forearms. He smelled damp earth. The rhythmic creaking of crickets seemed to slowly fade in, although he knew it was only himself, tuning in to the sound. The air was passing into that stage of particulate darkness, as if made of fine charcoal dust. He saw a firefly drifting slowly across the parking lot, parallel to the ground, and stepped forward suddenly, confused, feeling through the outskirts of his skin the pristine sense memory of his own cupped hands, closing together, the whisper of the insect on his palm—

When he remembered to look at his watch it had been twenty minutes. He went back into his room, which now seemed to blaze like a stage in the deepening dusk. Carol answered on the first ring and he heard the hiss of wet tires on wet pavement, all the boomerang howls of the traffic on Broadway. He'd left the door to his room standing open—this was how confident he'd come to feel in this place—and he stood for a moment ignoring Carol's voice, listening just to the racket of the city in the background while keeping his gaze on the motionless night. He couldn't remember the last time he'd so palpably appreciated the drama of the telephone.

"There was a guy talking and talking. I practically had to glare him to death to get him to get off the phone. Do you think he's still hanging around? He went into the deli and now I don't remember seeing him leave."

"Calm down, baby." Frazer inched over and pushed the door closed with his toe, feeling regret. The stale motel lamplight closed around him.

"Don't tell me to calm down."

Frazer laughed. One of his favorite things about Carol was her ceaseless narration of grievances; he never wondered what was on her mind. That kind of mysterious woman was for hopelessly loving, not living with.

"So this situation isn't quite as entertaining as it was two days ago. For one thing I'm going stir-crazy. I'm scared to leave her alone in the house. I'm all freaked out so I can barely concentrate. I can't even imagine what she's doing right now."

"She's not doing anything. She's doing whatever it was she was doing when you left."

"Oh, great! Jesus, Robbie. She might be running up and down Broadway completely naked this very minute. I keep looking around expecting to see her go by with her hair on fire or something. I'd lock her in but we don't have the right kind of lock."

"The last thing she'd ever do is leave the house. Are you kidding? She won't even get up off the floor."

"Now she does. She's obsessed with the streetside windows."

"Keep her the fuck away from the windows."

"No, the blinds are down, but she keeps creeping over to them and kind of perching there all stiff and wide-eyed like she's some kind of woodland animal listening for something. I swear I've seen her nose twitching. You know how squirrels look when they're really freaked out? She looks like that."

"More evidence there's no chance she'll run out of the house."

"You're probably right but I wish she would." Carol laughed a little.

"Hang in there, baby."

"If she isn't in squirrel posture she's ranting at me about our shitty security. The super was out in the hallway mopping and she went off about how our place isn't secure and we're really fucking her, blah blah, she won't be surprised if it's all a fucking setup, blah blah. And the worst is she ruined my paper—after you left I went and got the Sunday paper to have something to do so I wouldn't go nuts and then I went out again for about *five minutes* and when I came back she had totally ruined it."

"She's just clipping the coverage about herself. She likes doing that."

"No! That's not even what she was doing! She had the paper spread all over the floor and she was crawling around on it with a Magic Marker X-ing out people's faces and going 'Pig! Pig!' She fucked up the whole thing."

"Jesus. Who'd she X out?"

"How should I know? Henry Kissinger."

"What else is she doing?"

"Not much. Crying. Smoking."

"Why don't you just talk to her a little? Make friends."

"Oh, fuck off."

"You were getting along great when I left."

"Yeah, well, then you left. I don't know if it's because I'm another woman or what, but as soon as you left she started to really antagonize me. Pulling rank. In *our* goddamn apartment."

"What do you mean, pulling rank?"

"I don't even want to talk about it."

"Telling you what to do?"

"I sincerely don't want to discuss it. I'll get mad. We fought, and then we stopped talking, and now we're in a truce, I guess. She's pretty much staked out the living room and I'm hiding in the bedroom."

Frazer lay back on the motel bed and laughed. "Oh, man. You know what? I love you."

"And I hate your guts. When are you coming back? You said you were going up *for the day*."

"You haven't even asked me how it's going."

"I'm sorry," Carol said. "How's it going?"

There was often this moment in their conversations, when Frazer's love for Carol, or what he thought of as his love for her—perhaps it would be better described as his gratitude, for their script, his role, her familiarity, the fixed rhythm and ritual of their life against which he felt a freedom he'd never felt when he was alone—unexpectedly vanished. It was usually due to some excess of one of the very constants on which their married life was built. In this case, her selfishness of outlook, which prevented her from ever fully registering what he was doing, even when it was for her benefit. It was true that he had fallen in love with her for the same reason: She was, in her selfishness, extremely entertaining. And generally, except at moments of weakness, he valued nothing else so much. But at those moments of weakness he wanted something entirely different. Some clearer sense of their partnership.

"Really," Carol was saying. "Tell me everything that's happened. Have you found her?" He hated it even more when she sprang to pro forma attentiveness; sometimes, like now, he found it actually insulting.

"Just about, but I'll be a few more days. And I think we've spent enough time on the phone. You run on home and try to be a good girl."

"Oh, Robbie. I really do want to hear—"

"Bye baby," he said, and hung up.

The next day he returned to Wildmoor and found a rusty chain across the drive between two posts. On one of the posts hung a little sign that read, HOUSE TOURS MONDAY AND FRIDAY, 10 A.M. AND 2 P.M. PLEASE COME BACK! He idled a long minute with the end of his rental car sticking into the road before he had the presence of mind to back up onto the shoulder and turn off the engine. Then he ran over to the sign in the manner of someone being targeted by sniper fire. Even after seeing the state of genteel, mild dilapidation the house was currently in he couldn't help thinking of those tales of miserly paranoia and weirdness on the part of the wealthy and old. Fifty cats, foot-long fingernails, and a million dollars sewn into a mattress. Cars rusting all over the lawn and high-tech motion-detection trip wires concealed in the dirt. That he couldn't see cameras bolted to the trees didn't mean they weren't there. But still, he couldn't resist getting close to that sign. It was a flat piece of wood so weathered it looked almost silver, with the letters painted on it in black. It wouldn't be right to say he recognized the handwriting: Rather, he recognized the ability to have unrecognizable handwriting. Jenny could have been a professional sign painter. Back when they'd all lived in Berkeley she'd done Mike Sorsa's truck for the house-painting business. That time seemed far too remote, haloed in nostalgic gold light, to have been barely six years ago. She'd been nineteen years old. Weeks's startling new girlfriend. Frazer remembered sitting with her in the driveway of the Stannage Street house while she perched on an overturned milk crate, with the little cans of bright paint all around. He'd first met her just a few months before, when he'd needed somebody to paint him a banner for an action he'd planned to disrupt Berkeley's homecoming game. Sorsa had brought her and Weeks to a meeting and afterward she'd come up to him and said, "I'll do your sign"—a flat statement, not a question or an offer. Like an asshole, he'd grinned at her; he'd assumed she was flirting with him. Later, he'd watched her slash out one three-foot letter after another on his huge bolt of muslin, kicking the bolt progressively unrolled with her foot, this slight quiet girl creating a brash declaration at a feverish rate. She'd been working with a piece of soft chalk glued to the end of a stick—just to sketch out the letters beforehand, make sure of the spacing. The stick was so she didn't have to crawl around on the muslin; she worked too fast for that. She'd fully grasped the assumption in Frazer's grin, had coldly ignored it, and then, for a long time, him. He'd had to campaign hard before she'd talk to him again. The banner, of course, had been spectacular. Because flawless, remarkably authoritative. He'd felt like kissing her the day of the action, when the whole hundred-foot length of it, rolled up and rigged with some system of weights that she'd thought of, had regally unfurled, on cue.

He touched a finger to the letters on the sign: bone-dry and dusty. He dared himself to step over the chain and go running up the drive and let the fates do the rest. Then he got in the car, turned it back around toward Rhinebeck, and drove slowly away. When he had first been getting to know Weeks and Jenny he had been something of a hanger-on, a haunter of them; he'd known that. That they hadn't truly liked him, or wanted him. He hadn't let it stand in his way. There are so many things one can do to impose upon people, to carefully but firmly attach oneself, when the people offer no opening or encouragement at all. He had thought of it, then, as politics by other means; he'd needed Weeks, and needed to be counted as one of Weeks's friends. It hadn't bothered him to appear at their house unannounced, with a six-pack of beer or a small bag of weed or nothing but his relentlessly cheerful, impenetrable, apparent obtuseness. Many times, before he'd persuaded Carol to marry him, he'd gone to her house after being violently, permanently banished. "Don't you know you're not wanted here?" she'd once shouted. To which he'd shouted back, "Why should I care whether I'm wanted in the place I want to be?"

Heading back to Rhinebeck, roughly north, the road ran parallel to the river for a while, perhaps half a mile inland, but soon began to angle east, leaving the river even farther behind. When Frazer saw a fork to his left, heading west, he took it. The new road was narrower and poorer in quality; if he was driving west, Wildmoor now lay south of him, in the strip of forest defined by the Rhinebeck road, the river, and this road. It occurred to him that this road, with its long graveled patches and deep potholes and near-invisible center line, might be leading him to some back entrance to the Wildmoor property, and he began to feel light again, carried forward by instinct. He watched through the trees to his left for some point of entry but saw only a fieldstone wall running alongside, with many stumbles and gaps, and beyond it lush, silvery grass and then dense green trees. The road was angling more north than west after all; eventually, after what had probably been a few miles, he saw the river just beside him through the trees. The road hit a stop sign, and then the trees closed in, and he had entered a town. He took the first left and dropped nearly nose-first down a steep side street that ended abruptly in a tiny parking lot. He parked and got out of the car.

The hill he had come down was thick with trees but showed the sides of a few houses farther up; he seemed to be standing on the last of several large stair-steps to the river. Beyond the parking lot the railroad tracks ran nearly level with the water. The parking lot was attached to what he realized was a small stone railroad station. The side street he'd come down, which had seemed to dead-end at this lot, turned sharply left again, and climbed back toward the town. He could smell the slight salinity of the river, its hidden sea tides. Because it lay now directly in front of him, he was blinded by the light from its surface. And behind him, the leafy, secretive town. The station had no company on the sharp elbow of road; this small purchase between the bluff the town clung to and the water would not have accommodated anything else. Frazer felt the pleasant dislocation he felt in dreams, when unnoticed travel suddenly brought him to some fantastical place. He walked into the station and found that in the rear of it were stairs leading up, through double doors, onto a small promenade overhanging the platform. From here one could watch the boats on the river and, he realized, the trains coming and going, without being jostled by the crowds on the platform. But there were no crowds; the day was hot and still and silent. He had noticed a ticket window in the station but no attendant; that person might be hidden away, in the cool stone interior, asleep. Frazer lay his arms on the warm stone rail and gazed out over the water at the west bank, almost a mile away. He could see on the river's shifting surface signs of the deep currents, pulling slowly and powerfully against each other. Upriver, the arched silver thread of a bridge. After some time he felt, through the stillness, some very slight humming in the soles of his feet, and then, from a great distance, he heard the long hoot of the train. He smiled; it would be fun, actually, to watch the train come in from here. He wondered at what point in this tiny town's life such a pastime had been popular enough to have warranted the building of the promenade.

When the train did come, it exploded into view very suddenly. Frazer watched its ridged silver top come to a halt beneath him, and then three people, each interestingly foreshortened by his bird's-eye perspective, emerge from different parts of the train and move into the station. The train, having no one waiting for it, pulled away. One of the people was Jenny.

Why are instants of reunion so empty? Perhaps because they are too anticipated, too muffled already at the moment of their coming with every previous imagining to make any mark of their own. They refer backwards, to all the length of time that has defined itself as the prologue to this cataclysm, and to all the flawed imaginings themselves, in each of which this moment is strangely dilated, expansive, arrested. As if gemlike calcification has dripped into each invisible interstice and created a moment suspended but not dead—more alive. He supposes he has always imagined having the leisure to move through this moment as he needed to, finding his hold on it, feeling for the next best step, when in actuality, when the moment comes, it is if anything more fleeting, compressed, truncated, by virtue of all it was supposed to contain over and above all other moments—it is shorter, and contains even less. He doesn't have time now to think of all the other times he has approached a meeting point, heart pounding, mind frantically tracing its shapes, bright calcification dripping into his pores, dilation of all senses, extension of temporal units and intensification of material particles, only to see the person simply seated at a table, on a bench, cross-legged on the grass, bent over the newspaper, staring blankly into space, watching him approach with the unsurprised air of someone who has always expected him to approach, this instantaneous accumulation of unremarkable details like a thunderclap ending his heightened state, ending even his recollection of the state, catapulting him, with slight but helpless resistance, back into the world of the plainly living, each tick a plain second, each moment elapsed that much less of his life. He'll shake hands, embrace, nod at the person. No sunbursts or seven-part chords. By the time he is sure it is Jenny, her black hair still hanging an inch or so shy of her shoulders, her stature still small, step swift, back straight, she has long vanished through the doors into the station and he, unbeautifully, unclimactically, runs down the stairs and catches her just outside the station entrance, the cool vault of the station on one periphery of his gaze, on the other the afternoon as it appears in the parking lot, oppressive now, unpleasantly hot. He can hear the repeatedly rising shriek of some summertime insect. He has caught up to her, a small woman in a blue T-shirt and blue jeans and sneakers striding quickly toward a car, and has no choice but to reach out and touch her elbow as she is speeding away from him. The other two people from the train sweeping off to either side, one into a car, one on swift practiced foot up the steep road. She wheels around at his touch and then ceases to be anything but a marker of arrested time, standing there with her mouth slightly open, her breath snatched from her, eyes unblinking, staring at him in almost life-stopping shock. So it does happen that way, sometimes.

"Hello," he says, quietly.

After a long moment she stirs, only enough to release a last overlooked feather of breath. " . . . Hi," she breathes. And then is even more still than before.

"I'm Ted," he says, after a moment. It's a random choice.

"I'm Iris," she whispers.

"Is there somewhere we can go?"

She nods.

"Do you have a car?"

Nods.

"I do, too. Should I follow you?"

Nods. Her stare has taken focus; he sees something rising in it, something more specific than her shock that he's here. Then she says, almost inaudibly, "Is he—?"

"What?"

"Has something, is—" and then she seems to hiccough. He understands now.

"No," he says. "He's fine."

"Oh, God," she whispers, covering her eyes with one hand. For just an instant, as if a valve had been opened, she cries, without motion or sound—he simply sees the tears seeping through her fingers. And then as quickly, before he can speak or touch her or do anything, she wipes her hand hard on her jeans and says, "We shouldn't stay here. Come on."

2.

The gift of inconspicuousness is rarely given to those who most need its protection. And so it was that Frazer, two weeks earlier, had deplaned in San Francisco wearing an intentionally bad, sadly styled toupee that hid his trademark cueball, and a long-sleeved blue shirt with cuffs buttoned that hid some other prized identifying marks. The rest of his costume had been similarly limp. He wore a plastic Bic clipped to his shirt pocket, and a pair of loser's Naugahyde dress shoes. Bakelite frames with plain glass, and a cheap zipper windbreaker. Landing at the airport, he'd ducked into the men's room for another quick look and felt truly embarrassed, not of the clothes so much as the miracle of implication by which his body, thus concealed, sent a message of terrible weakness. A harrowing sense of self-loss overtook him as he stood there, staring with deflated disbelief while other men passed back and forth, between the door and the urinals, or sometimes pushed around him to wash their hands in the sink. It had seemed very different in New York, when he'd emerged from preparations in the bathroom to reveal himself to Carol. "Oh my God!" she'd shrieked, fleeing in horror. He'd felt sort of bold and funny then, but he didn't anymore.

He caught a cab curbside and took it to Market and Powell, got a cup of coffee, walked a few blocks south, and caught another cab. "Over the Bay Bridge," he said, assuming his persona of colorless loser. He slumped in the backseat and slurped his coffee, being careful not to let it splash onto his shirt. Out the cab window downtown swung away, and then the cab plunged into the Yerba Buena tunnel and the roar of the traffic closed in and the cab seemed to double its speed. That felt good. He had been so dislocated he had almost forgotten to relish the sense of moment, of cinematic significance, of homecoming San Francisco always gave him. It had been several years since he'd become a New Yorker, but returns to San Francisco never failed to shift his center, to reawaken dormant awarenesses. He would feel, as he was beginning to feel now, like a graduate returning after decades to his school; moved by certain intensifications of beauty, and by the diminution of everything else.

Once inside the apartment Frazer pulled off the toupee and ran a soothing palm over his skull. He slipped off the glasses, which had left grease marks on the sides of his nose, shrugged out of the windbreaker, and unbuttoned the shirt, yanking it free of the waist of his slacks. He was wearing a gray T-shirt underneath that said STILLMAN'S GYMNASIUM, from which the sleeves had been removed. Frazer was one of those people who always felt hot, who shed clean, copious sweat all year round and in wintertime improvised outerwear from loose flannel shirts because coats were too heavy. Being so deeply rooted in his body, his mind would constrict when he was physically uncomfortable, and he had been so itchy and hot upon arrival he had had difficulty clinging to precaution, and hadn't noticed his surroundings at all.

Now he looked at things, half-listening to the girl who had answered the door as she poured her voice toward him, the sound of it incomprehensible and pauseless and full of anxiously musical rises and falls. The apartment was beautiful and orderly and calm. He noticed smooth, cool surfaces everywhere—the silver stereo console, with its strip of green light like trapped pondwater; the coffee table, a slab of green glass on a polished wood stump. Thick cream-colored shag on the floor. The blinds were up, but the vast room was still pleasantly dim, like a cave. There was an aquarium the size of a coffin against the far wall, making a murmurous sound. He couldn't see anything in it but rocks.

He turned back to the girl, whose name was Sandy. Earlier that week Sandy had spoken at a memorial rally for a revolutionary "cadre" who in the space of four months had kidnapped a daughter of San Francisco's most prominent family, converted her to their cause, robbed a bank, and then along with their convert been cornered in L.A. and killed, in an hours-long shootout with cops that had led to a fire. The fire had burned so hot nothing had survived except teeth and some bones, which were still being picked from the ashes—like everyone she knew Sandy had seen the whole thing on TV, and though the cadre alive had turned off lots of people, with their gruesome spectacular deaths all their dubious acts had been laundered away. Sandy had always been too shy even to shout slogans as part of a crowd at an antiwar rally, but on this day she'd given a fiery speech and been cheered. As the rally was ending and the crowd was dispersing a strange, dirty girl had slipped up. "I knew the dead comrades, Sister," the girl whispered. "There's still ways you can help." The girl *was* one of the dead—or rather, the police would soon learn that three cadre members they thought they had killed were somehow still alive. So that in one dizzying May afternoon, Sandy had turned from a timid wallflower to a fierce public speaker to a terrified, not-quite-willing savior. At which point, naturally, she'd called Frazer.

Frazer knew her, though not well. She hadn't yet hooked up with his old friend Tom Milner back when Frazer lived here; she had been a girl of some contiguous circle, sometimes at big parties, usually piously listening to somebody play the guitar. He had slept with her once, but nothing beyond the historical fact of the encounter remained with him. When she'd called it had taken some time before he'd realized who she was.

"Is this your apartment?" he asked.

"God, no. Tom's turtle-sitting. It belongs to some guy from his job."

"Wow. Very nice."

She nodded, and then said, as if her thoughts were on delay, "Sort of gross."

"I wouldn't mind. This guy's far away, right?"

"I think he's in China or something."

"How'd Tom get such fancy friends?"

"They're not really friends," she said defensively.

"I'm just kidding around, Sandy." Wow. Was she tense. "Is Tom here?"

"He's getting lunch for them."

"And where are they?" He was bouncing on the balls of his feet, tense himself now, preparing.

"Okay, um." She'd blanched a little. "You ready?"

Past the fish tank the vast living room gave onto a corridor hung with nicely framed photos of distant-looking locales, and a few of those long, skinny vertical pieces of paper with Chinese calligraphy on them. This might have been the first time his mind—disordered and overwhelmed as it had been by the density of the past day's events, by Sandy's telephone call and the all-night discussion with Carol and the scramble to get his disguise and the rush to the airport—had focused on Jenny. Until now he had given no thought to what exactly he would do with these people. Once he and Carol had agreed to get involved things had been too swift to focus on details. Now Jenny, always resident in some chamber of his brain but for the past few years forcibly exiled to those most remote, floated effortlessly and inevitably forward and he understood that one significant problem was solved. He would entrust the day-to-day contact to Jenny. She wasn't merely the only person he could trust in this way, she was the best he could imagine. He would just have to find her. More focused now than before, he made himself set Jenny aside for the moment and shifted his thoughts back to what lay before him. One door along the hallway was ajar, revealing another cool, dim room with a free-weight setup and a luxe sheepskin rug on the floor. He caught a glimpse of a large photo of a white man posing importantly in karate pajamas, and allowed himself one more brief thought of Jenny. That would have amused her. Another door opened onto the bathroom, and then there was a door at the end of the hall that was closed. Sandy knocked very lightly on it, in what he recognized as some kind of code, and after a long moment during which a miniature rugby match seemed to have erupted inside the room, the door opened a crack and Sandy leaned in and whispered, "That guy I talked about, Frazer, is here." The door shut again, then reopened, and Sandy nodded at Frazer and stepped aside to let him in, without following. He heard the door close behind him.

It was so dark in this room that the gray twilight he had left behind in the hallway blazed like noon in his vision and at first he couldn't see anything. There was only the smell, a pungent sex-and-locker-room smell overlaid by fathoms of stale cigarette smoke, and the overwhelmingly motionless heat. The windows were shut, though outside was a blazing summer day. As his eyes started adjusting he could see that the blinds were down and that blankets had been tacked up as well, so that he only knew that some fraction of natural light must have penetrated the room from his awareness that the blankets were brown. And from his ability, now, to make out the room's contents. This room must have been the smallest apart from the bathroom in the entire apartment, and while the rest of the apartment exuded a vibe of Zenlike order and calm, in here was a rampaging mess. There were empty wine jugs and soda-pop cans and straw wrappers and sticky paper cups and balls of cellophane and grease-stained sacks and other food-speckled pieces of garbage all over the floor, intermixed with used tissues and ripe-smelling articles of clothing and bedding. The mattresses, probably dragged here from some other room, were propped up bunker-style against the windows, and it didn't look as if come nightfall they got pulled down and slept on. Whatever sleeping was done here was done on the floor. At thirty-one Frazer was suddenly aware of how young younger people seemed to him. Twenty-year-olds, when he'd been in his late twenties, had seemed almost like peers; now they seemed to him like children. Spooked, false-bravado-burdened children. These were staring up at him like three wild near-fledglings disturbed in their nest. They were stiffly seated Indian-style on the floor in a little half-moon, an arrangement he guessed had been the source of the rugby-match noise, and they had stuff in their laps and on their shoulders, weighty, cumbersome-looking stuff that he belatedly identified as ammunition bandoliers and large guns. Two machine guns and one single-barrel shotgun, with the barrel sawed off. "Whoa," he said, without stopping to think. His eyes had started running from the smoke; whatever drugs he might have sampled in youth before getting hooked on the great drug of exercise, he'd never been able to smoke cigarettes. They made his heart race in an uneven, scary way. His heart was racing now. "I'm not armed," he said, willing his hands to remain at his sides, though they wanted to float upwards, palms out.

Even through watering eyes he could see them clearly now: the married couple who called themselves Yvonne and Juan, Yvonne blond and wild, Juan short and compact, with small round glasses and huge hair, a huge beard. And Pauline—the girl they had kidnapped. Pauline was the one with the shotgun. "Have a seat," Juan said, nodding curtly at the floor. Frazer got himself onto the floor, wobbling unaccountably, perhaps from the heat. Pauline was seated to the left, Juan—who clearly meant for Frazer to negotiate solely with him—to the right. Yvonne was seated in the middle, looking sullen, as if she didn't like Juan doing all of the talking. She was startlingly dimpled—Frazer saw them when she tightened her mouth. A sprinkling of freckles on the bridge of her nose. But it was Pauline Frazer kept stealing looks at. She was tinier than he'd realized she'd be from her pictures; she didn't seem much more than twice as tall as her gun. And she was prettier, too, in a way that brought Frazer in mind of pale, solemn women in long sweeping gowns gazing out from the dusk of old oil paintings. Although now she had circles dark as bruises under her eyes, and like the other two was so evidently food- and light-deprived as to have turned slightly green. Frazer realized they all might be sick. He wished he'd thought to bring vitamins.

After a beat of awkward silence he said, in the way he'd rehearsed to himself, "I'm saddened and angered by the deaths of your comrades. They were murdered, but they died fighting for what they believed in. I've felt for you, the past several days. I was happy when I learned I could help you."

His speech seemed to startle and disorder them completely—he had his vision of the fledglings again. They widened their eyes, swallowed, and glanced frantically at each other. Pauline's head dropped forward so that he couldn't see her face anymore.

"Um, thanks," Juan managed. "We appreciate your sympathy and—feeling for us. And for our comrades. They were our friends and our comrades and we will avenge them." He seemed to have located his desired rhetoric again. "Their deaths will be avenged, bullet for bullet. Have no doubt about that."

"It took the pigs five thousand four hundred bullets," Yvonne said suddenly. "They said so in the paper. That's six hundred bullets per person."

"I know," Frazer said. "It was insane, disproportionate slaughter. Those cops had such blood lust—"

"They needed so many bullets because our comrades were fighting so hard," Yvonne interrupted.

"Would you shut the fuck up?" Juan said, elbowing her, so that his gun, which he had cradled in his arms, jumped with his movement. "I'm doing the talking."

"Hey," Frazer said nervously.

Juan didn't seem bothered. "Now we're under siege, like our comrades," he said. "We need to know what you'll do to help us."

If at any moment in the past twenty hours, perhaps while gazing out the window of the plane, mesmerized by the unfolding of the continent, Frazer had possessed the quietude to form an expectation of his encounter with these people—to imagine, say, that his plan for helping them would be greeted with immediate enthusiastic gratitude—he now learned his expectation had been wrong. The three fugitives were affronted, in their triadic way, from the instant he opened his mouth. He began at the beginning, with his idea for moving them East, having assumed they'd be desperate to leave the West Coast. Though he hurried to explain about the idea he'd had for a book, and the money it would make them, and all the revolutions, or perhaps expatriations to sympathetic foreign lands, it could buy them, their attention was already gone. At the mention of East they'd gone wide-eyed again, and Yvonne and Pauline had begun poking Juan.

" . . . wouldn't just be some money-making venture for you but more importantly a way to get your message out, tell your side of the story, especially now—" was what Frazer was saying when Juan finally broke in.

"We can't leave California!" Juan said. "Is that what you're saying?"

Frazer blinked at him carefully. "I know it seems risky. The airports are all being watched, and bus stations and stuff, and your pictures are everywhere. But I have a plan—"

"No, no, no! I mean, we can't leave California. We—we're at *war.* This is our *battleground.* Our comrades died here, and this is the terrain we know, and a soldier sticks to terrain that he knows, we can't just take off, are you crazy? We can't! No! Jesus!" Juan jumped up, gripping his gun—he was short but he was powerful, Frazer realized. He seemed to have jumped to his feet without the aid of his hands, simply shot straight up into the air. This was when Frazer had seen that, in spite of their obvious fractiousness, the trio could chime. They had a single gaze trained on him now: defiant, distrustful, and even, in Pauline's case, contemptuous. Frazer felt, within the horrible general heat of the room, a specific plume of heat emitting from his scalp.

"You know," he said, "I don't know about you, but when most people commit what's considered a crime in a certain—terrain, and then events keep confirming they're still in that terrain, even as recently as last week, such that thousands of FBI agents are crawling all over the *terrain* day and night looking for them, maybe even finding and killing a bunch of their friends in the process, they move. They move to new terrain!"

"So you're saying it's our fault our comrades got killed?" Yvonne cried.

"No! I'm saying you're in danger of getting caught or killed too, serious danger, especially here. You'd be safer almost anywhere else. In the East you could lay low a while, marshal your resources, live to fight another day. Unless you're interested in dying a martyr's death, in which case you should just walk out onto Telegraph Avenue and wave your guns around and I'll go home and save myself a lot of trouble and a lot of money, if you don't mind me mentioning money."

Frazer could see Yvonne's dimples—from the tight mouth, not a smile—again. Juan was shifting from foot to foot edgily. Pauline had started worrying a clump of her hair, staring into her lap. After a moment Juan said, with a significant look at Yvonne and Pauline, as if trying to recover their moment of union, "You're right if you're saying we need money. Money's an evil and we don't seek it for ourselves. But we need it. We can't survive otherwise."

"I understand that. And that's why you need to come East—to survive. Leaving California doesn't mean giving up. It's a strategic move to ensure you don't have to give up. I mean, look at you! Stuck in this tiny room, without light, without space to stretch out and breathe, eating—" he gestured around at the scatter of take-out-food garbage. "If you come East with me, I can guarantee you a place where you can breathe and relax and think clearly and plan your next move. And where you can, if we play our cards right, replenish your funds."

"Doing what?"

He was careful to not show impatience. "What I said. Writing a book. About your views, why you've done what you've done, like in your communiques, but longer—" Juan was grimacing.

"I don't know," Juan said. "A book seems so, I don't know."

"Bourgeois," Yvonne said.

"But it's another way of waging war. A war of words. And it would help you make money."

"I prefer manifestos. I mean, Mao wrote a book. Definitely. It just seems like, in this country books are such shit."

"I agree," Frazer said. "Though I think that's even more reason—"

"It's enough to have to think about going away. It's true that our struggle is an international one. We're in solidarity with freedom fighters all over the world. We should be able to be anywhere. But California's the place where our comrades got killed." Juan sat back down and they all became blank-eyed and silent.

After what he felt was a lengthy, compassionate pause Frazer said, "At least will you think about it? The money you'll make will be worth it. And until it comes through I'll support you myself."

"Why?" Yvonne said.

"Because I'm on your side," Frazer said, meaning it. And that was when Yvonne smiled at him, dimples and all.

They batted more questions at him. How would they get there? In cars . . . Whose cars? Those of various friends . . . What kinds of cars? A Lincoln, an Olds—but the tone was shifting, from one of challenge to one of anxious curiosity. They asked about things he hadn't even thought of—How many nights would they be on the road? Which roads would they take?—and in response to these questions he simply made up answers. Because he could see, now, that the more authoritative he acted, the more they took to him. At one point Juan said, "If we decide to do this book, will we have to type it out? Because I can type, but these two are useless." To which he responded, as Pauline and Yvonne hotly broke in that they were not useless, "Are you kidding? This is a professional setup I'm getting you. You'll have a transcriber, a ghostwriter, whatever you want. That's standard." And again, he had noticed that his authority seemed to draw them toward him. But they hadn't yet decided—they would have to hold council in private.

After a while a tiny knock came at the door—it might have been repeating itself for several minutes without having been heard, because they had finally thought to ask what he, Frazer, did, and he had started telling them about racism in professional sports, and they'd seemed interested, and he'd been speaking with great animation.

The knock was Tom, with their lunch and a new jug of wine. "Hey man," Tom said to Frazer, ducking his head in greeting. "Long time no see." Tom seemed nervous, which surprised Frazer now. He himself felt terrific.

The three fugitives dove for the wine, raking up sticky, stained cups off the floor. With not quite as much interest they unwrapped the food, although Frazer noticed Juan open a hamburger, squint closely at its surface, then close it and hand it to Pauline. "Maybe you'll have a chance to come to a decision after you've eaten," he suggested, and they all nodded, without another glance at him. Frazer let himself out.

He found Tom and Sandy back in the living room, slowly eating from a sack of their own. They turned their two gazes toward Frazer with what seemed like reluctance, as if Frazer were a surgeon coming out of the O.R. to give the bad news to the family. "So this is pretty surreal," he said cheerfully.

They kept looking at him in the same defeated, dread-filled way until Tom said, like a man with a concussion, "Are you getting them out of here?"

"That's up to them," Frazer said. "I hope so."

"Oh, man," Tom said, with what Frazer recognized, even through Tom's stupefied tone, as real feeling. "I need them out of here *now*. My friend's back in a couple of days."

"Stop worrying. Why'd you call me if you wanted to keep worrying?"

In response to this Tom and Sandy stared at Frazer not only as if they hadn't known him for years, hadn't moved in the same large, loose, yet loyal and right-thinking circle as he had, hadn't viewed him as someone of rare capability, but as if they hadn't even met him before. Then they went back to eating their lunch.

"What's the special thing about Pauline's burger?" Frazer asked, after a minute.

"Huh?" Tom frowned at him.

Frazer grinned. "*Pauline*," he said, making quote marks in the air with his fingers. "What's the special way she likes her burger?"

"I don't know what you're talking about, man."

"The burgers you got them. Jesus, Tom. Were they supposed to have certain toppings or something?"

"Uh, no. I mean, yeah. One was supposed to be plain. No ketchup or pickle or anything. Pauline doesn't like toppings."

"Blech." Frazer made a face involuntarily.

Tom shrugged. "They hardly eat anyway. They just taste stuff and toss it aside."

A few more moments passed with no sign from the room down the hall and no conversation in the room where Frazer stood. He strolled along the walls, looking unhurriedly at the aquarium, the pictures and calligraphy scrolls. "This guy's into Oriental stuff," he commented to Tom.

"He's a karate instructor," Tom said. "He's in Japan or something right now, but he's coming back. Soon."

"White-guy karate instructor, huh? Jenny would get a big kick out of that." Frazer took a beat to chuckle reminiscently. "What about her, anyway? You heard from her lately?"

"What?" said Sandy sharply.

"What?" Frazer answered, turning, with raised eyebrows, to look at her.

"What do you mean? She's with you, isn't she?"

Frazer laughed. "Did she say that?"

"Say that? She left here with you! You were taking care of her."

"I still am. I set her up in a great situation, but you know how independent she is. She doesn't need me to hold her hand every second. Lately we've just fallen out of touch. That's the way it is in New York. She's a real New Yorker now."

"But she's not even in the city. That's what she says in her letters."

"No, of course, right, but she's in New York State." Frazer's heart had sped up.

"I guess. I thought she might be in New Jersey or something. She lives near a river."

"The Hudson?" Frazer said.

"I don't know."

"What's the postmark of her letters?"

"I don't know. They're for William. She sends them to Dana in Boulder and Dana recopies them and sends them to William. But the last time I talked to Dana she said Jenny sounded real good. Doing well. I can't believe you're not in touch with her."

"That's the way it goes when people leave the city—it's really hard to stay in touch. Does Dana have her address?"

"Yeah. When William writes he sends the letters to Dana and they do the same thing going backwards. She sends them to Jenny."

Frazer turned away again and stared at the aquarium. Many of the smooth rocks turned out, on close examination, to be turtles. "I guess William writes her a lot," he said after a minute.

"God, yeah," Sandy said.

"How is William?" Frazer heard himself say, though he suddenly felt the same way Tom had sounded: concussed.

"Oh," Sandy sighed. "Every time I go see him I cry. I don't think it cheers him up much."

A sound came from the end of the hall and Sandy leaped up and ran out of the room. A moment later she was back.

"They want to talk to you again," she told Frazer.

Things were much as he'd left them. The recent lunch detritus had been incorporated into the rest of the trash on the floor and the threesome were in their half-moon formation, guns on their laps.

"We've made a decision," Juan said. "We accept your offer, on, um, some conditions."

"Of course," Frazer said encouragingly.

"We're not *moving* to the East or anything—we're just holing up there for a while, like you said, to lie low and regroup. And get funds."

"Completely understood. That means you'll do the book, to get the funds."

Juan shrugged wearily. "I guess so." Frazer saw Yvonne clandestinely poke Juan in the thigh. "And we're really grateful," Juan added. "I hope we haven't seemed unappreciative. We can see you're a genuine brother. It's just—these have been some bad days." Yvonne and Pauline had been watching Juan intently, even promptingly, during this speech. Now the two girls looked anxiously at Frazer. Juan was looking at his boots.

"This is great," said Frazer, calmly and commandingly. "I have a couple of conditions of my own. They're all for your safety. Number one is, while we're traveling, you have to do what I tell you. It's going to be dangerous, and I don't want us wasting time arguing. If you're going to trust me with your lives, you've got to go all the way. Or I'll withdraw my support."

They were staring at him with one face again. Juan said, coldly, "What's number two?"

"No guns on the road. You've got to leave your weapons here."

"No fucking way!" Juan leaped to his feet again, gripping his gun; though it had been lying untouched on his lap it arrived in his hands right-side-up and front-forward. Frazer felt his palms go wet instantly, as if he'd dipped them in water.

"Juan!" Yvonne screamed.

"I'm sorry," Juan said, with a terrible calm that dismantled Frazer's own calm completely, "but we are in a state of war, and we cannot be defenseless. There's no fucking way we're giving up our guns."

"He's just afraid of us," said one of the girls. Frazer gaped; it was Pauline.

"That's not true!" he said.

"You're asking us to trust you but you don't trust us," she said coolly.

Frazer felt his jaw working like a piece of stuck machinery. "You don't understand," he said. "We might get pulled over, you'll be in disguise but you can't disguise a gun. We can't drive across the country with guns!"

"So how do we get our guns over there?" Juan demanded.

"What? Get them—you don't need to. I'll get you new ones," Frazer heard himself saying. "My God, is that what you thought—I was saying you shouldn't have guns? I—wow. Misunderstanding," he said, with a strangled sort of laugh. His T-shirt felt glued to him.

Suddenly, Juan laughed as well: a short, barking laugh. "Fuck, man. You got me going. I thought you were telling us to give up our guns."

"Yeah, no, I know," Frazer said, grinning weakly. "Not at all. I mean, what have we got here, these are, uh—"

"This is a twelve-gauge pump-action shotgun—modified, obviously," said Pauline.

Frazer blinked at her. "Uh, yeah. I can replace that on the other end. Of course."

"I'd rather have a fully automatic," she said.

"Shut the fuck up," Juan repeated. "I'm doing the talking, remember?"

For the rest of that afternoon, as the sunlight faded behind the brown blankets, and fresh shelves of cigarette smoke filled the air, and the jug of wine rapidly emptied, they'd hashed out—never far from a hair-trigger moment, but never at one again, thankfully—the complex arrangements that had then unfolded, over the next several days, just as Frazer had said that they would. The tedious but uneventful car shuttlings, one by one, first of Pauline, then Yvonne, lastly Juan. The renting by Carol of a foolproof new safe house, an old farm an hour's drive from Manhattan. And finally, the storage of the numerous guns among Frazer's old friends until their owners could someday reclaim them. Frazer had put Tom in charge of the gun-storing task, which Tom seemed to accept as an improvement over storing the fugitives. By now the guns are presumably scattered throughout the Bay Area, a secret set of coordinates mapping the world Frazer and Jenny once shared. Their once large, loyal circle: is it loyal at all anymore? It's hard for him to know. He's been in New York too long to have any measure of what those people feel for him, let alone for each other. Sandy had called him when the fugitives washed up at her door, and later Dana had given him Jenny's post office box number. But Sandy and Dana have always been at the farthest edges of his awareness, mere acquaintances. Acquaintanceships don't seem to change over time; they are never substantial enough to accrue more mass, like planets in formation, or to blow apart like oversized stars. He doesn't know if he can say the same of his link to the woman in front of him. They've gone up the little road out of Rhinecliff and into the country. He is right about her not liking bridges, but now thinks he's wrong. Taking the left turn onto the bridge road with his car sliding briefly from the frame of her rearview, she can't see his eyebrows lift in surprise, and carefully following her, blinker on, he can't see the fine vein in her neck jumping slightly. Once on the far side of the river she leads him nearly five miles along the dead-level two-lane roads that run haphazardly through open farmland and empty fields like paint stripes laid down by a drunkard. She's changing roads as often as there's a new road to change to; he's beginning to think that she's trying to lose him. Again. Except for the fact that she's flawlessly toeing the speed limit. Trees close in and their road begins to climb; a forested abyss opens to the left, and after they have climbed and climbed, hugging rockface on their right—at every turn she slows to a crawl, and he hears her honk lightly, before creeping around—he can see, far below, a creek lying as noiseless and still as a string on the floor of the canyon.

And then they are out in the open again, but high up—he feels the elevation in the cool bite of the air pouring in through his window. She changes roads again, and again, and the shadows of their cars lengthen out in front of them. They're pointed east now, back in the direction they came from. At a sign for Twin Lakes

Camp she turns onto a dirt road and they bounce past picnic tables and fire pits, a tent or camper van every fourth or fifth site. It's midweek and, being barely June, still somewhat early in the season. Not many people. Out of the corner of one eye Frazer sees a girl sitting hunched beneath the frame of her backpack while the guy she's with yanks at her shoulder straps. Blond and bored, faintly scornful expression. She's grimacing; then she's gone behind a bend in the road. Glimpsing such a girl so briefly, you might almost think it was Pauline. Frazer wonders how many people across the land are having that experience this very instant.

The road ends in a lot by a lake. The lake has a thumbnail of gravel-strewn beach, an old lifeguard's chair lying toppled across it. There's one other car in the lot. Jenny parks as far away as possible from it and then takes off up a well-worn trail leading away from the lake. Frazer follows her. After just a few hundred yards of gentle climb and thin trees the trail opens onto a field of grass that then vanishes over a cliff. The entire river valley lies beneath them; in the middle distance, through shimmering afternoon haze, Frazer sees the river itself, a thin silver line. Beyond that, a rumpled greenish-gray obscurity of mountains and compounded haze and smog. Before them is the farmland they've driven through, miniaturized. The fields are green, yellow, black scored with green lines; the air is gold. The day seems to have been drained of all but the smallest sounds, which rise toward them from the valley with weird precision; Frazer hears a dog barking, perhaps miles away, and the thin mosquito buzz of a motorcycle. The field is large enough for football; at the farther end of it are several middle-aged-looking people in bright clothes taking pictures of each other. For all their relative nearness they're inaudible, gesturing excitedly and silently, like mimes. Jenny walks to the very edge of the cliff and sits down. From here it's possible to see that this cliff isn't a sheer bald wall like the ones in cartoons but a confused descent of crumbling dirt and treetops, but Frazer still feels his stomach turn over. He sits down next to her—not right beside her, not touching her, but not more than a foot from her shoulder. Intimately near. He would like to be sitting opposite her, studying the ways in which two years have changed her. Instead he stares out at the valley, feeling her angry curiosity moving over him quickly and lightly, as sensible as touch. She wants him to speak first but he's not going to. She pulls her smokes out of her jeans pocket, a pouch and papers, and raises her knees against the slight breeze to roll the cigarette. With her hands busy she doesn't manage to beat him to the match although she tries, this small fact about him coming upon her less as a memory than as a reflex in her body. The last, pleasurably dilated action of smoothing the cigarette's seam interrupted suddenly by an instinct to grab for her matches before Frazer has struck one and leaned close to her, the insistent bald dome of his head nearly brushing her bangs, his cupped hands near her mouth. She has avoided thinking of him for so long that her uncomfortably exhaustive knowledge of his particularities is returning too late. He has already struck the match, his hands cupped to protect the small flame against the currents of the air but also to smuggle more of his body into the exchange, under cover of courtesy. Frazer always cups his hands around the flame and leans near, even when indoors in a place with no drafts. Some men embrace all the retrograde aspects of gallantry because they've intuited that to be gallant is to take sexual hold of a woman, however obliquely. She thinks Frazer is one of these men. She's always thought so, since their very first meeting. One of these men with the terrible instinct and energy for approaching any woman from every angle. Perhaps not any woman. The flame touches the tip of her cigarette and she inhales sharply and sees the ash form and glow; when she glances up Frazer is there, filling her vision, looking back at her intently. She feels herself flush. He keeps her gaze another beat and then sits back again, shaking the match out, and the valley and the river and the sky, which he briefly blotted out, reappear.

Two years have taught him patience. That surprises her. He's generally frenetic with speech and not much of a listener, which means that once you get him talking he'll betray himself five different ways within minutes, but he's resolved to force her to speak first, and he isn't giving way. He's practically erupting with impatience, but he isn't giving way. She finishes her cigarette in what seems like one continuous inhale, flips it away, and rolls another.

Finally she says, "You alone?"

"Yes. What do you think, that I'm here with the posse? Come on, Jenny."

He sees her start a little at the sound of her own given name. "You never know."

"Of course I'm alone."

"How'd you find me?"

"Why'd you make me?" He shoots another look at her as he says this, and thinks he sees her flinch. Such a delicate thing. Like the spider's work: spin one thread and give it a test. Sidle up and down its length with an eye toward the next one. "I talked to Dick and Helen, the night you took off."

"I had to, Rob. They were getting suspicious. They didn't like having me there."

"They didn't act like they didn't like having you."

"Of course they didn't, to you. They're your friends. They didn't want to admit they were scared."

"They only sounded scared after you left. They went to work in the morning and when they got back that night you were gone. No note. If you were afraid they were getting suspicious, then you did the worst possible thing."

"I'm sorry, Rob."

"And left me holding the bag."

"I'm sorry, Rob."

"*And* trying to come up with some plausible explanation for why you spooked and ran that *didn't* have to do with their darkest suspicions, which they were certainly having, but only after you left."

"I'm sorry, Rob," she says again, refusing to fight with him. To even really look at him.

"And you never contacted me," he concludes. Saying this, he

feels a peculiar sensation of tightness, almost itch, in his throat. From the thin air up here, probably. She says nothing to this, so that the truth of it is left to hang, even longer, between them.

"How'd you find me?" she repeats, finally.

"It wasn't hard. Your pen pal talked to me about your new job. And your go-between gave me your post office box. They both thought I'd just lost track of the info, because I'm such a busy guy. They never dreamed you'd try to shake me. Because we're all friends, remember?"

She flushes again, and he knows this time it's not because of him. Seeing her at the train station, being so beautifully, perfectly surprised by her, the old sensations, in their return, had been transfigured—for a moment, he'd hovered with her in a new medium, derived exclusively from their pairing, charged in the old way but purged of the old taint. Now the old taint is back, with its unwanted passengers. Her hand, at "your pen pal," has literally flown toward her throat, although she's halted it short of its target and taken hold of her T-shirt. "You talked with Will?" she says, her voice just a half-tone too high.

"Sure."

"I mean, you saw him?"

"Sure. I told you. I said he was fine."

"I didn't realize you'd seen him."

"He's entitled to visitors." This sounds surly, but he can tell that the idea of his, Frazer's, recent physical proximity to her snatched-away lover is peerlessly horrible to her, though she tries not to show it.

"How is he?" she persists.

"He's fine, like I said. He's not so nuts about the food. Don't you get lots of letters from him?"

"Of course, but not directly. Dana forwards them to me, so it's slow. Maybe one every month."

"That's it?"

She nods.

"You'd think he'd write more," he says. Hating himself.

"It's that we both send our letters through Dana. That takes time."

Ah, he hates himself. If you're going to be cruel, be cruel! Stick with it! But he can't. He says, "I'm just kidding around. He was itching to talk about you when I saw him. He couldn't, you know, but he sent his signal. He was itching to talk."

"What did he say?" Then the hand flies up again, this time over her eyes, just like at the train station. "Oh, shit," she whispers.

"Sweetheart." He hasn't called her this in a very long time. Saying it, he feels a hole blown in his chest. He tries to take her hand from her eyes but she shrugs away from him.

"Anything?" she says, still blindfolding herself with her hand.

"Of course. Um, he said, 'I hear soldier's got a new line of work.' Grinning the way he does. When he mentions you." She nods, eyes still concealed. He casts about wildly for a phrase or two more. "He said, 'Keep watching over things for me.' Things means you. He doesn't know you took off without telling me. He thinks we've been in touch all this time. Because he wants me protecting you. Because he loves you. Sweetheart. Please. Uncover your face." He should have been an actor. Or at least, the one living an alternate life. Because, now as in the past, once the terrible pain of reassuring this woman of another man's love is commenced—once his throat, with its thickened walls of flesh and its central hard knot, has miraculously formed the first words, he could go on and on. He could smile and mug and retell anecdotes of this other man's devotion as if it means nothing to him, although he does retain for himself the fraudulently casual use of endearments. *Sweetheart.* He gets a charge out of this, though he knows she dislikes it. Now he says, "I would have been fucked if he knew I'd lost track of you. Because he counts on me to make sure that you're safe. I know you think you can take care of yourself, but that's not enough for him. I vowed to him I'd take care of you." Then she takes her hand away from her eyes and looks at him through tears, and he feels stricken mute. She puts her face on her knees, and a small bell of solitude settles around her. Frazer's left at the lip of the cliff, staring out at the void.

For a while there's nothing but drifting, disconnected sound. Birdcalls, the hollow undertone of a jet somewhere out in the atmosphere. He's afraid of hearing definitive proof she's still crying but strains his ears all the same. The brightly colored group of middle-aged couples angles across the field behind where he and Jenny are sitting, back toward the trailhead; the breeze shifts, and their gay, indistinct voices carry over a moment, then fade. Finally Jenny sighs, wipes her face with the hem of her shirt. When she turns back to him he's startled. He dreams of this distilled gaze of hers all the time but on the few occasions she's meant it for him, he has quailed before it. He's looked away, as he looks away now. "Rob," she says. He nods, waiting. "When you see William, you don't tell him, do you? About that time we fucked up."

About that time we fucked up. Frazer abandons caution and looks at her. He doesn't know what he was thinking: There's nothing particular there. "You mean," he says, elongating his words as if groping around in the black vault of memory. "You mean, the last time you saw me? When was that, anyway? I must have a newspaper clipping somewhere that could help peg the date. Maybe it was March 1972, when I saved your ass from prison. I have this vague memory of seeing you then. Is that the fucked-up time you're thinking of?"

"Rob."

"Of course I haven't told him. I always assumed you would, as part of some holy-moly purifying ritual. 'Forgive me my terrible sin, but I had sex with Frazer.' Isn't that your thing? Pure heart, pure life. You can't hold down a job in the capitalist system at the same time as you fight for revolution and you can't lie to your lover at the same time as making sure you're perfect soulmates who never power-trip each other! Right? Every time I go see him I think he's gonna try to punch me through the Plexiglas window but he's just all smiles and all love because you never told him. You're scared to."

"I am not! It's just not something I would ever disclose in a letter—that's *real* cowardice. When I tell him it'll be to his face.

And what about you? You haven't had Carol taken away, you could tell her to her face, but you haven't."

"Me and Carol don't believe in monogamy, so I don't know what you're talking about."

"Oh!" She leaps up in frustration. "Why are you here anyway, Rob? Why did you come after me?"

She's standing now, angrily planted, but he knows she'd rather stride off across the green field, down the worn trail, and get in her car and leave him. He can remember any number of their arguments in the past, arguments ostensibly about ideas but really about his persistence, her refusal, that have ended this way. With Frazer left alone, carefully avoiding all movement because to move is to reanimate a world stopped in its tracks by her violent departure and to reanimate that world is to allow the shroud of humiliation, still hanging uncertainly in the air the way silence hangs uncertainly after a door slams, to complete its descent onto him. He always needs a few moments to get ready for the shroud. He likes to wear it as lightly as possible. In the past Jenny did a lot of her storming off and leaving him in the parking lot of a pancake diner where they'd go on nights that Carol was with her women's group or her acting class and William was teaching his seminar or working the night shift, nights that were frequent, and they almost always fought, and insulted each other's characters and reviled each other's beliefs, but they kept doing it, didn't they? And didn't that mean something? Didn't it mean something bound them, somehow?

She's wearing a pair of old, faded, paint-covered jeans that Frazer hasn't been looking at closely, but now that she's standing, hands on hips, poised to depart, and he's leaning back on his elbows and pretending to gaze unconcerned into the distance while actually looking at her, he can see that these jeans, so splattered with recent activity, are a pair she's had for years and years, a pair that used to be nice, and that he remembers because they have seams on their fronts. Pointless, decorative seams, stitched with gold thread to form a thin ridge of denim running like a highway stripe down the centers of her thighs, over her kneecaps, and the rest of the way to her ankles. These were Jenny's signature jeans. He remembers one night years ago, when they all still lived in California, and when none of them were in prison, and when they were feeling that unalloyed excitement about being together, about being a group of friends that felt more like a family, like the sort of dream-family nobody had and that doesn't exist. Carol had been trying for weeks to talk them into playing a game from her acting class and everyone had been pretending to think it was stupid, but this night they were all high and goofy, and William said, Let's play Carol's game. And perhaps because they all secretly wanted to, or perhaps because it was William suggesting it, on this night they agreed. Scattered through the house to find scarves and stockings for blindfolds, then reconvened in the living room, laughing nervously, sucking last hits off joints or last slugs from bottles for more kick, or more courage. Carol explained that the point of the game was to pretend as if one was a newborn baby, or an alien. Without knowledge of anything, not furniture or carpet or LPs or human beings or beer bottles. The game only involved turning off all the lights, and blindfolding themselves, and crawling around on the floor trying to imagine they didn't know what things were, but somehow they all sensed, as the lights went out and the eruptions of *Ouch!* and *Shh!* and *Fuck you, man!* finally faded away into eerie, shuffling, shifting, sighing hush, that the game wasn't going to be about amnesia. Hands found shoulders, faces, tried to identify with the minimum of touch. Recoiled or lingered, were received with breathless stillness or flinched from. Frazer, inching out of the living room onto the smooth, cool wood floor of the corridor, came against a person sitting perfectly still, and was so startled he gasped—then extended one finger very slowly before him until he found a bent knee, felt the ridge of denim running over it. Jenny.

His hand meant to fly away, but it didn't. Tentatively, questioningly, he followed the ridge with his finger. Surprised by how much care was needed, in his blindness, to keep it squarely beneath the pad of his fingertip. He could hear her breath then, as careful and slow as his touch. Down the incline of her thigh and over rumpled territory to her waist. She didn't move, and so he extended the line, upward, over the warm curve of her breast, the shock of her nipple. Hard. He almost came, closed his hand around her, but that wasn't the game that he'd started, and though this threshold would become one of the premier erotic episodes of his generally eventful and unrestrained sex life, it lasted only for a sliver of a second before he forced himself onward, his line up her body uninterrupted as it left her breast, skimmed over her collarbone, traced her neck to the down-dusted earlobe and then moved away, through her hair, to the void. From the living room he heard a crash, and then a peal of laughter: Carol's. He swiveled in panic, thinking the lights might come on, and crawled hurriedly back to the living room like a dumb frightened animal.

There are the famous jeans now, wash-worn almost white and caked with dots and streaks of different kinds of paint. Their tantalizing ridges obscured. Take your cue from the pants, Rob, he thinks. The past is obscured. Now, the future. The middle-aged couples are gone. They're completely alone.

"Sit down," he says. "I'd rather say this without yelling."

All the while he's been looking for her he's also been rehearsing, not with unease but with fidgety eagerness, even euphoria, the speech he'd deliver. But now the moment has come and the speech is gone, in a tumble of parallels and hypotheticals and other half-baked attempts at suspense. *Say a person like you,* people *like you. Principled people, pursued by the state they oppose! Time running out . . . needing refuge, as you did—and do—*

Instead he says, sounding dully pragmatic, "Your current situation doesn't look like much of an improvement over living with Helen and Dick. That old lady doesn't pay you, I bet. Or she can't pay you much."

"What are you saying?" she asks, and from the stillness of her face, her concealed alarm, he can tell he's guessed right.

"What I mean is you don't have a plan, Jenny, do you? You're running, from everyone, from *me*, even, but you don't have anywhere to run to."

"I might."

"Oh, really? Where?"

"None of your business."

Then he knows that she truly has nowhere to go, and knows as well that she knows it. His excitement, his almost evangelical joy at the opportunity that has befallen him—them—returns to him, and some of the speech along with it. "What if I were to tell you that I've recently met with some people. People whose principles we basically agree with, though we might find their tactics a little way out. People who are in trouble, the way you've been in trouble, although I should say they're in trouble to a way, way, *way* bigger degree. They need a safe haven immediately. What would you say to all that?"

"I'd say that you'll probably help them, and they'll be far more grateful than I was."

"Not me. You. You'll be the hero who helps them." She's resisting the vision, but he's expected her to, at the outset. "Because you have the underground know-how, the wisdom. *Yes*, I'm saying you have nothing to lose, it's the truth, but more I'm saying you have everything to gain! Jenny, listen to me. These people, who need us—who need you—aren't just any group of people. They're people who have such a sensational story to tell that if they could just get a safe haven, and write it all down, they would make tens, maybe hundreds of thousands of dollars. For their cause, and for the people who help them. But," he holds up a cautioning hand, "it's tricky. Because these people need someone aboveground, who's not compromised, to make the arrangements for them. *And* they need someone belowground—like you—to take care of the everyday things. The grocery shopping. The phone calls. Someone like you, who can serve as the go-between—between these people, for example, and me."

"But I only move around because I have to. It's risky for me."

"Nowhere near as risky as it is for people who are in *Time* magazine every week. Who are on fucking TV every *night*, Jenny, whose story is wanted by *everyone*—"

Now she's staring at him, very pale. "My God," she says. "You're not talking about who I think you are, are you?"

"What if I was?" he replies, and his long effort to contain himself finally fails. He grins giddily at her.

"This is just what I was always afraid of," she gasps. "You think you're so suave, and you're really so reckless! You think you're discreet but you *talk*—don't tell me you came from those people to me. You met with those people, and then you came and found me!" She looks around wildly. "I'm going."

"Don't do that," he says.

But she's not even staying to argue. Before he can take in what's happening she's back on her feet and then actually running from him, her form receding across the deep field and slipping into the trees. He's abruptly, completely alone. One half-circle around him the trees Jenny's disappeared into, the other the far-off horizon. Himself at the center, as if he's awoken on top of this mountain and everything else was a dream. He hears a ship's horn, perhaps down on the river, perhaps a hundred miles away on the sea. Under these weird acoustical conditions it seems he might hear her heart if he tried. He hasn't heard her car engine. He shoots up and goes sprinting across the field himself—you can take the quarterback out of the game but you can't take the game out of the quarterback—and bursts through the trees into the parking lot, but it's empty, apart from his car.

3.

There's the long way and then there's the very long way, much farther west into mountains before turning east by way of angling south, which means rolling gradually down through the foothills instead of precipitately through the gorge. Even though she's on none of the roads that she used to come up, she's still glancing in her rearview so often she keeps crunching onto the shoulder. Rule number one is don't drive, and if you must, please don't drive like you're sleeping or drunk. She tries not to drive all the time, but now she's a regular face on the train. Known and liked by the different conductors: another rule broken. Hey, Iris. Going down to Poughkeepsie today? Knowing it's bad that she smiles and says Hey. Bad that she's friends with the ticket seller at the station because he sits all day reading the paper. Bad that she's a familiar face in Rhinebeck, also, in spite of sometimes shopping down the river in Poughkeepsie, and getting her mail two towns over in Red Hook, and saving serious emotional collapses for the spot she's just left, because the view is worth the risk of the bridge. Bad that she's rooted in the transient train, the anonymous post office box, precisely the places that Frazer has managed to find her.

And because she's taken the very long way she hasn't managed to get back before tea. She's usually ensconced deep in the house by now, after having boiled the water and spilled the box of cookies onto the dish and decanted the milk into the creamer and dropped the cubes of sugar in the sugar bowl with tongs—Miss Dolly is scrupulous about the use of tongs, to prevent spread of germs—and carried the rattling tray onto the porch with the old woman bringing up the rear in her fragile, methodical way. And then politely ducking off to some project-in-progress, before any visitor comes up the path. By that time she'll be lying well out of reach and very nearly out of sight beneath the library ceiling, on her jerry-rigged scaffold with a bowl of soapy bleach-water, gently wiping away at one hundred years of brown pipe-smoke residue. And listening. Hiding from the ritual of teatime but anxiously listening. *How's that lovely Oriental girl working out? So-and-so saw her at Buell's Hardware shopping for tools. Where is it she hails from, originally?* Coming around the last bend in the Wildmoor road she can see that someone has already arrived, and unhooked the chain, and turned around the little sign from the side saying HOUSE TOURS to the side saying JOIN US FOR TEA. 4–6 P.M. DAILY. It's just ten past four. Miss Dolly's visitors are all extremely punctual and ancient, the men thin and erect and slow-moving, like large wading birds, the women tiny and blurry and loud. They all seem to have lived on the river for eons, and never had jobs. Whoever has unhooked the chain has left it lying in the dirt across the drive, and after she bumps over it she gets out of the car and pulls it properly off to one side, noticing as she does that there's a small white streak of bird shit on the sign. She scratches it off with her thumbnail. The sign looks old and faded already. It's one of the first things she made when she came here.

She drives the rest of the way through the trees and tries to slip in the back door, but then someone calls out "Iris!" from the porch. "Yes!" she calls back. Her voice snags and she falls over coughing. Too many smokes. "Come visit with us for a minute!" The speaker, unsubtly sing-songing, is clearly relishing some innuendo. Not Dolly, but Mrs. Fowler, the lady from the historical society who leads the house tours. Jenny's heart picks up speed; the body's quick fear, always five beats ahead of the brain's. Still, she keeps moving and hacking toward the front of the house until she comes into the dining room and catches sight of herself in the huge sideboard mirror. Gray-skinned and red-eyed and with hair like Medusa's, matted up from the wind, sticking straight off her head. She looks cringing and hunted and ugly but she also looks like herself, an upsetting coincidence, and though she can't now put particular words to it, her shock has something to do with existence, with the continuing presence of *her* through these worlds upon worlds. She wants to sit down, on the nearest solid surface, but all her hand finds is the shiny gnarled upright of a thronelike velvet chair, and it doesn't seem right to sit there. Is it all right to sit on the floor? Her body gives a panicked twitch the way it used to when she was so miserably high on something William had given her that she was secretly sure she was dying, that each labored beat of her heart was its last, that her lungs were somehow blocked from filling properly—she would involuntarily twitch out of fear she was dead. She leans heavily against the thronelike chair until the room stops moving and then sneaks a look at her reflection again—no real change. She turns very carefully around and edges her way through the rest of the house to the porch with her eyes on the floor. Miss Dolly is perched in her usual chair, stiff-necked, looking slightly bemused. Mrs. Fowler is bent over the tea tray, but when Jenny comes out she nearly pounces on top of her. "You've had a visitor!" she trills. Jenny has long suspected that Mrs. Fowler's ideas about her involve rock gardens and tea ceremonies and slender bamboo writing tools; that Mrs. Fowler, a connoisseur of the Arts of the Orient, is stubbornly awaiting from Jenny some endorsement of her, Mrs. Fowler's, very own aesthetic gifts. Mrs. Fowler has previously attributed Jenny's avoidance of her to mist-enshrouded Oriental remoteness. Now she seems delighted to have Jenny on the spot. She picks an envelope up off the tea tray and waggles it suggestively. "I *knew* you had an admirer. From the way he asked questions about you, I could just tell that he'd met you before. He was trying to be subtle but I'm a very canny reader of men! And he just now dropped by here again with some adorable story about wanting to ask your advice about having his house painted. We tried to make him stay for tea but he wouldn't, he just scribbled you a little note and then asked for an *envelope* for it. I was just saying to Dolly, We've got hot tea right here, we ought to steam it open! For heaven's sake I'm teasing you, Iris. I'd never. Are you all right? You look green. Have some tea. Sit right there and I'll get you some tea and we can open the envelope."

"Quit fussing, Louise," Dolly says. As usual, an exercise in sharing Mrs. Fowler's excitement has given way to irritation. Like Jenny, Dolly tends to disappear from the house when Mrs. Fowler gives tours; this is one of the reasons Mrs. Fowler so regularly comes to tea.

"No, thank you," Jenny says, trying to make a casual grab for the envelope and instead falling sideways into one of the porch chairs.

"There's lemonade. Miss Dolly's *famous* lemonade, of course," Mrs. Fowler says, waving the envelope around busily, in the style of a symphony conductor. She winks over her shoulder at Dolly.

Dolly ignores her. "I bet it's all those fumes you're working with," she tells Jenny. "What about those fumes in the porte cochere? I don't know if you should be using that paint-stripper stuff on the porte cochere. It might be bad for my bluebirds."

"Your bluebirds!" exclaims Mrs. Fowler.

Miss Dolly regards Mrs. Fowler remotely. "The bluebirds that nest in the porte cochere," she says.

"That's so darling!"

"That's what birds do," Dolly says. "Did you hear me, Iris? If those fumes are making you look so green, I bet they'll fry those little birds."

"I had no idea you had nesting bluebirds—I'll have to add that in to my tour. I thought they said those PCPs or whatever they are have killed off all the bluebirds. Oh, did you want to look at this, Iris? What do you say, Dolly? Should we let her look?"

Once Jenny has the envelope in hand she tries standing up. "Excuse me," she begins.

"Oh, no." Mrs. Fowler pushes her, gently and firmly, back into her chair. "Miss Dolly and I have been climbing up the walls with curiosity, haven't we, Dolly? You're so mysterious, Iris. Won't you just tell us a thing or two? Where in the world did you meet this young man? You never seem to have pals or go out or do anything except shop for paint. *Tell us*. Dolly, make her tell us."

"Please recall our agreement," Dolly says instead, in her bland, unoiled voice. "Regarding room and board."

Jenny nods. "Of course," she says.

Mrs. Fowler blinks at Dolly. "What agreement?"

"Regarding room and board," Dolly says.

"No male visitors," says Jenny. "This man wasn't visiting—I don't know him. He must have made a mistake—"

"Oh, Miss Dolly. That's so unromantic and unrealistic. This is *1974*. The girls are going to do whatever they want no matter how you try to stop them. I know that with my girls, I'd much rather have the boyfriends coming by the house than taking them out God knows where. Just the other day Maureen—"

"Even if he was a boyfriend, which he wasn't," Jenny says, "because I don't even know him, I would never have him visit—"

"Please correct me if I am somebody's parent," Dolly says. "So far as I know I am nobody's parent. Whenever I have taken a boarder at Wildmoor I have forbidden lady visitors if the boarder was a male, and male visitors if the boarder was a lady, and it hasn't been because I'm somebody's parent. It's because it's my house!"

"Of course it is," says Mrs. Fowler.

"No matter how many folks come tramping in and out at three dollars a pop. It's my house."

"And thank goodness for that!" Mrs. Fowler exclaims. "When I see some of these lovely old homes come separated from their owners it just breaks my heart. Like at the old Bellingham place? When the last Bellingham finally gave up and sold it to the state for the back taxes? They turned it into a park, and they didn't even give it a budget for oversight or preservation or anything, just stuck an 'Open, dawn to dusk' sign at the gate and a line of Porta Potties on the drive. You go over there now and there are all these people who haven't got anywhere better to go barbecuing hot dogs on the lawn. Remember that mosaic of lovely little colored tiles in the bottom of the fountain? Somebody's pried those up, every single one of them. It doesn't even matter because the fountain is practically a public swimming pool. It just breaks my heart."

Miss Dolly lets this discourse dribble off into silence. "All I'm saying," she concludes at last, "is it's my house."

After a time Mrs. Fowler says, brightly, "More tea?"

"I'll take a splash," Dolly says. "Iris, I need to hear how things are coming for the Fourth."

"Good," she says cautiously.

"Have you got my ball?" By this is meant the yellow croquet ball. The yellow croquet ball supernaturally vanished last summer, at Dolly's yearly Independence Day picnic. Even the determined bushwhacking of dozens of guests at the time, and the denuding of the ground through the subsequent winter, have failed to produce the lost ball. It has been one of Jenny's most urgent tasks to locate someone who will sell her a yellow ball pro rata, as Dolly is reluctant to buy a new set—this was the errand that had taken her down to Poughkeepsie this morning, returning from which she had found Frazer waiting for her—but so far she has not been successful.

". . . no," she says.

"No?" Although the project has been ongoing for some time, without any progress, Dolly seems newly amazed by this setback. "No? How hard can this be? Did you try Buell's in Rhinebeck?"

Jenny nods. She had not wanted to try Buell's in Rhinebeck—she hadn't wanted to try anything in Rhinebeck. Being the nearest large town, Rhinebeck is a place she has sought to avoid. But the demanding nature of the yellow ball quest has sent her into nearly all such dreaded places, one after the other.

"What did Buell say?"

"He said if he gave you the yellow ball, then his set will be missing the yellow ball and he won't be able to sell it."

"Did you tell him who it was for?"

"Yes."

"And he still wouldn't do it?"

Jenny shakes her head.

"Did you tell Buell he's not invited to my Independence Day picnic this year?"

"Oh, Dolly," says Mrs. Fowler.

"Well, fiddlesticks," Dolly says. "And by that I mean something much worse."

"I'll try again tomorrow," Jenny says.

"I think you'd better go down to the city. They've got to have some outfit that replaces croquet balls. Haven't they got everything in Chinatown? You'd know your way all around there."

"At this point you could get a new set for the cost of her train fare," Mrs. Fowler says, rashly.

"Unfortunately, you don't know half as much about this as I do," Dolly snaps. To Jenny she says, "You go down to Manhattan tomorrow and I bet you'll find it. We've got to get this thing taken care of. There's a lot else to do."

"Of course," Jenny says. At the thought of going into Manhattan her heart must have sped up, but it feels more like it's beating through sludge. *Thump . . . Thump . . .* "Excuse me," she murmurs.

"You are excused," Dolly says, lifting her teacup.

Making her way off the porch and back into the house, and holding the envelope as inconspicuously as she can, she hears Mrs. Fowler say, "I wanted to find out about her boyfriend."

"I don't pay her to have boyfriends," Dolly says.

In truth, Dolly almost doesn't pay her at all. She is frightened by how much Frazer seems to know about her—that her situation isn't good but truly bad, that she's far from indifferent to money. When Dolly hired her they'd agreed that her pay would be room and board plus a small hourly wage for her work, and that she would keep track of her hours. For the first few months Dolly had paid her, but now, whenever she tells Dolly she has worked, say, one hundred fifty hours this month, or thirty hours this week, or any chunk of time, large or small, Dolly tells her to wait until she reaches a good round number, because it's such a production to go to the bank. Meanwhile giving her a very small allowance, which keeps her in groceries and train fare and gas and supplies for the housework—which keeps her, Jenny knows. Period.

She has to light a cigarette before she opens the note, and then she has to smoke the whole thing. Her nails are so bitten she can't get a hold of the envelope's flap and finally, in a burst of irritation, she just rips the end of it off with her teeth. The tiny piece of paper inside says, in Frazer's childlike scrawl, RHINEBECK MOTEL ROOM 10 PLEASE COME TRUST ME HEAR ME OUT

—FRAZER

FRAZER'S FRIENDS Dick and Helen, a professor and his aspiring-writer wife, had lived in Riverdale, the Bronx. Frazer had met them during his brief career as the athletic director of the famously incendiary little college where Dick still taught, halfway upriver between the Bronx and Wildmoor. Jenny had gotten the sense Dick liked knowing Frazer but didn't like Frazer, while Helen disliked knowing him as much as she disliked him, but they were both the kind of people determined to feel they were daring. They had subscriptions to the *Evergreen Review* and season tickets for avant-garde theater. Dick's specialism was the nineteenth-century American novel but he was really an experimental poet, as yet unpublished, whose heated defense of one of his contemporaries against the assaults of a rival professor was being published, letter by letter, in the journal of the Modern Language Association. It would be Jenny's task, among others, to archive these letters for a book Dick thought he might publish. Helen had been a housewife until the past year, when their youngest child had gone off to college. This was the change that had prompted them to do something they would never have dreamed of otherwise, and hire a housekeeper/assistant, so that Helen could go every day to the tiny Greenwich Village apartment she'd rented for use as a study, to work on her novel.

Frazer had told Dick and Helen that Jenny "needed a place to lie low for a while" and that it was best if they didn't know more. She had to admit he'd been skillfully vague. He'd made it seem, on the one hand, that she might have a boyfriend who'd gotten abusive. On the other hand, he'd implied she might be a bona fide fugitive from the law. Either way Dick and Helen couldn't say no to her without seeming hard-hearted, or square. Together they had worked out her story: Jenny was the daughter of old family friends, living with Dick and Helen to establish residency so that she could apply to a New York State school. Her name was Sally Chen. She planned to be a doctor.

Dick said to her, "One of the truly great things about academic life in this country, Jenny, is that it has always embraced people of every race and every nation. White, black, yellow, red. So it'll make perfect sense to our acquaintances that Helen and I would have known Chinese people. *Sally*. Sorry. Should we celebrate?"

Dick and Helen made a point of living their lives as much as possible free of American commercialism. They had just been to the South of France, and had brought back—smuggled back, in two suitcases taken over empty for the purpose—quantities of handmade cheeses as well as brandies and wines that weren't available for sale in the States. "The artisanal aspect of cuisine is being completely effaced," Dick said, cutting into a round of cheese carefully, like a surgeon, to create extremely minuscule wedges, "by the corporatizing of agriculture, by commercialism—basically, by all the wonderful social ills our nation is so good at manifesting and spreading to other parts of the world. Have some cheese, guys," he said to Jenny and Frazer. "And wine. Let's not forget about the wine."

"Right on," Frazer said. They lifted their glasses.

"Can you taste that?" Dick cried. "If you had a more acidic wine, the cheese would taste chalky. That's what's being lost, all this knowledge—this *culture*. To freedom," he added belatedly.

The arrangement lasted for barely six months. "I think," Dick said to her one night, choosing his words with ostentatious care, "that you are a person of substance. A person that, under better circumstances, I could imagine as a very close friend. Don't you think?" And another time: "The whole thing with not knowing your story has gotten kind of hard for Helen, because she tends to assume the worst. If you feel the same sort of respect for us that we feel for you, you might clarify things and put Helen's mind at ease. I mean," he held his hands surrender-style, laughing, "just a hint. By all means please don't tell us who you are! Just the broad strokes. Are we talking multiple felony indictments or, ah, first offense? Maybe just a bad vibe that made you want to get away for a while?"

And then at last she had woken with him in her room, leaning into her bed, his old-cheese-and-tobacco breath hot on her neck. She'd sprung up. "Are you sleeping okay?" he had whispered.

"Yes, thank you," she said, and cringed from him until he went back to his room.

The next morning, after they'd both gone to work, she packed her bag, put on her cleaning gloves, and wiped everything in the house. It took hours. She went through the kitchen drawers and wiped every fork, knife, spoon, and utensil. She wiped the spices in the spice rack and the Tupperware containers in the fridge. She went through the apartment room by room wiping even things she'd never touched before: the Rockwell Kent engraving in its frame, the Paul Robeson records. She saved the bathroom for last. When she arrived there she stood over the toilet she had cleaned once a week on her knees. She felt as if she'd never really seen this toilet before. Then she wiped it, for the last time, and left.

SHE'D CHOSEN Rhinecliff at random: She'd decided to go where one fourth of her money would take her. It was not very far. In Rhinecliff she had stood for a long time on the deserted station platform with her duffel bag and her accordion file, looking out at the river that had lain alongside the train the whole way from New York. She smelled rotting vegetation, but also brine. She sniffed, hard. It was low tide, and the ocean smell somehow seemed stronger, though the ocean was now two hours farther away. She'd finally walked out to the front of the station, called a taxi, and asked for the nearest motel. There had only been one, miles inland near a town called Rhinebeck. Everything riverine, *rhine*-something. The motel had subtracted another huge chunk of her funds, but then the ad for the Wildmoor job had appeared in the Rhinebeck *Gazette* the next day. Later she would learn that the ad had been running for months without any responses, because Dolly rarely made payments, a fact known all over the town. But she was an immigrant, unknowing, without options. She agreed to take board as a part of her pay. Late October, 1972. She would remember the Nixon placards at the ends of the secretive drives that slipped off through the yellow-leaved woods from the long country road.

She chose Red Hook for her post office box because it was barely a town; the post office sat by itself just past a desolate intersection, and served scattered farms, or so she guessed reading the flyers on the bulletin board. She called herself Iris Wong and subscribed to the Rhinebeck *Gazette*. Once it started coming she drove to Red Hook two or three evenings a week, after the post office window had closed, and took the slim accumulation of papers to a neglected little park on the river with a lone vandalized picnic table. She never saw anyone using this table and she didn't use it, either. She read the papers in the car. She would tackle the AP capsules first, whipping open each of the two or three papers to the national news page and skimming it with eyes narrowed and head slightly averted, as if she expected to be struck blind by the newsprint. After she'd gone through them all without finding any mention of herself she'd start over, a little more calmly, and actually read, from beginning to end. There wasn't much to be learned about the state of the larger world, or even about the state of the Rhinebeck area, from this newspaper, full as it was of church spaghetti-dinner announcements and tips for keeping Canada geese off the lawn. But she perversely enjoyed that aspect of it—enjoyed the sense it gave her that she, too, was imprisoned. She couldn't be expected to do anything for now but familiarize herself with her cell.

November, December. The New Year, January. Her ritual with the paper had turned into a lazy indulgence. She would leave the engine on, blast the heat and the radio, slowly smoke at least a half a pack of cigarettes. One day at the beginning of February she read in the paper dated January 28, 1973, that cease-fire agreements had been signed in Paris, to end the war in Vietnam. The article had been reprinted from the *Times*: *Mrs. Nguyen Thi Binh, Foreign Minister of the Vietcong Provisional Revolutionary Government, wore an amber ao dai with embroidery on the bodice, an unusual ornament for her. Mrs. Rogers, wife of the Secretary of State, wore a dress with a red top and navy skirt*. The man she loved was in prison, and she herself was a fugitive for the things they had done to protest—no, *demolish*—this war. Now it all had been calmly concluded, the outfits of the various parties described as if for a society column. She remembered letting the paper fall into her lap and lighting a fresh cigarette, then pulling the cuff of her shirt up over the heel of her hand to wipe away the condensation on the windshield. The sun had just set on the far side of the river, the afterglow a cool wintertime pink, like the flesh of a melon. The leaves were all gone from the trees, and against the suffused evening sky the bare branches formed a dark filigree. She heard, somewhere near the river's surface, the frantic honking of geese settling down for the night. It had occurred to her that perhaps she should keep this article, as a memento. After one more cigarette, and one last look at the fading sky, she'd thrown away the rest of the papers and driven back to Wildmoor, but when she got there she threw away the article, too. It seemed empty, a memento of nothing.

BEFORE, IN her previous life, she had been a bomber. She and William had bombed several government targets, mostly draft offices, always deep in the night when no one would be killed. They'd known nothing better seized attention than violence, and that the rightness of theirs would be obvious, dedicated as it was to saving lives. They'd meant to persuade the most hawkish, resistant Americans, and been sure that they could—but after she'd gone underground Jenny realized they'd never known quite what they faced. They had known only like-minded people. Even so-called conservatives around the Bay Area had held views not so different from theirs. Jenny's life at Wildmoor was the first time she was ever submerged in that part of the country she and William had meant as their audience, against which they'd fought with such hope, and so little success.

The scale of her situation at Wildmoor was exceedingly small, finite, knowable. A world of twenty-odd people or less, all living in the rhythms of a distant time, more like her vague ideas of 1933 or even 1893, the year Dolly had been born, than 1973. A true Shangri-la for its natives. After living there for a couple of months she looked up the legend of Rip Van Winkle, having seen reference to that person everywhere—it was the sort of thing that had been no part of her California education—and then began to see everyone around her as a race of Rip Van Winkles, still asleep. What would these people think if they were ever to take the train to the city, or even drive a half hour in their cars to Albany or Poughkeepsie, where the year 1973 was steaming along in all its anger and confusion without them?

The local trait found its most extreme expression in her new employer. She had never known someone with money—transcendent, atemporal money, money of such a baffling magnitude as to require only one intervention with the plane of reality to have eternal, irreversible effects. The kind of money impervious even to its own disappearance, over a couple of centuries of folly and abhorrence of labor. She had thought she knew all about class, she recognized the names and faces of the titans of American industry, had come to understand that none of these people were other than several lucky steps from the sort of hustling her father had done, lucklessly, all his life—but she'd never known someone with money. And never having known someone with money, she had never encountered what she now recognized as an axiom, that the rich are incurious. She had arrived at Dolly's with an autobiography that was neither too exciting nor too bland, too local nor too foreign, too complete (no one remembers her life thoroughly) nor too full of strange holes, yet Dolly had never asked for it. Dolly had never asked her any questions at all, beyond, "Have you got your own car? That's all right. You can drive mine." It seemed to come as no surprise to Dolly that "Iris Wong," "Chinese," "from San Francisco," should materialize to meet Dolly's around-the-house needs. And Jenny found that, far from being grateful for the reprieve from scrutiny, she was increasingly driven to make herself known. Increasingly angry at not being asked. She knew better than to offer information that was not solicited, yet she increasingly volunteered tidbits that weren't even true. "My parents never really understood my interest in drawing," she announced one day, as Dolly sat watching the bluebirds in the sycamore tree. "My grandfather Brinson was a great collector of drawings," said Dolly. "I wonder if we could get down some of the drawings he brought back from Peru, and hang them in the sun room."

Then it was still Dolly's unrealized plan—Mrs. Fowler's, really, but Dolly needed the money—to open the house up for tours, but with Jenny's arrival the plan gained momentum. Mrs. Fowler had decided the restoration work itself could be called an attraction. Jenny put herself to the task of learning restoration as she'd once taught herself to handle oil paint, to repair her old car, to assemble a timer and fuse. She began using the scrapbooks of

Wildmoor in the local library, since Dolly's own records of the changes the house had been through were all buried somewhere in her rooms, so that the excavation of them was its own separate task. One day, reading, she came across the accounts of a party Dolly had given to celebrate the marriage of a nephew, in 1954. Dolly had invited the entire towns of Rhinecliff and Rhinebeck, as well as her social equals up and down the river. When the guests had arrived, they were divided in two—the river people ushered into the house for caviar and champagne, the townspeople sent down to the field, to the far side of a rope strung nearby the gazebo. The townspeople as one had walked out—it was 1954, after all! They weren't serfs!—and Dolly had professed herself truly bewildered. But after a town representative explained peoples' feelings to her she'd apologized in the newspaper, and added that she planned to be buried in the Rhinebeck cemetery, which was public, instead of her family's plot. The insult was forgiven.

Not long after, standing in the aisle of the hardware store reading down her list of supplies, Jenny heard someone say, near the register, "So now we have the privilege of giving the old bitch three dollars to look at her house. I guess she's finally broke."

"She deserves to be," someone else said.

When Jenny emerged from the aisle, with her supplies in her arms, the speakers, two Rhinebeck men, turned and stared at her. One was the proprietor. He'd been friendly the first time she'd shopped here. He rang her up on this day without speaking.

"That's her," she heard him tell the other man as she went out the door.

SHE NEVER meant to become a familiar face anywhere, yet she'd find herself chatting with people. Introducing herself to the hardware-store owner, the train conductor, the librarian. Compensating, she knew, for her strangeness—not just her strangeness to this town, but her lone Asian face. Trying to outflank suspicion. Sometimes she longed for a companion, to fulfill this desire for acceptance. A confidante, to make sure that she didn't break down and confide in the plumber. It was more and more difficult for her to trust her intuitions, her judgments, her decisions. The one-year anniversary of the day on which William had been arrested in their bomb-making workshop by FBI agents; the day on which she had fled her apartment with two grocery bags of her snatched-up belongings; the day on which Frazer had driven her in the whistling darkness down I-5 to the Los Angeles airport came and went and she failed to notice until several days later. The oversight made her feel panic, as if she had spoken aloud in her sleep, or gone into town naked, or committed some other rash act of exposure.

Beneath all this self-criticism was the thought that she tried not to think, of how terribly lonely it was to be in this alone. She pretended her longings were purely pragmatic: A companion would give her the gift of another perspective. Two were more likely than one to make crucial corrections, to compensate for extreme paranoia, or extreme tendencies toward the sense of invulnerability. She was capable of veering in the latter direction, though never for long. But even brief veering was reckless, like jerking the wheel while driving. You might jerk off the road, and then you'd be a jerk. That was just the kind of stupid, drunk-seeming funk her mind lately slumped into. Jerk/jerk. Drunk/funk. She had a growing catalogue of dangerous sins a partner might help her confront, chief among them the irrational but insistent idea that her time was almost done; that perhaps, in just a few more months, she'd be able to come out. Completely. She had always hoped, half-believed, that time was the answer, as if her problem were like anything in the physical world, subject to erosion. Or perhaps it was a narrow window of opportunity she awaited, a confluence of attitudes and events that could occur any moment. If this was true, she might have already missed it.

The Watergate hearings began her first summer at Wildmoor. She listened to them as she worked, finally painting the upstairs bedrooms, which she'd fully prepared while the weather was cold. She'd stored furniture, vacuumed great bales of dust, chosen colors and gotten them mixed. Gently scraped eons of shape-dulling paint off the moldings, covered countless complexly paned windows. The radio she listened to was a cheap little transistor she'd found in the stables, perhaps forgotten by some short-lived, never-paid, handy-man predecessor of hers. It could hardly hold on to a signal; every few minutes static would rise like a sandstorm and drown the words out. She'd climb down from her ladder and yank the antennae. Finally it occurred to her to put the radio on an extension cord, and then she lashed it to her ladder with duct tape and tweaked and adjusted it constantly while she never stopped painting. The little radio taking on siftings of paint like an outward expression of static. A spectrum of static in buttercup yellow and sea green and cabbage-rose pink. She felt almost happy, to finally have vigorous work. Or perhaps she was happy to feel herself drawn in again by the life of the nation. Sometimes Watergate felt as surreal as a dream, because she had no one with whom to discuss it. No one beside her to gasp—really gasp—when Nixon's ex-secretary let fall that everything was on tape. She had rushed out of the room, in her amazement actually scrambled down from her ladder and rushed from the room to the head of the stairs—and stopped there, hearing Dolly's bland voice drifting in from the porch. Hearing teatime visitation in session, the sound of the landed who lived on this river. The sound of the "set," anchored in ancient greatness, where even the dirt and the trees justified them. For them there was no vivid convulsion in the life of the nation. There was no odor of change on the air. There was not even the melancholy of national shame that the "average American" felt. Theirs was a nation transcending such temporal things. What must that be like, she had thought, turning back from the stairs with her brush in her hand. That complacence that said, I have no need to watch the strange signs, to scent change on the wind. I have no need to pay any attention. It certainly wasn't the thing that drove Nixon to tape conversations. That was the act of an insecure, paranoid man, never sure of his empire. On the river empire was eternal, even when funded by three-dollar tours.

When the first room was painted she rented a sander to start on redoing the floor, and sent a mushroom cloud of sawdust to the sixteen-foot ceiling. Sawdust settled thickly all along the painstakingly repainted moldings. Because the summer had been so humid, and the paint so slow to dry, the sawdust seemed as if it might stick to the new paint forever. It didn't, but only after three days of additional labor. She'd let herself cry when this happened; and then she took back the sander and decided to paint with no thought of the floors for as long as she could. She would deal with those later. The first night she could finally shut all the windows, because the paint had all dried and no scent of it lingered, was the night of first frost. Only early September. For the fall she planned cleaning the library ceiling. She did a final dustmopping of the freshly swept floors after taking up all of the dropcloths. As she stood looking over her work Dolly came to join her. Dolly had looked at the rooms perhaps three times a day every day for three months. Now she said, "I don't remember that shade on the wainscoting."

"It may be off by a tone or two. It's hard to match these historical colors."

"I don't mean the tone, dear. I mean the color. I don't recall having drab gray wainscoting when I was a girl."

After a long silence Jenny said, very calmly, "I used the scrapbooks in the Rhinebeck library for all of the colors, and then you approved the paint chips."

"The scrapbooks I donated? Did Mrs. McNulty go through them with you?" When this had been confirmed Dolly said, still with a touch of displeasure, as though an unfair point had been wrested from her, "Mrs. McNulty does a wonderful job." Dolly's eyes narrowed at the wainscoting.

"They're wonderful scrapbooks," Jenny heard herself saying. "I've learned so much from them. I read about that big party you threw."

"That must not have been me. I'm not one for big parties."

"You had a big party in 1954, when your nephew got married."

"Did I? I much prefer just hosting tea."

"I wondered whether that's why you began hosting tea. To open the house to the town, after closing it to them."

"I'm not sure what you mean. Tea is just a tradition. My mother held visiting hours, and my grandmother, and all our set."

"But anyone can come to tea. Not just your set."

"You'd have a hard time finding any of my set anymore."

"What I mean is, you wouldn't let people who were not of your set in the house, at your nephew's big party."

Dolly looked at her for what seemed the first time. "That was a long time ago. I hadn't realized how much things had changed."

"Things are still changing," Jenny said. To stop herself saying anything else she went quickly downstairs.

IT WASN'T UNTIL the late fall, when the leaves were yellow on the trees again, and then on the ground, and brief flurries of snow had begun, that she understood what the Watergate scandal might mean for her. She'd been to Red Hook for the papers, and had a letter from William. In the papers were the reports of the president's having fired the special prosecutor and abolished his office, and the attorney general and deputy attorney general having resigned. Congress seemed daily more in favor of Nixon's impeachment—but these things she already knew from the radio news. In the letter was this:

"We've finally come back through the looking glass to the side that is sane. When even the crooks in the government are ready to call the president the biggest crook of all, I can see the conditions for general uprising we once feared would never arrive. The "average American" wants Nixon out. The critical faculty we tried so hard to inculcate with regard to the war has arrived with regard to the White House. I wonder how I—*or any person like me*—would fare now, brought before the robed judges, in this altered climate."

Attached was a short note from Dana. "William asked me to get you the name of this *very good friend*. William thinks you should look this friend up. Write to him at the address below and set up a phone call."

The language of the note, the *good friend* that she should *look up*, was obviously William's. She hadn't known Dana and William corresponded with each other independent of her. That behind her back the two of them pondered something so private as her, Jenny's, fate. It annoyed her, or at least, something did. She was aware of a childish unwillingness in herself to realistically face what surrender would mean. When she imagined it, she saw herself among the neatly dressed, anxious visitors to San Quentin, placing her hand on the Plexi partition with her palm matched to his, somehow feeling the warmth of his skin. Not herself on the far side of the glass, without even William among her rare visitors. She couldn't really imagine surrender at all. Although she was amazed to realize it, she and William had never discussed what they'd do if they got separated. They had endlessly discussed what they'd do if they both were arrested, but they had never discussed, perhaps because it had never occurred to them, what they would do if only one of them was caught. Every action they had ever done they'd done assiduously together. That had been part of the power of it, that their every movement was in tandem. Then his arrest seemed to come as a freak, a complete accident. On his way home he'd planned to drop by their workshop, a garage that they rented, to pick up a tool. She'd been at home making salad to have with their dinner. Listening to the police band, as was her around-the-clock, paranoid habit. Peeling a carrot, listening less to the cops than for William's footfall on the stair. Lasagna in the oven. Sometimes the harvester's scythe falls and you are left standing. Running through the apartment with grocery bags, grabbing your things. But why? she asked. Why was she spared? A true marriage, he'd once said, was one in which the fear of outliving the other rendered minor the fear of one's death. His arrest had been like his death to her, and she'd wanted to be dead as well. But she'd known that she had to live on, to wait for him, and this was the thing that she felt she lived for. His suggesting she turn herself in somehow seemed like his cutting her loose, though she knew this was not what he'd meant.

She wrote back, "I'll let you know when I reach our good friend," and glued the slip of paper with the lawyer's name and phone number on it into one of her shoes, underneath the insole, so that all day long she had to step on it, and think of it. Merely calling the lawyer wouldn't mean she had chosen surrender. But a week passed, and then several weeks more, and she still didn't call. As winter deepened she sometimes went down to the river and sat watching the train. That close to the water the wind was much worse; she would smoke, without gloves, as her fingers went bluish and stiff. It was the same train on which she'd arrived here. She remembered what satisfaction it had given her to find that the Wildmoor property ran along the same tracks, as if staying nearby would ensure that one day she'd get back on and finish the trip. Now she knew that the train went to Canada. Sitting blue and numb on the dead grass, looking down at the dross that washed up from the river, she would feel the train register itself first in her bones, amplify her teeth-chattering before it burst into view and she saw, as it streaked past the curve, a conductor's pale face and raised hand, briefly waving to her before whipped out of sight. She would pretend she was ruminating the plausibility of it, the chances she'd save enough money, the chances of crossing the border, but she knew—as she might not have known if the train were just a little bit farther away, if it were gliding on the river's other side, if it were merely a wail she heard in the night—that the train was a dream. She didn't have the documents or the money, or Canadian friends.

Then, as February began, something happened having nothing to do with her own ruminations, and she stopped hesitating and flew to the phone. In Berkeley, a band of masked, armed, black-clad women and men kidnapped the nineteen-year-old daughter of one of California's premier families. The girl's last name was as well known as Fremont's, familiar to all Californians from big granite buildings and vast public parks. The kidnappers were a revolutionary cadre that nobody had heard of before, but they claimed kinship to a long list of better-known threats, like the Weather

Underground and the Black Panther Party. The kidnapping had taken place in full view of the neighbors, Berkeley graduate students and young couples who'd thrown themselves on their floors as machine-gun fire shattered their windows and the screaming girl was dragged from her house wearing only a bathrobe, and dumped in the trunk of a car. All over the country the kidnapping was greeted with outrage and horror. It even made the front page of the Rhinebeck *Gazette*. If William was right—if Watergate had made mainstream Americans more sympathetic to radicalism—something like this would exhaust that new sympathy quickly. She didn't know anything about these kidnappers, who they were, what they hoped to achieve, but she could see they were being portrayed in the worst possible light. She had dreamed of a window that might open for her. What if Watergate really had opened it? Now the public's dismay at the kidnapping would close it again.

And so one freezing morning she boarded the train at Rhinecliff, at an hour unusual for her so she'd see no conductors she knew, and rode farther south toward the city than she'd been since the night she had left. She got off at Peekskill. Here the river emerged from the vise of the highlands and pooled open again to the width of a lake. Beside the quaint station were a few scarred benches facing the water and the cement plant a half mile away on the opposite bank. "If it's raining I'll meet you inside," she'd told him, "but if not I'll be out on a bench. The wind is brutal off the river at this time of year. I'm sure we won't have company."

The lawyer, when he finally came, turned out to be much younger than she'd expected. She had imagined a salt-and-pepper moustache and eyebrows, some sort of socialist party survivor who'd seen darker days and far worse situations. Instead he was smooth-cheeked and handsome, with a pair of steel-framed glasses to lend gravity. His voice, when he said hello to her, had the hard city edge she had heard on the phone. Then it had been persuasive; in person she found it too dissonant, matched with his face. "Nice spot," he said, pulling his collar tightly around his neck.

It was a dark, windy, quintessentially upstate New York day. Clouds the color of pewter rolled over them, pushed by strong wind. The air felt pregnant with snow, a worse cold than dry cold would have been. She had been waiting for almost half an hour, in her thin jeans and an old leather jacket that was missing two buttons, and a sweatshirt rolled up for a scarf. She couldn't feel her hands or her toes, but she was used to it. She hadn't bought winter clothes since she'd been here. She'd never had enough money.

"I won't keep you long," she said, feeling embarrassed. She realized that in some part of herself she had actually wanted the older, grandfatherly man. The one who would arrive with a gruff nod but a warm gaze, who would be knowledgeable and relaxed, having won harder cases than hers more times than he could count. She suddenly longed to be sheltered by someone like that. Instead she was huddled outside on a bench with a very young man, and their meeting so far felt as awkward and fraught as a date.

He was watching her, waiting, and so she finally choked out her question. "In light of the current political climate," she began awkwardly, in the way she'd rehearsed. When she was finished he said, after a moment, "I think it's fair to say that the current climate is pretty much the same as it's been. No deals for fugitives. They'll talk to you once you surrender. It's safe to assume that coming in on your own will help out, later on."

"I didn't just mean the climate inside the Justice Department. I meant the political climate in general. The Watergate scandal."

"I'm not seeing the connection."

"With abuses of power at the executive level so certain, it struck me there might be more sympathy now for the radical movement."

"I don't know about that. You'd be safer just putting that out of your mind. It won't bear on your case."

Now she no longer felt she was just quoting phrases of William's. The young lawyer's tone was so breezily certain she wondered just how young he was. Was he younger than her?

"How can you say that?" she demanded. "The government's prosecutorial habits are always political."

"Sure, but the charges against you are serious. I'm not trying to stick up for Nixon. I think the guy's as crooked as they come. But you can't say the executive office did criminal acts, so my criminal acts aren't important."

"It's not the so-called crimes, it's the underlying reasons for them. *You* can't strip our acts of their context and say they were crimes, and at the same time strip something like Vietnam of its crime, and call it a legitimate venture."

"Vietnam was a war. A distinct body of law applied to it."

"That doesn't make it right."

"No, but your case will be decided on law. I agree with you, Jenny. But we're talking about your chances in the justice system. We're not in ethics class."

This made her wish for the meeting to end. She stared across the water at the glowing cement plant. Although it was midday the sky looked like dusk, and the plant's green and gold lights shone intensely. A plume of white smoke, perhaps steam, emerged and was steadily snatched by the wind. The river looked like the ocean downstream at its mouth, green and full of harsh chop. She said, barely hearing herself over the wind, "I don't have any money."

"We don't need to talk about that."

"We will. Maybe there's no point in our talking at all. I'll have to have a court-appointed lawyer."

"Would your family help?"

"My mother died when I was a baby. My father isn't sympathetic to my views."

"Enough said. Jenny, if you go forward with me I want you to assume money isn't an issue. Money will be worked out somehow. The issue is, do you want to go in? Do you want to surrender?"

The white plume was still steadily torn from its smokestack. She sighed; she must sound like a truculent child. "Let's pretend that I do."

"What happens after that will have a lot to do with how much you cooperate."

"I won't name names."

For the first time she was aware of impatience. "Then you'll have a hard time," he said, crossing and recrossing his legs. "I hope you weren't expecting me to tell you that there's some kind of Watergate amnesty for the government's enemies. Your only advantage is the stuff that you know. You had a large circle of friends when you lived in Berkeley. Your boyfriend was convicted of bombing draft offices. At the time they were claimed by something called the People's Army and no one believes that was just him alone, or even just him and you. You see, I did my homework before coming here. If you surrender and offer no information you're going to get a very hostile reception."

"I can't betray friends. I don't mean to drag you back to ethics class, but it's a principle for me."

"Maybe you have information that doesn't involve your close friends. Things you've heard on the grapevine."

"Like what?"

"Information about this kidnapping would help you. A lot."

She knew she shouldn't be surprised this had come up, but she still wondered whether he sensed this was why she had called him. Flamboyant behavior elsewhere in the Left; sudden desire to get herself cover. "Not my circle," she said.

"Same hometown. You might know someone who knows one of them."

"I don't, and if I did we'd just be back in ethics class. I'd be willing to talk about general things. Common techniques, types of targets—"

"You wouldn't betray *kidnappers*? That's beyond the pale, Jenny. They snatched a little girl. God only knows what they're doing to her."

"She's not 'a little girl,' she's a nineteen-year-old college student, not that that means she deserved to be kidnapped. They say they're treating her in accordance with the Geneva Conventions."

"Oh my God, that's not even the most absurd thing they say. You can't really believe that."

"I don't yet disbelieve it! Almost the entire world believes the worst of them. Who's left to believe the best, if not us?"

"Kidnapping's not politics, regardless of what those clowns want to claim."

"I'm not in agreement with them, I'm extending them the benefit of the doubt. Isn't that part of your *legal* discourse? Kidnapping's not a tactic I'd ever embrace."

"I hope not. And don't talk about what you have or haven't embraced, even hypothetically. I'm not representing you yet."

This stung her. "You haven't exactly said whether you would," she said, after a minute.

"Of course I would. But you haven't said whether you want me, and I'm not sure you do. I'm not sure you're ready to go through with this. If you become my client I'll do everything in my power, but you'll still face the same choice. You'll feel a lot of pressure to talk, and not just from the government. You may feel a lot of pressure from yourself. You don't want to go to prison for ten years, maybe more. I'm not saying we're certain to lose. I'm not saying you should abandon your principles, either. I'm saying you need to face facts. There won't be any Watergate amnesty."

She'd flushed from his tone, but she knew he was right. Perhaps she'd already known. William was in prison, she realized. Sometimes she realized this incredible fact with fresh force. William was in prison, and his capacity to gauge the political atmosphere was not the same as it had been when he was out in the world. She'd wasted this young lawyer's time. In some way, though, she'd enjoyed it. She'd liked arguing with him.

"I understand," she told him.

It was time for the city-bound train. Before he turned back toward the station he said, "It's too bad you don't know where those kidnappers are. That would be worth at least three Watergates."

"Really?" She knew it was a peace offering.

"Oh, yeah. They'd throw out all the charges and make you an FBI agent."

"The worst fate of all!" she said, laughing.

"Write me." He put his hand out and she took it. Even through the numb chill she could feel his hand's warmth, and the shock, the warm touch, made her stomach turn over with longing. She pulled her hand away quickly.

"I'll write you," she said.

IT WAS HARD, she had to admit, to give the kidnappers the benefit of the doubt. They'd taken weeks to convey their demands, and when they finally did she had the sense of a panicked all-night study session, or a coffee-soaked chainsmokers' mad argument that had collapsed in indiscriminate compromise. There were pages on typewritten pages. There were declarations of principles and sociological tracts, and a mythlike explanation of their symbol. There was a long list of other revolutionary movements with which they shared ideological ties or—perhaps this was meant as a threat—"logistical/material reciprocity arrangements for ammunition, supplies, and ground troops." There was a tape with the victim's voice on it. "They've chosen me as a symbol of the problems of capitalism, Mom, Dad; and I think if you try you can see what their point is." The victim detailed—clearly reading, her voice strangely girlish yet dull—the demand: that a week's worth of "good, healthy food" be distributed to every California resident whose annual income was below the poverty line, or who suffered some form of social marginalization, for example was a recently paroled criminal, or a resident of the state's substandard low-income housing, or otherwise verifiably poor. Every person in need must be fed. The food was to be distributed, no strings attached and no hassles, starting in no less than a week and continuing for no less than a month, anywhere that was not a social services center or some other record-keeping arm of any level of government and preferably at normal supermarkets where The People were accustomed to going, so as to make it convenient. The distribution was not even the actual ransom, but a goodwill gesture, after which ransom talks would commence. Periodically the girl would pause, and a rustling of sheets would be heard. "I just had to turn over the page," she murmured at one point.

Lying flat on the scaffold she'd built beneath the library ceiling, watching the colored lozenges of light from the faux-Flemish windows moving over her legs as the March sun came through the bare trees, gently swabbing the foul brown stains with her soap-lathered sponge, Jenny still had the transistor beside her. After its dizzying summer and fall the Watergate scandal had been in eclipse for the whole of the winter. Congress wanted the tapes, the president had refused them, and now it was up to the courts to decide. Like the rest of the audience—the sofa citizenry, she thought ruefully, whom she'd been forced to join—her attention had been taken up by the kidnapping everywhere Watergate let it go slack. But for her there was also the oddly secretive family dimension that the rest of the sofa folk knew nothing of. The ransom demand was picked apart in the Left-leaning press. It was grandstanding, self-righteous and impractical, out of touch with the actual needs of The People. A one-time food handout was just the kind of ostentatious paternalistic gesture the United States government was fond of making in the Third World countries it had previously helped to destroy. This must have frustrated them, Jenny imagined—to have labored to come up with a ransom that would clearly denote them as selfless and noble, and then to have it thrown back in their faces. Even the most radical guests on the student-run radio show she could sometimes tune in said things like, "With the movement dying out, you can't be surprised at these macabre developments. It's like a corpse twitching. You could call this the decadent stage of the Left; if there was ever a golden age, this is our signal it's over." She felt mingled outrage and shame, and a certain fiery defensiveness for the cadre, hearing comments like these. Yes, they were probably crazy. But who with legitimate, fervent belief hadn't also been looked on as crazy? The kidnapping was a public mortification for the Left, an occasion for shirt rending and excommunication, but it also gave Jenny the sense of One Nation she'd felt during Watergate summer. Except that this nation was hers, her own nation-within, sharing borders yet pursuing itself on an alternate plane.

A few weeks after their meeting she wrote the young lawyer No. "You were right," she explained. "I'm not ready for this." She took the train back to Peekskill to mail the letter, so he would only have that place linked to her. Then she hoped for relief. In the weeks since they'd met she'd been desperate to see him again, even just to say No to his face. He was the first person in almost two years she had spoken to truthfully, and so it wasn't her desire so much as her failure to anticipate her desire she found so unnerving. She had dreams about him: mortifyingly sexual dreams in which they made desperate love to each other, which weren't even as bad as the abstract emotional dreams, in which she "knew" that he loved her. She wished she missed William as she'd missed him at first. She tried to summon those waves of blind pain she had felt at their first separation, even tried to revisit the worst lows of their history together in the hopes she could "plumb from their murks certainty?" of her love. She finally wrote William to explain her decision and felt guilty for some of her phrases: "Your idea that the robed judges might now be more kindly disposed gave me hope, but it isn't the case. You or anyone like you might do worse at present, or so I am told *by a very good source*."

The Rhinebeck library sat on the town square, a graceful little building of cut stone and stained glass that had a kinship to the Rhinecliff train station. The two had been designed by the same architects, hired by a titan of railroads who had summered out here and who'd wanted his guests to embark from the train—and page through the newspaper, and bow head in prayer (there was also the wonderful church)—in the splendor to which they were accustomed, but on a quainter, more countrified scale. "Our historic river valley," Mrs. McNulty would say. "Everywhere you look there's a door to the past." She had become fond of Jenny for her supposed role as a restorer. When Jenny first ventured into the library not for the Wildmoor scrapbooks but for West Coast newspapers, Mrs. McNulty kept confusedly bringing her clippings about Queen Anne décor; but after some days she perceived that the errand had changed. Now when Jenny dropped into the library, always trying to seem casual, she would find the most recently arrived *San Francisco Chronicles* and *Examiners* neatly laid out stair-step style, the dates showing, at the large corner table she liked. "Please don't, it's all right, Mrs. McNulty," she said, but it kept happening. Sometimes while she read, a new bundle of mail would come—the newspapers came on delay, as always with libraries. She'd hear Mrs. McNulty humming and clipping the string with her small pair of scissors. Then Mrs. McNulty would come to her holding the new ones like freshly baked bread. "Oh Iris, I'm afraid you're homesick," she'd say, setting them down.

The girl's family had responded to the demand for the goodwill gesture with a fastidious attention under which the demand could only look absurd. "We're sure grateful to those folks, honey, for shooting straight with us," the girl's father said to a lawnful of cameras. "And we're working away to see how we can meet this demand. But the thing is, it's a little bit vague. A week's worth of food, over the course of a month—we're thinking, a few times a week for a month? We just want to be sure we get everything right. As for the numbers—well, honey, I hope you can convey to these folks that, in a big state like ours, it's not easy to find everybody who's poor. We have so many ways of calculating that number, and it's likely to be such a big number—and that doesn't make anyone happy. But that's the way that it is. We've got some folks here who are praying for you, and are helping us out just so much—they're mathematicians and statisticians. And they think—well, their estimate is that maybe we're talking about half a billion dollars' worth of food." Here his voice cracked. "And I have to say, there's no way I can do it. But I'm going to do the very best that I can."

The response came within just a few days, another tape at the door to a radio station—the tapes seemed to drop from the sky, and bore no fingerprints. "These people want you to know, Dad, they didn't mean to make a demand that nobody could meet.

Um—what you said, about doing the best that you can, that's just fine. Just do it, really quickly, okay?" But the girl's nervousness seemed to alternate now with a different, peeved tone. "These people want you to know they're not crazy. Don't try to make them look crazy. Their message is a political message, it's about poverty and the problems of capitalism, and I'm a symbol of all that, as they said. They are fulfilling the conditions of the Geneva Conventions . . . in accordance with the Codes of International War." She had a script, but she seemed to be straying from it. "And if you'd tell Mom the way she keeps crying—that's really depressing. It's like she's standing right next to my grave."

Doing the very best that he could seemed to involve, in the end, compliance with some of the least advisable of the cadre's demands, and disregard of many of the others. With the dispatch of exceptional wealth the girl's family set up a food-distribution command center and rented a flotilla of refrigerated trucks. And then, pointing out that the cadre had insisted they do so, they hired to distribute the food only welfare recipients, paroled criminals, and other often-unemployed individuals. There was a predictable range of results. A few ex-cons told the papers they were grateful for the second chance in life. One truckful was hijacked at gunpoint. Others vanished in more subtle ways. Where the trucks did arrive unmolested, workers hurled the food hand over fist out of the back, while crowds trampled each other. An eight-year-old boy was knocked out by a frozen whole chicken.

Jenny knew she shouldn't have found it surprising how skillfully the family was able to present itself as the beleaguered party, doing its best to accommodate, but outflanked on all sides by plain greed. Public sympathy for them kept increasing; they were the quintessence of noblesse oblige, they were doing the best that they could, and who doesn't prefer the rich who give a crumb of their wealth, to the poor who rush forward to take it? This was where the Left lost its last shred of patience. Only this band of irresponsible adventurers, they complained, could have made the rich so sympathetic. The one observer of the spiraling affair who seemed displeased with the family was the victim herself. The food program debacle unfolded, and like a missile the third tape arced out of the sky. "It seems to me you're not doing your very best at all, Dad," the girl said, and now she was starting to sound really angry. "It looks like that food program was a complete total sham. I know it's a tax write-off anyway. Isn't it, Dad? And I just have to wonder, I feel like if you or Mom, or Alexa or Katie was kidnapped I would just do whatever it took. Which is not what you're doing!" She didn't seem to be reading a script at all anymore—or perhaps her kidnappers had started to know how she spoke, how she tended to phrase things. Perhaps their new scripts showed a talent for slickness they seemed to lack everywhere else.

When March came to an end Jenny drove to Buell's for wood stripper, paint, new dropcloths, and a safer stepladder. It was warm enough to work with open windows again and she could start the restaining job in the upstairs conservatory; soon enough it would be hot and humid, and the stain would goo up like molasses and never get dry. In the course of the winter opaque bumpy ice had closed over the river, but now they heard the ice groaning and cracking at intervals all through the day. Sometimes it went *pop!* with a suddenness, like a shotgun. As she drove back to Wildmoor with the ladder sticking out the back window, the newly mild wind filled the car; spring still had the power to move her, to make her feel burgeoning change. It was always a short, vivid, heartrending spring in this place. White filigree cherry tree blooms, the hot pink apple blossoms; crocus and daffodil and narcissus spearing out of the ground. This was her second spring here. The autumn would be her third autumn. When she thought about this her enjoyment evaporated and instead she felt something—despair, more credible each time it came. She shrugged it off harshly, as if despair were an irritating though well-meaning person with a hand on her shoulder. Turning south between fallow gold fields, parallel to the river, she could smell the sea brine on the air. Sometimes, driving this road in a deep reverie, she would feel as if snatched from the car by a hand and raised high in the air. She would see the Atlantic tide pushing kelp miles up the river, and the Atlantic itself, spreading out from the foot of Manhattan. And Manhattan's wild spires casting shadows halfway to Ohio, and then the vast carpet of grass racing toward California. Her life there, and her shadow life here. She would see all of that and herself seated in Dolly's car—and then it would end and she was in the car, driving again. She pushed in the car's cigarette lighter, and turned up the radio loud when she heard a voice say another tape had arrived from the cadre. She pulled over to the side of the road and lit her cigarette there; she'd never mastered using lighters while driving. She was always afraid she would weave and be stopped by a cop. The tape, like the three before it, was broadcast after assurances from the newscaster that it had not been at all shortened or altered. The girl's voice sounded hollow again, as it had at the start, almost two months before. "Today is April 3, 1974. I have been given the following choice: to be liberated to rejoin my family, or to join these comrades in their battle. My decision is made: I will stay with these comrades forever, because theirs is the only just battle there is. They are my family. My old family did not care for me; this new family does. My old family did not care for the poor; this new family does." To go with her new life the girl had taken a new name: Pauline. Jenny felt her gaze space out, refocus. She realized irrelevantly that the windshield was spattered with bugs: it had gotten that warm. Sitting there on the mill road from Red Hook, with the old fields stretching away. All the old fields going to seed and the old stone wall crumbled in places and bristling with weeds. She felt an odd tremor, from what source she could not have said. There had never been a Watergate amnesty; there had not been a window. Still, she felt something slide quietly shut. She tried to restart the car and it let out a horrible shriek, because it was already running. The post-tape commentary began, and even the newsmen made no effort to hide their revulsion. It made you disgusted, one said, to imagine the tortures the poor girl had endured, to say something like that.

Getting back to the house she was surprised to see that even Dolly had the television on. "Brainwashed," Dolly said from her chair, as the newscasters droned.

"How do you know?" Jenny said. "How do you know that she doesn't agree with them?"

"Oh, please," Dolly said, with a voice full of scorn for the people that would have to be agreed with. "Not a girl from a family like that. Not a girl like her."

TWO WEEKS LATER the cadre held up a bank and made off with fifteen thousand dollars, "Pauline" clearly visible on the security tapes, looking either brainwashed or eerily calm, depending on your view. The money would fund The People's Liberation. The bank happened to belong to a prominent business partner of Pauline's father. Then the cadre disappeared; they seemed to have slipped through the dragnet with remarkable ease. Over the protests of her family the attorney general declared Pauline a criminal, no longer a crime victim, and issued a Wanted poster with her face. The Left-leaning press scolded those of its own who stole Pauline's poster to decorate their apartments. They were equally displeased with the people who were spray-painting things like WE LOVE YOU, PAULINE! onto buildings. Jenny floated in clouds of wood stripper, lightheaded and vague, as the radio droned and the languid breeze failed to siphon enough of the fumes. Unthinking and wood stripper–stoned. Unmolested by Dolly or anyone else. In the late afternoons when the teatime approached she would lurch from the house for a walk, and drink in the fresh air. The house, still a shaggy King Lear despite all of her efforts. For more than half of the mile-long slope that led down to the water it stayed visible at the top of the hill, though it sank by degrees. Lines of trees began to appear as the slope grew more steep; the trees seemed to form doorways through which, as you looked riverward, the water loomed larger and larger. There was the gazebo just past the first line, giving a view of the water in front and of the uppermost point of the house, its ridiculous tower, behind. Then at last the house sank out of sight. The grounds had been laid out a century before to look carefully wild, like an English farm going to seed, but now the effect was much more natural. The screens of trees had widened with decades of new growth, and grown gaps where some old trees had died. And the fields were truly overgrown with weeds now, not made to appear that way. There really were moors, and a sense of forsaken remoteness, though once you reached the last vista before the drop-off you saw the railroad tracks just by the water, and the electric lines just beside them.

Coming back to the house she sometimes felt such pleasure in the progressive unfurling of the landscape, such a sense of poignant recognition as the battered old house rose again from the grass into view, that she would forget how unlike her it was to pretend this was hers. Forget her deepening shock, the first time she'd gone walking and realized the property went on for miles. The days grew longer, and if Dolly was ensconced with a tea visitor she could slip back in through the side door, and go up to the second-floor ballroom, where the gold light that bounced off the river poured in through the giant windows. She could move with her crisp shadow over the boards through the turning dust motes, as the air started losing its heat. She had bought painters' lights to offset the dramatic shadows of the late afternoon, but this also meant she could work late at night, after Dolly was sleeping. That was its own lonely pleasure, working at night when it grew really cold in the room, and the velvety darkness outside sometimes echoed with owls, and she knew that her bright yellow light could be seen miles away, from the river's far side.

And always the radio on, somehow underscoring her loneliness more than relieving it. She had plenty of distance from Dolly but still, late at night, she would turn down the radio low. In the vast nighttime hush she could play it quite softly and hear. The contrast of her life with the world outside sometimes felt too great on these nights. The radio was like a tiny porthole in her drifting balloon. One night in the middle of May her evening music broadcast was interrupted by the news that the cadre had finally been traced to a house in a Black neighborhood in Los Angeles. They were surrounded by FBI agents and local police and SWAT teams. All twelve members, including Pauline, were presumed to be there. Calls for surrender had been answered by gunfire. "We take you live to Los Angeles," the newscaster declared, and then a maelstrom erupted in the small radio such as she wouldn't have thought it could hold. A badly stammering reporter who could barely be heard. Such a roar of gunfire she thought it was war. Smoke, the reporter was saying, rising out of the house, a smoke bomb—no, orange flames could be seen. No, that's fire, he said. We're told that these are . . . the rules of engagement . . . they say that they'll call for surrender again. I'm up here on a neighboring roof. Oh, my God. That's a real, that's a very hot fire. Those deafening booms that you hear, we're told that's ammunition they had in the house, blowing up from the heat. Through the smoke a lone person was seen, crawling out the back door, and was quickly picked off by the SWAT team. Jenny had stopped in mid-stride with a big can of wood varnish hanging from her hand, her breath frozen inside her, the weight of the can almost pulling her over. It wasn't until it had ended—fifteen minutes? an hour?—that she found herself standing this way. Slowly, she set down the can, her right arm muscles wildly trembling. And then turned the radio off. Never imagining that in the twilight beyond what she'd heard, the three fugitives somehow spared death were driving north on I-5, being bundled into an apartment. That on the opposite coast, in New York, Frazer's telephone was ringing, in the middle of the night.

Part Two

1.

They had been driving for more than an hour on a succession of small rural roads, creeping along at just under the speed limit although it was near five o'clock in the morning. A waxing moon hung fuzzy and huge just above the horizon. The damp of the summer night strangely translated the moon's weak gold light through the air, so that though it was dark you could see a great deal—shadowy forms of dense woods, lone trees, smooth dark hills reaching to the horizon. She had been staring out the window a long time. "Rob," she said. "When Pauline joined the cadre—are you sure it was truly her choice?"

"I had doubts too until I met them." Frazer paused. When he spoke again his voice was so certain it almost sounded grim. "She's riding with them, for sure. You'll see what I mean."

The stars were just starting to fade when they found it, a faint dirt track climbing a long grassy slope from the road. The car shuddered on the uneven ground. They were almost at the top before they saw the house, small and dark, with the dark woods behind it. From here you'd have warning long in advance of anybody heading toward you from the road. As if to prove this she saw Carol standing outside, waiting for them. Carol was wearing shorts and a large sweater and was hugging herself against the dawn cold. Frazer touched Jenny suddenly, seized her hand—he hadn't even tried to touch her when she'd shown up at his motel room door, when she'd sat in the doorway with him for hours, smoking, arguing, settling what she would do, what she wouldn't. His hands had stayed carefully far. Now he seized her hand just as their long ride alone was over; she no sooner felt it than he let go again and they'd come to a stop. Frazer rolled down his window and Carol ran over and said, "Pull around back where the other car is," and turned to lead them to the rear of the house.

When they had parked he sat a beat without moving, and she thought he was going to speak. Then he simply got out of the car, and so she got out, too.

"Hi, Jen," Carol said. "We were worried about you." Belatedly they jerked forward and hugged. In the brief moment of the embrace she looked up and saw Frazer watching. He looked away quickly.

Carol detached herself and said to Frazer, "I need to get back to the city for work. I've been waiting all night for you guys. What the hell took so long?"

"Where are they?"

"Sleeping. Finally. After marching all over the house like crazies, doing 'security checks' and complaining about every goddamn—"

"Carol," Frazer said.

"I'll go in," Jenny said, quickly pulling her things from the car.

The back door was a rickety screen in an old wooden frame; it whined as she eased it open. She heard a sound like small rubber balls tumbling: mice. Inside she set her things down and waited for her eyes to adjust. She was in a small kitchen: all the usual things plus a table and chairs, and several full-looking grocery bags on the table. She trailed her fingers on the wall, turned through a doorway to a small vestibule at the foot of a short flight of stairs. Through a second doorway was a room growing gray with the dawn. A few curtained windows, another door at the far side that was closed, the dark shape of a couch. She didn't know where the fugitives were, she realized. Whether they were upstairs, or downstairs, or behind the closed door. She heard the screen door squeak open and then Frazer was in the room with her. "Jen," he whispered. She heard an engine cough, start. "Carol's tapped out and she wants to get back to the city. So I'm running her back, because we're leaving the other car here for you. You'll need money. Shit. This is—shit. I have forty. Okay? Next time I come I'll give you enough for a month. But write that down, so I don't forget. Jenny? Write down what I gave you and keep track so I know what I've spent. Get a notebook or something."

"Okay," she said. Her heart was banging, the way it had banged at the station in Rhinecliff when she had walked out and seen him and not known where she was, who she was, anything. The car, the car that she and Frazer had arrived in, was pulling around to the front of the house with Carol at the wheel. She followed Frazer to the door. Carol did not look over at them.

"I'll be back soon," Frazer said. "I've been away from home for weeks dealing with this, so I have a whole lot to catch up on. But you can handle it until I get back. Keep cool," he added, as he strode away quickly and climbed into the passenger seat. Frazer and Carol drove off without waving good-bye.

BY EIGHT in the morning the heat was rising, along with the noises of insects. Deafening chirrs, rattles, buzzes; so many variations of drone from invisible sources, each a note she parsed out with her ear but the whole somehow unified also, in a rhythm like waves. She sat at the kitchen table, paralyzed, waiting for some sign or noise from somewhere. Finally she went outside and tried to find a place of repose there, in the overgrown grass, but the soft patches it promised from a few feet away were all equally prickly and crawling with bugs when she got to them. Even from a few yards off the house shrank drastically. It seemed to be capsizing in its ocean of grass. She stood looking up the hill to where the dark woods began and climbed up to the ridge, and down to where she knew the road lay, out of sight. She crossed her arms tightly over her breasts; she felt cold although it was hot. Nothing about the house and the long golden hillside it sat on didn't feel abandoned, as if it was all an old luckless homestead that the owners had fled. Up an S-shaped pair of ruts from the house was a barn and an almost dry pond. She waded slowly through the grass to the barn and pulled its heavy doors open, belatedly starting with fright, as if the three fugitives were inside. But it was only a flock of pigeons exploding above her, in the dim space of crisscrossing rafters; she watched them arc through the pale beams of light falling in through the roof. The barn was full of dark shapes, smelled of moldering hay. She backed out and latched the doors shut again.

The house was still eerily silent when she returned to it; nothing had changed except that there was more light, and more heat. She eased one of the kitchen windows open and right away the screen door began to slap in its frame from the breeze; she rushed to latch it, but she still didn't hear a roused cough or a footfall. In the front room motes of dust turned in the light coming in through the drapes. She carefully opened a window here, too. The door off the front room that had been closed before was still closed. A second door that stood ajar revealed the bathroom, an old toilet with a pull-chain, an old tub with a green copper streak where the faucet was leaking. Leaving the bathroom and going to the foot of the short flight of stairs she could see a patch of sunlight at the top: a door upstairs was open. She climbed up, creaking no matter how slowly she went, and at the top found the open door, the only door there was, leading into a little low-pitched attic room with a single low window. That was all; now she had seen every room in the house but the closed room downstairs. There wasn't even a cellar. The attic room was bare except for a single narrow bed against one wall, a frail-looking table, a lamp and a frail-looking chair. Along the opposite wall was a thick rectangle of dust on the floor. It was about the same size as the bed, as if it had been moved in one piece from beneath it, or rather, she realized, as if another bed had been moved from above it. She got down on her knees beside the bed and flipped up the threadbare coverlet it was made up with, to look underneath. There was a thick pad of dust down there, too. So they really were here. They had taken a bed from upstairs, and moved it downstairs, behind the closed door. Somehow this small confirmation that she wasn't alone was less reassuring than startling, like the footprint on the sand in *Robinson Crusoe*.

The exposed stretch of dust, the shadow of the bed they'd removed, stirred and began to disperse in gray clumps when she opened the single window to let in the breeze. The sun was high now, and the cramped room was hot. She'd begun pouring huge beads of sweat. She was tired, she realized. She hadn't slept in a day, not since she'd risen early to go to Poughkeepsie and come back to find Frazer at the train station, waiting for her.

She climbed onto the bed, which stank faintly of mildew. For a moment her loneliness swept her and she thought she would never descend into sleep. But she was so tired that the next time she opened her eyes it was dusk. Now the bare room was softened and blue, with cool air pulsing in through the window. Outside she could see the dark form of the barn, and closer, the texture of a huge maple fading with the last of the light. Even the insect symphony had grown smaller and simpler; single crickets creaking tentative up-notes, and something else, a soft whirr. The best time was dusk, she realized. The sharp baring light bled away but the night hadn't come. That was the fugitive's hour, when the darkening air felt like shelter, yet you still had your eyes.

Downstairs the front room was as shadowy as it had been when she'd first seen it that morning; the one door was still shut. She tiptoed into the bathroom and peed without turning the light on. She put her hand on the chain, then thought again and simply put down the lid. In the doorway from the front room to the kitchen were her duffel and accordion file; she'd forgotten about them.

Frazer seemed to have brought her here, left her here, eons ago. Passing through the kitchen and pulling open the screen door she caught her breath and stood still. Someone was sitting on the step, a hunched form in a blanket facing away from her in the direction of the hill climbing up to the barn, and beyond, to the woods; and then the dark ridge giving way to the sky, strangely pale from the afterglow. After a long moment the form didn't turn to her so much as it twitched aside slightly, shifted in the most minimal, barely animate way while still giving her room to step out.

It was the man—Juan—as she'd sensed it would be, from the wideness of the hunched, shrouded back. But nothing else about him was familiar. The photos she'd seen in the papers had shown a grinning boy with curly hair and a blunt nose and round cheeks, a midwestern farm kid, robust; because the pictures only ever showed his head and shoulders she'd had to extrapolate the rest of the body, and she'd imagined him tallish and tapered. But he was small and compact, like a barrel with legs. And though the face was the part she had seen, in the flesh it was equally startling and strange. Beneath a globe of wild hair and a beard and a small pair of wire-rimmed glasses his face was dull, its lines muddied. His eyes were obscured in dark hollows but she could feel him staring at her from what seemed to be deep, inert shock, as if she were an apparition, a supernatural event thrust upon him that jammed all his modes of response. A crumpled pack of cigarettes lay in the grass by his feet. He seemed to have carried them outside and then let them fall from his fingers, forgetting about them. "Hi," she said, because it was the only syllable that seemed appropriate for utterance by itself, and she couldn't imagine uttering more than one syllable now that the air felt so fragile and tense, with this motionless man staring at her. It was strange to hear her voice, smaller amid the noises of insects and leaves than she'd thought it would be.

"You're not Carol," he managed, and his voice did no better than hers, rattling out through what sounded like a quagmire of phlegm and fatigue and smoked cigarettes.

"I'm Jenny. Carol and Frazer's friend."

Juan nodded without interest; he'd been told about her. "Where is he?" he asked after a minute.

"They've both gone back to the city already."

"I don't remember him coming."

"It was early this morning. He'll be back soon," she added, although nothing about Juan's tone suggested he cared if he ever saw Frazer again. "And I'm here, to take care of the day-to-day things. To help you, with whatever you need."

But Juan—if it really was Juan, if it really was one of the former notorious twelve when you counted their captive; the impetuous brandisher of shotguns; the now-leader of the two that remained of his three-quarters-slaughtered army—had tipped his forehead down onto his fist, as if the weight of his head was too much. The darkness deepened around them, and so many minutes went by she thought he might be asleep. Guiltily, she felt her appetite stirring. She hadn't eaten since a quick roadside burger she and Frazer had gotten on the way out of Rhinecliff the previous night, but being hungry right now seemed perverse. She'd finally located the source of the dread she'd been feeling since dawn. It was death. It didn't hang about Juan like a shroud, or sit at the back of his eyes like a nightmare he'd had. It was nowhere that she could pinpoint, since she didn't know what to look for, but she still had the sense it had dusted his skin with its ash. In the end his nine comrades had been burned, so the previous day's papers had said, so completely each charred bone had to be picked from the ash, one by one. They'd been found wearing army gas masks that had melted and fused to their skulls. She felt her stomach flip. Juan's form still hadn't moved. She could barely tell him apart from the house now. The stars had grown bright in the sky.

"I'll make something for us to eat," she said, although now her appetite truly was gone. She took a step toward him, back toward the door, and again he twitched aside. So he was still awake.

She squeezed back through the door. When she found the kitchen light and turned it on her reflection in the window over the sink spooked her. For an instant she thought someone else was outside, peering in. "Juan?" cried a voice. And then edging into the doorway from the front room with a hand over her eyes was Pauline, or the person who must be Pauline. Jenny felt as if she were watching the sort of old movie in which the lead character is surprisingly revealed to have a dark twin; that the twin is played by the same actor only deepens the strange sense of oppositeness. The gold-haired debutante of the newspaper and magazine photos seemed not even coincidentally linked to this girl. Pauline's hair was ragged and dyed a ghastly dark red, between fresh blood and beets. Jenny had imagined her tall as well but she was tiny, not just short but reduced drastically to her bones. Her skin was so pale it seemed bluish, except for purple stains under her eyes, which were vast in her face. Her filthy T-shirt and blue jeans hung around her like sackcloth. She stared at Jenny with shock, as Juan had. "Why's the light on?" she said.

Outside Juan had risen and opened the door. "Doesn't matter," he said, coming in. Pauline turned to Juan and seemed to forget Jenny was there.

"I woke up and you were gone," Pauline said.

Juan, upright but slumped, as if he'd been hung from a hook, gazed back at Pauline, and even through his deathly fatigue Jenny thought she saw a movement of habitual surprise, as if he still couldn't believe that he saw Pauline standing in front of him. "Where's Y?" he asked.

"Sleeping."

"You should sleep too."

"I can't."

After a moment Juan brushed past Jenny, as if he had also forgotten her, and with an effort rooted into the grocery bags on the table. She went to help him, to see what there was, but it was only a bag of potato chips and a box of cornflakes, a soup can, a banana—castoffs from Carol's pantry. All the rest of the bags contained nothing but huge jugs of wine. One was already open and practically empty. Juan pawed into a cupboard and came up with a tall, dusty glass which he filled from the jug to its rim. He handed the glass to Pauline and poured one for himself. Pauline stared into it for a minute, took a small sip, and then began to drink it off steadily, as if the glass contained water.

"Our Code forbids drugs," Juan began, leaning heavily on the counter as he recorked the jug, and it was a beat before Jenny realized he was talking to her. "But our leader drank wine, when his worries were clouding his thoughts. Wine's a natural thing, wine and grass . . ." Juan seemed to decide that the lesson was not worth the trouble. A door opened at the back of the house and suddenly the third of them, Yvonne, was approaching the doorway, her matted blond curls standing out from her head. She was wearing a thin cotton halter that clung to her breasts, and thin panties, and nothing else. Jenny could see her large nipples, the dark hair curling out at the tops of her thighs. She was vital and tall, with grainy peach skin and an elfin nose covered with freckles. Whatever storm they had endured, she seemed to have stood it the best, or perhaps she'd once been even taller and stronger, an Amazon. She stared at Jenny impassively.

"The comrade Frazer told us about," Juan said to Yvonne. "Jenny."

Yvonne nodded.

"You want some wine, baby?" Juan said after a minute.

Yvonne nodded again.

Juan had his own wine in one hand. With the other he hooked a finger through the loop on the jug and a finger into a third dusty glass in the cupboard. Then without another word or glance in her direction they melted away again, out of the kitchen. She heard them bumping through the darkened front room, through their bedroom doorway. The door slowly scraped shut.

DRIVING WEST from the farmhouse the road threaded between forested hills without a lot or a dirt track cut into them, and through gold agricultural valleys that never held more than one fatigued pile of wooden farm buildings, or one sprinkling of lying-down cows. Every few miles there was a sign for a town, but

Jenny could not even see where these towns were. Only once did she descend into the heart of a settlement, something called Ferndale that consisted of a post office, Agway, and church, and she didn't dare stop; she sank deep in her seat and slid past, a pair of eyes and a cap of black hair above the wheel of a rusting red Bug. She had always thought of Rhinebeck and Rhinecliff, with their fences and farms and their view of the Hudson with its barges and tugs, as the country, but they were really outposts of New York, strung along New York's river. This felt like a lost land, connected to nothing.

She was twenty minutes past Ferndale and forty minutes away from the farm when she finally came on a junction of the small local road with a four-lane state highway. There were newspaper boxes at the curb here instead of inside a quaint general store. She bought the *Times* and something called the Monticello *Examiner*, and set out to explore what must be Monticello. It was a largish small town, down-at-heels, with a blacker and shabbier side, and three grocery stores. She cased all three, although she knew as soon as she found it she'd go back to the black one, where there wasn't a single new car in the lot. When she did she parked in the confusion of rusting cars and empty shopping carts and did the shopping as fast as she could, arriving at the register with a tonnage of cans—canned soup, chili, spaghetti, beans, corn, tuna fish, and even something that claimed to be bread in a can. "You digging in," the cashier commented. She yelled across the store suddenly and Jenny's palms began to tingle with prickly heat, but it was only a summons to a long, lanky boy with a comb in his hair to load the groceries into boxes and get them out to her car. The boy's hair was a fluffy brown corona; after he'd put the groceries into the boxes and the boxes in a cart he paused to pull the comb free and give his hair a bunch of expert little yanks, as if he thought it was sagging.

"You from Vietnam?" he asked Jenny as they crossed the parking lot.

"No!" she said, startled. She realized she'd forgotten to come up with a story. She couldn't be "Iris Wong, Chinese, from San Francisco" anymore. She stared at the boy with alarm.

"Sorry!" he said. "Not from Nam. Okay, not-from-Nam, where you from? I'm just asking a question."

"New York," she said finally.

"City?"

She nodded.

"Aw," said the boy in admiration. "Some real bad luck must have landed you in Monticello." They had reached the Bug by now and she began to struggle with the handle that opened the hood. "My brother went to Vietnam," the boy went on, taking out his comb again while he waited. She finally got the hood open, and the boy began to heft in the boxes of cans. There were five boxes and only two of them fit. He opened the car's door to put the other three on the backseat.

"What happened to him?" She started scooping out her change bag for a tip as the boy shoved the last box into place, and eased his upper body carefully free of the car, without marring his hairdo.

"They got him," the boy said. He grinned, as if embarrassed. "He was fast but they was faster." He held out his hand for the tip with a goofy flourish. "I am not supposed to take *gratuities*, but those boxes were heavy. Good luck," he added, and his gaze seemed suddenly penetrating when he trained it on her. Her heart jumped.

"Thanks," she said.

Back on the state highway she tried a new road and after fifteen minutes was in a town much larger than Ferndale but smaller than Monticello, called Liberty. She found the post office quickly, a surprisingly grand marble building. There were a few other cars in the small lot, a few other people on the sidewalk, mailing letters in the outside mailboxes and going on with their days. No one looked particularly at her. Inside the post office was cool and cavernous; it seemed to have been built for a town that expected to be larger and more consequential. Only one window was open. The woman behind it did not say anything as she approached, merely cast a cold, impassive look in her direction, and remained motionless.

"I need a post office box," she said, her heart racing in a riot of fear and also excitement, just as it had the first time she had done this, in Red Hook.

She filled the form out swiftly. Now the whole story had come to her. Alice Chan, from New York. Landscape painter. "I travel," she said casually, as she wrote, "but I pass by here often."

"You can't be leaving your mail in the box for weeks on end, and letting the box get clogged up. We don't allow that. You can't just be letting junk mail pile up in your box. You've got to empty it regularly or we'll empty it for you. Right into the trash."

When she had her key she moved around a corner and out of the woman's view, to the long wall of tiny bronze doors. The new box had a bronze eagle on it. She didn't much care for the symbol, but it was beautifully done in relief. Old, like the rest of the building. She ran a finger over it, then tested the key to make sure that it worked. The box was like a miniature of the lobby she stood in: cool, dim and empty. She peered into it, but only saw a blank wall opposite, no sorting area, no canvas bins piled with letters. She closed the box, pocketed the key.

After the post office she found a good phone booth in the parking lot of a boarded-up diner and called Frazer at home. It was early enough in the morning that she knew he would be there. Carol answered, her voice hoarse from a late night; in the background Jenny could hear the intimate squeak of the bedsprings, the rustling of sheets. "Hi," she said.

"Hang on," Carol said sharply.

There was a flurry of muffling sounds and tense murmurs; then Frazer came on. "I'm just on my way to the store," he said. "To pick up some milk."

She hung up and checked her watch; then she hugged herself, waiting. Just past ten A.M. Fifteen minutes seemed unendurably long. She wondered if she should go sit in the car, or pull the car around the back of the building where it couldn't be seen from the road. It looked incongruous, parked alone in the diner's empty lot. Almost no one was driving by on the road, but as one car passed, and then, long ticks later, another, she could swear that they slowed down a little. She had her back to the road, a hip canted in the attitude of casual waiting, but in the quiet she'd begun to imagine police cars pouring up the long hill toward the house, the blurred wheel of a helicopter blade rising over the ridge. Black-clad SWAT team snipers creeping down through the grass on their stomachs. Somehow the druggy-seeming, dead-eyed indifference of the three fugitives to their new situation had quadrupled her usually manageable paranoia, as if each of them had a soldier's freight of it they'd unstrapped and shrugged onto her. The previous morning, her second morning in the house, she had awoken with the dawn light, starving, after eating a bowl of dry cereal for her dinner. Feeling her way into the kitchen, she'd found Juan there, hunched under his blanket again. He seemed to have worked open the second jug of wine with the use of a penknife, but now he was dragging the blade through the flesh of his arm. "Don't," she gasped, and when he looked up at her he might have thought she was either Yvonne or Pauline, he seemed so unsurprised. "I don't feel it," he said. Then he stood up wonkily and she thought he would pitch past her onto the floor. "This is only a dream," he slurred, clutching the jug with the unbloodied arm and weaving back toward his room.

When she called the street phone Frazer answered immediately. "What is it," he said. She was only supposed to call him this way in the case of a dire emergency, and now she wondered how she could convince him, without his having been in the deathly still house. She tried to explain, but of course he did not understand. "Are they writing?" he asked.

"Rob, they're not eating."

"They weren't so bad off before. I saw them eat in California."

"That was in California. California's their home. Here they're like—fish out of water. Lying there." She didn't want to say *dying*.

There was silence on the line, or at least there was silence from

Frazer. She could hear the traffic on Broadway, like a cyclone of honking. "I'm scared," she admitted.

"Keep your cool."

"I don't know how to help them."

"Of course you do. If anybody knows what to do, it's you. Just get them busy. We don't have unlimited time."

"I know that."

"For the moment they've pulled the good vanishing act, but they need to make the most of the moment. They need to pound out that book."

"It doesn't seem like they care. It doesn't seem like they care if they live."

"Bullshit. I don't believe that. They're the warriors, Jen. They have balls. Bigger balls than I've got. Remind them who they are."

"How can I do that, when I'm not even sure who they are?"

"*What?* They're the most important people in the country, that's who they are! They've scared the pants off the government, they've made the average American think, Is this some wacky dream? Is our society really so flawed that we've spawned these hard cases who won't take the shit? And the answer is yes. The richest girl in the world has said This is a lie, I'd rather shoot up the place. Jenny, we can't stay on the phone for much longer, I'm on the corner of Broadway and 116th and somebody might hear me."

"Then come up here! Talk to them like you're talking to me. They need it, they need something—"

"I'll be there two weeks from today. I know, my schedule's crazy. This week is out, this weekend is completely impossible, next week is out, but next weekend I'm coming. Don't worry. By then they'll have written a pile."

SHE WASN'T SURE if it was true that they didn't care whether they lived or died; but it seemed to her that all their energy, what little there was of it, went toward drinking wine and avoiding daylight. The night after her encounter with Juan she'd been awakened again, by a sound of voices; the voices were low, but she'd left her bedroom door open to help with a breeze. Again, they were down in the kitchen. "You're the one who always talks about karma." The oddly familiar small voice of Pauline.

"That's not karma." Also a woman: Yvonne.

"If Juan hadn't stolen that thing in the store . . . if he'd just acted straight like he says—"

"Straight people don't buy bandoliers. Juan was thinking. And it would have been fine if that pig—I hate those rent-a-cop assholes—"

"But we didn't need it, everybody had two. We didn't need a bandolier."

"Since when do you know what we need? Since when are you the least authorized to have a fucking opinion?"

Now both girls fell silent, and she didn't even hear the creaks of the old wooden chairs. She lay perfectly still so as not to make noise with the bedsprings. It was the first time she'd heard Yvonne speak. Yvonne's voice was bossy, attention-desiring. It reminded Jenny of Yvonne's body when Jenny had seen it, barely clad in its tight underwear. Though her tone was low, almost a stage whisper, her voice seemed too large for the furtiveness of the discussion. Whatever they were talking about, it was clear that they wouldn't have spoken that way with Juan present. And Jenny also felt sure it pertained to the deaths of their comrades—even more so when Yvonne added, ending the silence, "I know you think it's Juan's fault. But what about you? You were supposed to give us cover, and you were too slow."

"I don't think it's Juan's fault. I'm just—" Pauline started crying. "I'm sad," she wailed, her voice, even while wailing, so soft Jenny barely could hear it.

"Shhh. Oh, Polly. Shh. He'll wake up." Now Yvonne's bossiness was more like the reproach of a mother. Jenny heard a creak as someone rose, then liquid being poured—another jug of wine.

"Careful," Yvonne said. "You'll spill it." After a few silent moments—"I'm sad, too," Yvonne said. "I'm so sad I feel dead."

"I wish I was dead."

"Shut up." And then, more carefully, "You can say that to me. But don't ever say that to Juan. You know why."

"'The brave don't fear death. The weak desire it,'" Pauline said, clearly quoting.

Coming into the house now with the first load of groceries, Jenny was surprised to find them in the front room, although with all the windows shut, the drapes drawn, and a thick haze of smoke in the air. If they had been talking before she opened the door, they were silent now. They looked up at her like one person, but without expectation or interest. Pauline was curled on her side on the couch with a newspaper crossword on the cushion in front of her and a pencil dangling loosely from her hand. Juan and Yvonne were lying on the floor. The small radio that had come up in the car with them from Carol and Frazer's was on, barely tuned to a station; she thought she could hear snatches of big band beneath a constant wash of static, but while the radio was loud in the cramped room no one moved to turn the dial, or turn it off. Outside the day had been hot for hours, and she could smell them, their unwashed bodies pungent and sour, their stink intermingling with the smell of their wine. "I brought you the paper, and the news magazines," she said. Last week had been the week of black smoke and orange flame on the covers of *Newsweek* and *Time*, and the headline, "Surrounded!" Between the covers, the radiant family photos of all twelve of the comrades from their previous, normal American lives. That had been before the nine bodies were positively numbered as nine, and each ID'd by its teeth, and Juan and Yvonne and Pauline were confirmed to be missing. This week marked a lull, and other stories had reclaimed the front covers. "It's good news," she said, holding the pile out toward them. "You've disappeared without a trace. The FBI is intensifying its manhunt in L.A. and points south, all the way into Mexico. You've been spotted on the West Coast from Canada to Tijuana, but nowhere in the East."

Juan had managed to sit upright while she was talking, and now he took the week's news from her hands. She saw an ugly fresh scab on his arm. "Thank you," he said. For a long moment he didn't seem to know what to do next. Then, "Intelligence," he murmured, and passed *Time* to Yvonne, and the newspapers to Pauline, keeping *Newsweek* for himself. Pauline gazed down at the front pages. Yvonne fingered *Time* idly.

"I was thinking," she said. "It might help if you wrote down your feelings about your lost comrades. Your remembrances of them. It might help you—I know you're in pain."

They were suddenly staring at her as if she had suggested their comrades be resurrected and then murdered again. "That's none of your business," Yvonne said.

"We're fine," Juan said harshly. "We'll get to that book when we get to it."

That they would think she was only trying to prod them into writing their book, as if she were Frazer, made her discard her caution. "I didn't mean the book. I meant that maybe, before you can do that, you have to write about them. Write a eulogy for them."

"We'll eulogize them with the blood of the pigs they were killed by!" This was Juan, suddenly full of fire.

"An eye for an eye. That's enlightened."

"That's the revolution, Sister," he sneered.

She lingered another moment in the doorway, gazing back at their six hostile eyes fixed on her; then she turned away into the kitchen and went out the back door. She sat down on the bumper of the Bug, the rest of the groceries still in the backseat, and lit herself a cigarette. She was remembering what Frazer had said—not about their being the most important people in America. Nor about how they were warriors. It was what he'd confessed to her after they'd argued and glared and subsided that night in his Rhinebeck motel room—that the three fugitives had seemed so young to him, the first time he had met them. He'd meant that he, Frazer, was illegitimately old—too old, he'd worried, to keep their confidence. But they *were* young. Not young like the kid who had carried her groceries, but still young. Frazer would have laughed at her if she'd said this to him. Juan and Yvonne were only a few years younger than she was, twenty-two or twenty-three. Pauline had just turned twenty. Not such big differences, but they felt big to her. At twenty-three she'd been beginning her life underground, and she couldn't say she hadn't also been undisciplined, and terrified, and aflame with self-pity. She'd done and said stupid things out of anger, and an almost suicidal urge to be caught. And herself at twenty? That was the first year she'd been with William, before which she had known almost nothing. Both these ages of hers, looked at now, seemed like children to her. She was amazed that each one was herself, and not so long ago.

WHEN FRAZER HAD found her in Rhinecliff she'd been in the middle of a letter to William. The letter of his she'd been answering, almost four weeks old now, had said this: "I've been thinking a lot about zealots. How they taint the whole lake of ideas they drink from, and taint everyone who might share that lake with them. I assume you know the 'comrades' I mean; you keep up with the news." The first time she'd read this she'd actually been annoyed, that their need for a code seemed to have unleashed in William a tendency toward pompous phrases she'd never suspected. Now she didn't just feel guilty for having thought such an unkind thing of him. She was in a house with those very same "zealots," and she had to conceal it from him. She refolded his letter, and listened; it was early morning, and they didn't seem to have stirred out of bed. She took out her own letter-in-progress and skimmed it critically. Every day since leaving Wildmoor she'd tried to finish it, but she was stymied by the number of things that she had to leave out. Finally she started fresh and wrote an account of her quest for the yellow croquet ball, as if she were still at Wildmoor. She'd do better next time. How could she know right away how to translate this new situation? She had to be honest with William while at the same time dropping no clue the prison censors could possibly grasp, and although this meant, basically, lying to William, she still wanted to think that it didn't.

The truth was that her whole correspondence with William,

which she constantly thought of and poured so much energy into, in some way made her miserable. The first time she'd written to him she had signed the short note, in code as obvious as it was foolproof, from his "sister." He'd responded chastely as her "brother." And this had seemed wonderful, that in the midst of their crisis, in one small respect, they had both understood what to do. Yet the template was limited. Though William's letters were more daring than hers were, they still seemed impaired. She knew the letters could only ever be indications, puffs of smoke from far sides of a canyon, but more and more they seemed to her the essence of her connection to William, and that connection seemed less and less strong. Dana only resealed William's letters in new envelopes, but tearing the envelopes open Jenny felt a cool draft. And so how must he feel, reading her declarations, already blunted and constrained by their code, and then in Dana's slanting, regular hand? So different from Jenny's own, her pointy insistent block letters, her underlinings and loud exclamations. All of that was ironed out in Dana's transcriptions, and perhaps a little of Jenny's love was lost also, like steam. She still had his wonderfully formed, upright writing, like notes on a staff, but now it kept to a strange measured tone: "I love you very much. I'm finding good work to do. I've been thinking a lot about zealots." They'd never written letters to each other before his arrest because they'd never had to, and perhaps it wasn't a skill they possessed and meant nothing in terms of their love. But still, she believed in the romance of letters, and her stomach hurt when she read his. His letters arguably lacked nothing, but she couldn't stop searching them for an intangible something, the orthographic equivalent of his hands on her skin.

As always, she felt him more fully once she'd put his letter away again in her battered brown accordion file with the limp ribbon for tying it shut. The file was the one thing she'd taken from Dick and Helen's apartment; it had been in the trash, and had *Tax Yr '64* scrawled hugely across it. It was so full by now she kept thinking the ribbon would break, but she managed to tie it shut, squeezing the file with her knees. Now she could lose herself the way she longed to lose herself in the letters. She thought of their bedroom in Berkeley, the windows open to the breeze, the slight light from the street sifting in. She thought of their mushy old bed, the mattress from Salvation Army that had made a soft dent right away in its center for them, as if they were musical instruments set in its case. Then she thought of his body. The reddish-blond translucence of his hair. The undulations of the blue vein, so prominent though deep within his skin, on the underside of his penis. Her eyes flew open, as if she'd been caught, though the real reason she'd stopped herself was that it disturbed her how quickly these details had faded. For a long time she'd been remembering him by reference to her previous attempts to remember. She didn't know when she'd last remembered, just by reference to him.

SINCE THEIR FIRST morning in the house a box of writing equipment—a typewriter, a reporter's cassette-tape recorder in a Naugahyde carrying case, bales of loose scrap paper that seemed to have been scooped up off somebody's floor, spiral notebooks, notepads, and several rubber-banded bundles of ball-point pens and pencils, all violently deformed at their ends from long, powerful chewing, which meant that they and everything else had been harvested from Frazer's home office—had been sitting untouched just inside the back door. When she went downstairs a few minutes later to see if the box contained any envelopes better than the ones that she already had, it was missing, and the front room door closed. Putting her ear near the door she heard the tentative pops of the typewriter keys. *Pop . . . pop pop pop.* Then, silence. A coffeepot had been unearthed and a warm inch of coffee still sat in the bottom. She filled a cup and let herself out the back door. The day was buzzing and humid, high June; she walked around front, past the side window over the kitchen sink, past the front-facing window over the kitchen table, and stopped there, out of sight of the rest of the house. Without going farther she could tell that they'd opened the windows. She heard Juan's voice, carried out on the breeze. "No. Every word should go in like a knife."

"I was thinking about it all night," Pauline said.

"It still sounds like a fucking Hallmark. 'Evan, you were the man of my dreams.'"

"Oh, just let her," Yvonne said, annoyed.

By that evening they'd moved from the typewriter to the tape recorder. The typewriter had been silent for stretches of hours; had then pecked like a hen thoughtfully; had sometimes erupted in great fluid bursts, like a rain of small rocks on the roof. At some point it had crashed on the floor; Jenny heard the bright ding of the carriage returning. Compared to those sporadic spasms the tape recording was a constant vague dirge. Someone droned on at length, stopped short, droned again in the same shaky rhythm. Someone else paced and mumbled intently. The tape recorder made a loud *clack* as it was turned on and off, like a branch being broken. She crept around the kitchen making toast and heating soup from a can, but when she knocked to see if they wanted to eat, all their efforts derailed. "Ah, shit!" Juan cried as she peered through the door. Now they had to start over again. They couldn't have background noise—that was why the windows were all shut again, and, less obviously, why the room's only lamp had been snuffed by a blanket. "*Listen*," Juan said. There was nothing to hear but the night-insects sawing and creaking. But had there been noises like this back in Berkeley, Juan wanted to know? Just *exactly* like this? And listen now—Pauline and Yvonne tilted their heads, as if to sharpen their ears. A night flight was passing over, so far above that if it were daytime they would just see the jet as a tiny white flake in the sky. Its slight noise like a faraway ocean—but what if there was some Harvard-trained FBI pig who could hear that and say, "That was Pan American flight 405 heading from Chicago to London at thirty-nine thousand feet on June 9—let's search all points underneath its flight path?"

It wasn't until the next morning that she had any idea of what

Juan had been talking about. The noise of the car's doors awoke her. Going to her window hugging herself against the early chill she saw the three of them crawling over the car like a scavenging pack of street urchins. She pulled on her jeans and went downstairs and out the back door, feeling the cold dew on the soles of her feet. For a moment she just took them in, seeing them outdoors and beneath sunlight for the first time. They were bloodshot and fevered and pale. Their hair was lank, and their clothes looked too big. Carol had bought the car used, with cash, and never registered it, but there had still been an old insurance card and owner's manual in the glove box. These had now been thrown onto the grass. The map she had bought on her trip into town had been hurled forth as well, and little balls of tin foil and dirty pennies and cigarette butts were raining onto the ground. From opposite sides of the car Pauline and Yvonne began yanking out the mats and digging into the seat cracks, all the while casting burning glances at each other as if to say, See? I thought of it! Juan slowed down, then stopped; he leaned heavily back on the car and for the first time looked at her.

"What are you doing?" she asked.

Pauline and Yvonne didn't glance at her. "Finished eulogy," Juan said, and from the gravel in his voice she could tell they'd stayed up the whole night. "Gotta go." Juan heaved himself off the car with one arm. She saw he was holding the car keys. She'd left them clipped to the sun visor.

She took a careful step forward. "Go where?"

"Go deliver. A radio station. Pigs'll know we avenge our comrades." Juan raked a hand through his thicket of hair. "Come on," he said to Pauline and Yvonne. For the first time Jenny noticed a small package perched suspensefully on the roof of the Bug. From its size it could have been a sandwich, but there was something so disturbed about the way it had been wrapped, in many sheets of note paper secured with scores of different-colored rubber bands, that any person who saw it would find it suspicious. "Radio station?" she said.

Pauline and Yvonne had backed out of the car. "We have to get our tape *out there*," Yvonne said, as if Jenny were dense.

"But that eulogy was supposed to be for you, to help you—to heal you and help you move on. You can't take it to a radio station." None of them seemed to hear her. Juan was shrugging off his work shirt, then winding it in a loose mitt around one hand, and with that hand grabbing the package. "Okay," she said. "That's good, you don't want to get prints on the tape. And your precautions last night, about background noise—I understand all that now. I hope I didn't compromise things. You wouldn't want to undo all that effort by driving into town in broad daylight to a radio station, when no one even knows that you're on the East Coast."

"You can quit with your protocol lecture," Juan said.

Now she'd run out of patience. "You can't just get in a car and deliver a tape! Have you forgotten that there are people out there who'd be happy to kill you?"

"I'll kill them! Come and watch me."

"Give me the keys, Juan."

"Don't tell him what to do," Yvonne exclaimed. "He's in command here, not you."

"Every day that we're silent's a crime on our comrades," Pauline piped up hoarsely.

She tried to ignore them and win over Juan, the commander. "Give me the keys, Juan," she said in a comradely tone. "Even if you're not seen, if you leave that tape at a station around here we'll get agents all over the place."

"We're not going to *leave* it at a station," Juan said with disgust, getting into the car. "We're going to *mail* it to one."

"There'll be the postmark."

"We'll mail it to someone who'll mail it *for* us."

"Who? Everyone you've ever known is under surveillance!"

"You told us to do this!" Juan roared, jerking out of the car again—he wanted to lunge, but he couldn't get far without letting go of the wheel. "We want this tape on the radio *now*, we're gonna swear vengeance *now*—"

"You said so yourself!" Yvonne said.

"I meant you should do it for *you*, not to broadcast all over the world!"

Juan got back in the car, slammed the door shut and started the engine. The car jerked and belched as he stomped on the gas. "Come on, Y. Not you," to Pauline.

"But what if you're caught?" Pauline cried.

It still seemed possible this was a ruse, a game of chicken, but Juan shoved the Bug into gear. It hopped forward and then stopped again. Pauline, suddenly sobbing, was struggling with the passenger-door handle. "Polly," Yvonne admonished. Yvonne had both her palms pressed down over the door lock so Pauline couldn't lift it. "We'll be back, Sister, stop. Sister, stop it!"

"Goddammit, I'll go!" she said finally, running up to Juan's side of the car. "I'll do it, I'll do it right, just get out of the car. If you're caught it's the end of me, too."

"When the pigs took your old man, did you just shrug and say That's okay? Go ahead Nazis, take my old man?" Juan yelled wildly. "Did you?"

At last Juan had turned off the engine and handed over the keys. Going inside she felt their three gazes suspiciously tracking her progress. From her room she got her letter to William and her postal supplies, so that once she was out of their sight she could repack the tape. Before going back down she glanced out the window. They were there, clumped together just next to the car. They knew they had to let her do this, though they weren't yet sure if they could trust her. She wasn't sure, either. Her first thought when she was finally driving away was of burying the tape miles off, where it would never be found. But she knew that she wouldn't. She'd been thinking again about death. The first year after William's arrest she'd never slept well, never through the whole night, and she still woke sometimes with a shock, as if William were dead. Yet his death was impossible to her; she knew this, because she couldn't be grateful for his life as it was. Did death seem more likely when someone had actually died? She thought the reverse must be true. Which was why mourning had to be done, vengeful eulogies written and broadcast. Maybe they were all trying to believe in death, the three of them to grieve properly, she to grieve less—she glanced back and saw them small in her rearview as the hillside rose up. Then they dropped out of sight.

2.

Four days later she was at the phone booth beside the boarded-up diner on the outskirts of Liberty again. By now it was so familiar she entered it hardly noticing what was around her, and reflexively yanked the door shut. She dropped the battered plastic bag in which she hoarded small change on the booth's metal shelf, and began to sift through it for dimes. The bag was also full of lint and dust and other particles that weren't currency. In the heat that quickly built up in the tightly closed space she could smell the sweaty metal of the coins, and the less identifiable fragrance they'd picked up on their thousands of journeys. She sometimes gained a delicate feeling of comfort from a telephone booth. Feeling less displaced than placeless, and kept company by her fistfuls of captured but transient coins. Although her daily visits to this booth, since she'd mailed the tape, had been so brief as to be almost instant. That was as per her and Dana's traditional system: she would feed the phone coins, hear the line open, hear her loud heart. When

Dana answered she'd say, "Did you get something?" When Dana said No, they'd hang up.

Today Dana said, "Yes. And I want you to tell me right now what this is."

"I can't. You'll understand why later on. When you take it out of the envelope, wear dishwashing gloves. There's a second envelope inside. Don't touch it at all. That's the part to deliver."

"I've already done that. I already opened up the outer envelope with gloves, and got out the inner envelope, with gloves, but it isn't just paper." Dana's voice was thin. "I can hear something rattling in there."

"Don't shake it. Just deliver it like I told you."

"Fuck, Jen. What did you send me? Did you send me one of those things that the roadrunner sends the coyote?"

"No! How can you think—" She tried to put the cradle of the phone between her shoulder and ear and dropped it instead, so it banged on the glass of the phone booth. She grabbed it again. "How can you think I would do that?"

"Then tell me what it is."

"Listen to the radio after you drop it, and you'll know what it was. Then you'll see why I can't tell you now. But it's safe for you, Dana, I swear."

"I can't believe that you're doing this to me!" Dana said, hanging up.

The next morning they were all up by six, tripping over each other in the kitchen and knocking the coffee out of each other's cups. The radio was already tuned to their A.M. news station, and Yvonne sat at the table with a notepad and pen poised in front of her, white-lipped and tense. "We need to take notes on how they present us," she said. "They'll do an update of the case, but they'll also convey attitude. What the sentiment is." Juan had set the tape recorder next to the radio for the same purpose, but this made the radio scream and distort even more. "Piece of crap!" Juan exclaimed. Pauline carefully shifted the dial a hair and Juan said, "Don't you touch that again! Do you want us to miss it completely?"

At eight Juan dropped down to the floor and did push-ups while whistling. After a few he collapsed on his stomach, rolled onto his back. He lit a cigarette and smoked, staring upward.

By ten their vigil had disintegrated. Every day before this they had felt it might play any time, and so their anticipation had been diffuse, and immune to final disappointment. Now they all knew that the tape should play some time this morning. The chance that it wouldn't drove them away from the radio, and toward it again. They jittered past each other, pretending to be doing other things.

At a quarter to noon she pointed out, "It's just nine forty-five in the morning there. Stations open up late, especially college ones."

"But they broadcast all night," Yvonne said.

"The graveyard DJ, but they're in the sound booth, not the office. They don't go in and out the front door."

"How do you know?" Yvonne said.

At twelve-thirty Pauline was overcome. "Change the station!" she said.

"This is the news station. If they're going to play it anywhere around here, it'll be on this station."

"I'm going to listen to the car radio," Pauline said, grabbing the keys. "I'm going to find a better station."

"Get back in here," Juan shouted. And then—

"Polly," Yvonne screamed. "Polly! Come back, come in, now!"

She was back in the room instantly, and then they were all clustered around the tiny radio, as the announcer interrupted the regular programming to join station K___ in Boulder. Without further warning Yvonne's voice burst out of the speaker. Yvonne flushed slightly and adjusted her posture; a flowering of her sense of self-importance, yet there was something uncertain about it. Yvonne was not taking notes, but anxiously watching Juan for his reaction. Juan was gazing hard into the distance, ignoring Yvonne. Yvonne's section was a meticulous cascade of facts: of time, date, duration, snipers, 'copters, rifles, riot-gas canisters, injured black bystanders, corpses, and cost to the taxpayer. The facts on the ground, the particulars; then Juan seized them up and charged toward universals. Juan must have been waiting for his cue as tensely as if he had to deliver the speech now, on a stage. From on high he found murder and greed; he could see Vietnam; he indicted, convicted, condemned. The kitchen looked suddenly strange, as if it had just dropped around them. Midday sunlight, a heap of filthy cups and plates. Pauline was motionless in her chair, her eyes dark and opaque, her lurid hair standing out in a shock from her head. Juan was saying, "But the pig did not put out his fire until every warrior was cut down in the act of unleashing a last shot of defiance. And the pig did not put out his fire until each body was charred and the skin drifted upward like paper. And the pig did not put out his fire until only the bones were left over, and then even the bones crumbled up. The pig's greed is always his undoing. When he finally put out his fire, he assumed he'd destroyed all twelve comrades, because there was no way to know any better. Now he knows he was wrong.

"What happened? How did three warriors fly from Los Angeles? They knew vengeance would have to be theirs. How did they sleep on the ground in the shelter of trees, right under the FBI's nose, like a pack of wild dogs with no fear? They were not afraid to eat the garbage scraps of the citizen-pigs who waste food endlessly. They were not afraid to pull your pizza scraps right from the trash, pig, they know how to live like the man with no home, the poor man who's their brother. We were there on the bench in the park with the crust of your sandwich. Our clothes didn't smell so good and our manners weren't nice. Did you see us and turn a blind eye? We were there right in front of your face. And when our friends came to mourn us and swear vengeance for us, we were there too. We came forward and said, Do not cry.

"We understand that the Chief of Police of Los Angeles had some awe for the weapons we use. According to the *Los Angeles Times*, after slaughtering our comrades in a battle that was more than a hundred to one, almost a thousand pig bullets per warrior, the Chief picked a number of our warriors' shotgun shells out of the rubble because he admired their size. He had them made into gift lapel pins for his underlings. Did you desire a souvenir, pig? We've got something for you that's much better, but don't hold your breath. It'll come when you're least prepared for it.

"To our friends: Don't think we are cold. It was horrible watching our comrades get burned to their deaths. But we live for the struggle, and die for the struggle. We don't fear our deaths anymore."

The tape seemed to go on forever. The words now seemed ancient to her, not elegy so much as things that should themselves be elegized, artifacts from the deep past. All over the country, at that instant, hundreds of thousands, perhaps millions, were listening to this. Did the three of them realize, themselves? They had never heard themselves as she had, driving down a country road with the radio blaring and paralyzed suddenly by their crazed, keening screed. It was possible that their own voices were an echo chamber around them, beyond which they grasped nothing. There was something so lonely about it, the three of them standing and sitting, and hearing themselves as they'd been just a few days before. And then, as if the storm's fireworks had ended, leaving only a slow, steady rain, Pauline's section began. Jenny thought she saw Pauline stiffen, though her face didn't change.

"A____, that scarf never left your hair, did it? It was a gift from your father, and you loved him so much, though he scorned your beliefs. You never stopped hoping you'd reach understanding with him. And B_____. You had trouble at first with your rifle, but you just worked harder. You never complained. That's how you were all your life, so determined and quiet. C_____. You always stood with your arms crossed and your blue eyes on fire, so mad when we weren't being serious! Then you would laugh too. Perfect friend in good times, perfect soldier. I know you fought hard . . . " Behind Pauline's staticky voice the kitchen was still. "And Evan," Pauline said. Then she paused. When she resumed she was less audible. "I never had a brother, but when I met you I thought you were my brother. We both grew up like birds in gold cages. Always being admired. Afraid that if we escaped we would never survive. We had so much more to overcome than the rest of our comrades. Yet you changed, and you promised I'd change." Listening to herself, Pauline seemed to grow more and more stiff; now the stiffness dissolved and she crumpled, and started to cry.

"I can't listen to this!" she said. She shoved her chair back and ran from the room. Yvonne dropped her pen and stood up.

"Don't," Juan said. "Let her go."

"What if you'd died and left me alone?"

"I'd expect you to save your tears. Do you fear death? I don't. My death will be righteous. Our comrades' deaths were righteous."

"God, you're a fucker. Are you happy they're dead?"

"No, I'm not happy they're dead. You're a moron. What I'm saying is your tears are an insult to them." Juan sounded as if he had tears of his own, but since he couldn't cry without contradicting himself, they seemed to be boiling off him through his pores. "Would you shut up?" he screeched at Yvonne. "I'm still trying to listen!"

At last the tape ended, and as Yvonne had predicted it was followed by a tumult of update: three still at large, field agents, new focus on Boulder. Jenny felt a wash of heat slide down her skin. "Oh my God," she said, thinking of Dana. But Juan had seen Yvonne clearly at last, and Yvonne had fallen into his arms, and Pauline was still locked in the bathroom, and so no one responded.

LATE THAT NIGHT the door of her bedroom flew open. Pauline cried, "Someone's coming!"

Jenny flew downstairs into the front room and in the dimness saw Juan pressed against the side wall, hopping into his blue jeans, and Yvonne rushing past toward the kitchen. "No lights," Yvonne hissed. In the kitchen Pauline dropped to her knees beside Yvonne at the front-facing window, pressing her face near the sill. The window was open, and Jenny heard the sound more distinctly—a car engine, straining in its highest gear and seeming to stutter from very slight taps to the gas. It came slowly; there was no sign of lights. Juan sprinted out the back door and returned with a rake in one hand.

"We don't have anything," he panted. "Not the first fucking means of defense—"

At last the shape of a car emerged out of the darkness, and felt its remaining way toward them. The car halted somewhere near the big maple and a silhouette emerged, its gait familiar, traveling swiftly. "It's Frazer," Jenny said, still frightened in spite of herself. The back door opened and Frazer made a strangled noise, seeing their four dark shapes. "Ah—" he cried.

Juan flipped on the light. "What are you doing? Why the fuck were you trying to scare us?"

"I wasn't trying to scare you, I was trying not to wake you."

In the harsh sudden light from the bulb they all stared at each other. "I thought," Jenny said after a moment, "you were coming next weekend."

"I felt like coming early. To see how it's going." He glanced around at Juan and Yvonne and Pauline. "I have a surprise for you," he told them. "It's out in the car. The backseat. You want to go bring it in?"

After a long moment the three of them filed out the back door. "Not you," Frazer murmured to her. They heard car doors open, and Frazer pulled her upstairs.

Once in her bedroom he turned on her. "Are you crazy?" he said. "What's the matter with you? I've left you with them for *ten days*. You're supposed to be handling them!" All his edgy tics were going full throttle—pulsing eyelid, beads of sweat on the brow, one hand opening and closing as if it were squeezing a ball. He hadn't been driving without lights not to wake them, he'd been driving without lights not to be seen by his unknown pursuers.

"I am, Rob," she began, annoyed by her instinct to mollify first, before showing her anger at him. Who was he, to be lecturing her? "It's not easy—"

"I guess not! I guess it's not easy helping them get their promise-of-apocalyptic-vengeance manifesto on the radio."

"Is that why you're here?"

"I would have come the minute I heard but I'm trying to use some precaution, unlike the rest of you. Can I guess whose tape recorder they used? And whose *tapes*? Dana called this afternoon. She's extremely unhappy."

"They tried to take the car and mail it themselves!"

"You're supposed to control them, Jen. You're supposed to keep these lunatics alive!"

"Until you have your book and your money?"

He seemed stung. "It's not just about money. Though I seem to remember you're in for a share of it, too."

"I've got to survive."

"So do *they*. That's my point."

"Then why aren't you yelling at *them*."

He stared helplessly at her a moment, as if about to say something else; then he yanked open her door and went back down the stairs. She could hear Juan and Yvonne and Pauline coming through the back door, dropping things on the table. She lingered at the top of the stairs, but he didn't come back. When she went down he was unpacking grocery bags into the fridge, with the three of them watching him mutely. The surprise was a feast: thick steaks, potatoes, a bucket of chocolate ice cream that was soft from its ride in the car, vegetables for a salad, a bottle of whiskey and two of red wine. "I know nobody's vegetarian, because you ate burgers at Sandy's," Frazer was saying. "Pauline likes a plain burger, right? I bet that means plain steak, too. For the rest of us there's A-1 sauce"—with a flourish—"and a shitload of stuff for potatoes. The oven works, I made sure of all that when we rented this place. There's more in the trunk, but don't peek—save some stuff for tomorrow."

"What's all this for?" Juan managed weakly.

Frazer laughed—a fake-sounding laugh, she thought angrily. "I've really confused things by coming up early. This weekend I was going to pick up your writing, remember? I jumped the gun a little—I'm sorry. I'll get a couple days less of your writing, but that's only fair. We'll still celebrate. That's what all this is for."

All three of them seemed confounded—by Frazer's appearance, by the food, by the mention of writing. But at the word *celebrate* Yvonne seemed to home in; her gaze narrowed on Frazer as if he'd just said the one thing in the world that she found most distasteful. "I know that you're just being nice," she told him, "but we're struggling for our brothers and sisters who've never had what we all got at birth, just for being born white. In terms of all that this is so self-indulgent."

"It's not self-indulgent to celebrate when you have a good reason."

"Well, we don't!" Yvonne said. "We can't *celebrate* while our comrades' ashes are still blowing into those shacks our black brothers and sisters in L.A. have to live in. Who'll never afford to eat steak in their whole fucking lives."

"Sometimes you're too much of a saint," Juan told her suddenly. "Don't be so proud of yourself."

Yvonne stared at Juan, silenced.

"Look, my fault," Frazer said. "I went overboard. Let's just not waste this stuff, okay? It won't happen again."

Yvonne had flushed deeply; she seemed to be containing a huge conflagration just under her skin. Pauline was watching her with what Jenny felt she recognized now as anxiety, but if Yvonne's emotions were as obvious as weather, Pauline's were indoors and shuttered and draped. "I guess we'll see you in the morning," Yvonne said, and turned on her heel and walked out. Pauline followed her quickly. The bedroom door slammed.

Juan hadn't moved since he'd admonished Yvonne; he was propped up against the door frame. He seemed on the verge of saying something in summation, but then he only said, "Good night, man." He left the room and the bedroom door opened and slammed shut again.

Now she and Frazer were alone. For a moment she pretended to be absorbed in listening for noises of argument or reconciliation from the downstairs bedroom, but there was only silence. She felt Frazer watching her. "Jenny," he said.

"I'm tired, too. I'll see you in the morning." She started upstairs, and he snapped off the kitchen light and followed. "Rob," she said warningly.

"Just to talk."

On the stairs there wasn't even the faint sifting of moon- and starlight through the windows; she couldn't see him at all, but she could smell him, the always surprisingly sweet scent of his skin, strangely familiar though he had never been her lover, or rather, though he'd just been her lover that once. She knew how near he stood from his heat and his breath. "Then talk here," she said, sitting down on a step.

"What if they come out?"

"We'll hear them."

He hesitated, but not as long as she thought that he might, and not petulantly. Finally she felt him sit down on the step just below her. He found her hand and she let him hold it; he held it gently, as a friend might. He didn't clutch it or stroke it. "I'm sorry I yelled," Frazer whispered.

"It's okay," she said. She felt suddenly so comforted to be allied with someone, even if it was Frazer. After a moment she said, though she'd been afraid to, "They haven't started their book."

"I figured. I'll get them in gear."

"How?"

"Would you stop worrying? If you want to keep worrying I'll have to leave, or I'll solve all your problems."

She laughed. "You're the same asshole, Rob."

"And you're the same." He stopped talking and reached for her.

"*No*," she said, pressing him back.

For a moment she just heard his breathing. Then, "You can't blame me for trying," he joked.

She found his head in the dark, kissed its crown quickly, and stood. "Good night, Rob," she said, finding the banister.

"Good night, sweetheart." And then he stood also, and made his way down.

• • •

THE NEXT DAY was tall and dark blue and much cooler than the few days before it. She and Frazer dug a fire pit in back of the house and lined it with flat stones that they found up and down the hillside. Juan dragged dead branches out of the woods and threw them carelessly into a pile. Inside Pauline and Yvonne cut vegetables for a salad. They had tuned the radio to music and set it up in the window, so the music moved out on the breeze. But a pall still hung over the day, deepening by the hour. The three fugitives seemed to have repaired their rift of the night before by turning a blank, sullen face to Frazer. When they sat down to eat in the late afternoon Juan and Yvonne and Pauline only picked at their food. None of them spoke; she and Frazer were left talking to each other, like nervous hosts trying to keep a bad party afloat. She was growing angry with them—for shoring up their unity by snubbing Frazer, for behaving like children about the good meal, which she wanted to relish but now somehow could not—when Frazer finally shoved his plate aside, and everyone else set aside theirs as well, although they were crowded with uneaten food. "Did I say I had another surprise?" Frazer said with a show of great cheer. "And you guys, don't keep me waiting anymore! Why don't you bring out the pages you've got and let me take a look at them." She caught Frazer's eye but he only smiled at her.

After a moment Juan said, "You first, man."

Frazer strode off and they heard his trunk open and boom shut again. When he reemerged from the side of the house he had a long, slender gun in each hand. He stopped a short distance from where they were sitting and propped the guns against the trunk of a tree. "How about a trade?" he suggested.

Juan, Yvonne, and Pauline were all staring at the guns. "A trade?" Juan said.

"A trade. Or maybe I should hold on to these until you've kept up your end of the bargain? Because I have the weirdest feeling, I don't know why, that you haven't even started to work on the book. Maybe it's the way you've been acting like you don't understand why I'm here. Maybe it's that I slept on the front room couch last night, and when I woke up I noticed the big box of paper and shit that I gave you, and everything in it is your eulogy tape written five hundred ways, and not a page of the thing we discussed. Am I right about this? There's no harm done so far, but I'd like you to be open with me."

Yvonne and Pauline had turned pale; Juan was gaping at Frazer as if he were choking on something. "And you'll hold on to those until we've kept up our end of the bargain?" Juan said. "Those aren't even real guns! What do you think we are, man? What are you trying to do to us?"

The two girls looked wildly from Frazer to Juan. "Not real guns?" said Yvonne.

"They're rifles," said Frazer.

"Air rifles," Juan said. "BB guns. Did you think that I can't tell the difference?"

"You said you would help us!" Pauline said. "And you made us all give up our guns and you said you'd replace them."

"I am replacing them."

"With those?" Juan exclaimed.

"Not *even* with these unless you show me you've made a real start!" The trio was suddenly silent. "I am helping you," Frazer went on, in a quieter voice. "But you, you've got to pull yourselves together. I know you're in pain but you have to get moving. People look up to you, did you know that? Did you know there's graffiti about you on the walls of the college I got fired from? I walked past it yesterday. It says how much they love you, and that their hearts are with you. That made me feel good, to know that you're here, and safe, and that I had a little to do with that. I am helping you. But you have to fucking help yourselves, too."

"Don't tell us what to do, man," Juan said, but Jenny saw his eyes glitter, and she thought he might cry right in front of them.

"I'm not," Frazer said. "I'm not telling, I'm asking. I'm asking."

For a long time they all stared at their gore-covered plates. The wind picked up and Jenny felt goosepimples prickling her skin. "These play guns are pretty ridiculous," Juan finally said. He got up slowly, unkinking his knees, and then he crossed the grass to where Frazer had put them and picked the guns up to look at them.

"I know," Frazer said, "but I've had delays and these came to hand, so I wanted to get them to you. At least you can do target practice."

"We've had delays, too, but we'll get it together," Juan sighed. "We'll keep up our end of the bargain. Am I saying the right thing?" he demanded.

"Yes, baby," Yvonne said. She went and put her arms around his waist. They made a strange tableau, Juan standing with arms extended, a long gun in each hand, and Yvonne softly wrapped around him.

Frazer stayed, talking easily, pouring whiskey and wine, as the western light slanted more steeply, and their shadows grew long, and the campfire fell into embers. By the time he was standing to leave, as sunset began, he had brought them around. They were all laughing, even Pauline; they were lazily sprawled on the grass in the quickening wind. They had finished their steaks. Frazer told the story of one of his firings, imitating the pop-eyed indignation of his strait-laced colleagues, the sangfroid of the black kids he'd coached, his own half-goofy, half-swaggering triumphs, and she lay in the grass being warmed by the whiskey, and watching. When he really was leaving—he didn't want to, he didn't! . . . but he had to get back to the city—Yvonne abruptly embraced him, a belated apology, and then Juan and Pauline did as well. "You too, Jenny," said Frazer. She stood lazily out of the grass and went toward him, the pleasant haze of the whiskey around her, and let herself be enfolded. "See?" he whispered, his breath in her ear.

"Venceremos," Frazer called out to them, as he started his car.

EARLY THE NEXT MORNING she was sitting high on the hillside above the house with a mug of coffee and a book when she heard the back door, and looking down saw the three of them slowly emerge. They didn't see her, mixed in as she was from their vantage with the forest behind her. Juan put his hands on his hips and looked assessingly at the long open slope the house sat on. Then, after an awkward transition, as if he were throwing himself in cold water, he started to run.

Once he was actually moving he moved with surprising ease. Yvonne and Pauline followed, Yvonne readily, Pauline less so. Pauline wasn't clumsy, but she seemed to require more mediation between herself and the earth. Jenny could imagine her erect on the back of a horse, or slicing through the water with an elegant crawl, but jogging seemed wrong for her. Still, Pauline jogged after Juan and Yvonne with unsure, choppy strides, and vanished as they had behind the far side of the house. Juan and Yvonne reemerged a beat later, abreast. When Pauline reappeared she was already a half lap behind. By the end of the exertion, which did not go on long, Juan and Yvonne might have circled the small house ten or twelve times, while Pauline's orbit had grown so slow, and so far out of sync, that Jenny couldn't count any of them correctly. Pauline sank down on the back step and put her head on her knees while Juan and Yvonne did a series of toe touches, and then Juan shook Pauline by the shoulder, she rose, and all three went back into the house.

The brief spectacle weirdly thrilled her; she had to set her book down and stare over her coffee at the hills growing haloes of gold in the strengthening light before she understood why. When she was a child she and her father had lived for a while in Japan. Seeing Juan and Yvonne and Pauline run like that, in their tight little circuit, had made her think of gym class at her Japanese school. All the boys and girls wearing identical brilliant white trousers and shirts and soft caps and thin sneakers; sometimes they'd played team games, with balls, and when they all grew too hot they would thoughtlessly take off their shirts, boys and girls, even when they were twelve and thirteen. But mostly they'd jogged. All of them, paired, in a winding defile in their blinding white clothes with their footfalls in perfect accord. Singing, they'd jogged through the streets of their cramped little town, while the old people waved. Singing, they'd risen out of town on the gravel-paved road that soon turned into dirt. Her first few times, gasping and blistered, she had fallen farther and farther behind, and perhaps she'd been taken back down by an older classmate. But soon, as with the language, as with dress and regime and friendship, she grew able to do it. They had jogged, a great body of children, as if they were going to war. Past the wet scrolled eaves of the frail ancient houses, and the eaves of the temples with their banners of prayers. She remembered the road out of town, the stones denting her thin canvas sneakers, but sprinting past tiredness and pain to a fleet-footed joy. They would jog endless miles, the whole day, though this couldn't be true. It was school, after all, and they had all the usual subjects. But it was jogging en masse she remembered, the small wooden shrines on the roadside far out in the country, the long-distance walkers bent over their sticks, the road level between the drenched fields, distant hills rising round from the green, level ground. Their town miles forgotten. She tried now, but she couldn't remember a single adult.

She found them in the kitchen, red-faced and a little bit trembly, all smoking in silence. "You jogged," she said, and they looked furtive, even embarrassed. "There's better places to jog than just in rings around the house," she went on. "There are all sorts of fields, when you go left from the barn. I think this place was a dairy farm once. Most of it's hilly, but some of the fields are level. There are pastures back there. And you can't see them at all from the road."

As she'd thought they would, they seemed a little resentful that she was suggesting anything to them, but they also seemed, though reluctantly, curious. "Security," Juan said shortly. "In the house, behind the house, and right near the house are secure."

"What about the pond?" Yvonne asked him.

"What about it?"

"We could go swimming in it."

Juan looked at Yvonne witheringly, and Yvonne sighed and

shrugged, but after that Jenny felt more encouraged. She could tell that they longed to be outside; they longed to *do something*. Frazer had put them at ease, and she was starting to think that the secret was just taking action. You couldn't leave them to transform themselves.

Over the next few days, while they were slumped on the couch drinking wine, or perhaps more adventurously clumped outside around the fire pit drinking whiskey, she started to inquire about the things they'd done before. When their comrades were all still alive, had there been—exercise?

"There was physical training and war games," Juan said. "Always limited, obviously, by our urban setting, and the importance of staying low-profile."

"Right," she said.

Another morning she remembered Frazer's mention of target practice. "So, you used to do target practice?"

"More than *that*." Juan seemed amazed by her ignorance. Hadn't he told her about combat training? Though it was true that once Pauline was with them, the cadre hadn't been able to go outside anymore. "We stayed sharp," Juan explained. They'd practiced search-and-rescue, ambush, self-defense, although it had been hard in a three-bedroom railroad apartment. Tripping over electrical cords, freaking out downstairs neighbors.

"Of course!" she agreed.

Finally, one morning Juan handed her a supply list as she was preparing to go buy the papers:

wine
beer
cigarettes
whiskey
one (1) bag approx 5 lbs unmixed cement
one (1) lg bag sand or gravel

The cement turned out to be for old flower pots and paint cans Juan had found in the barn; filled with it, they were stuck onto short lengths of broomstick, to serve as barbells. The sand was for filling up socks, which were tied off with twine and then made into loops, to be ankle and wrist weights. The barn had also yielded a few stacks of shaky sawhorses and these were set up in one field for an obstacle course. In another Juan paced out a half-mile loop, and soon the weeds there were flat from the number of times he and Pauline and Yvonne had run over it. The wrist and ankle weights were a process of trial and error; Pauline's ankle ones were too large and kept flying off her feet, so she was always looking for them in the grass, and her wrist ones chafed her from the twine. But Juan sat squinting beneath the front-room lamp for hours one night with a needle and thread, and modified them with a T-shirt he tore into strips. He made a schedule:

8 A.M. rise
8–8:30 washing, eating
8:30–11:30 field training: physical strength/readiness, combat strategy, weapons (when weapons arrive)
11:30–12 ego reconstruction
12:00 lunch

"What's ego reconstruction?" Jenny asked.

"Cadre stuff, can't discuss that," Juan said.

Once Juan and Yvonne and Pauline had worked out a routine she constantly saw them jogging, through the overgrown pasture uphill from the house, or up the dirt track that made a long S from the house to the barn. They were usually so far away they were just jerky movement against the landscape, but even then she could almost immediately tell them apart. On his stout piston legs Juan moved squarely, with almost no bounce, like a human bulldozer. Yvonne bounced and bounded in arcs like a deer or a colt. Pauline was the slight form that always lagged badly behind. They ate now, and stayed awake in the daytime, and asleep in the night; she wasn't startled by their unsteady movements at dawn anymore. They went red, and then brown, from the sun. Even Pauline slowly took on a healthier tinge, and the dark circles under her eyes correspondingly faded. Sometimes they fought, but with rediscovered and intense energy, as if fighting were a heady relief after weeks of grim union. The sawhorse hurdles were too tall for Pauline, and when the wind blew the right way Jenny heard passionate disputations; Pauline once came running full tilt toward the house with a red-faced Juan chasing her. And yet at the end of the day they would lie in the grass drinking beer—even their drinking seemed somehow more wholesome—and going over the progress of the day with earnest absorption, talking over goals met and goals still fallen short of, race times, numbers of repetitions. They'd found tools in the barn, an electric bandsaw and a lathe and a handsaw and drill and all sorts of other surprising and functional things, and Juan finally took the handsaw, Pauline watching, and shortened the hurdles.

One night Juan said, in the middle of dinner, "We'll resume combat drills tomorrow. We ought to be in good enough condition. If we aren't we'll have to get that way, fast." He didn't look at anyone particularly when he said this, but the comment seemed directed at Pauline.

"What about weapons?" Yvonne said.

"We'll use the stupid BBs, for something to carry. We need to get our asses in gear. We spend too much time just sitting around."

"We're not just sitting around," Pauline said.

"If you think you've been having it tough you ain't seen nothing yet, Princess."

"We don't have enough people anymore for combat drills," Pauline added.

"Sure we do. Two-on-one."

"That's not fair."

"We won't team against you. It's more like me and Yvonne play each other, and one of us gets you as a handicap."

"Ha, ha."

"Don't pout, Polly," Yvonne said.

"Fuck you," Pauline said. Yvonne laughed.

"Actually, I was thinking that Jenny could join us," Juan said, and suddenly Pauline's face seemed to darken for real. "To even things up," Juan said, turning to Jenny. "You can team with Pauline."

"I don't really like war games," she said. She was watching Pauline, as Juan wasn't. Pauline's eyes weren't glistening, her mouth wasn't trembling, but she was sitting so tensely, her fork suddenly stilled, that it seemed she might shatter if someone disturbed her.

"You should do it for the exercise, regardless of what you like or don't like," Juan was saying, "because the revolution needs your body to be strong. I know you have a good mind, I can tell that—"

"Why can't I be with you or Yvonne?" Pauline interrupted.

"Jenny'll be a great teammate."

"But I'm the least experienced. I should be with one of you."

"She's the least experienced. Compared to her you're an old pro. You won't be the rookie. You'll like that."

Jenny interrupted, loudly. "I'd rather not anyway."

"You'll like that," Juan was repeating. "Won't you. Hey. I'm talking to you."

Pauline was looking at her plate. "Yeah," she said, after a minute.

"I'd rather not, anyway," she repeated, but now Pauline looked at her for the first time.

"Come on," Pauline said. "We need someone to even out the teams."

"I could team with Juan or Yvonne."

"No," Pauline said. "Team with me." She was adamant now; she waited for consent almost fiercely, while Juan and Yvonne, sipping beers, forking up their spaghetti, seemed to consider the issue resolved.

"All right," she said finally.

"Great," Pauline said, in a tone that did not seem sincere; but then Juan looked pleased, and suddenly Pauline also looked pleased, while Yvonne had looked pleased all along.

THE OBJECT of the game was to make it to the goal without dying. They chose the house's water cistern for the goal, hiking up to it together through the woods, over and around the huge boulders, sometimes sinking knee-deep into leaves from the previous fall. On the way back down they split into teams and scouted good ambush spots. Pauline chose a large boulder with a crack down its middle, so that from behind it a slice of the forest below could be seen.

"They'll give us a five-minute head start. When we head off, split up so that they see we went two different ways. Then we'll meet here and try to ambush them."

"All right," she said. "Pauline, listen—"

Pauline turned without another word and began picking her way down the slope.

When the game started Jenny had trouble finding the split boulder again, and expected Pauline to be waiting impatiently when she arrived, but Pauline wasn't there. The five minutes had passed. Five more went by, then ten. She was feeling alarmed when Pauline came unsteadily toward her, one tree to the next, and finally dropped down beside her. Pauline was breathing hard, and the blue vein at her temple was jumping. "I led them the wrong way and then lost them," she whispered.

"I was starting to think you were hurt."

Pauline gulped another few breaths. "I was fine," she said shortly. "I don't see why you'd think I was hurt."

"It's not a criticism."

"You only got here first because you came directly. I was trying to lead them astray."

After a moment Jenny said, "I know you didn't want to be on the same team. You could have let me tell Juan that I'd rather not play."

"I don't care. It doesn't make any difference."

Pauline's gaze flicked away. Looking at her so closely, at the dark eyebrows like wings on the fine-featured face, the blue veins at the temples that never appeared in newsprint, Jenny could see that the bruiselike eye circles hadn't faded away so much as been somewhat obscured by Pauline's darkened skin. "Are you all right?" she said. "You look tired."

"Shh. It's sloppy to talk. They might hear us." After a moment Pauline added, "Of course I'm tired. It's impossible to sleep with all the mice in that house."

"I hardly ever see mice anymore."

"Just because you don't see them doesn't mean they're not there. They're more careful, that's all. Shh!" Pauline sat up suddenly. Jenny sat up, as well. Before Pauline had arrived she'd been listening to a strange little bird perched above her that made a sound like a car's engine trying to turn over: *eh eh eh eh eh eh*. Now the bird started again, in a different location. Below was a flicker of movement: the top of Juan's head, re-eclipsing behind a tree trunk. Then Juan burst from his tree in two long strides, reached another wide tree, disappeared. He was just below them. Pauline slowly stood up, one hand on the boulder. Jenny heard the wind sigh through the canopy, so far above that she couldn't feel it. The tree trunks creaked softly, like ships. Juan emerged from his shelter and ran, and Pauline leaped out into his path. "Ha!" she yelled. "Bang you're dead!"

AT THE END of their first week of training Juan declared that they'd done well enough to take the next day off. That evening he and Yvonne and Pauline made as if to carouse until late. They turned up the radio loud and tuned in a rock station. They opened fresh beers. Jenny took hers onto the porch and sat staring out at the gathering dusk, but she'd only been alone a few minutes when the door opened behind her. To her surprise it was Juan; he stepped out with a chair and sat down next to her. "What's so riveting out there?" he asked.

"I'm just looking for the first star." She expected him to snort with derision, but instead he turned from her face, to the sky, and surveyed it with interest.

"What'll it be?"

"I don't know. I don't really follow the skies. I just like to see the first star. Sometimes it'll be a planet, like Jupiter or Venus. Sometimes it's just whatever of the really bright stars is in the part of the sky that you're looking at. I don't even know which constellations should be out right now. Summer ones, obviously, but I have to see them to know what they are."

"That's still a hell of a lot more than most people know."

"It's a bourgeois indulgence, stargazing," she said, mostly to tweak him. She guessed it was something he'd say.

"I didn't say that. I think it's cool, that you know all this stuff."

"It's just the fruits of isolation and boredom. See how much trivia you know after living like this for another few years." As soon as she'd said this she wished that she hadn't. She knew the fugitive life worked much better when you avoided reference to the future. The twilight had accelerated as they were watching, and suddenly she noticed not just the first star, but three different stars burning hotly in three different parts of the sky. "Shit," she said, and Juan noticed them too.

"So much for keen eyes," he said. They heard the clatter of dishes from the kitchen, Yvonne singing along to the radio. "You know, you could be a real leader," Juan said suddenly. "Quit this 'I'm in retirement' attitude. You've got the chops. And you've got a brown skin."

"What does that have to do with it?"

"You owe your people your leadership. You can't go denying your race. You don't just owe the revolution in general, you owe your people in particular."

"Human beings are my people."

"But that's denying your race!"

"Just because I'm a Japanese woman, you can't define me in terms of just that. And I'm not in retirement. I don't know what you mean when you say that."

"I don't see you lifting a finger for the revolution."

"How about what I'm doing right now, devoting myself to a madman like you?"

Juan surprised her again; his laughter rang off the porch. She remembered, with odd disconnection, their first few weeks here, the funereal stillness and silence. Now Juan laughed so loudly that although she heard the door open behind them, she didn't really take notice of it. "All I'm saying," Juan said, "is your skin is a privilege. Your Third World perspective's a privilege."

"And all I'm saying is, stop saying I'm from the Third World when I'm from California."

"You'd make an exceptional leader, that's all that I'm saying. Hey, Princess," he added, and she turned and saw Pauline in the darkness behind them. She'd come out when the door creaked, Jenny realized. She'd been listening to them for a while.

"Pull up a chair," Juan said. "Where's Y?"

"Making pudding."

"Take a load off. You're spooking me, just standing there."

"I wouldn't want to butt in," Pauline said, and she went back inside.

Now it was dark, and in the dense spill of stars Jenny couldn't find the first three she had spotted. "Pauline dislikes me," she said after a moment, when she was sure Pauline really had gone.

"She's just jealous. She likes being the belle of the ball."

"What does that mean?"

"She knows how important she is. The Publicity Princess. But she's still got to learn that there's no substitute for a Third World perspective like yours. Brown, yellow, black, red: those are four things that she'll never be. And she isn't just white, she's a filthy rich white. Y and I are from the Midwest, and I'm not saying our town wasn't racist, or that we don't have a taint that we'll never repair. But at least we're blue-collar. We can relate to working brothers and sisters all over the world. Pauline's a big step behind us that way, and she'd like to pretend that she isn't. That's why you're a good lesson. She sees your reality and knows that she won't ever know it. Like I tell her, she can't kill what she is. She can only atone."

"You don't really say that to her?"

"Her consciousness is our responsibility. It's up to us to undo the wrong thinking she's done all her life."

"But it's wrong to condemn her because of her background!

She can't be faulted for where she comes from. That's as bad as racism."

"You can't say that I'm racist," Juan said earnestly. "I've always wished I was black. Not just wished it, but willed it. If any black man came to me and said Change places with me—regardless of if he was poor, or in prison, or was suffering in ten different ways, I would do it without thinking twice."

"That's just guilt. And it's selfish."

"Maybe it's selfish, to want the kind of integrity that you can take for granted."

"I don't have more integrity than you do, just because of my skin. I wish you wouldn't use me as an example of something I don't believe."

"I could use you as an example of humility, too, but you're almost too humble. A racial leader should be more prideful. Our leader was humble, but he was also a hard-ass. He was one motherfucker, and in this world that's just what it takes."

Juan fell silent and she could see him tipped back staring up at the sky, perhaps finding his leader immortalized there in the stars. Everything that he'd said rankled her, and yet his belief was total and serene, more serene than any aspect of him she'd encountered so far.

A FEW DAYS before this she'd heard a commotion after everyone had gone to bed, and returned downstairs to find Pauline tugging her twin mattress through the bedroom door into the front room while Juan and Yvonne, in the double bed, writhed with their heads under pillows. "Polly, stop," Yvonne said. "They're just mice. You're way bigger than them."

"They're not in *your* bed," Pauline said, struggling to flip the limp mattress over. "See?" she cried, when it faced downside up. There was a hole in the ticking about as big as a fist. "They were in there!"

"Get the fuck back to bed!" thundered Juan.

The furor hadn't died down until Jenny stuffed the hole with balls of newspaper, difficult enough because half the pages strewn around the room Pauline wanted to save. They'd all been annotated in one way or another. Under a headline that read STANDARD OIL CHIEF MAKES PROJECTIONS the photo of the frowning oil chief had been embellished by a black felt-tip frame and captioned TYPE 1 OFFENDER. Other pages carried articles about the fugitives themselves. "Not that one!" Pauline kept saying. Finally the hole was filled up and Jenny sealed it over with the wide roll of cellophane tape that she used for her letters. Her fingers were stained gray from the newsprint, and the grime got all over the tape. "Do another layer," Pauline said. "Another piece at the bottom. No, longer. Like that."

"Say thank you!" Juan yelled from the bedroom. "She's not your goddamn maid, Princess!"

The next day Jenny had set out wooden mousetraps, more from a desire to feel efficient than to catch and kill mice, and then they'd found the first caught mouse squeaking weakly and trying to tear itself free. Amid shrieks of horror she'd scooped it up, run out the back door and thrown mouse and trap into the pond. Belatedly she'd feared the wooden trap would float, prolonging the mouse's awful death even more. But the injured mouse was heavier; it sank. Coming back to the house, Yvonne gave her a huge mug of wine. Pauline was on the couch, tightly wound in her sheet, with a cigarette burning. "Such a disgusting way to kill them," Pauline whispered. "And it doesn't even work!"

Juan had said, "That's what Princesses get for complaining so much."

The morning after she'd stargazed with Juan on the porch Jenny drove to the hardware store in Monticello, then in Liberty, then simply stayed on the state road and asked in every town that she passed. "I'm looking for something that takes care of mice without hurting them. Or killing them," she explained. Most of the store owners looked at her blankly, but in the fifth store she tried the owner held a hand up to tell her to wait, and after a few minutes returned with a metal grate box. It had a handle on top, and a dial on the side like an egg timer. "It's humane," he explained. "I don't know if it works. I've never actually sold one before."

The next day they resumed combat training. When she and Pauline had reconnoitred behind the branches of a fallen pine tree, Jenny said, "I'd like to show you something, later on. It's a sort of experiment."

"Shh," Pauline said. "You know we're not supposed to chitchat."

"Come upstairs after they've gone to sleep."

Pauline hesitated, then jumped. Something had snapped in the brush, but it was only a chipmunk. "What kind of experiment?" Pauline said. "Don't you want to show Juan?"

"Not really. I just want to show you."

She could tell that Pauline didn't want to appear interested. "Then just say what it is."

"Then just come up and see."

"I think I see them. Be quiet!" Pauline said.

That night Jenny stayed awake in the attic room reading as her watch ticked past one, then one-thirty, then two. Finally, feeling strangely stung, she turned off the lamp and lay staring into the dark. She wasn't sure how much later it was when she heard a soft step on the stair. Pauline knocked, barely making a noise, and she got up and pulled open the door. Pauline slipped in and shut the door behind herself and waited in the dark while Jenny lit the lamp. Then they both stood awkwardly, like the first guests at a very small party.

"I haven't been in this room since we came up here to get the other bed," Pauline offered, after a moment.

"There's not much here," she said, gesturing.

One of her snapshots of William was propped on the bedside table, and she saw Pauline notice it, and then pretend not to have noticed. She picked up the photo and handed it to her. Pauline took it by the edges, and studied it closely. "So this is him," she said, as if the two of them had discussed William so often that he had become, in their discourse, simply "him," when they'd never discussed him—or anything, for that matter—before.

"That's him," Jenny said.

When Pauline put the picture down again she walked to the room's single window and peered out, shielding her eyes from the slight glare the lamp put on the glass. Her gait seemed exaggeratedly casual in a way Jenny hadn't noticed before—it was in the slouch of Pauline's shoulders, and the way she shoved her hands deep in her pockets, in the loose-jointed pose that she struck at the window, one hip canted slightly, like a very young hood on a street corner. As always her drab hand-me-down T-shirt and jeans hung obscuringly on her, but Jenny thought she could see a previous manner of holding herself to which Pauline's swagger was grafted. Pauline's head still rode with perfect uprightness upon her neck, and her back, for all her shoulder slouching and hip tilting, was still straight as a rail, as if she'd been trained from a very young age and to an extent that she couldn't undo in ballet, or at least in posture. And she was still beautiful, despite her thinness and her hair, which looked to have been cut with garden shears, and the unyielding dark circles under her eyes.

"So what's the experiment?" Pauline asked.

She'd slid the mousetrap under her bed, and now she got onto her knees and retrieved it. It had a doorway on one side, a very small flap of metal that only opened inward. On the opposite side was a second door, very large, that unlatched from outside and swung outward. Inside simply looked like a box, but when the egg-timer-type dial was wound the box ticked from within, like a clock, or a bomb. Pauline ventured forward to look at it. "It's a weird metal box."

"It's a mousetrap. A humane mousetrap. It catches them but doesn't hurt them. They're supposed to go in on their own. Then you can release them, wherever you want."

"Why would they go in?"

"Supposedly because of curiosity. The directions say mice like to explore. They hear the tick and want to know where it comes from. You might have to wait a while for the first mouse to get trapped, but once it does more and more mice come to see what it's doing. Then you've got a box full of mice."

Pauline shuddered. "Ugh. I wouldn't want to touch them."

"You don't have to. You don't even have to watch. I can do it myself."

"No," Pauline said, and Jenny noted with interest that something like pride had sprung up in Pauline's flecked green eyes, like a pair of small flames. "I'll come watch. I don't mind."

Downstairs Juan's snoring was penetrating the closed bedroom door. Jenny eased open the door to the kitchen and felt a soft explosion of movement, as if tiny projectiles had launched. Behind her, Pauline cringed. Then the kitchen was still, and the only sound was the soft squeak of the trap, swinging on its handle from her hand. She lit a candle, dripping its wax onto the lid from a can until the candle could stick. Pauline gingerly opened a cupboard, and poured two mugs of wine. When the dial wouldn't wind any further Jenny let go and a soft, steady ticking emerged. She set the trap on the floor and climbed onto the counter with the candle and her wine. Across the room from her Pauline had climbed onto the table, and tightly wrapped her arms around her knees. The candle guttered, its glow swelling and fading. Soon they'd drained their mugs and refilled them in silence, and the larger silence that had grown up around the fine grain of the ticking seemed inviolate; even Juan's snores just enclosed and refined it.

When the mouse came Jenny heard its approach like a whispered, irregular ticking that offset the tick of the trap. She saw Pauline start and sit forward. The mouse trotted out of the baseboard, circled the trap anxiously, angled toward it, and then backed away. She felt her heart beating, as hard as the mouse's, she thought. Suddenly the mouse crept inside and they heard a soft click and a brief, confused shuffling, as the mouse tried to reverse what had happened. Pauline loudly gasped.

"Shh," Jenny said.

In the dim light they could just faintly see the small whiskered nose at the grating. For long minutes the mouse would click in thoughtful circles, and then all at once it would fling itself wildly around; it would be silent; then it would squeak, anxiously. She was so intent on the trap that she didn't see the second mouse until it was practically in. And then a third mouse appeared. For the rest of the night, drawn ever more by the ticking or by the sounds of their increasingly numerous comrades—orgiastically gorging on cheese? shredding a fresh, somehow overlooked cushion?—mice trotted, circled, sniffed, and eventually pushed themselves into the trap, until it was full as a nest.

The candlelight was slowly replaced by a dim, foggy dawn. Jenny slid off the counter and lifted the trap by its handle, shocked a little at the wild explosion of life, the rapid uncontrolled pouring of weight from one side to the other as the mice renewed their efforts to escape. Pauline covered her ears, but Jenny thought she saw a spark in Pauline's face, in the way she quickly jumped off the table and opened up the back door, holding it for Jenny to carry the trap through. She stepped out into the wet dawn, feeling it like a salve on her eyes and her blooming hangover. In resignation or foreboding the mice grew still again. She shifted the trap from hand to hand as she walked through the long grass, Pauline close behind her. The trap was heavy, like a pail of water. The grass was softly razored on its edges and sopping from presunrise dew. Soon their jeans were soaked, and their sneakers were squishing and burping. Past the barn, past the small lily pond. They reached the first fence line and she set the trap in the grass and clambered over, then held out her arms for the trap. Pauline blanched. "Go on," she said. "They're locked in there. They're not getting out." She could feel the weak bulb of the sun, edging over the ridge line.

With a burst of resolve Pauline picked up the trap, and it shook with renewed consternation. She thrust it over the fence at Jenny quickly, as if it had burned her. Jenny took it and Pauline climbed over.

Just short of the woods Jenny stopped. She was sure that they'd gone far enough, but at the same time she already knew that this act was one she would perform again soon, that this was only the first instance of a new ritual. She set the trap into the grass while Pauline dashed away, as far as she could go while still keeping the trap within view. Jenny stepped as far away as possible herself, then lifted the door and leaped back. At first there was nothing. She kicked the trap lightly and leaped back again. "That way!" she whispered. Absurdly, she shooed with her hands. Then they came pouring out, little silver-gray creatures, and streamed off through the grass toward the trees.

MOVEMENT FLICKERED outside a window, and her pulse, as it always would, quickened. But it was only Juan, laying a plank across two chairs and picking up his barbell. Then it was Yvonne, snapping open a blanket. And finally it was Pauline, rooting through the kindling pile for a newspaper crossword she'd claimed to be finished with, twice.

Jenny closed her journal and gazed at the light slanting in through the window. The doors and windows were open, and the thin kitchen drapes billowed up and fell back silently. She was alone in the house. They'd been outside for hours, as they were every day, as they'd once been inside every day, with the windows sealed shut, the drapes drawn, the air thick and stale with smoke.

She put her journal upstairs in her room and went outside, to join them.

Juan lay on his plank, his feet braced in the grass, the sound of his effort unobtrusive and rhythmic, like a distant axe falling. Yvonne lay in the grass, unabashedly watching his body. Jenny was starting to be able to imagine what they must have been like when they first fell in love. High school students, Yvonne tall and awkward, at odds with her body, Juan a C student, track runner. Both instinctively solitary, lacking intimate friends. Somehow they discover each other. Yvonne watches Juan at practice—not a boy, but a *man*, with a man's burly body, circling the track in his team-issue sweatsuit. His strides are short but inexhaustible, they endlessly repeat, he is carried around and around the track at the same steady rate, lifting a hand to her each time he passes. Later they will make love, as if they are vampires who feed on each other. Later still he'll be drafted. He won't die; he'll live.

"Do you think it's a good argument?" Yvonne asked, referring to the book she was reading. "I wish you would read this book, baby. It reminds me of that thing you once said. How we all wear a mask, yet there's nothing beneath it. Our real selves are a put-on, a mask. Isn't that what you said . . . "

Juan answered her between exhalations, his thoughts piecing together, a phrase at a time. Pauline interrupted, "Four letters, a word that means 'still in dispute.'"

"You've asked me that one twice before," Juan complained.

Yvonne had a beer, and she shared it with Jenny. Without words, they passed the can every few sips. Another calm rhythm. It was their last beer, and later on, or tomorrow, Jenny would get in the car and drive to get more beer, more wine, more cigarettes, even more whiskey.

"Wait," Jenny suddenly said, and Yvonne's hand, passing the beer can, was stilled in midair. Juan stopped with his arms extended, the barbell above him. Pauline's pencil hovered.

Far below, on the barely used road, was the sound of a motor. They listened, keeping utterly still while it hurtled toward them like a comet. Then it passed, with a sigh.

"Just a car on the road," Yvonne said.

Now the hillside was blue. They could feel the night dew settling out of the air. A firefly drifted past, blinking.

Juan breathed, "Four hundred," and let the barbell sink onto his chest. They all shifted, erasing the brief interruption. Soon they'd go in and make dinner.

3.

Juan had shut himself into the barn with a secret project and dire warnings to the person or persons who dared interrupt him. That left Pauline and Yvonne doing physical training on the dirt track between the barn and the house. They jogged the two S curves downhill, tagged a mark, jogged back up, tagged again. Soon Pauline was a half lap, then a full lap, then one and a half laps behind. On her next downhill leg she skipped tagging the mark and dropped onto the grass. "You're not done!" Yvonne called, striding down.

Pauline stared at the sky. "I feel sick. I haven't had breakfast."

"Who needs breakfast? I've stopped eating breakfast. Brothers and sisters all over the world survive on one bowl of rice every day. Not like the kind of pigs you grew up with, gorging themselves on three meals a day and getting so fat that they're completely apathetic."

Jenny couldn't endure this; she set her book down. "Poor people don't survive on one bowl of rice because it's *better.* Try telling them they shouldn't have three meals a day."

"Sister," Yvonne said to her, "why make conflict when we're struggling together? Here we are in this beautiful place, blessed with the time to hone our minds and our bodies before the next test, and you go out of your way to make conflict."

When Juan finally emerged from the barn he had a long object under his arm which he threw on the grass when he reached them. It was a toy gun—a toy machine gun—which was made out of wood. Crude and flat, it was still unmistakable, like those black scarecrow silhouettes of a farmer leaning back on a fence Jenny sometimes saw propped up in gardens on the small country roads. "I'm fed up," Juan said, "of training with no arsenal! From now on we train with a full set of weapons. I want to make handguns, machine guns, and shotguns. That's all we can do until Frazer shows up with our arsenal."

Juan had worked out a system to make a good gun in just three or four hours, and after the first in each style was done he could go even faster, by using the completed guns as patterns. In the barn they all watched him run the stub of a pencil around the tight inside curve of the trigger, along the length of the muzzle. Once the shape was hacked out of the plank with the bandsaw it was just a matter of rounding the corners to make it "3-D," as Juan said. The gun came out "2-D" in that while it was as thick as the plank it was cut from, it was basically flat. "3-D" meant rounding the slab of the muzzle into something resembling a tube, although not really hollow.

It was another mania, Jenny thought, like their combat training and perhaps even their eulogy tape. The activity might stem from some clear objective, but soon enough the objective was lost, while the frenzy of action kept going. In no time they'd made full sets of "weapons" and then they kept making more, as if adding to a precious stockpile. Soon the barn floor was covered with Juan's many false starts, some ruined by unsteady handling against the blade of the saw, at the silhouette-cutting-out stage; some ruined after that, in the making-the-gun-3-D stage. Once the girls had been fully instructed they worked with wood chisels and hammers and pocket knives, and, less serenely, with the bandsaw as a sort of a lathe. This was Yvonne's innovation. The bandsaw was turned on, so that its shrieking complaint filled the barn, and then the gun-in-progress was held at arm's length until the wildly vibrating blade just nicked it, sending little chunks of wood like bullets in unpredictable directions. Juan said, "You shouldn't fuck around with a tool you don't know how to use," and, "That's good, bitch. That fucks up the blade," but it was clear that Yvonne's recklessness threatened him in some way. He tried to cut guns out more and more quickly, with a lot of gazing into the distance, so that they came out with wiggles on top of the muzzles, or with no trigger guards, or with very short grips.

One afternoon when Jenny looked in on them Pauline was sitting cross-legged in a far corner hacking at a crude gun with a chisel she gripped in her fist. She suddenly flung the chisel, with incredible violence, toward the back of the barn. It struck against the wall with a *pow* and thumped into the hay. "I got a splinter," she said.

"Good luck finding that chisel," Juan said, without looking up. "Move your ass while you remember where it landed."

"I got a splinter," Pauline repeated.

"Your hands can use some splinters and calluses, woman. That's a little tiny step to redemption, getting a sliver from doing hard work."

"Oh, Jesus," Pauline said.

Juan put down the gun he was drawing. "Whenever you're ready," he said.

Pauline didn't move.

"Move your narrow ass and find that chisel!" Juan yelled. "We only have two fucking chisels!"

"Make me, Adolf!" Pauline yelled. But she finally got to her feet, very slowly, and spent a long time brushing sawdust off her knees, thighs and backside. Then she started picking her way toward the spot where the chisel had fallen.

There was no longer any way to pretend, Jenny decided, that they were preparing to work on their book. They weren't exactly avoiding it. But the book was like "ego reconstruction," whatever this was: an activity they saw themselves as performing because they had the intention. And yet they never did it by day because they said it was too hot to sit in the house writing, and they never did it by night because by then they were always a little too drunk. Now a heatwave had settled on them. The house had a thermometer by the back door, a novelty one that was glued to a mountain landscape in a cheap metal frame. "A hundred," Yvonne read one morning, squinting wetly, wearing nothing but cut-offs and a bra. "It's a hundred!"

"It's more than a hundred," said Juan. "That thing stops at a hundred. Not that the piece of crap works."

"It does work!"

"That's not mercury in there, that's food dye."

"Last week it said seventy-five."

"Then it ain't never worked. It ain't never been seventy-five since we've been in this dump."

"That picture looks like California," Pauline said. "That picture looks nothing like here."

"Ain't no California I know."

"It looks like the Sierras."

"Didn't you have a nice castle in the Sierras?"

"The Cascades, and shut up."

"You shut up!"

"*You* shut up!"

Every day that week Jenny drove into Liberty, partly to get away from them but mostly because she expected a letter. Typically weeks felt like months, and she always expected her letter from William too soon. Now a reply wasn't just due, but well overdue. Finally, though, something lay in the dim little box. She stared at it, her fingertips tingling—then she snatched it and tore open the envelope. The thick square of many-times-folded notepaper within, written over so densely that dark tangles of ink showed through on the reverse, was so familiar to her that for an instant she misrecognized it. But it wasn't a letter from William, it was her letter, to him. The only other thing in the envelope was a small slip of paper on which Dana had written, *Don't write any more or send anything. I've moved. Sorry. Dana.*

She stood a long time holding the various pieces of paper, the tiny bronze eagles repeating in rows all around her. The lobby was silent and empty; she made her way blinking into the daylight and then into the car. Another car pulled into the lot and she drove away quickly. When she arrived at her pay phone there was somebody in it, a traveling-businessman type with an unknotted tie and his jacket slung over his shoulder. She drove up and down like a perturbed animal trying to reclaim territory until he finally left. Then there was no answer at Dana's. She got back in the car and drove to a small park and waited, her head in her hands. After half an hour she drove back to the phone, but there was no answer again. She was pressed so intently against the handset that the shell of her ear throbbed with pain. She closed her eyes against the sun beating into the booth and suddenly the line opened; she had almost forgotten that it was still ringing. She heard the soft hissing inside the wire, the sound of the void between herself and Colorado, and then to her bounding relief Dana's voice said, tentatively, "Hello?"

"Dana," she breathed. "Dana, it's me."

Dana's voice leaped over hers. "I said not to call!"

"But Dana—"

The line went dead.

When she called back Dana snatched up the phone. "Don't do this," Dana said.

"Don't hang up, Dana, don't, Dana, don't—"

Dana interrupted harshly. "I got sick. And I saw the doctor. Don't try to act like you're surprised."

It was her turn to pause. She heard the hiss inside the wire again, but it seemed subtly altered, as if an element that was not aural, that she could feel but not hear, had been added to it. She thought of something her father once said. Her father had always been uncannily good with cats; he'd been able to discipline them, to command their respect and control their behavior. "It's all in the way you go *pssst!*" he'd said. "There's two different *pssst!* sounds to get their attention. One sounds like the wind in the grass, which they love. One sounds like a snake, which they fear." To her the two *pssst!*s were exactly alike. Her hands were pouring sweat; she was surprised to see that she was still holding the returned letter tightly. It was stained from her palm. "Is that clinic still there on the corner?"

"I think so, but I can't go there now."

"Please go, just for a checkup. It won't take very long."

Dana was using the silence to signal her anger, not to make a decision. At last she said, "I'll be there in about half an hour."

Their conversation lasted just a fraction of the time Jenny waited for it to begin. "That thing you sent me made me very, very sick," Dana said. "You can't imagine what things are like here. There are doctors all over the place. That location, where I left it, there are people working there who've been examined maybe five or six times. And then they found me."

"There's no way they could have, unless you weren't careful."

"You're blaming me?" Dana seemed to be struggling to control her voice. After a moment she said, "I don't understand why you got into this."

"I'm helping them. The way you help me."

"You're in no position to help anybody."

"How did they find you? Did they see you? Did you tell anyone?"

"God! Don't insult me."

"Then they've only talked to you because there's a—flu in the area. They're just talking to people who live there."

After a long pause Dana said, "Remember how Sandy talked at a memorial service? For those people who died of this illness? The doctors are tracking down everybody who spoke there, and everybody they know. They talked to Sandy about three weeks ago. Now she's run off to hide with her sister."

"Did she tell them anything?"

"She must have told them she knew someone in Boulder." When Jenny didn't say anything Dana added, "I came back from work and they were sitting on my porch. In dark suits and sunglasses, the whole fucking deal! With your letter right there on my table."

She couldn't seem to keep the shake out of her voice. "I'm sorry, Dana."

"Be sorry for yourself. If Sandy told them about me, then she must have told them about your great admirer. And he knows where you are. He must be how you got into this."

"You know where I am."

"Not exactly, and I wish I knew less."

"I'm sorry," she said again. She felt sick, as if the unidentifiable element inside their connection hadn't been a wire tap but a poisonous gas. Their conversation seemed poisoned.

"I'm hanging up now," Dana said. "We've been on for five minutes."

IT WAS a long time, several shoppers going in and coming out again with their bags hugged to their chests or in ramshackle carts that they pushed to their cars, but then she saw the boy step out the front door and light a cigarette standing in front of the store's big glass windows, against the placards announcing store specials. He cupped his hands around the cigarette and craned toward it, but with his neck stiffly bent back, as if trying to keep something balanced on the top of his head. She realized he was holding his Afro away from the flame. Somehow the deliberateness of his awkwardness made him look practiced at what he was doing, though she could tell that he wasn't a smoker. He glanced over his shoulder into the store and then moved sideways, away from the line of sight out the windows. When he'd moved far enough he tilted back against the cinder block wall and surveyed the expanse before him, taking only occasional, very quick drags.

He was a beautiful kid, and the instant she thought it her eyes filled with ridiculous tears. Watching him, she understood exactly the pleasure he felt. He was taking a cigarette break like a man, savoring his aloneness. It was a startling contrast to her own cracked up, desperate condition. After talking to Dana she'd felt she couldn't bear to be alone, couldn't bear going back to the farm, couldn't possibly stay on the road she was driving so badly, and so she'd found herself here, staking out a bag boy. She put her sunglasses on and restarted the engine before he could see her, but at the same time the boy peered forward, and then he flicked the butt away in a long arc and began to walk toward her. "Hey!" he called cheerfully. "Not from Nam! You sure eat. I thought those groceries would last you a year." Just then a small middle-aged white man, the sort to walk tilted forward as if always looking for something, ventured out the store's doors and squinted tentatively at the lot.

"Thomas?" he called.

Drawn up short, the boy turned around and waved to the man across the hundred or so feet between them with great sweeps of his arm, as if directing a distant airplane. "Over here, Mr. M."

"Are you staying or going?"

"I ain't sure."

"If you're going, punch out." The admonition was distracted and mild. Then the man went back in.

"That's the boss," the boy said, arriving at her window. "He's as blind as a bat."

"You seemed worried he'd see you were smoking."

"I don't *worry*. Mr. M thinks I'm too young to smoke, but I'm eighteen years old." This seemed to remind him to unhilt his comb. "You here to shop?" he inquired, as he worked on his hair.

"I'm just driving around."

"That sounds cool. I'll drive with you."

"I think you're busy," she laughed, but then she realized he wasn't kidding at all. He was sprinting back into the store. As soon as he disappeared inside she tried to make herself speed away, but before she could even debate it he was coming back out. "Days like this they don't need me, but Mr. M lets me stay if I want extra hours," he panted, climbing into the car. "I just had to punch out."

Once they were driving she felt calmer and more reasonable. There was no reason to think she was endangering this kid. She hadn't endangered the Liberty postmistress, or the man who'd sold her the mousetrap, just by talking with them, had she? She followed his directions through the outskirts of town to a lonely brown structure with one slotlike window before she caught wind of what he was doing. "Is this a bar?" she exclaimed. "You don't look old enough to drink."

The observation offended him deeply. "Bet I'm older than you. This bar is my regular place, wait and see. They all know me in here."

Inside the bar felt murkier than it might have at night, when the small lamps and the pinball machine would cast more of a glow. Now they were washed out by the weak sunlight through the slot of a window, and that light didn't go very far. There were just a few people, two older black men at the bar and an older black woman behind it. As they walked in the bartender gave them a withering look. "Two beers," the boy said. "Or just give me a Coke," he complained. "I'm just here with my friend."

"How old are you?" the bartender asked her.

"Twenty-five."

"Whoa!" said the boy.

The bartender raised her eyebrows. "Thomas ain't even sixteen. Don't believe what he tells you. Why aren't you at work?" she demanded. "Don't make me lie to your mother."

"I'm off *early*," said Thomas, aggrieved.

When they'd slid into the booth farthest from the bar, near the window, she said, "Maybe we shouldn't stay here."

"Why, 'cause of how mean she was? Oh, she's always that way. She likes me. My brother brung me in here all the time."

"I'm sorry about your brother," she said after a minute.

"Why? Ain't no big deal."

"It is a big deal. He was killed in a terrible war. He should be with you now."

Thomas looked narrowly at her. "Shit," he said after a moment. He laughed briefly.

"What?"

He shook his head. "I don't know your name," he realized. "My name's Thomas, did I already say that?"

"I'm Alice."

"Alice, don't be mad." He cast a backwards glance over his shoulder, but the older people at the bar were ignoring them now. He still lowered his voice. "I was just shitting you, Alice. My brother ain't dead."

"He's not?"

"No."

"Well, I'm glad to hear that," she said tentatively.

He seemed much less comfortable now. "Where do you live, anyway? I never see you in town."

She took a sip of her beer, fizzy and cold, and let it burn down her throat while she thought. She didn't know when she'd last sat in a bar and just let the time pass. "Outside town," she said finally. "I live with this lady I work for."

"You're a maid?"

"Pretty much."

"Is it just you and her? That sounds lonely."

"It is," she said, and for a minute they fell into silence.

Soon her beer bottle was empty and before she could stop him Thomas went to the bar for another. "On the house," he said, setting it down. "See? It's my bar, even if I can't drink." She waved her thanks at the bartender, who waved her off, shrugging.

"Why'd you tell me your brother was killed?" she asked him, after taking a swig of the beer.

"Just kidding around."

"Was he drafted?"

"Why?"

"I'm just asking."

Thomas twisted around in his seat. With another quick glance toward the bar, he fished his cigarettes out of his pocket and gazed down at them. "She'll rat me out to my mother for sure," he said irritably. After a while he added, "He was drafted but did not report. Then he ran off and never came back. So it's like he's dead. Maybe he is." His Coke was finished but he poked his straw around in the ice cubes in an exploratory way, as if he might locate more.

"You shouldn't be ashamed of what he did."

"It don't make any difference to me. He can do what he wants."

"My dad did the same thing. But in World War II, not Vietnam. He was angry that the government put all the Japanese people in prison."

"Who put all the Japanese people in prison?"

"The government. After Pearl Harbor. Not prison, but a camp that was just like a prison. Even if you were an American citizen, if your parents or grandparents were Japanese you got put into prison because you might be a spy. We were at war with Germany and Italy too, but if you were German or Italian that was fine. It was just the Japanese that got put into camps."

"I never heard that in school."

She shrugged. "They never teach it."

"You're shitting me, right?"

"No. I'm not." She threw back another long draught of beer. "How much do they teach you in school about slavery?"

"Right on," Thomas grinned. "They don't teach us shit about that. But I hardly go, anyway."

"Oh, Thomas. That's bad. You have to go to school."

"You're just saying what bullshit it is!"

"You still have to go. That's what they expect you to do, as a young black man. Not go to school."

Thomas considered this a while. "What happened to your dad, anyway?"

"He went to prison for a couple of years. Real prison, I mean." Her heart had gained speed; she couldn't believe that she'd let herself mention her father. She wrapped her hand tightly around her beer bottle as if the cold could pull her back into line. The bottle was still beaded with chill water from the cooler, but like the last, it was suddenly empty.

"Alice," Thomas was saying. "Hey, Alice. Don't cry."

For a moment she didn't know why he was calling her that. "God, look at me. I don't drink much. That beer made me sappy."

"At least your dad and you see eye-to-eye. My dad's not around, but if he ever got hold of my brother, my brother would *wish* he was in Vietnam."

"What makes you think that we see eye-to-eye?"

"You said that you thought war was bad. So you're like all the antiwar people. And your dad must have been that way, too." It was just an observation, a pleased notation of one possible harmonization in a generally discordant world. She looked at him, facing the single small window, his young face slightly dusted with light. Admiring her from that strange manchild zone of fifteen. The comb came out of the pocket again, and he lazily tugged at his hair: afternoon-off contentment. While she faced away from the window, her face near his, yet shadowed. She tried not to stand up too quickly.

"I have to go, Thomas," she said. "I have to get back to work."

"Aw, but you're telling me so much great stuff. You got great stories, Alice. Maybe we can meet up tonight when you're done with your job."

"I don't think tonight."

"You won't come by the store for a year. You got too much food last time."

"I'll come by anyway."

"Cool. Shake on it." He stuck out his hand, and she shook it. "I have a magic touch with older women," he warned her.

Outside he lit himself a cigarette, in his awkward, amateurish, impressively particular way. She wondered if it was just coincidence, the random crossing of their paths at a time she was desperately lonely, that had made her say so much to him. Or was it something about him, himself? Once William had said, of winning people to the cause of revolution, You have to get them while they're tender and young. He'd mostly been joking, but for a while afterward she'd imagined an invisible eye on the young, not yet shut, the way that the skull of a child is supposed to be not fully fused—so that being permeable to the world was a physical thing, that no matter how hard you tried not to, you lost as you aged. Thomas declined her offer of a ride to wherever he lived—I dig walking around, he explained. And she was relieved, and disappointed, and it was all she could do to depart casually. She'd broken a rule talking to him, and she knew she wouldn't let herself see him again.

"Hey," he said as she started the engine. "Thanks for telling me all of that stuff."

Driving off she still wasn't sure why she had. Her father's attitudes weren't things she hoped to alter or even fully understand anymore. She'd long given up brooding on his appalled opposition to her political beliefs, in spite of the fact that he should have been more likely than the average person to agree with her. Her father had been so embittered by the internment and his imprisonment for resisting the draft that when they'd moved to Japan, he'd meant to expatriate permanently. He must have thought there he would finally get some respect: he wouldn't be shunned by white people because of his race, and he wouldn't be shunned by his race, because he had failed to kowtow to white people. Resisting the draft as her father had done hadn't ever been a popular or noble position among the interned Japanese. It lumped you in, however unfairly, with the fanatical Emperor-worshippers, the few real America-haters who made everyone else look so bad. And so her father must have hoped the Japanese would embrace him as heartily as the Japanese-Americans had cast him out, but things hadn't wound up that way. In Japan he'd emerged as indelibly and hopelessly American. It had been in his slight advantage in height and his unerasable Los Angeles accent, in his casual dress which in Japan just seemed sloppy, in his inability to master Japanese. While she'd seemed to absorb Japanese in her sleep; leaving California she'd been shattered, but she'd also been nine, and by the time her father decided to move them home again she was fourteen. She remembered sobbing on the plane, all the way back across the Pacific. In Stockton there had been a dutiful visit to a school psychologist with an office in the municipal building, an occasion mostly notable for the perfect, child-high replica of the Statue of Liberty that had sat on a stand in the lobby. She had been transfixed by this, had reacted to it as if it were a challenge and a joke, had circled it and been reprimanded for trying to touch it and had then sat thinking irritably and irresistibly about it all the while that her father, uneasy and surly himself in a new suit and shoes, had sat with one ankle tensely propped on one knee and his hands in a casual pose in his lap, trying to explain the five-year hiatus in her education. "The school system there is superior," she remembered him saying. And then he'd added, into the arctic silence that had greeted this comment, and in a stammering tone unlike him, "That is, superior compared to other foreign countries. Not compared to American schools."

There had been tests of the sort she imagined were given to retarded or incorrigible children, flashlights shone in her eyes and then bright wooden puzzles and ink blots and reading aloud. California had looked so astoundingly different to her, not just because she was no longer nine, but fourteen. Not just because she had lived in Japan for five years. Not just because the psychologist had seemed disappointed when she passed all her tests, or because things were smaller, stripped of childhood enchantment, more uncanny the better she'd known them before. There had been something else, an aura of fraudulence in the burnished sunlight and the dense floral yards and in the bland self-absorption of faces. In Vietnam at the start of that summer a monk had immolated himself, and the ghastly flames eating his body had been shown on TV. Now her father was declaring a truce in his one-sided war on the land of his birth, but it was at the same moment she'd started to grasp why he'd waged it. It had been at her school in Japan that she'd learned about the internment. She'd never heard of it in California, where it had happened, or from her father, to whom it had happened, and when she'd asked him about it after school that day he'd just said with annoyance, "Why ask about that? All of that was a long time ago."

But to her it had seemed like a key: to understanding him, to knowing him, perhaps even to being his daughter. Her discovery of what he'd endured was the beginning of her discovery of history and politics, of power and oppression, of brotherhood and racism, and finally, of radicalism; but it only drove them to fight with each other. As she grew increasingly involved in the antiwar movement she and her father fought with increasing fury, but not increasing complexity—never about issues, never about the war itself, only about her arrogance, or perhaps it was her stupidity, or her naivete, in daring to oppose it. *What do you know?* he would shout. She moved at eighteen to Berkeley without finishing high school; in spite of how well she had done on the tests, the Stockton psychologist had put her back three grades, perhaps to make a point about the superiority of American versus Japanese schools. In Berkeley she enrolled in a night class on modern political science at a local community center, with the idea she might eventually transfer to a college that didn't require a high school diploma. Her teacher was a clean-shaven senior at Berkeley, who'd just been thrown out for taking over the dean's office a few credits shy of his B.A. degree. By the end of the term they'd become lovers. This was the calm way in which William denoted what for her was an unprecedented development. She had never before had a lover. Until him, she'd never even been kissed. If the connection she felt to her father had already been tenuous, her involvement with William destroyed it completely. There had been one catastrophic visit from her father to the apartment she and William were sharing. The fight that erupted, in which her father and William began trading astonishing insults, had been even worse than she'd feared, and her worst fears had been suitably dire. After that she and her father, in what was the least hostile position they both could arrive at, simply broke off their contact. William became her world, his language her language. She remembered thinking to herself, and sometimes even daring to utter aloud that They Had Become Lovers. And she remembered the joy she'd felt being propelled, by a manner of speech she would never have used, toward a life she had never imagined.

Now that life was entirely gone; Dana had cut the last thread, all because Jenny had stuck her neck out for a trio of "comrades" who would never have done that for her, she would bet, and who still hadn't written a word of their book. She was furious by the time she was driving the last few steep yards up the hill. She slammed the Bug's door and strode toward the pond; they were skinny-dipping, something she'd been able to deduce before even reaching the house from the gay trail of clothes scattered over the grass. As she came level with the tea-colored, peat-stinking pool, she saw Yvonne waving to her and Pauline sitting carefully sunk to her shoulders, hair still dry. "I need to talk to you," Jenny announced, surprised at how calm her voice sounded. Juan splashed up to Pauline from behind and plunged her under the surface. Pauline came up, screaming and sputtering.

"Motherfucker!" Pauline cried.

Pauline and Juan thrashed and churned in the murky water while Yvonne waded out, splashing mud off her knees and her thighs, and then turned back to watch them benignly. "Take a dip, Sister," Yvonne said.

"Some other time. I need to talk to you. All of you."

"What about?" Water dripped off Yvonne's breasts and from her jumble of pubic hair. "Jenny wants to talk, comrades," she called.

Pauline and Juan paddled away from each other. Juan tilted back and submerged his head under the water, as if being baptized, and when he came up again his hair lay plastered darkly on his skull. "You look hot, Sister. Take your clothes off. Let us all see your natural skin."

"Goddammit, I need to talk to you!"

"Nakedness ain't no big thing. That don't hang you up, do it?"

"I'll be in the house. Don't keep me waiting." She saw Pauline, sunk to her neck, look alarmed as she turned on her heel and left them.

And she was glad to observe that all three of them seemed apprehensive when they ventured in the back door, their clothes sticking wetly to them, their hair dripping in ropes. She'd emptied their writing box onto the table. "Hey," Juan said. "Get out of there."

"Have you done anything? *Any*thing?"

"That's none of your business. Like I told you, we do it at our pace, not yours."

"Frazer's coming back next week to see what you've done."

"We're going to write it," Juan said stubbornly.

"When? Outside of this place the world's still going on like before. They're still looking for you. There's no reason to think they won't figure this out, pretty soon."

"Oh, my God," Pauline murmured, twisting her hair.

Juan said, "I never underestimate pigs, and pigs should never underestimate me. Let them come here. I'll cook them for breakfast!"

She didn't leave the house again until they were actually in the front room rolling a blank sheet into the typewriter. "This won't take long," Juan said. "It's pent up in our minds. It'll feel good to spit it all out." Outside she followed the slender aluminum pipe that came from the back of the house and traveled up the hill, lying almost out of sight in the grass. Even after it entered the trees the climb was steady, as the pipe angled in joints around boulders, or slipped through a crevice between. It seemed not to have rained in a while, but the cistern was full. Without pausing she stripped and sank into it.

The cold felt unbearable but she stayed in, and washed herself with numb hands and raked her puckered fingers through her hair. Her limbs and torso and even her breasts gradually lost all feeling, until she was only aware of a pain in her bones. She still didn't get out; the loss of all sensation felt good, the most aware of her body she'd been in a while. Like a backpacker or a pilgrim or every other kind of nomad she'd been without real privacy for so long that it seemed as if her body had vanished. Now it was just a vehicle, a shield, a tool. That it had ever housed beauty or pleasure seemed very unlikely. She closed her eyes, and saw William; the oval of sweat that would dampen his sternum. Sometimes she could arch up and transfer this sweat to herself. Past the door of the bedroom, their home: they were finally living alone. In the dark space defined by these things is her pleasure, opening like a stain. The first time it had happened to her she'd been so dazed already by pleasure that when she'd heard a strange noise, like an animal's wail, she hadn't realized it was coming from her.

William Weeks. Later, she had tried to see him as the world had, studying his arrest photo in the newspapers. His full mouth was there but his eyes were opaque, not the eyes that she knew. His eyes as she knew them were bedroom eyes, superficially sated, but with a subtext of starvation in them. Eyes linked to the way he would fuck her, with reproachful frantic whimperings, as if he'd been deprived. He often, in the full light of day, had a sexually calculating, restless, predatory expression on his face, the same expression she sometimes saw when he was on her and arching to push farther in—a decadent look, as if sex with her were as ruinous as a drug addiction. Of course none of this was conveyed in the photo. There he looked like a former teen idol, corrupted by nothing much worse than old flannel workshirts and long hair. His prettiness had made him the sort of boy young girls fall in love with because they haven't yet stopped loving girls, but he had also been the sort of man a certain type of woman particularly desires. After they had been together for more than two years she had understood that she wasn't the only one, even once they were sharing a home. But she had been the central one, somehow unrivaled. She could not fathom why.

Now she was distorted and blue in the cistern's deep water. She reached for herself, pressing a hand between her legs, but no sooner had it flared than the impulse was gone. She looked up, at the cathedral-like structure of trees. Although the canopy was dense she could sense where the sun was; it had sunk a good way since she'd been here. She had to flop and flounder to get out of the cistern because now her whole body was numb. While she was sitting on the cistern's edge with rattling teeth and gooseflesh, waiting to dry off, she noticed that the hugest of the boulders had skidmarks behind them, as if they were traveling, more quickly than most geology travels, downhill toward the house.

That night she was plunged into feverish dreams. She stood on shipboard with her father in the port of Hawaii, but this Hawaii was a Technicolor afterlife, as if the terrestrial one were mere shadows. These mountains rose in untouched velvet folds to the darkness of space; this sea was the color of fountain-pen ink. Floral scents were so strong she could taste them like soap in her mouth. Far offshore a huge waterspout stood, like a glass pedestal. "I'm swimming out there," she said. "Don't do that," her father said. "Jenny." She awoke strangely clutched with emotion. In the kitchen she encountered Yvonne, brewing coffee. "We're getting to work," Yvonne chirped, as if Jenny were a hallway proctor in high school. "I'm going for a long walk," Jenny told her. But only a short way up the hill the surge crested and dribbled away. She had been impelled out of bed by the strong sense that someone expected her, and now she knew this was false. Slowly, she walked back to the house. The front room door was closed. With what seemed to be her last strength she crept back up the stairs and lay gingerly down on her bed.

Some time later she was startled awake by the door to the front room banging open. "It's too hot," Yvonne said, from the foot of the stairs.

"If we leave that door open, and the bedroom door open, the air'll move better," Juan said.

"Where's Jenny?"

"She went out. For a walk."

The kitchen tap came on with a squeak, and a water glass filled. The refrigerator door sucked open and thumped shut again. Jenny closed her eyes. Some time after this, or perhaps immediately after this, Juan yelled, "Don't waste tape if you're only rehearsing. Goddammit! We don't even know if you're done with it yet."

"I made all those changes," Pauline said.

"I haven't heard any changes. It goes on the tape when it's done, and it's done when I say." After a pause he said, "So read."

"Okay," Pauline said. Then came another pause, as if she were preparing herself; perhaps pushing her ragged hair behind her ears with several small nervous movements; or biting down quickly and hard on the corner of her thumb, as if trying to get a good chunk off before being caught. Pauline had scores of twitchy little tics that Jenny had absorbed without being aware, so that lying there, with her eyes closed, she was surprised by how detailed her imagining was. The corner of Pauline's thumb—the inner corner, on her right hand—was flattened from gnawing and healing, as if the flesh had been neatly sliced off. ". . . New ideas, real ideas, were in the air all around me. But it wasn't until I fell ill, from purely natural causes, that I truly began understanding the travesty of my life until then, and the rightness of my future comrades' beliefs. I was so ill that I lay down all day. I heard a voice that was so sweet I thought I was dreaming. But I wasn't dreaming. The voice belonged to the comrade who was caring for me. Not content just to be a good nurse, he was reading aloud to me, for hours on end. Later I would learn that the stirring words I was hearing were from *Capital*, by Karl Marx, and *Soul on Ice*, by Eldridge Cleaver, and *Blood in My Eye*, by George Jackson. Of course I'd heard of these books, but in my blighted old life I hadn't thought them important. More and more I longed to see the face of this kind and wise person, this brother who was trying to teach me. I begged him to take off my blindfold. 'Can't I just see you?' I said. 'The words matter, not me,' he explained."

Juan interrupted. "No blindfold."

"No blindfold?"

"I already said to get rid of the blindfold."

"You already said I can't be in the closet."

"For the last fucking time, you were not in a closet."

"Was it a pantry?"

"It was a *room*. Maybe not like the nice rooms you're used to."

"Well, what do I know," Pauline said, "I was wearing a blindfold the whole fucking time."

"She has to explain why she couldn't see him," Yvonne said, in a peacemaking tone. "It's sweet. She fell in love with his voice."

"I don't care if she fell in love with his voice or his dick or whatever."

"Don't talk about him like that," Pauline said.

"You hardly knew him, Princess. I might not have fucked him, but I actually knew him. Get rid of the blindfold. It's bullshit."

"It's true."

"It's not true to the point of the story. There's things that are facts that in context don't help make the point."

"Then why can't I see him?"

"You *can* see him! Why the fuck do you have to not see him?"

"Because," Pauline said. At last she said, "It just mattered more when I couldn't see him, and then I did finally see him."

"Figure out some other way to do it."

Pauline's expression must have spoken for her because Juan added, "No one said it was gonna be easy. This is the real fucking deal. This is our *book*—" In frustration he kicked something, the tape recorder or typewriter, so that it left the coffee table and came down with a crash on the floor, and although it was far from an unfamiliar noise, Jenny jerked upright. Her back was not just damp, but streaming with sweat. The room seemed to react to her movement. It quivered, then fell still again.

"What was that?" Yvonne said.

She reeled from her bedroom and onto the landing. The three of them had emerged from the front room to look up the stairs. After a moment Yvonne said, "I thought you went walking."

"I started but I felt . . ." She let a vague gesture name her condition, and with that she realized she was sick.

"Did we wake you?" Pauline asked.

"I woke up on my own. I was thirsty."

She thought she felt a tense line of inquiry, connecting the three of them to her; but if she had, it fell slack and dissolved. They were drifting away to the kitchen. She followed, one hand tight on the railing to get down the stairs. It struck her that their actions were overly natural. She could remember other moments of terrifying acuteness endured during fevers, although for some reason she never recalled all the things she'd discerned. "Is that true?" she demanded abruptly. She felt the fever's mingled weakness and weightlessness moving her forward. "You kept Pauline locked in a closet and wearing a blindfold?"

They all turned back to her. She thought she saw Pauline redden.

"I heard you," she added. "I didn't mean to eavesdrop, but I did."

"Sister," Yvonne said with amazement. "Are you sure you're okay?"

"In those communiques you used to send out, you said you were treating her better than prescribed in the Geneva Conventions. You said you let her exercise and read the papers and eat with you. 'We knew we'd never prevail by punishing her. We always let her see that we're true friends of liberty.'"

After a moment Juan said, "All that's true. But she had to be blindfolded in the beginning, so she couldn't ID us. That's standard, for her own protection. You know that, Jenny."

"What about the closet?"

Juan grinned helplessly at the ceiling. "Ah, Christ. So you overheard that old debate."

"Pauline," she said. "Why don't *you* say something?"

"Sister!" Yvonne said. "You can see for yourself that Pauline's not some helpless prisoner."

"I could get in that car and drive off any time that I want," Pauline said suddenly. "I'm more committed than you are."

"Don't talk to her that way," warned Juan.

"Oh, she's so great. I'm sick of it! Everything I do is wrong, and everything she does is right!"

"That's not true," Jenny said.

"Let's see you accomplish *one fourth* of what Jenny accomplished. Let's see you come from a nonwhite-skin background—"

"Oh God," Jenny said. "Don't." The staircase was buckling beneath her. They were still arguing as she crawled upstairs, clutching the banister. Back on her bed, time slowed down to a crawl. Her bedsheets were drenched with her sweat but she was shaking from cold. She kept rising and closing the window and later realizing she still hadn't closed it. Noises, the noises of dogs yapping, although there weren't dogs, and of traffic, although there wasn't traffic, filtered to her from outside. She didn't know if it was then, or later, that she thought of the call of the soup man. This was a noise that she'd once tried to memorize and instead she'd forgotten, and even forgotten her attempt to remember. Now it sounded with force in her mind. It had only ever come on summer nights, when it was too hot to sleep soundly and yet so late that everyone had gone inside to try, and the streets were left utterly still, the air beneath the street lights showing yellow and viscous from the unmoving haze and the peculiarly Egyptian-seeming leaves of the ginkgo tree drooping like pendants—the keening seemed to come to them from miles away, carried somehow through the air on no breeze, sounding like the last cry of a mortally wounded coyote. It always pierced whatever depth of sleep and she would come conscious with her heart pounding and her hair standing straight up on end. Street light filtering in through the windows, the steady guttering sound of their fans, the underwater movements of her insomniac father like a deep sea fish, passive and depressive. All that seemed to gel, as if time were too thick to move forward. As if she were hovering over a bottomless well. Even the actions they took would seem shrouded in stillness. Her father was always wearing a robe belted over his pajamas, and a pair of thin slippers like footprints of cardboard with a dirty cloth band running over the knuckles. She would be wearing her nightgown, no slippers. Hand in hand they would pad down the dank, pungent stairwell five floors to the street. Looking back up she might see their window, in the top of the ginkgo, a lone square of light broken up by the leaves. Perhaps there was just one night like this, but she remembered it somehow as ceremony, exemption, deep sadness, the depth of the well of their life in Japan. The soup man would have seen their lone light, or perhaps he'd been waved at, to wait, by her father. When they emerged onto the sidewalk he would be standing next to his cart. His instrument, in her memory like a kazoo with a twist in the middle, which she linked to its uncanny cry, would lie mute in his hand. A small object that had somehow taken the sound of the soup man's loneliness and cast it like a line across miles. Of course now the memory was marred by illogic. Why was he peddling his soup in the dead of the night? Why were she and her father the only two people who bought? Of some things she was sure: that the man's cart was square and had two wheels and a long handle; when he wanted to move it he had to both lift up and push. There was a trap door on top and when the man opened it she heard liquid slapping within, like seawater restlessly trapped in the hold of a ship. She understood that in that country, hot things on hot nights could be cooling. It was an axiom that seemed to be bound to the natural laws of that country alone. The soup she didn't really remember. Were there noodles? There must have been. And rich broth full of salt. They ate silently there on the street, gave the man back his bowls, climbed back up the stairs. Sweat pearled deliciously from every pore of her body beneath the long nightgown and she would feel cool, and then sleep as if drugged. One night like this, after the strange pilgrimage to the street in the dark in her nightgown, and the soup, and her own cool sweat, there was an earthquake near dawn, which she slept through.

Perhaps she didn't remember this during her fever; perhaps it was there in her body but not found by her mind until later. Perhaps, after her fever had broken, and she saw Pauline in her doorway, the memory of the soup man came for the first time and tinged all the hours before. Pauline was watching her tentatively—she was holding a bowl of soup. "Jenny," she said. "You've been sick. You've been—talking. Sometimes you would seem to wake up and talk to us, but then what you said wouldn't make any sense. We didn't know what we would do if you didn't get better. We can't call a doctor. What would we have done?"

"You were here?" she said, sitting up weakly.

Pauline nodded. "All of us were."

"It's just you now."

"They're sleeping. It's late. It's past three in the morning."

"You should be sleeping, too."

"I couldn't," Pauline said. "Do you want this soup? It's cooled off, but I can go and reheat it."

She nodded, mutely. A few minutes later Pauline was back, with the soup now steaming. A slight smell of char wafted off it. "I think I burned it," Pauline said. And then, with frustration, "I know how to cook. I used to cook complete meals. I was good at it."

"That's okay," Jenny said. She lowered her face to the soup, and took a careful spoonful. To her surprise her stomach growled with desire; she began eating quickly.

"I'm sorry I said that to you," Pauline said, watching her. "About how you do everything right and I'm sick of it. I didn't mean it."

She felt newly focused, as if the soup were fresh blood that had gone to her head. "I heard you arguing with Juan about a closet," she said. "And a blindfold."

"I know, but you don't know the context. Those points aren't important."

"You seemed to feel they were important."

"You don't know the context," Pauline said again. "I don't want to explain."

Jenny thought of Juan's words: There's things that are facts that in context don't help make the point. "Before I'd met any of you, I asked Frazer if he was sure you were staying with them out of choice."

Pauline was suddenly hard-eyed and silent, and Jenny remembered her at the beginning—before combat training, before summer sun, before food. A pale blue wraith made of stone. "Jenny, we were all really scared when you were having your fever. And I really did want to apologize. But you don't know what you're talking about, okay? You don't really know me."

"Okay," she said, after a moment.

Now Pauline seemed less certain. "Can I show you something?" she asked. "If you're not really tired."

"I've been sleeping all day."

Pauline went downstairs and came back a few minutes later with a brown document envelope addressed to Frazer. Its flap had been torn open but the metal brad and its matching hole were still intact, and with the brad the envelope had been neatly reshut. "Not the envelope," Pauline said. "I just took it from Frazer's to organize things, when we were still in New York. Look inside."

Inside was a slim pile of clippings. Most had been torn out rather than clipped, although torn with great care. There were pages from *Newsweek* and *Time* with six holes down the center where the staples had been. Leafing through the pile Jenny looked for the black-felt-tip underlining she'd come to recognize as Pauline's signature, but these pages were largely unmarked. In some places a light vertical line in the margin indicated that something of note lay nearby. She remembered the features from *Newsweek* and *Time*, sweeping overviews of Pauline's case that had been rich with pictures but poor in detail. Just a few lines had merited notice from the subject herself: an expulsion from school and the loss of a job, each mention as slight as the inked lines with which she had marked them. The newspaper clippings were meatier. They were from Bay Area tabloids that Jenny hadn't seen in over two years; they weren't the kinds of things subscribed to by the Rhinebeck library. Subtleties she never would have noticed without the long absence now seemed sharply familiar: the quality of the paper, the typeface. On the backs, parts of ads like old landmarks. The most recent clipping bore a date from just after the shootout. IN THE END, read the title, COPS, AGENTS MAKE NO DISTINCTION BETWEEN "VICTIM" AND CAPTORS.

Going back through the earlier clippings, she saw they were all on this theme. NEW NAME, BUT OLD ROLE: AS THE FAMILY REBEL. And, KIDNAPPED HEIRESS MAY HAVE HAD MORE IN COMMON WITH CAPTORS THAN INITIALLY THOUGHT. The expulsion, from a girls' convent boarding school, had been for sneaking out and talking back to a nun. The job loss had been from a restaurant: she had taken a job as a hostess, though she didn't need money, and had later been fired for supporting the bus boys when they tried to get their pay raised to minimum wage. The idea that Pauline had always been some sort of antiestablishment rebel had been explored by the scandal-minded media even before she'd announced that she'd come to see her captors as comrades. But it had always been minor, not much more convincing than the contrasting portrait of her as intensely devoted to tennis. "You don't have to read them all," Pauline said.

She put down the clippings and fingered the bedsheet, worn and pilled and now damp with her sweat; the night breeze pulsed in through the still-open window, but it no longer chilled her. She watched Pauline watching her: with satisfaction? with hope? She finally said, as if treading on glass, "You must be glad to have finally found comrades who share your same views."

She thought she saw some small portion collapse; as if, within the full bird's-eye sweep of a complex, unknowable city, one building had fallen. "Yes," Pauline said, quickly putting the clippings away. Something had not been said that she'd wanted to hear; or something had been said that she hadn't expected; Jenny watched helplessly, as Pauline closed the envelope, carefully pressed flat the small metal brad, then took up the used bowl and spoon. And there, for a moment, Pauline seemed at peace—as if the small gesture of tending to something unhooked her from whatever she felt. "It's almost morning," she said. "We should sleep." She went back downstairs before Jenny could answer.

Jenny turned off her lamp. When her eyes adjusted she saw dawn had already begun. The few forms in the room slowly gathered themselves into view. Downstairs a lamp was still on; she listened intently, and heard the soft rustling of paper. That sound, and the faint lamplight sifting upstairs, felt like safety to her, though she knew they were not. They reminded her of the last stage of sickness in childhood, when no longer sick, but still treated with care. That exceptional feeling of safety, and freedom. Downstairs, in the bedroom-cum-office, with its overflowing desk of business papers and its collection of particularly cherished and difficult plants crowding all of the sills, her father would have fallen asleep in his chair with the light on. If she stole down for a glass of orange juice and his door was ajar, she would hear his restrained, haughty snoring. She'd have his thin ray of light to see by. This would have been early childhood, Stockton, before they moved to Japan. She didn't know why she thought fondly of that house when it had been so uncomfortable to her. It had always been too small and too crowded with junk, like a garage or an attic. The boundary between private house and open-to-the-public greenhouse had never quite been determined. There was the sideline in appliance repair; half-deconstructed mechanisms would be gathering dust on the tables, on old sheets of newspaper. Her father's indifferent bookkeeping would have strewn sales slips everywhere. In the huge handmade urn near the door was their massive jade plant, like some vegetal form of an elephant, all winding coarse trunks and great rubbery ears; the dim light would reflect off the leaves. They never dusted or vacuumed or swept, but her father did wipe every leaf of that tree with a damp cotton cloth once a week.

She remembered lecturing him in that house every year on her birthday, detailing why her new age was the best age to be. Six was the first year of school, when it would be novel but not yet a grind. Seven was the quintessence of lucky, the most lucky she'd be all her life. At eight she was still young enough to have fun, but old enough to appreciate it. He would listen to her without comment, continuing some household task. Sometimes he might close the discussion by saying, "I'm sure that you're right about that." Now it seemed like a melancholy exercise, these proofs that the future would never match up to the present, but at the time she'd felt so optimistic. Each year trumped the last and advanced closer to the ideal. And she remembered, years later, believing with the force that was thousands who believed just like her, that her generation was surely the luckiest, best, and most blessed. Her father's generation had been the good Germans and the humiliated interned Japanese and the racist white sheriffs and the callous corrupt government, while hers had just grown more enlightened on each of their parents' mistakes. They had tasted their century's horrors before they themselves gelled into cowards or bigots. Young enough to have fun, old enough to appreciate it! Unsurpassedly lucky! That kind of moral certainty carried with it a joy that couldn't be reconstructed in memory, once it was lost.

It was suddenly almost sunrise. Moving by inches, she got out of bed and went to the window; but gingerly as she had moved, the old floorboards still creaked. The downstairs lamp quickly snapped off; its faint glow vanished out of the stairwell. She heard Pauline rise from the couch, with the same pointless stealth, as if in this house they could hide from each other. Pauline slipped back into her bedroom, and pulled the door shut.

4.

The night before Frazer's arrival they packed up the writing box and hid it under Juan and Yvonne's bed. They had obviously learned not to leave the evidence, or lack of evidence, of their progress lying out in plain view. When Frazer arrived the next day they held council with him underneath the big maple. Jenny watched from high up on the hill, pretending to be reading. The conference looked friendly and calm. It ended with everyone rising and the two girls and Juan sauntering toward the house. She began to walk down and when Frazer saw her he walked up to meet her. His expression, while not overtly angry, was sardonic. One corner of his mouth was pinched upward.

"So," he said, reaching her. "They've done nothing."

"They're doing something, Rob. They finally seem committed to it. They talk about how great it'll be, to have the chance to explain how they feel."

"Do they talk about how great it'll be, to have the chance to make back all my money?" As soon as he said this he seemed to regret it. "Juan tells me they've been putting the whole thing on tape. He won't let me hear the tapes, or even look at them. He says he doesn't want confusing input until they're all finished. Is this a crock of bullshit?"

"They are taping. I've heard them."

"Then what are they saying? Give me something to go on, Jenny. I just want some goddamn reassurance."

She hesitated. "I don't hear individual words. They always keep the door closed. They can't write with me eavesdropping on them."

Frazer glared, disappointed. Then he laughed. "You're so generous, sweetheart. Maybe we're two of a kind. I brought them the gun that they wanted. I kept up my end of the bargain." Below them the back door swung open and Yvonne leaned out.

"What do you want?" Yvonne yelled. "Tuna fish sandwich, or cheese?"

When they had shouted back and forth about lunch and the door slammed shut again she said, "Just one?"

"Don't tell me they've turned you into a gun lover."

"No. I'm just afraid they were expecting something more."

"I'm afraid *I* was expecting something more."

She couldn't say anything to this. She watched him as he cast a hard gaze at the opposite hills, the vein at his temple jumping, the smooth dome of his head bright with sweat. Frazer's strange, prominent skull featured a shelf of bone just above the eyebrows that could make him resemble Neanderthal man or a glowering genius, depending on his general expression. She couldn't decide which he favored right now; his jaw was jutted forward, restlessly working, another tic that betrayed deep anxiety. She could feel her own pulse speeding; she'd been hoping for something like the right moment, but she'd known beforehand that a moment like that wouldn't come. The book she was holding was only a ruse, to conceal her letter. She had written to William all over again, though she'd been no more free than before to explain where she was. And now she'd had to explain what he would feel as long silence, as well. At least she'd had a stroke of brilliance and borrowed the typewriter from them, to type it. She wouldn't have to ask Frazer to rewrite her love letter. That was one humiliation she still could avoid.

As if he somehow sensed the drift of her thoughts, her effort to find the small upside, Frazer said, "At least it's a beautiful place." He sighed, looking off at the warm, buzzing hills.

"Rob," she said. "I have something to tell you. And a favor to ask."

TEN MINUTES LATER she was standing in the kitchen with Juan and Yvonne and Pauline, as Frazer's car roared down the hill. "Doesn't he want his sandwich?" Yvonne asked.

"No," she said.

"Good. Fuck him," said Juan. "I'll eat his goddamn fucking sandwich, fucking dishonest fuck."

She chewed her own sandwich without appetite. Frazer had blown up when she told him what happened with Dana. In the days since that phone call she'd felt more and more certain that Sandy had given up Dana's name to throw the cops off the trail; not knowing that Jenny had mailed Dana the tape, she would have thought Dana still was the cleanest of all of their friends. Sandy never would have named Frazer no matter how scared she was; she'd introduced Juan and Yvonne and Pauline to Frazer herself. But Frazer just said, "I still can't believe you sent out their damn tape! If they'd just had the patience to wait, that could have been chapter one of the book. That could have been our *exclusive*, I could have called up that editor weeks ago . . ."

Handing him the letter at this moment was even worse than she'd thought it would be, but there were no moments left. "You know people everywhere," she was saying. "If you mailed it to someone in Mexico, maybe, and they mailed it on—"

Frazer was turning it over and over in his hands, as if trying to see into it. "Thick," he murmured. "Didn't Dana recopy these for you?"

"I typed it."

"Oh, wonderful. Can I guess whose typewriter you used?" He closed his eyes and stood still a long moment, as if hearing something that she couldn't hear. She could see his jaw working, his pulse hammering in his neck. "I'll do my best," he said finally. "But it's not really the first of my worries."

Her face burned. "I didn't ask to be the first of your worries. If I had my way I wouldn't have asked you to do this at all."

"I know you wouldn't." Frazer got in his car, slammed the door hard and started the engine, but his window was down and she came to it and looked at the letter, which he'd tossed on the passenger seat. "I'll take care of it, Jenny!" he said.

The car's vibrations shifted the letter, and a wind had risen that seemed the forerunner of rain. "It'll fly out the window," she said.

Frazer opened the glove compartment, threw the letter inside with his jumble of maps, and slammed it shut again, hard. "How's that?" he yelled.

"One fucking gun," Juan was saying. "'That's not exactly what we agreed on.' 'Well, it looks like we're *all* just a little behind.'" Juan minced and sneered when he did Frazer's line. Then he said, "Clear the table. Let's take a look at this thing."

The gun was a Smith & Wesson snub-nosed revolver, with its own cop-style holster; Juan explained all this as he cleaned it, and buffed its outside with a T-shirt, and lay it down, darkly gleaming, on the table. He was already wearing the holster. Alone at the center of all their attention, the gun seemed to have an aura of intelligence, as if its coiled stillness was deliberate, and its potential lunges also matters that it would decide. It didn't seem at all related to the BB guns, with their faux wood grain and their slender black snouts and the gentle *pew pew* sound they made. Compared to this the BB guns were like fireplace tools. This gun stared back, through tiny, bright, metallic eyes.

Outside it had started to rain. The rain came down in ropes; all the colors seemed drained out of things, and the wind lashed the trees. Jenny went to the door and gazed out, her back to them, and the force of the rain misted her through the screen. Through her whole conversation with Frazer she had been so concerned for her letter, and how he would react, she had not lingered over his saying he'd brought them a gun. They had been talking about guns from the start, and she had always realized guns might one day appear. But the idea of guns and the actual presence of one weren't at all the same thing. Behind her, even the hardened threesome who sawed off their own shotguns were silenced by the gun's magnetism. Now that Juan had put on the holster she couldn't imagine him taking it off; and then she knew that he couldn't, either. From this minute he would constantly wear it, as if before he'd been naked.

The rainstorm had not slackened at all, and the rich wholesome smell of wet earth, such a strange counterpoint to the gun, billowed into the kitchen. Yvonne suddenly said, "I can't stand it, I've just got to feel it!" She leaped up from the table, squeezed past Jenny and ran out the door. Then Pauline moved away from the gun's circle also. Jenny thought she would follow Yvonne, but Pauline came to stand in the back door as well, and silently they both watched Yvonne run shrieking over the grass. She turned to see Pauline's face, and Pauline looked back at her—not communicatively or blankly, not coldly or warmly, only looked at her briefly, and then looked back outside. Pauline did not seem to feel the same dread that she did. After all, Pauline had been as insistent on being rearmed as her comrades. The rain's wind blew Pauline's hair slightly off of her temples; then Yvonne splashed back onto the step and they wordlessly stepped back to let her inside. "It's cold," Yvonne gasped.

Only Juan's concentration had not left the gun for an instant. He didn't look up at Yvonne in her plastered-down T-shirt, with her breasts in clear view. "One gun," he said again sourly. "What the fuck do you do with one gun? Oh, anything you want. You just have to get in and out fast. If you're cornered you're dead, because none of your comrades are armed. But haven't you heard about guys robbing banks with one gun? Sometimes even *no* gun. They just make a gun shape with their hand in their pocket, and all the dumb people believe it. One gun. Hey," he said loudly to Pauline and Jenny. Yvonne had left the room to change clothes, and Juan had realized he was speaking to no one. "You can hijack a plane with one gun. A plane's the one place where one gun is as good as a hundred. Hijack the plane, go to Cuba. Some comrades I knew did that once."

"Who?" Pauline said, finally.

"Before your time, Princess. A guy that I knew who lived on the East Coast helped these other two guys leave the country. I think they'd blown up a Dow Chemical plant. My friend heard that hijackings to Havana were happening all the time on flights from New York to Miami, but the hijackings were never reported. The airlines didn't want to show how goddamn easy it is. The government didn't want to show how many people are wanting to go to Cuba all the time. The papers are all in on it. My friend went to the library and sure enough, there were all these little wire service reports of successful hijackings on the very back pages of newspapers, and on the front page are the stories about the one or two hijackers who failed, usually because they're so dumb they don't even have a weapon. And not only that, but he learns the airlines tell pilots to do what the hijacker wants, because they're afraid of having passengers die. So everybody's trying to play down that you can basically go to Cuba, no problem, if you pull out a gun." The reminiscence had vastly improved Juan's humor. "I hadn't thought about that in a while."

"Did they make it?" Pauline asked.

"Who?"

"The guys. The Dow Chemical guys."

"Fuck, of course they made it. My friend drove them to the airport and then he went home and listened to Liberation News Service and sure enough, late that night he hears flight whatever's 'diverted' to Havana. Read off the wire. It sure wasn't in the *New York Times* the next day. I didn't believe him at first, but I redid his research and it's all true. Between ten and twenty hijackings a year to Havana, and you never hear one word about it."

"When was this?" Jenny asked.

"Four, five years ago. It's less now, but I bet you it hasn't changed that much. There's no foolproof way to stop people. What are they going to do, make everybody unpack their suitcase before they get on? Go through everybody's shaving bag? They can only hope less people think of it."

"You know a lot about it," she said.

"At the time I thought, if I ever had comrades who needed my help in that way, I ought to be ready to help them. I never thought I'd be one of them."

"We could never hijack an airplane," Pauline said, staring out at the rain.

"Why not, Princess? What's a better long-term plan?"

"I don't know," Pauline said. "Isn't it your job to figure that out?"

Before Jenny had even registered what had been said, Juan snatched the gun off the table and aimed at Pauline. "What's with your fucking mouth, Pauline?"

"Stop it," Jenny murmured. The hair on her neck had sprung up.

"It's not loaded. He just finished cleaning it," Pauline said, but they still didn't move.

"What are you doing?" Yvonne said, coming in.

"Hijacking a plane. You know. 'Nobody fucking move. This is a hijacking.'"

Yvonne seemed to think it was funny. "'Maybe you should have a cocktail, sir,'" she said. "'Bag of peanuts? Would you like a cigarette? Pinch my ass, Mr. Hijacker.' I'm the stewardess, get it?"

With his free hand Juan yanked the kitchen chairs out to face forward, like rows. "All right, Princess," he said. "You be the hero passenger. You look mild-mannered and square but it turns out you're some kind of Green Beret. Try to subdue me."

"No thanks," Pauline said.

"Okay, maybe you're the screaming bitch who's so scared she can't keep her mouth shut. 'Oh, no! What will we do?'" Juan pulled a long face.

Pauline kept silent, staring at the gun pointed at her.

"Maybe *you're* the hero passenger," Juan realized, turning the weapon on Jenny. Loaded or not, the gun pointed at her made her armpits turn damp. The temperature had dropped with the rain, and the wind that touched her felt like fall. Her skin goosepimpled all at once, as if obeying a command.

"Maybe I'm the pilot," she said. "Stop pointing your gun, sir. I'll take you to Havana."

"How do I know you won't try to overpower me, and turn me in to the pigs?"

"It's not worth it. We'd rather go along with you than risk anyone getting hurt."

Juan let his arm drop and threw the gun on the table with a loud clatter, and Jenny felt release flooding through her, as if tranquilizers had entered her blood. "Don't rule it out," Juan told Pauline. "Running and hiding forever just isn't my style."

FOR THE REST of the day the rain continued, though it ebbed to a drizzle. No one so much as mentioned doing combat training. Juan kept leaping through doorways quick-drawing the gun from its holster. Then it was dusk, and Pauline and Yvonne began dinner. The house had never seemed so small. Since the night Pauline had brought her the soup Jenny had sometimes felt the strange hyper-alertness that follows a moment of intimacy, as if their conversation had been left incomplete, the point felt but avoided. Pauline had rebuffed her question but then she'd brought up the clippings; that had seemed like an invitation, as if the subject weren't closed after all. When Juan had sneeringly pointed the gun at Pauline, and then her, though she'd known it was just a new form of his usual strutting, for an instant she thought she had felt the three fugitives' tightly knit union fall slack. For an instant Pauline was cast out completely, and even Yvonne had looked inconsequential, and each of them seemed solitary, the way Jenny felt that she constantly was. She'd wondered if the gun, the very thing that joined them as comrades-in-arms, was actually working on them in an opposite way. And again she had glanced at Pauline's face for some fleeting message. Pauline had been flushed, with anger or fear or embarrassment or all of those things. But if she'd felt brief alliance with Jenny, from both finding themselves at the weapon's wrong end, she had never let on.

The rain finally stopped while they were eating. They ate in silence, the four of them hunched at the table, Juan still wearing the holster and gun. She wanted to rip it off him. After dinner Juan announced they would work on their book. Juan and Yvonne and Pauline went into the front room with their unfinished beers and pulled the door shut behind them. She went upstairs and sat down with her journal, but she couldn't write in it; she uncapped her pen and just sat there, tensed over the page. The air in the house felt close, sickly. The moment of refreshment the rainstorm had brought was long gone. She heard the big maple dripping. And then she heard them; she felt unsurprised, though her stomach turned cold. They had been shut in the front room for barely half an hour. The shape of the dispute ascended and ascended, rising and falling in smaller waves up toward a peak; she couldn't make out the words. She recapped her pen, lay the pen in her journal, closed the covers around it, and walked to her door. The argumentative peak had snagged clouds and brewed thunder; she heard the lightning-bolt crash of a large piece of furniture thrown or, she realized, a body. Someone screamed. She yanked open her door in time to see Pauline rush past the foot of the stairs with the bright print of a hand on her face. "I don't care, I don't care!" Pauline screamed, running into the kitchen and out the back door. Yvonne hovered in the front room; Juan blocked Jenny's way at the foot of the stairs. "Stay out of this, Jenny," he said.

"Don't you touch me!" she yelled, shoving past him.

She couldn't make out Pauline in the dark, but she heard the barn doors creaking open with effort, and then the barn light, its bare lightbulb, came on. She found Pauline sitting on one of the moldering haystacks, loudly sobbing, her thin hands hanging between bony knees. When she saw Jenny she shot to her feet.

"Leave me alone," she said. "Leave me alone!"

"What happened? Why did he hit you?"

"I know it's a trap, I'm not talking to you. Like that time in ego reconstruction? 'Tell us what you *really* think of Juan's leadership. We *really* want your honest opinion.' And then I gave it, and everybody said that I was insubordinating. Well, fuck you! Fuck you! Fuck you!"

"No," she said. "That's not me. Pauline." She heard her blood sounding loud in her ears. Pauline looked feral and unrecognizing, as if her words were instinctive defenses, claws bared, haunches tensed at a threat. Jenny remembered a trip she and William had taken—they had driven miles and miles up Highway 1, past Mendocino, all the way to the place where the highway cut in from the coast, the one place in the state where it did this, because the coastal range there was impassable. The Lost Coast, only reached by a harrowing, steep, wet dirt road with a sign at the mouth that said CLOSED. ROAD IS OUT. GO NO FARTHER. They'd seen the ocean yawn open beneath them as they came through the pass and inched down, gravel showering under their tires. They'd seen a gray whale burst out of the surf like a missile, just yards off the beach. The last bend of a long mountain river, pulling a delta of mountainous rubble and downed giant trees and fine brown sand on its way out to sea. They had hiked up to shelves of wild meadow, hearing only the harsh cannonade of the ocean and the barking sea lions, seeing the dark shapes of the whales below on their epic migration; and when they'd returned to their camp, between themselves and their tent had been a small golden bobcat. Seated compact on its haunches, its tail curled around, its ears sharp and upright, its spectacular eyes trained on them. "It's so beautiful," William whispered, advancing. "No," she'd said, stopping him. "Don't be stupid."

"Pauline," she said, trembling. "Pauline."

"Why do I have to choose?" Pauline screamed at her. "Don't make me choose!"

"Hey, baby sister, hey, come on," Juan was saying, behind them.

"Leave her alone," Jenny said, but Juan strode in and took hold of Pauline and she scrabbled at him frantically, not to escape but to keep him.

Yvonne had come in as well. "Oh, Polly," she said.

"Don't make me choose," Pauline sobbed.

"Of course not. Choose what? What the fuck did you say to her, Jenny?"

"Nothing," Jenny said. She could not make her mouth utter anything else. She could only watch dumbly as the three of them, fused to each other, as if tied together to run a strange race, hobbled out of the barn.

"WHAT I REALLY ought to do is build a block first and then mount the gun to it," Juan said the next evening at dinner. "You and Y both learned to shoot on shotguns, and a handgun's a whole different creature." He explained to Pauline patiently, "You're small, but you can brace yourself against a shotgun so the kick doesn't throw you, remember? With this gun it's more like," and Juan mimed shooting the gun with his arm extended, and his hand flying back from the force. "It's going to be hard for you to have the accuracy you've achieved with the shotgun. You're going to get frustrated."

"I could hold it with both hands," Pauline said, reaching out toward the gun. Juan barred her from it and Jenny saw her face spark with annoyance.

"That's fine on the shooting range," Juan said, "but not on the fly."

At last, Juan relented; they could shoot without the block for a few rounds and see how it went. Jenny followed them into the barn and stood in the barn door, watching. Was it an act, Pauline's seeming eagerness to handle the gun? Was it apology, for whatever she had done to incur Juan's wrath the previous night? Before leaving the house Pauline had briefly disappeared into the bathroom while Juan dug in the trash for their empty soup cans. Now the cans filled the barn with a strong stench of old coffee grounds, sour wine and wet cigarette butts. "Joining us?" Juan said to

Jenny genially. "You must be a good shot. Oriental people always have exceptional aim. They're inherently good marksmen, they're good at precision sports like pool and golf, they're good archers—"

"I've never touched a gun in my life," she said coldly.

"Oh, I don't believe that," Juan said. One by one, Juan balanced the cans on the spine of a sawhorse. "Just say the word if you want to take a shot at it. Get it? Take a shot at it?" Yvonne, always his best audience, dissolved, giggling.

But when Yvonne got the gun she became serious, even grim. Her chin crinkled and her lower lip jutted out slightly, while the rest of her body seemed fused to itself and the floor. The mass of muscle above her kneecaps tensed and shifted. Yvonne punctured the back wall of the barn several times and then, with her very last shot, a can flew in the air with a *pang*. The rest of the cans tumbled onto the floor from the movement.

"Good!" Juan yelled. Yvonne grinned.

When Pauline's turn came she brought a wad of toilet paper out of her pocket and began twisting it into small balls. Juan went into paroxysms.

"What are you *doing*?" he said. "What's the Kleenex for?"

"Earplugs."

"Oh my God—wake me up, Yvonne. Earplugs."

"You know that my ears are fucked up! I still hear that ringing sometimes—"

"'The pigs are at the door!'" Juan enacted. "'Okay, I'll just put in my *earplugs*.'"

Pauline threw the balls of tissue angrily onto the floor and wrapped her small hands around the gun's grip. Her stance seemed overdone; her feet were planted very wide. Her narrow shoulders shrugged up toward her ears.

"Wait," said Juan seriously, stepping up behind her. "Get your shoulders down. You've got to compensate for the weak one. Push your arms good and firm in their sockets."

Pauline wasn't disastrous, but she was badly thrown by the recoil, and only sheer stubbornness seemed to keep her arms stiffly extended. From her first shot they trembled with effort. Unexpectedly she tried shooting one-handed and her shot flew to the ceiling; there would have been an eruption of terrified doves if the doves hadn't all fled already. "Whoa!" Juan said, hitting the floor. "Holy Jesus! Hand over that thing!"

Jenny finally left them and went back to the house; from her bed she could hear the *POP, POP* of the gun; in the end she must have fallen asleep to it. The next morning she found them all in the kitchen, writing little notes back and forth to Pauline on a notepad. "She's *deaf?*" Jenny said, looking at her in horror. Pauline looked back and frowned. She took the pen and wrote, *You have to write, Jenny*.

"Oh, my God," Jenny said.

"It'll pass," Juan said, shrugging. "She has sensitive ears. It happened before, and it passed." Pauline was watching him with impatience; he looked at her and she pointed sternly at the notepad. "Oh, I'm sorry, Princess," Juan laughed. He took the sheet and wrote, *Talking about what a sensitive Princess you are*. Pauline whacked him, but she was smiling; if she was frightened by her sudden deafness—and Jenny was sure she saw, at the back of the green-flecked eyes, fear—her fear was outweighed by her obvious pleasure in being pampered by her comrades. For the rest of that day Juan and Yvonne and Pauline passed little notes back and forth, giggling and hitting each other, or reading and tearing to shreds with a show of annoyance. Jenny could almost have thought they had deafened Pauline deliberately, so that they could play a conspicuous game of shared secrets that, whether by design or not, did not include her. By dinner that night Pauline's hearing had begun to return, and then this was a new game: Juan and Yvonne would say things to each other in Pauline's presence but in normal tones, and Pauline would yell, "What?" Or, alternatively, every minor announcement was bellowed: "I WANT MACARONI FOR DINNER!"

She wondered if Pauline, in those in-between days when she had no longer been simply a captive, but was not yet a comrade, had felt the way she was starting to feel: neither satisfactorily with the group nor completely outside it. They had all laughingly offered her the notepad and pencil while Pauline was deaf, they'd done nothing outright to exclude her—but she'd had nothing she wanted to say to all three of them, and that was the heart of the game, that the three were as one. The next day Pauline was back to normal and they decided to work on their book. Now Jenny eavesdropped on purpose, but she learned nothing about why they'd fought. She did learn at least one of the reasons the project was taking so long. They couldn't seem to make the first statement without delineating the premises on which it was founded; and every premise required its own proof beyond all possible doubt. "U.S. imperial incursions into peaceful Vietnam," Yvonne began. "Wait a minute," Juan said. "We can't forget that the French were in Vietnam first." "So we can't say it was peaceful?" "It's not that, it's the way the world's powers *collude* with each other to exploit the brown peoples. The way we *colluded* with France." "We colluded with France?" Pauline said. And it went on like that, endlessly. The foundation of their worldview sank swiftly into the past: condemnation of the war required dissection of the Kennedy administration's foreign policy, which demanded criticism of the imperially minded rearrangement of national borders in the wake of the Second World War, which led to a long meditation on the rise of the nation-state. Gone were the days when they'd been happy to make incendiary, irresponsible statements with no basis in fact; and the further they beat back the brush of the past the less effort they gave to the present.

That afternoon they were still working when she heard a car laboring up the hill. Jenny went down to the kitchen, and the three of them emerged from the front room. Juan said, "What the fuck is Frazer doing back here already? He said he'd give us another two weeks." She looked out the window and saw, instead of Frazer's battered brown coupe, a blue four-door come around the last turn of the drive.

"It's not Frazer," she heard herself say, "unless he bought a new car." But she knew, although she could only see the barest hint of the person inside the sedan, that it was someone unknown.

"Upstairs," Juan said to Pauline.

A solid, blond, red-faced white man, perhaps in his mid-forties, was coming toward the back door. He had an off-duty look to him. Pauline's last pounding step had sounded at the top of the stairs and now Jenny and Juan and Yvonne were all locked there like statues. The man seemed to know the house; a stranger would have tried the front door, not knowing it barely got used. He passed from view through the window and reappeared right away in the door. "Afternoon," he said cheerfully. "Sorry to barge in on you folks." They didn't manage to utter a word of response. The man opened the screen tentatively. "I'm Bob, the owner. Where's—Dierdre? I'm lousy with names. For a second I thought you were her," he added, to Yvonne.

None of them knew if Yvonne should be Dierdre or not. "Bob," Juan repeated. Jenny felt her skin crawl. She knew it was only her paranoia that made this man look like a cop, but what must they look like to him? Juan had a dully fixed look to his face, like a reptile eyeing a fly. The man said, "Are you Dierdre's husband?" and shook Juan's stiff hand, and then Jenny understood suddenly, and Yvonne must have, also.

"I'm Dierdre's sister," Yvonne announced boldly. "And this is my husband, George. And this is our friend Judy."

"You all having a good holiday? Wife and I both grew up in these parts. We wish we could get back here more. I thought Dierdre was meaning to be with her kids here all summer."

"She did, but she just took them down to our mother's for a couple of days," Yvonne said. "Our mother lives in Pennsylvania," she added, warming to the exercise. "In Philadelphia."

Jenny felt a bead of sweat leave her armpit and draw a wet path down her side. The man had shaken her hand very briefly and turned his gaze back to Yvonne. Juan was still staring hard at the man but the man only glanced toward Juan courteously. "Excuse me," Jenny murmured, and slipped from the kitchen. The front room was a riot of ashtrays and unwashed wine glasses and empty potato-chip bags and heaps of newspaper and inexplicable detritus like Juan's flower-pot barbell; they had been living here with no thought for whomever the house was owned by, as if the house would vanish into the ground the instant they moved out. Now she saw the accumulated damage of months, the blackish-purple splash of spilled wine on the couch, the ashes and dirt that had darkened the carpet, the beer bottles kicked in the corners, and this was not even the barn, with the block-mounted gun and the silhouette shot full of holes, or the pasture, where the grass was stamped flat in an oval-shaped course. Juan had taped a list to the wall hugely titled CODE OF WAR and she ripped this down and was crumpling it into a ball when the others came out of the kitchen. Bob stopped in the doorway and she saw him take in the room very quickly before turning away. "Because the number Dierdre gave me doesn't work," he was saying. "I might have took it down wrong. You don't have it?"

"No," Yvonne said. "She just moved."

"It's nothing important. I just like to have a number for my tenants." Bob cleared his throat. When he'd turned away from the front room Juan and Yvonne had been just on his heels, and now the three of them were crowded in the little vestibule between front room and kitchen, at the foot of the stairs. Jenny hovered behind them. Bob's back was encased in a thin brown windbreaker and she wanted to plant both her hands on this jacket and catapult him from the house. Juan was still staring at Bob as if he were a steak to be carved up and eaten and she understood, suddenly, the great impulse that he was restraining; Juan could murder this man. He could actually kill him. "Do you want us to give Dierdre a message?" Yvonne asked, steering Bob toward the kitchen. But Bob resisted; he looked up the stairs.

"Anything I should know?" he asked. "Roof leaking? Plumbing all right?"

"Fine," Yvonne said, rather sharply.

He finally followed her back to the kitchen. "I hate to intrude on a person's vacation. Just tell her to make sure, when she mails me the key, to include an address. I'll need it to refund her deposit. I somehow never got it from her."

"She's been so absentminded. She moved . . ."

At last he was standing outside, with the three of them crowding the door like a barricade. Jenny tried to remember that most people trust. He would take what he'd seen as the basis for standard regret, might not refund all the deposit. It's people like us, she thought, who mistrust everyone. She had spent years of her life trying to instill mistrust in the average person. Your leaders are misleading you, she might say, and misspending your taxes, and killing your children—not just strange foreign children, but *yours*. Very few people listened. Now she relied on that stubborn, instinctual trust. Yet this man lingered on the grass. "That your car?" he asked, indicating the Bug.

"Yes," Yvonne said.

"You might need a new muffler." He bent to look, hands on his knees. "Say," he said, straightening again. "Say, would it bother you all if I took a short walk through the fields? It's been a long time since I've been here. I come by to check on the plumbing and errands like that, but I never just amble around." He must have seen something in all their faces; he blanched suddenly. "On the other hand, I don't have time," he amended. "You all didn't rent out this place to get bothered by me."

"It's all right," Yvonne said. Jenny saw Juan take a pinch of her flesh and squeeze, hard. Yvonne slapped him away. "Go ahead. It's your home, after all."

"No—no. That's okay. The wife's waiting in town, anyway." He zipped his jacket and nervously took out his keys. Suspicion or some even more dreadful feeling seemed to tug at his sleeve, but he pulled himself free. "You kids have a nice summer," he said, getting into his car.

PAULINE rushed downstairs covered with dust. "I was under your bed," she told Jenny. "He's gone, right? He's gone?"

"For the moment," Juan said.

Juan seemed strangely clarified and calmed; in the face of an actual crisis his disproportionate swagger, his hair-trigger temper, his preening self-importance were gone. Under Juan's direction they tied blankets and clothing and food into four equal bundles, and buried them in the woods in a pile of rocks they'd once used during combat training. "I never thought I would say this," Juan said, "but if pigs come here, run. Run like fucking antelope, to this spot, grab provisions, then melt away into the woods." Two BB rifles, and one handgun; that was no arsenal, thanks to Frazer, and it left them no choice but to run. "We'll survive," Juan told them as they retraced their steps, and in spite of the fear that she obviously felt, Jenny thought that Pauline almost floated with joy. Juan had finally said it was all right to try to survive.

Back in the house the three of them quickly sorted their actual writings from the litter of writing equipment, and now it seemed fortunate that these comprised just a few messy sheets and a half-blank cassette. The writings were compressed into a pocket-size package, and wrapped and rewrapped in a plastic trash bag. They returned to the woods and Juan buried the package as well.

Then they all agreed that Jenny should drive into town and call Frazer immediately. "Ol' Bob-O," Juan said. "He might not have suspected a thing. Nine out of ten that he didn't: We're fine. One out of ten and we're dead. I'm coming with you," he told Jenny. "Let's go to the big town, with stores. And don't argue with me."

THEY LEFT Pauline and Yvonne, terrified, with the one gun and the last of the wine. "I know you've been mad," Juan remarked casually as they drove off, as if they went driving all of the time. Being in a car, undisguised, in broad daylight, for the first time since becoming a nationally sought fugitive, now didn't seem to perturb him at all. "I know you're mad about stuff with Pauline, and I'm glad we've got some time alone to talk. I've been wanting to talk with you. Damn," he added, looking out the window. "This is beautiful land, you know that? You can look at land like this and almost forget what a sick, fucked-up country this is. Anyway, understand: for Yvonne and for me, Pauline's truly our sister. Know it, all right? She's our family. And we fight. And all families fight. And I know that you know how that is."

"I do," she said, mostly to make him shut up.

The drive to Monticello hadn't changed, but now every shifting inch jarred her, the way shifting light jars someone with a migraine. Juan kept talking, his face pointing into the wind, the late afternoon sun flashing morse code off his glasses, his words, an endless stream of them, snatched by the wind. Something about his mother . . . his mother would have loved all these hills. His mother had spent all her life on the flat fields of Illinois, so that any kind of wrinkle in the land used to get her excited. There was this one field they used to drive past when he was a kid where, who knew how, a huge tree had grown up in this dent in the field, so that even if the farmer had gone to the trouble of pulling the tree out, the dent still would have been there. Tripping up plows, etc. So the tree had been permitted to stay, and it made an oasis in the unchanging field, this deep bowl of greenery. This thrilled his mother. "Oh, there's my tree!" she would say. Did Jenny know that of all of their twenty-four parents, his mother had been the only one to have said she was proud of them? A reporter from the *Chicago Tribune* tracked her down, and she said she didn't really understand their methods, but she understood their beliefs, and she was proud of them. "That's what she said. She grew up poor. Yeah, my mother was poor," Juan said, suddenly abstracted.

She called Frazer from a telephone booth at the end of Monticello's Main Street. "I'll call back," he said. "At the usual place?"

Craning around to look back at the car, she realized she couldn't see Juan. Sunlight blazed at her off the windshield; was Juan waiting quietly there, sheltered by the reflection? She felt sure that he wasn't. "There's no time," she told Frazer. "I'm just calling to say visit early. Like maybe tonight. Okay? Bye."

"Wait, wait, wait. I'll buy milk. It'll take me five minutes."

"I can't wait, just come up! We'll talk then."

"What the hell—has somebody got sick?" Now a note of alarm shook his voice. He'd never felt this, she realized: nearing danger, its sights fixed on *him*. Frazer's desire to play savior was real, but it was fueled by his flawless good luck. He'd always been so uncommonly lucky, he'd never had to be selfishly prudent. He'd never had to choose between self-sacrificing battle and ignominious but self-preserving retreat. He was ardently loyal but she'd always been nagged by the fear he was also untrustworthy; he never expected a problem, and so perhaps wasn't built to withstand one. Perhaps, when the problem arrived, he would run for his life. It wouldn't make him any worse than she was; his tone of alarm made her fear for herself, and so she said the one thing that she knew would snare him, and not scare him away. "They haven't written a word."

"Motherfucker! Okay. I'll try to be there tonight."

Leaving the phone booth she saw Juan coming back toward the car. He had a pleased smile on his face, as if Main Street offered a rich tapestry to consider. At least it was near five o'clock; the few stores here that weren't out of business would soon be closed for the night. The sidewalks were deserted. There was the store that sold fishing supplies, the Singer store for sewing materials, the Maytag repair outlet, the five-and-dime with a wilting Fourth of July display still in its window. They had entirely missed the Fourth of July, she realized—how many weeks ago had it been? Seven? Eight? "I don't even want to know what you were doing," she told Juan. "I called Frazer. Let's get out of here."

"We just got here! Come *on*. Ten minutes. And give me some of our money."

"What for?"

"Things. Didn't I say not to argue with me?"

"Ten minutes," she said finally.

"And the money, Jenny." She gave him a twenty and he said, wheedlingly, "Could I have some more, Jenny? *Please?*" Whistling, with Frazer's money in his hands, Juan strode off down the sidewalk.

She checked the parking rules sign at the curb and then turned off the engine and pulled the keys from the ignition, absently crushing them in her hands. After a while a sweaty metallic smell told her what she was doing and she dropped the keys onto her lap. *Little hands!* William had often said that. *Little hands but big deeds*. She had been very good at wiring explosives. Deft, and unafraid. She'd learned from him quickly and hadn't needed him to check on her work. Somehow she had not had a splinter of doubt when she put them together. She remembered, coming home from Japan, the way her long absence from English had stripped every English cliché of its comforting chime. Suddenly there were the tepid and fraudulent words: Do unto others, and, If at first you don't succeed, and, Might does not make right. It had struck her, coming home to a country in which she felt foreign, that they were lessons taught in the same way that vaccines were punched into your arm on that bad day in grade school, lined up in the gym in your ankle socks with the sleeve of your Peter Pan blouse harshly shoved to your armpit. Lessons punched in when you're young so that when you grow up, you won't really believe them. Might does not make right: a stunning truth, robbed of its force by a numbing cliché. The mind might believe, but the body has trouble. Power has the power to seem natural, and to live in your gut like an ulcer: your secret certainty of your defeat, finally, at its hands. And yet Power was only people, war makers, money-possessors, with elaborate tools to use. This had been the belief that impelled her, when she learned to build bombs. Feeling as she thought the Christian Reformers might have felt when they seized the Good Book for themselves. Except bombs weren't inherently good but inherently evil; she and William had set out with their bombs to expose the real evil of government violence, not to recommend violence to everyone else. Then the ground started tilting beneath them, or perhaps it was they who had tilted the ground; perhaps they had been wrong to fight Power on its terms, instead of rejecting its terms utterly. *Little hands*. Something about this memory made her cringe now. Juan emerged from the five-and-dime with a bulging sack under his arm, and entered a store called Margot's Modern Fashions. She lit a cigarette and smoked it furiously until her head wobbled from the smoke and the heat. She'd smoked two more before Juan came out again. "What size are you?" he asked, coming up to her window. "Dress size, not jeans size."

"I don't know."

"You must know. It's a number. For example, Yvonne is a ten. You're smaller than that."

"Four or six, maybe. Why?"

"Four's what I think. You and Pauline are about the same size."

In a much shorter time he'd returned from the store again, now with two bags. She started the engine and was squealing away from the curb before he'd fully shut his door.

"Hold on! Take this turn," Juan said.

"Why?"

"I want to look around! Come *on,* Jenny."

Off Main Street were cracking sidewalks, uplifted by the roots of old trees, and Monticello's surprisingly pretty old houses, dignified and decrepit, set at the backs of deep lawns. The street was quiet, except for the voices of children coming from the backyards. She slowed down and they took in one block, then another. Farther from Main Street the houses were smaller and in worse repair, but the yards were more lush. "What did you buy?" she asked him.

"You'll see when we're back at the ranch."

"You didn't spend all the money, did you?"

"Don't worry about Frazer's money. We won't need his money much longer."

"What does that mean?"

"It means that it's time for a change. It means we forgot who we were, but we're starting to remember again. It means we won't be no exotic zoo show anymore."

"I don't know what you're talking about," she said irritably. They had entered a part of town where the unrestrained plant life had defeated the buildings completely. Small shotgun cottages hid in the trees, and the drone of insects was almost as loud as the drone of the Bug. The scene was pleasantly swamplike, as if they were puttering along in a boat. Then she saw, loping through the pattern of sunlight and shade, a familiar figure with a great crown of hair.

"Oh God," she said.

"What?"

"That kid. I met him once." She covered the side of her face with her hand.

"You know him?"

"I don't know him." She was trying to subtly speed up, but the car's solitary presence on the street had caught Thomas's attention already. "Hey," he said, coming toward them. "Not-from-Nam. Alice."

She slowed down, then stopped. "Hi," she said. She felt her heart in her throat. She wished she could signal to him to move on from them. She saw the comb in his pocket, but he didn't reach for it. He looked older somehow, and then she realized that his face had very slightly hardened against her, developed a shell of defense it had not had before. She'd never come back to see him.

"How you doin'?" he said, with emphasized casualness.

"Okay," she began. "My job . . . "

"Hey, that's all right. This must be your boyfriend. Good thing I didn't make my move, right? Hey, man." With his hairdo-maintaining grace Thomas leaned into the car across Jenny, extending his hand. "How you doin'?"

"I'm good," said Juan, taking the hand. She braced herself for the brusque dismissal, but instead Juan said, "What's your name, brother? I'm George. Sounds like you know her."

"I know Alice. I'm Thomas," he said.

"What you doin'?" said Juan.

"Just walking."

"Get in."

"George," she said.

"Get in," Juan repeated. "Ride with us."

Once they were moving again she began to wonder if Juan longed to be recognized. She barely saw where they went, while Juan twisted around toward the backseat congenially. He was saying things like, "You think all white folks look the same? Bet you've seen me before. Or a million dudes like me." Thomas laughed. "Where you live, man?" Juan asked him.

"Just there," Thomas said. "Where you got me."

"What you got planned for later?"

"It's my day off," Thomas said. "Ain't nothing to do in this town. Almost rather be working."

"Not for the Man. You should work for the People. Your People."

"My people ain't owning a grocery store," Thomas joked.

"Naw, that ain't what I mean," Juan insisted.

She'd circled back to the block where they'd started. "Where's your house, Thomas?" she asked, and her voice seemed too high. Juan interrupted.

"I'll tell you a secret," Juan said. "My name ain't George. And Alice here ain't my old lady. So you still got a chance." He and Thomas both laughed. "But she's my sister-in-arms," Juan went on. "She's been helping me out."

"I had a feeling she was helping out someone," said Thomas. His fresh spark, his openness, had returned. "She was doing some extensive grocery shopping."

"That's right. You want to help me out too, for a minute?"

"George!" she said.

"Sure," said Thomas. "Of course I'll help you."

"Are you out of your fucking mind?" she said. "Let him go!"

"It's cool, Alice," Thomas said, very kindly, and the simplicity of the gesture, of his using what he thought was her real, perfect name, almost made her start crying.

"Let him go," she told Juan.

"In a minute," Juan said.

They drove back to Main Street, and took in its full length again. Thomas wanted a Coke, and they stopped in front of a dingy luncheonette and waited while he went in. Nearby were the stone slabs and grim pillars of a bank, faceless as a tomb, and though built to be imposing, somehow almost unnoticeable. It was past five now; the bank had been closed for more than two hours. When Thomas came back Juan said, "Is that the only bank in town?"

"Think so," Thomas said, unwrapping his straw.

"Black people bank there, or just white people?"

"I really couldn't say." Thomas took a slurp of his Coke and then raised his eyebrows. "Uh-oh. This sounds serious."

"I'm just wondering. There's no other bank around here? Maybe out where your grocery store is?"

"Mr. Morton makes his deposit up here. I don't know why he would if we had one down there."

"Mr. Morton's the boss?"

"He's the Man," Thomas teased. "Naw, he's a nice man."

"It would be better to work for a black man."

"It would be *better* to not work at all."

The conversation was in its final stretch, and as their banter continued she drove determinedly back to Thomas's street and heard no objections. But when they reached Thomas's house Juan got out. "I'll walk him up," he said.

"I hope I'll be seeing you, Alice," said Thomas. "Don't forget how you said we would hang out again."

They loped away over the grass, Juan unconsciously mimicking Thomas's gait. Juan had only been making dumb, eager small talk, asking Thomas his age, if he still went to school, if he had any brothers or sisters, but her stomach was still clenched with dread. She could see them, although indistinctly, on the shadowed and shrub-obscured porch.

It was many more minutes before Juan came jogging back over the grass. He was flushed and excited. "Man!" he said. "That's a smart fucking kid."

She shoved the Bug into gear. "Don't act so amazed that a black kid is smart."

"Oh, bullshit. I'm amazed if a *white* kid is smart."

She was finally free to drive back to the farm. The sun was just setting when they reached the base of the hill the house sat on, and started to climb. The gold sunset light stretched the car's shadow over the grass, so that from a distance an observer might have seen on the bright face of the hillside a long black mark, moving slowly upward. Juan had been rambling and musing the whole way: "There's a reason we're different from trees," he observed. "Trees stay stuck in one place their whole lives, but a man's got to move or his brain starts to rot." When they got to the top Yvonne and Pauline came running out the back door with relief at the sight of them. "Sometimes, when you're not sure which way you should go, you just float with the current," Juan said. "Then you see. Then you see."

JUAN'S equanimity was still intact the next day, though his comrades could not seem to share it. Yvonne and Pauline were up and down from the kitchen table all morning, lighting second cigarettes while their firsts were still burning, peering through the curtains, slamming out the back door to gaze down the long hill from behind the fat trunk of the maple. Nine A.M. gave way to ten, then eleven, then noon. Jenny stayed in her chair with an effort, pretending to read. Juan sat across from her, feet up, contentedly paging through *Blood in My Eye*. "You did say it was urgent?" he asked, his voice not sounding urgent at all.

She studied him for a beat before answering. "I said you still hadn't written a word of the book."

To her surprise Juan guffawed. "Right on, Sister! That'll get him up here on the double."

It was past one when they heard a car's engine and saw Frazer's familiar brown coupe struggling up the long hill. The coupe parked and Frazer seemed to hesitate a long moment, twisted around toward his backseat, before he swung out and came toward them. Jenny realized Juan was wearing the gun, in its holster. "What are you doing?" she said, but then Frazer had reached them. He greeted Juan with a strained smile, ignoring the gun. "So that old devil writer's block's bothering you," Frazer said. "It's not easy for me to write, either—"

"Really? And you don't even have pigs named Bob dropping in."

This caught Frazer up short. "Pigs named Bob?"

"Pigs named Bob," Juan repeated. "That puts a damper on writing for sure. It's called a security breach. A bad one. The kind of breach you assured us we'd *never* have while we were here."

"Bob's the landlord," Frazer realized. "For fuck's sake, you knew there was a landlord. I told you that ages ago. He didn't see Pauline, did he? You acted natural, right?"

"Don't act like it's our fault! I don't remember anything about Bob the Landlord dropping in on us while we were here. You need to move us right now. To a better location."

"Move you? I don't have the money to move you. I paid for this place in advance, and it didn't come cheap. You have to finish that book—oh, Jesus. Hang on for a second—hang on—" Frazer went back to his car. Until now Juan had seemed to be toying with Frazer, as if he enjoyed Frazer's trying to make light of Bob's visit. Soon would come Frazer's acknowledgment that he'd been wrong after all, and after this would begin his exhaustive attempts to appease them. The balance of power would be all the while shifting toward Juan . . . Frazer had opened his rear passenger door, and suddenly they were seeing him help someone upright and out of the car. "You okay, Alan?" said Frazer. The person named Alan was a spindly young man: big Adam's apple, long legs and long arms, timid-looking, in running shorts and a T-shirt and jacket. He was blindfolded. Somehow that fact seemed no stranger, no more astonishing or terrifying, than anything else about him. Frazer eased off the blindfold, and Alan blinked and rubbed at his temples. Then he saw them; his eyes widened slightly when he caught sight of Pauline.

"Wow," he said. "You weren't kidding."

Pauline reddened; suddenly she turned and ran into the house. They heard her footfalls on the stairs, Jenny's upstairs bedroom door slamming shut, as if by hiding herself Pauline could erase the moment the young man had recognized her, or perhaps erase the young man himself. "Oh my God," Jenny realized. "Jesus, Rob, I didn't tell you to do this! I just told you to come right away, I didn't say to do *this*."

"Who the fuck is this guy?" Juan screamed at them.

Frazer still had Alan by the arm, as if to keep him from running away. "This is Alan," Frazer said, putting too much emphasis on the name, as if speaking to children. It was clear this introduction wasn't going the way he'd intended. "Alan's a very close friend. He's your ghostwriter, Juan." In response to Juan's stunned, pop-eyed silence Frazer added—gently, firmly, finding his footing again—"Isn't that great? Alan was one of my boys when I coached at that college I got fired from. He's a brilliant writer—he's been my assistant on the last two sports-activist books that I wrote. And he's a runner. Just like you, Juan. He's a miracle worker. He's discreet, he's smart, I'm paying him out of my pocket. We need to get this thing going. That editor I told you about is getting very impatient."

Alan had withstood his introduction like a person about to be tossed in a pit. He was cringing away from them stiffly, his eyes on the ground. "Rob, you should have told me you were thinking of this," Jenny said to Frazer. "You said you'd never bring outsiders here."

"Told you when? You hung up on me, Jenny, remember?"

Juan had found his voice again. "We asked you here to discuss our security, and you've brought us a *ghostwriter*?"

"Juan, before you asked me here, as you say, I asked you here, for the purpose of writing a book. We'll also discuss your security worries—" Juan unholstered the gun suddenly and aimed it at Frazer, undoing the safety. "Jesus!" said Frazer. "Don't do that. That's no fucking joke."

"I agree. It's no joke, it's a serious, valuable item. We owned a number of these items not so long ago. A handgun. A number of rifles. Some customized by us, which takes effort."

"That's a separate issue. If I don't have the rest of your weapons today, it might have something to do with the fact that I was ordered to come up here early."

"Don't interrupt me, man. I've got the loaded gun! You should just shut the fuck up and let me continue." Juan waited a moment for compliance; Frazer stared at him, silent. "Think back to a few months ago. You offered us safety, in exchange for a cut of our story. You made us put down our guns to travel, but that was just temporary, that was just so we'd *be more secure*."

"The only thing I care about is your security, Juan."

"Then why won't you arm us? Why the fuck are you stalling? Armed revolutionaries, that's what we *are*. That's the point of your stupid-ass book."

"*My* stupid-ass book?"

"Yeah, your stupid-ass book! It's just your way of grabbing our action. Books are for phonies like you who use words when they ought to *do something*."

"I'll just wait in the car," Alan said.

"Don't you move," Juan said. The gun was pointed again, now at Alan. Alan froze in his tracks.

She saw Frazer blanch. She could almost see his calculations: sedate, or confront? *Sedate*, she was thinking, *sedate* . . . "That's it," Frazer said. "When you can stop acting like a prick you just give me a call. Come on, Alan. What are you going to do, shoot him?"

"Shut up, Rob!" she yelled furiously, but Juan had already pounced; he grabbed Alan around the neck and stuffed the nose of the gun into the soft space just under his chin.

"Ah, agh," Alan gurgled in terror.

Now Frazer was visibly frightened; and it served him right, strutting in and out of the house, on and off the hillside, never knowing what it was to live here, waiting for his payday; she thought of something else. She walked quickly to Frazer's car and Juan said, without moving at all, "What're you doing, Jen?"

"Just checking something."

"All right."

"Juan . . ." Frazer said.

But Juan was saying to Alan, "Do you know what'll happen if you ever tell pigs where we are? That you saw us at all?"

"I won't tell," Alan gasped.

"I will find you, and kill you," Juan said. "I don't have reservations about rich boys like you."

"He's not rich!" Frazer said. "Alan made it through school on a track scholarship!" Jenny leaned in the passenger window of Frazer's brown coupe and flipped open the glove compartment. Her letter to William was still there. She pulled it out and stared at it. "For fuck's sake," Frazer said, the weight of the last straw dropped on him. "It slipped my goddamn mind, all right? Why'd you make me shove the thing in the glove compartment?"

Juan flung Alan away from him and Alan went tumbling at Frazer's car so that Jenny had to leap from his path. Alan dove into the car and flattened himself on the backseat, as he must have been flattened when Frazer had driven the car up the hill. Juan was no longer paying any attention to him; now he had the gun trained on Frazer again. "Give us money," Juan said.

"Money? How much more do you want?"

Yvonne searched Frazer's pockets and pulled out his wallet. "Ten dollars," she told Juan.

"You asshole," Juan said. "Come back with our guns and our new place to live and our money, and you'll get your dumb book."

"You're making a mistake," Frazer said as he rushed to the car. From the relative safety of the driver's seat he called out, "Jenny, give me the letter."

The envelope was warm, dry, her careful printing of the prison address somehow pitiful to her; she couldn't bear to hand it back to him now. *My darling*, it bluffed, it bullshitted, *you haven't had an answer from me in so long, but there's not any reason. I love you, so much.* She felt her eyes flooding with tears. "No," she said, but he might not have heard her. The gun went off: *POP!* Juan had fired a shot into the air. Frazer stomped on the gas, sending chunks of turf flying.

"And put his blindfold back on!" Juan yelled after them.

• • •

JENNY DIDN'T know how long she lay upstairs in bed, curled tightly around herself under the sheets, oblivious to the heat. The unopened envelope lay on the nightstand. From downstairs she heard their voices rising and falling, water running and being turned off. She squeezed her eyes shut and prayed to fall asleep, but her body seemed to wind itself more and more tensely away from repose; she couldn't even feel that her head lay heavily on the pillow. It seemed to ride just a hair's width above, and her neck ached from bearing the weight. Bands encircled her ribs: fear, she knew. Although she had never told William where she was, what she was doing, the unsent letter made her feel a new danger, as if she had set off on foot into mountains without telling a soul, and now knew she was lost. No one would realize they had to come looking for her.

She heard a car start. She had also heard footsteps, the back door, voices loudly debating together, but all of that she had ignored. She got to the window in time to see the Bug driving away.

Downstairs she found Pauline watching out the front window, clutching the transistor to her chest. It was hissing with static. "I'm too recognizable," Pauline said. "They wouldn't let me go with them." She wiggled the transistor's antennae, touched the dial, then hugged it tightly to her chest again, no more tuned in than before.

"Where are they going?"

"Into town. To survey the terrain."

"Why? What for?"

Pauline shook her head; she knew, but was not going to say. "He'll tell you," she said.

Juan had hidden his purchases when they got back from Monticello, but now she saw what they were; in the bathroom and in their bedroom, boxes of L'Oréal hair dye, combs and brushes and scissors, eyeliners and lipsticks and powder, lengths of Ace bandage, reading glasses for both men and women, pillow forms that must have been from the sewing-supplies store, had emerged from their place of concealment and been strewn everywhere on the floor. There were two dresses lying empty and twisted across the rumpled double bed. Both were conservative, even prissy, with cap sleeves and darts. One was pink and one yellow. Both were size four. Pauline watched as Jenny riffled the bedroom, but said nothing to stop her. The bedroom was ripe with the smell of sweat, and dust. And sex. Dirty clothes, overflowing ashtrays, empty bottles, plates crusted with food, cups lined with a skin of dried wine, were so thick on the floor she had to push things aside with her feet to take steps. She left the bedroom and went into the bathroom; in the bathroom was a blizzard of hair. When she returned to the front room Pauline said, blurting it out, "They'll be all right, won't they?"

"I don't know," she said after a moment. "I don't know what they're doing."

"Don't be angry, Jenny. Juan's in command. He has to tell you himself what he's doing. Don't leave!" Pauline cried.

"But you won't tell me what's going on!"

"You can still stay. Don't leave me alone. Find some music." Pauline thrust the radio at her. "Do the crossword with me. I found an empty one. I've been saving it."

Juan and Yvonne were gone for almost two hours. When she and Pauline heard the Bug on the hill again they both leaped up; Jenny rushed out the back door and stopped short in her tracks. Yvonne was made up and coiffed, legs shaved, in a powder blue dress, but it was Juan's transformation that stunned her. Juan's guerrilla beard was gone, exposing round cheeks and a cleft in his chin. And his hair was cut off—it fell neatly above his ears, and the ears, exposed, stood out alertly. His shirt was tucked in, trousers belted. He looked like a midwestern college kid studying crop yield. She might not have recognized him had they passed in the street.

"Not bad, huh?" Juan said, walking past her. "We clean up pretty well."

Yvonne was stepping out of a pair of sandals. "Those are awful," she said, walking barefoot the rest of the way to the door.

"Where have you been?"

"Town," Juan said shortly. "Hey, Princess. Don't look so freaked out." Pauline threw her arms around him; Yvonne came and smiled gaily and Pauline rushed to hug her as well.

"Give me the keys," Jenny said to Juan quietly.

"Later," Juan said. When he saw her face he said, "Come *on*. We just went for a nice country drive."

Behind her, Yvonne was still hugging Pauline. "I wish you could have seen the sights with us, Sister. I brought you a treat." It was a copy of *Newsweek*, with Pauline on the cover. Beneath her face the word WANTED had been crossed out and replaced with MISSING. "Isn't that wild?" Yvonne squealed, as Pauline held it and stared.

THAT NIGHT after dinner Juan called a council. "The reward offered for us is more than he'd get for a book, I would bet you," Juan said. "And he wouldn't have to split it up. He could keep the whole thing."

"He wouldn't do that," Jenny said, at the same time as Yvonne said, "He'd get busted for harboring," though this hadn't been what Jenny meant.

"Bullshit," Juan said. "Harboring's hard to prove, and he's smart. He'd make a nice deal for himself. It ought to be tempting for him." All through dinner the little radio had been tuned to the A.M. news station to the extent it could be tuned to anything, and in the silence after Juan finished speaking its whining and hissing seemed to scrape on the bones of Jenny's skull. "Anyway, let's start this fucking council," Juan said. Jenny rubbed her thumbs over her eyebrows and snapped off the radio irritably. Looking up she felt everyone's gaze on her.

"Sorry," she said. "It was bugging me."

After a moment Juan said, "You see, we're starting our council."

"I heard you."

"You need to leave," Juan clarified.

Between hearing his words and understanding them she experienced a very slight delay. "Right," she said, standing up stupidly.

She slept badly that night. The next morning she was still tangled up in her sheets, trying to block out the light, when Pauline came and lightly knocked on her door. Pauline looked oddly happy. "Come down," she said, smiling.

Downstairs Juan looked as if he hadn't slept either. His eyes were bright with manic calculation. He was unfolding a wad of notepaper. "Jenny," he said. "There's coffee. You want coffee? So, you know, we had to hold council, we had to vote, but it turned out good for you, we all voted for you. I know you hated us making you leave." Gripping both ends of the notepaper he scrubbed the sheets against the door frame to flatten them.

"I didn't hate it," she said. "I just want the car keys."

"But in our situation, it's not that we would ever have secrets from you so much as we feel responsible *to* you," Juan went on, ignoring her interruption. "We couldn't lay our plans on you until they were formed, and I had it all firm in my mind how and why things would go. Now I do, and I can answer your questions and deal with your objections, because I know that you'll have them. Day after tomorrow is Sunday, and we're going to hit that kid Thomas's store. Not with him, don't bugeye like that. He doesn't have any idea, it won't touch him at all. His boss makes the deposit into the drop safe at the bank on Main Street. He does it alone, and he's a very small guy—Y and I checked him out yesterday. We'll approach, boss'll hand it right over, and then we'll be able to get out of here."

It took her a moment to find her voice. "No!" she said.

"Just listen before you say no."

"No! This is your wonderful plan? Are you out of your mind?"

"I know it's not the kind of thing you like to do," Juan went on, seeming unsurprised by her objections. "You like to blow things up that belong to someone who can always replace them, like the federal government. You like to do things that make you feel morally superior but don't make any difference, except getting your lover's ass thrown in prison."

"Don't be an asshole."

"I'm just saying, Jenny, that you have to leave the moral high ground sometimes. Our high purpose now is survival. We don't have the good options. And we don't have your stash of cash, either."

She felt herself color; at the edge of her vision she saw Pauline's eyes widen slightly. She wondered if Pauline was surprised at the invasion of her privacy, or if she'd been part of it too, and was merely surprised Juan had told.

"Your two hundred thirty-two dollars and, uh, what." Juan consulted his sheets of paper. "Some small change. Don't be mad at us, Jenny. We went through your shit. It was ages ago. We just needed to know who you were."

"Fuck you, Juan!"

"Jenny." Juan stretched and looked at her perplexedly. "We made this plan with room in it for you. We want to make it up to you, that you'll never get your cut from the book. I know that's why you're here. I don't hold it against you—you've got to survive just like we do. The three of us agreed last night to give you a full fourth of the take, though we're doing all of the planning. It won't be the big bucks a book might have made, but it'll carry us all for a while."

Pauline, like Yvonne, was watching her with less suspense than confidence; they actually seemed to expect she'd relent, and not just relent, but become infected by their enthusiasm, which they'd caught from Juan—or perhaps the idea, like everything that they did, was a product of bad alchemy, a miniature collective insanity none of them could have sustained on their own. "No," she said. "No, I will not commit stupid armed robbery, Juan." When she looked at Pauline and Yvonne, they seemed truly surprised.

"Then you go," Juan said, suddenly brusque.

"Oh, Juan," Yvonne said. "That's so harsh."

"If she does the thing with us she stays, if she doesn't, she goes! You think we should keep her around as a witness?"

"I'll go gladly," she heard herself say. "I'll go now."

Juan only hesitated a moment, and then threw the keys at her. She raised a hand and felt them smack into her palm. Juan's and

Yvonne's and Pauline's six-eyed gaze, suddenly strangely opaque, tracked her out of the room, and then she was striding past the foot of the stairs and through the kitchen with its warm pot of coffee and out the back door. Juan had thrown her the keys in a fit of his idiot temper, and even now he'd be realizing what he had done. He'd come storming out, red-faced and thwarted. She only needed to drive into town and call Frazer. This was his problem, now. She was aware of feeling more than a little bit pleased that everything was backfiring for him. Crossing the grass toward the car she heard the back door open and shut, a strangely leisurely sound. She dropped into the Bug's driver's seat and turned the key in the ignition. There was nothing, not even a cough. She gave the gas a few pumps; still nothing. All three of them had filed out the back door and now they stood at wide intervals, watching: Pauline on the back step, Yvonne several paces closer, eyeing Jenny with stern disapproval, but still a fair distance away; Yvonne seemed to sense that this moment was a crisis in Juan's leadership he desired to resolve on his own. Juan had come up to the driver's side window; he stood there observing as she turned the key and stamped furiously on the gas a last time. "Excuse me," she said to him coldly.

He stepped aside with what was almost great politeness, and she shoved the door open and got out again. At the back of the Bug she yanked open the deck lid and stared at the engine. Juan came and studied it also. One of the spark plug wires was missing. "I only took it on the long, long-shot chance you'd say no to our plan," Juan remarked thoughtfully. "You can hot-wire a car, can't you, Jenny? Of course you can. You can do everything. I couldn't let you try jamming the works, once we'd let you in on it. But I really didn't think you'd say no. I'm surprised and I'll even admit that I'm kind of upset. It's not just that my plan'll work best with four people. We can do it with three: it's less elegant, sure, but we'll do it. I'm upset that you seem to have more sympathy for a store-owning pig than for the people we're trying to help. The People! *Your* People, Third World People—"

"When can I actually leave?" she interrupted impatiently. Juan's encouraging, comradely aura snapped off like a lamp.

"When you can't interfere with our plan."

"And when's that?"

"When I say! I guess we'll finish the job and take off, and you'll walk into town. Find a bus stop or something."

"I could walk to town now."

"But I'd stop you," Juan said. His tone was so simple it took her a moment to realize he was threatening her. He was wearing the gun in its holster. It was so much a part of him now that she sometimes forgot it was there. Her eyes fell to it and Juan smiled, seeing what she was seeing, and knowing what she had realized. "Just sleep on it, Jen," he suggested.

"I don't need to," she murmured.

"Who knows? Maybe you do. Because this—" and he gestured, at the shimmering maple above them, at the steep hill beyond, at the barn, and the woods, and the shriveled-up patch of the pond, and the summer, she realized. "This is over," he said.

SHE WAS SITTING on the floor of her room going through William's letters when she heard the Bug's engine start up. She went to the window in time to see Juan and Yvonne drive away, both in sunglasses, smoking, their windows rolled down, Juan's left elbow protruding, Yvonne's right, as if they and the car comprised one entity that had always been self-sufficient.

She went back to the letters but couldn't stand to look at them. She had meant to find a way to compress them, but going page by page through the thick bundle she couldn't find anything to cull but the occasional white envelope with her old alias and old post office box printed on it in Dana's neat hand, and even these she could not throw away. Most of them she'd discarded long ago, and the few that remained seemed like rare artifacts and their absence would not have diminished the bulk anyway. She removed them, replaced them, retied the bundle and stared at the wall. She heard Pauline coming upstairs.

"Packing," Pauline said when she reached the doorway. She said it as if she'd found Jenny slaughtering a chicken, or performing some other blood-curdling and difficult task.

"Just thinking about it. Don't worry, I'll pack soon enough."

"What is that supposed to mean?"

"Nothing." She didn't feel like arguing. She wound the leftover tail of twine around and around the letters. She'd been trying to imagine herself on a bus, her duffel on the rack above her, the accordion file on her lap, but she could only see it from the outside, like a scene from a movie. Her head dark and vague through the grit-coated window.

Pauline didn't move from the doorway. The cigarette that she held stayed unlit. She seemed irresolute, as if she might turn on her heel and leave. "You're making a mistake," she said finally.

"Let's not talk about it."

"You don't have anywhere to go. It's like Juan said: You're just making a self-righteous stand. What are you going to do? Who can you turn to? You've decided robbery is wrong on principle, but it won't hurt that man, and it'll help all of us. It's not his money, anyway. All his business comes from the black people of that neighborhood who don't have any other store to shop in. They can't get loans to start their own stores because the banks are so racist. So stealing from him isn't stealing. He profits from racism."

Jenny wondered how it was that Juan, whose analysis this obviously was, managed to take very plausible statements and make them sound trite. "I think that's probably true," she allowed. "It doesn't mean I'll add armed robbery to my rap sheet."

"Why was it justifiable for you to blow up a building the government owned? That's against the law, too. That's destruction of property."

"That was different."

"Why?"

"That was to try to *end a war*. These things aren't all on the same scale, Pauline. The lives of millions of Vietnamese, and thousands of young American men, aren't quite the same as the well-being of a bunch of lunatics."

"And that's what we are?"

"I don't know," she said after a minute.

"Because if that's what we are, that's what you are! You think you're a saint. Maybe you're just a little too proud of yourself." Jenny had heard this one, too; she could not remember quite where or when. But she didn't have the chance to say so; Pauline had slammed her door hard and gone back downstairs.

SHE KNEW it had been an unthinking insult, seized upon and fired off randomly, but for the rest of the morning Pauline's saying that she might be a little too proud nettled her. Her father had always been maddened by what he called her moral absolutism. And once when she'd criticized Frazer's self-promotion in the guise of political action, he'd dismantled her in return. "At least I'm not deluded about my desires," he'd said. "At least I know that I'm selfless *and* selfish. We all are, sweetheart. We're just human." One of the first things she'd loved about William was his tireless perfectionism; he never chose a target for an action without researching exhaustively first, without being able to demolish its potential defenders with chapter and verse, without knowing its board of directors or slate of officials, its funding, the whole range of its acts, bad *and* good, in the world—but had this rigor been vanity, too? If so, she'd been equally vain. She'd never wanted some ill-defined public glory, like Frazer. Even in their intimate circle of comrades she'd been relieved to let William take most of the credit. Yet she knew, in a way that now made her feel oddly abashed, that she'd longed to be morally perfect. That was either self-denying, or vain, or perhaps it was both.

She still felt sure that none of this touched on armed robbery. Armed robbery simply was wrong, and saying so wasn't endorsing the capitalist system, no matter what Juan might insist. For one thing, it did nothing to alter that system. For another—but Juan wasn't interested in arguments. "This ain't theory, this is practice," he said, brushing past her. He and Yvonne had overshot the Bug's usual spot when they came back from wherever they'd gone, and instead parked in back of the barn. By the time she was climbing toward them they were on their way down and the spark plug wire, she knew, had been plucked from the engine again and concealed somewhere. That afternoon Juan and Yvonne and Pauline went into the barn to rehearse. As soon as the barn doors swung shut she began on the house: she searched underneath the back steps, in the toilet tank, under the mattresses of their ripe, rumpled beds. When she lifted up Pauline's mattress she saw the patch that she'd made on the underside, eons ago. She ripped the lid off the coffee can and dug through the grounds. When she heard target practice and knew they couldn't hear her she walked up to the Bug and examined its engine again. She felt along the insides of the fenders and wheel wells and door panels, but she was more and more sure the wire was simply on Juan. Like the gun, it now went with him everywhere.

She thought of Frazer, probably stretched on his couch in New York, his glare drilling holes in the unringing phone. He hoped to be called and apologized to; he expected to always be needed. She willed him to realize that he was expendable—to grit his teeth, rehearse a smile of defeat, and drive back up the hill. But he was also too proud; too proud to imagine his fugitives could hatch a scheme of their own, not in spite of his help but because of it. This was a great part of their happy activity, she knew: the rediscovered pleasure of calling the shots. Of course they were too proud to have stayed Frazer's wards forever. She'd felt the same way when she'd left Dick and Helen: disgusted with them and afraid Frazer might compromise her, but beyond all that, fed up with being dependent. She'd hated being dependent, and Juan and Yvonne and Pauline hated it just as much. If their plan was to remake the world, then they had to be able to remake themselves. She understood that very well; at least that was one thing she could still sympathize with.

That night at dinner they were loudly optimistic. Juan said, "It's so obvious to me we could rebuild our cadre right here. The one mistake I've made is I took so long realizing that. Take that kid, Thomas. That kid's never heard of Black Power, he's like a powder keg ready to blow."

"You'd better leave him alone," Jenny said.

"I've gotten to like rural life," Juan continued, ignoring her. "I can imagine a headquarters here."

"'For Rent, Fishing Camp, on the Delaware River,'" Yvonne read, as they ate. "Fishing Camp—that's right on. We could catch our own food." Then she looked up at Jenny. "What about you, Sister? Wouldn't you like that? You love being in nature so much."

Only Pauline said nothing, and kept her eyes trained on her plate. After dinner Jenny sat in her room at the window, reexamining the things she'd lined up on her sill over the course of the summer. Things she'd found on her walks and felt compelled to slip into a pocket, which had always looked diminished when she found them again, slightly crushed, or dusted over with lint. The spiny rind of a chestnut; a smooth white bracket mold, like a tongue of spilled cream. The one thing that hadn't been damaged in transit was a robin's-egg shell that she'd cupped in her palm all the way down the hill. Someone, between dinner and her mounting the stairs to go to bed, had hung one of the size-four dresses, the pink one, on her doorknob. Compared to the blue of the egg the pink shade was a vile one, tainted with orange. The effort, whoever had made it, to tempt her with the dress, then the whole costume drama-in-progress, with its earnest makeup and its script and the greatness of its imagined results, almost made her laugh, it was all so absurd. Then she thought she might cry. Downstairs was shrill laughter and footsteps; they must be getting drunk. Their bedroom door slammed but then she heard someone mounting the stairs. Pauline appeared in the doorway. "You're still awake," Pauline said.

"So are you. I thought you'd gone to bed."

"They did. I wanted to talk to you."

Pauline looked much more resolute now. Jenny thought of Pauline's shooting stance, the wide legs, shoulders shrugged to her ears. "Pauline, my mind is made up."

"There was just something I thought of I wanted to tell you. Our old leader—before our comrades died our old leader once said when you're weak, you have to fight to get strong. But you can help yourself out by removing temptation. Like the temptation to go back to a life that's complacent and selfish. I had that temptation. My comrades needed money to keep doing actions, and I needed to remove the temptation. So I robbed a bank with them."

After a moment Jenny said, "You shouldn't tell me about crimes you've committed."

"But there's more. There's something else that I wanted to say: It helps us help them. Help the People. Because without it we just can't continue. Of course it isn't an ideal situation. Money is evil, there's no good way to get it. But it's a necessary evil, until the revolution changes everything. Until then, we need money. There's no good way to get it, and there's no bad way to get it. You just have to get it, that's all."

"That sounds like something Juan would say."

"Why can't I make you understand?"

"It's not your job to."

"Yes it is. Yes it *is*." Pauline sat on the floor suddenly, leaning onto the door frame.

When Jenny had come upstairs the room had been cool; now the chill night air was making her shiver. Pauline was biting her thumbnail, intense, but turned inward again. Jenny got up and closed the window, and realized it was the first time she'd closed it since they had arrived. She knew that she'd never imagined the four of them still in this place, as the leaves on the maples turned red, and the larches turned yellow, and magnificent weather refilled the small pond and then gave it a clear skin of ice. They were always supposed to be gone by the end of the summer. Autumn was coming, and none of them even owned socks. They had turned all their socks into wrist weights.

She lit a cigarette and held it out silently to Pauline, and Pauline took it and inhaled hungrily, without comment, and in that instance the undeniable nonaloneness of the past several months overwhelmed her. Of course she would only taste it when it came to an end.

"I'll stop bothering you," Pauline said, and she went back downstairs.

THE NEXT DAY she'd finally packed all her things—her blue jeans and T-shirts and the old leather jacket for when it got cold, her underpants and her modest collection of paperback books, the tools she'd accumulated that were too valuable to give up, like the big crescent wrench and the drill from Wildmoor that an ancient worker had abandoned; and the notebooks of her journal of more than two years, and her letters from William—when she realized her duffel and accordion file were too much to carry. She hefted one and then tried for the other and almost fell over. It would have been different if the duffel was something else, like a backpack, or if the file had a handle. She finally got the duffel hung over one shoulder, and took a tentative step. Once she got used to this she could try the accordion file under an arm. Juan came jogging up the stairs and eyed her coldly from her doorway. So far today he had been treating her not with goading argumentation or comradely persuasion or ostentatious indifference, but a sort of hostile minimality: she had spurned his great offer, and now he was finished with her. "We'd like to rehearse, and we'd rather not go to the barn just so you can kick back in the house."

"Then I'll leave."

"And put the bag down. You're not free to go yet."

"I'm just seeing how well I can carry it."

"Bullshit. Put it down."

"I'm not trying to sneak off, Juan," she snapped.

"Put it down."

She let the duffel bag fall to the floor; its impact shook the room. "You're a prick," she said, shouldering past him to get out the door. She felt her eyes welling up suddenly.

Outside was a late summer day, clear and warm but alive with cool breezes. The sky seemed huge for the mammoth clouds traveling through it. She walked the steepest and fastest way up to the woods but once in the dense mix of boulders and trunks she was forced to slow down. She picked her way through obstacles. She was near the split-boulder reconnaissance point that Pauline had picked out long ago, or at least thought she was. Now she couldn't locate it. She kept moving, not climbing or descending but just steadily crossing the flank of the hill. Then she reemerged in the open, in the uppermost pasture. From here the house looked like a toy left behind in the grass. The hillside was ragged with milkweed and goldenrod and other hardy things she didn't know the names of, the kinds of things that drift and root everywhere and don't need a particular place. She thought of her father, always trying to teach her to build chairs from scrap wood or grow food from seeds. Maybe that had been his way of describing internment to her. He'd always brushed off her questions about it, but maybe he'd been telling her things all her life. This is how you make a horse stable into a home, and a burlap sack into a bed. This is how you pack one little bag, though you're going so far for so long . . . She thought of her duffel and accordion file, waiting for her like a pair of old dogs. They seemed like so little and they still were too much. She hadn't learned very well. And her eyes, spilling tears that she chose to ignore, also burned from how badly she'd slept. She hadn't learned that, either. Her father had expected her to sleep well anywhere and under all circumstances. On the ground, in the back of the car. Across chairs in the bus station waiting room.

She closed her eyes and lay carefully back in the bug-teeming grass. After a while she had finally stopped crying. She knew the sun alternated with clouds from the shifting of warmth on her face. Some time later she heard the back door slam, the noise carried to her on the wind. When she sat up she saw the tiny figures of Juan and Yvonne moving over the grass. Halfway to the barn they paused for a moment, then parted. Yvonne dropped to the ground and began doing sit-ups. Lately she did them by the hundreds, bobbing and gasping with calm fixity, like a yogi. Yvonne had decided that they were too decadent with their meals, and begun halving hers; now she even tore her sticks of gum in half. Juan went on to the barn. A few moments later Jenny heard the *POP, POP* of the gun.

The next time she opened her eyes she must have been responding to the strange length of time that her face had been covered by shadow. Pauline stood over her. She sat up on her elbows and Pauline said, "I didn't mean to wake you."

"That's okay."

Pauline just stood there, not saying anything else. "Want a cigarette?" Jenny asked, to break the silence. Pauline accepted, sat down, leaned forward to take a light, began to smoke, without speaking.

There was a hawk turning slowly above them; Jenny watched it, feeling the way she might have on a boat, watching the horizon to keep from throwing up as the boat pitched and rolled. Clinging to belief in the tranquil apartness of that faraway point, from the tumult she found herself in. When Pauline finished her cigarette she ground it out at great length on the bottom of her sneaker. Pauline's old beet-colored dye job had grown out so much that an inch of brown showed at her scalp, strange and vulnerable-looking, like the fur of some blind newborn mammal. Then the wind picked her hair up and the pale brown roots were obscured. Pauline dug in her pockets and brought out her own cigarettes and a book of the matches that Jenny had brought back to the house when they'd first gotten here, from a gas station outside Ferndale. She had swiped a whole big box of the individual cardboard books of matches from the gas station's office while the attendant was under a car, because they went through their matches so quickly. They'd needed them to light the stove, and cigarettes, and since they were always lighting cigarettes outside, and there was often wind, they always used up many matches on just one cigarette; except for Juan, who had a trick for lighting a match with one hand, without tearing it out of the book. He'd bend the match backwards and then by some swift movement of his thumb make it ignite with particular violence. She'd once seen Pauline alone in the kitchen trying to duplicate Juan's trick with match after match until a whole book was splayed like a badly bent fork and the sulfur heads were all crumbled and Pauline's thumb, she imagined, was sore. Pauline didn't try to do the trick now; her hands were suddenly trembling as she handed Jenny a reciprocal cigarette and tore a match from the book to try to light them both. But she couldn't; Jenny took the matches from her. "Pauline," she said. "What is it?" The breeze had gained strength, and on it she thought she heard the *POP, POP* of the gun again, just for an instant.

"Please do this thing with us," Pauline said. "Do you remember the other night when I told you about what I did to remove the temptation? That was only to make sure I couldn't go back. It didn't let me go forward. It didn't prove to them I can be good, and not just a beginner."

"I don't understand."

"It's my job to persuade you to stay. To recruit you. You didn't think we'd be an army of three forever?" Pauline paused, watching her searchingly. "It's the first thing I've been given to do on my own. I don't get any help. And they know I won't let myself fail."

"What do you mean?"

"I mean they know I won't let myself fail. He could probably kill me." Pauline was flushed, oddly triumphant from the terrible confession. "I wasn't supposed to tell you that. You know I wasn't supposed to tell you that. But you won't ever tell them."

"No," she said. She was suddenly sweating, she realized. Profusely. She thought of the bright red handprint, Pauline screaming at her in the barn. She saw the hawk drop like a meteor into the grass. For a moment the hillside looked just as it had. Then the hawk rose again, without anything.

"He only wants you to drive the switch car," Pauline added.

Jenny was still staring at the blank patch of grass where the hawk had dropped down. What did it mean when people said, "I've decided . . . ?" Did anyone ever truly decide? A brand-new white purse set in place, her quick footsteps away; that had been a decision. And yet she couldn't recall when and where she'd *decided* to do that. "I drive the switch car, and Juan leaves you alone." It came out as a statement, though it was meant as a question. Her own voice sounded distant to her. "And then what?" she belatedly asked, but Pauline had stood up.

"He's in the barn. He'll want to know we can go with Plan A."

Jenny followed Pauline down the hill. Pauline moved hastily, almost eagerly. In the barn Juan was taking a break to reload. He was handling the gun with grave earnestness; seeing him like that, imitating the pure absorption of a child as his minion approached him, made her feel hatred for him like a rash of small spines bursting out of her skin. He looked up at Pauline without anything in his face but the fact that she'd roused him from deep meditation. "Jenny does want in," Pauline announced. "I've been talking to her about it."

Juan looked startled; he must have assumed and perhaps even hoped Pauline wouldn't succeed. But then he remembered to safeguard his pride; he turned to Jenny magnanimously. "It's a good thing I don't take back my offers," he said. "You're gonna have to catch up. We'll rehearse before dinner."

She stalked out of the barn tasting bile in her throat. When Pauline emerged a few moments after she pulled her aside, as Juan's shooting resumed.

"When this is over, you have to leave them." She wished there were proof of the moment, a receipt or a bell, to mark Pauline's decision.

Pauline seemed to hesitate slightly. "Okay," she finally said.

"HI, MR. MORTON," Yvonne called.

Then she would hurry to him, in a powder-blue dress from Margot's Modern Fashions, a light coat from the same on her arm. "Hi! Don't you remember me? Sandra. I'm back home for a visit." She would put her coat arm partway around him, take his arm with her free hand.

He would say, "Sandra?" his small, creased eyes blinking at her. He would feel the hard thing in his back.

Yvonne urges him gently. "Keep walking. Sandra Smith, remember? From check-out. Now I'm engaged."

"I don't remember . . ." he says, in a strangled voice. Fear, not resistance.

"It's a gun," Yvonne says. "I won't use it if you'll just walk with me. Let's turn here, okay?"

They leave Main Street, the bank still a half block beyond them, and turn down a side street that leads to a rear parking lot. The side street is blank, no windows, just some side doors to businesses closed on Sundays. Juan is there. "This is my fiancé," Yvonne says. "Why don't you give him the bag."

Juan holds out his hand, warmly smiles. In rehearsal this takes barely a minute. A car pulls itself free of the cars in the lot and comes toward them, Pauline at the wheel. A few miles away, in a second car, Jenny is waiting.

"Good!" Juan said. "Now we're driving, we're calm . . ."

Past four in the morning Yvonne and Juan drove to Ferndale and hot-wired a nondescript four-door sedan. The two cars came rumbling back up the hill before dawn. Pauline sat in the driver's seat of the sedan and gripped the wheel so tightly her knuckles turned blue. "Drive up to the barn and come back and don't turn off the engine," Juan said. The car rolled away, picked up speed. "California girl," Juan observed of her. "She said she wasn't sure she could still drive. Like she'd ever forget."

At ten o'clock Jenny was sitting in the Bug at an overgrown fishing access to a river so dry that she only saw piles of rocks, round and pale, and then sometimes a glint of reflection from deep between them when the sun left the clouds. Through the trees she could see the boat launch, a cracked, crumbling ramp of concrete. She was wearing her own jeans and T-shirt and sneakers; she'd refused to put on the pink dress. It was a grim day, intermittently raining: all the better for Sunday on Main Street. "Hi, Mr. Morton," Yvonne calls. It had occurred to them, belatedly, that Mr. Morton did not seem to have white employees. Did this mean he had never had white employees? She hurries to him, in the dress, with the coat, puts her coat arm partway around him.

Jenny thought of the white purse, the green dress. On that years-ago day that is somehow more real than this one, she looks like a girl who has just been to church, in a dainty green dress with white piping, white shoes, clean white gloves, the white purse to match. In the middle of the bright business day, waiting calmly at the elevator bank in the lobby, later going back out the same way she went in. Perhaps the guard senses a ripple, in a distant recess of his mind; she does not have the purse anymore but the lobby is crowded, twenty people pass by every minute, he doesn't know what he has noticed and may not even know that he's noticed at all. She takes the bus home as if sleepwalking, as if levitated, or drugged. Seeing nothing. Trying to shake herself free of the trance, for the sake of safety, but she can't. Floating into Tom Milner's apartment, where they've arranged to regroup and observe, she finds not just William and Tom but Mike Sorsa, and Tom's practically brand-new girlfriend—she's still really a date—Lorraine, gathered there, waiting for her. One look at her face and William knows she's done it right; and of course the bag is gone. Before anyone can say anything, while they're still staring, stunned, she and William walk straight to each other and lock mouths desperately, and the tension, though it doesn't break, quavers briefly with keyed-up laughter and admonitions: "Aw, come on. Save the pornography."

Tom Milner's brand-new girlfriend—he won't meet shy, loyal, nervous, impassioned Sandy until more than a year from this time—reveals she has made them a party: vegetarian chili heating up on the stove, a bowl of salad in the fridge, she's instructing various of them to get out paper plates, forks, napkins, she leads them onto the roof, the reason they're using Tom's—it has a view of the building—and there are lawn chairs set up here, as if it's a day at the beach, and a cooler of beer. It's only now that she registers how disturbed—not just disturbed, angry—she is that this girl,

Lorraine, is here. William wraps his arms around her from behind and she shrugs him off; she can't scold Tom, or even reveal her irritation, and so she's left with being angry at William. "What?" he whispers, with the hint of a warning: don't ruin our night.

"Nothing," she says. "But I'm nervous."

"I love you," he says. Waiting sternly until she meets his eyes.

She hates this pro forma exercise; what she really means, what she really feels, needs, craves, is hardly expressed by these words. These words seem like a fence to her, a little white line of pickets to keep things at bay. A formula to ward off other words, real words, words tightly bound to their meanings. But for William the utterance is like a dangerous thing he was taught to avoid. He says it with jaw jutted, with something like anger—I will possess this fatal weapon and use it!—and, finally, with the need for her to acknowledge the significance of his having chosen her.

"I love you," she says.

And then all of them are eating the chili and drinking the beer, conversing at first uneasily, then with greater fluidity as the sun, and the beer, go down. They gorge themselves, lean back, open fresh beers. Mike Sorsa fills his little silver pipe and passes it around and they get high. It's a mild, fragrant night; she watches the green lights from the port come on, the lighthouse beating its tempo on Alcatraz Island. It almost feels like any summer night's roof party. It won't be fully dark until nine; then Lorraine, somewhat self-importantly, takes the leftover chili downstairs—it was good chili; they've all praised her, grinned over it, dunked bread into the pot and licked it off their fingers in stoned primitiveness when they got sick of using their plates—and comes back up with candles and the transistor radio. Jenny is annoyed again by Lorraine's manner—it is proprietary, braggartly, as if Lorraine is the center of events and not what Jenny feels she is, a dangerous interloper. Lorraine's easy femininity also seems boastful. Jenny decides she hates these girls who flaunt their casual associations with the marginal while at the same time oddly emphasizing their traditionalness—these girls who always end up acting as caretakers, the ones who stroke the foreheads of the boys overcome by LSD, who gladly whip up omelettes for twenty at four in the morning, who are always to be found, the next day, gliding easily among the prone, pungent bodies on the living room floor, collecting the glasses and plates and wiping up the spills. She is thinking she hates them; though she is more likely to be a caretaker herself than a prone body on the living room floor. All the same she is more and more, perhaps because of the grass, not just irked but frightened by the ramifications of Lorraine's inclusion in their circle. And also, perhaps because of the grass, she is less able than ever to summon the strength to do something about it. What could she do?

It is the kind of thing, she thinks, that will lead to disaster someday.

But hours are passing, have passed. William has gone downstairs also, and returned swinging a full bottle of whiskey by its neck. Nice whiskey. "I think this qualifies as a special occasion," he says, smiling at her.

At half-past midnight she shudders suddenly, as if chilled. She's thoroughly lost track of time. "Shh!" she exclaims, and everyone stares at her. Lorraine looks at her with exaggerated concern, her eyebrows raised questioningly, as if Jenny were an inarticulate child.

"I just worry we're loud," she says, embarrassed. She gestures around, at the indigo night, the palms swaying along the avenue, the lights from the strip, two blocks away, where the deli and grocery are. All is murmurous, as are they, she realizes. They're not loud, they're not even the only ones up on a roof, drinking beer, getting high. It's the season of roof parties.

"You just worry," William teases, wrapping himself around her back like a chair. She leans into him, closes her eyes. She can feel his cock hardening against the base of her spine. He feels her feeling him and squeezes humorously; it's a joke of theirs, his uncontrollable hunger for her body. A fantastic joke she can't imagine tiring of. A sated drunkenness has overtaken them all. Tom Milner and Lorraine, around the corner of the hutlike structure that houses the entrance to the stairwell, are intensely necking and stroking each other; she can feel the heat washing off them, but with William against her, she doesn't care anymore. Sorsa, the quiet loner, is crouched near the roof's edge, cigarette pinched between his fingers, meditative and unmoved, it seems, by the pulse of sex behind him. She feels William work his hand beneath her shirt, under her waistband. When he fingers her she is already so wet he's sucked in by her flesh. She twitches, gives a jerk, as if her nerves are malfunctioning, and pushes against him anxiously; she hears his ragged breath. He sometimes comes, with sudden and great force, while touching her this way. Not touching himself at all. Then she hears Sorsa say, as if to himself, "One."

She looks up, feels Tom Milner and Lorraine break apart. William's hand, as if caught, slips from her. A long beat, in which nothing happens. Her throat closes.

Then, across the expanse of cottages, palms, streets criss-crossing, the quiet night in this low-slung, waterside settlement, traffic hardly audible, lights of the port glowing green, lighthouse at Alcatraz pulsing, the toy city of San Francisco not really visible behind the string of the Bay Bridge, downtown Oakland rising like an accident near the water's edge, as if, midway through its construction, someone had realized San Francisco lay just across the water, and so cancelled the project, the X___ tower, only twenty-two stories, rectangular and graceless, burps a ball of black smoke and orange flame; from the distance the noise is as quick and mundane as, perhaps, a dump truck letting go of its load. *Boom*. That's all. Then a streamer of black smoke is angling away, with the wind. She feels as if she's going to faint, *is* fainting, she's tumbling backward, then realizes this is because William, whom she'd been leaning on, has leaped to his feet with a whoop. "*Shh!*" she says—but they're all whooping, clutching their chests, pointing, reeling, amazed.

While she's started to shake, violently. Not because she did not know, before, the real scope of the thing she would do. She made sure to know, or she wouldn't have let herself do it. But nothing, no amount of mental preparation, has been equal to what it looks like. William sees her quaking, her teeth chattering, as if it's the middle of winter, and kneels quickly before her, grabs her hands, her *little hands*, squeezes them, as if she is a child. "Think of that being dropped onto people," he hisses. "Balls of fire dropped down onto children. Little children who look just like you."

"I know what I did," she says angrily, snapping out of her trance. "And I know why—*you* don't have to coach me."

AT ELEVEN they were suddenly upon her. Yvonne's blue dress was spattered with black blood and gore—Jenny saw her and screamed. "Shut up!" Juan yelled. Yvonne couldn't speak; her hand, her gun hand, was soaked in blood as if she had plunged the hand into a wound. Juan was bundling her into the Bug like a sack of potatoes. Pauline drove the other car across the empty oncoming lane and the shoulder and bumped down into the high grass in the ditch; the rear bumper sank out of sight. "What happened?" Jenny screamed at them. Pauline came running back across the road to the Bug, her hair flying behind her. Yvonne leaned out the door on her side and threw up and Juan pulled her back in, roughly, but with a palm on the top of her head to keep her from hitting it on the door frame. The way cops always do, Jenny thought. "What happened?" she screamed again.

"Just drive!" Juan said. But she was already driving.

She didn't remember the drive back; not in sequence, or as a sustained length of time. All the miles she'd driven up and down these roads now seemed to have been an accumulation leading up to this drive; she did not see what she did, didn't tell her hands to guide the wheel as they guided it. She held the memory of this drive in every cell of her body, and later it would seem that even those things that were happening now had already been part of the great mass of detail she knew. Yvonne sobbing hugely. Juan talking and talking, like a thread being pulled from his mouth, no island of silence or emphasis. Clean house pack call Frazer need to cars need to get another car maybe after nightfall go back for that car maybe no one but that one man saw have to travel they'll think it was local not the kind of thing state police local one-off thing . . .

Pauline was silent. She sat beside Jenny, her profile motionless, like a ship's figurehead. Homing in on invisible landmass. Seeing past the horizon—

They roared and bounced wildly up the dirt track to the house; now that they were on the property Jenny was standing furiously on the gas pedal until they were doing seventy, eighty; they almost shot up in the air when they came to the level. And they almost hit the maple; her eyes were trained on the rear view, on the length of the road you could see when you'd climbed from the valley. Not another car on it.

"Put it into the barn," Juan said, pulling Yvonne, limp and blood-spattered and vomit-stained, out of the car. He flipped her over to face the house and swung her arm around his shoulders. "Walk," he growled. "Come on, baby. Walk."

Pauline finally turned to her. "He's dead," she burst out.

"Get my duffel and file. Run!" Pauline heard an order; she ran; she ran across the lawn ahead of Juan and Yvonne as if to hold the door for them, then slipped through; the door slammed shut behind her. A beat later Juan was there with Yvonne. Jenny watched him struggle to reopen the door, then hold it with one outstretched leg while he handled Yvonne. She seemed to have fainted, but then she looked up at him, as if she'd just seen him. Her face collapsed, and he pulled her into his arms.

"Okay," he said. "It's okay. He's all right. That person was there to help him. Now they've gone to the hospital."

"I love you," moaned Yvonne.

"I love you. I love you." Juan hitched her arm over his shoulder again. They went in. Jenny started to cry; she tipped her forehead on the wheel and sobbed. The engine was still running. Her body shook as if someone were standing behind her and shaking it. She heard noise at the back door, and her head, like an object obeying physical laws, rolled to one side; she opened her eyes. Through her tears came a melting and wavering form, struggling, pulling something. Her duffel and file. Pauline had the file gripped to her chest and was tugging the enormous duffel through the grass; she dumped them next to the car as if they were an obstacle race she'd completed. "They're in the bathroom," Pauline gasped. "Cleaning. Juan says put the car in the barn and hurry!" Jenny swung out of the car and opened its back doors. She kicked the red gun onto the grass. The deposit bag was still sitting on the floorboards; she opened it, pulled out some money, and threw the bag on the grass also, then grabbed for her duffel and file.

"Get in!" she said to Pauline.

"What?"

"Get in! We have to go, now!" She could see Pauline finally flooding from panic, as if the news she'd delivered herself had just registered with her. *He's dead*. Pauline blindly turned toward the doomed house and Jenny seized her and manhandled her into the car, the way Juan had manhandled Yvonne, but with even less care. Pauline's brittle frame gave her a shock, as if she'd taken a gloved hand and felt only bones. Pauline twisted and recoiled and fell roughly on the front seat.

"Oh, no," she was sobbing. "Oh, no, no, we can't, no, we can't . . ."

Jenny stamped on the pedal and the Bug squealed in a half-circle and roared down the hill. Inside, above the sound of running water, the noise might have reached Juan, but if he came running out with his sleeves rolled up, hands white with lather, Yvonne's tears a damp patch on his shirt pocket, she didn't look back to see him.

They were down the drive, onto the road, before Pauline had voiced her whole protest. "We can't leave them!" she screamed.

"Leave *them*!" Jenny said.

But after they'd been driving long enough, turning, turning, turning, changing roads as often as there were roads to change to, Pauline's sobs winding down to just harsh hopeless scrapes in her throat, the pinhole that had been Jenny's vision dilated: grew huge. She slowed down. The faint yellow stripe of their road stretched away endlessly.

"You lied," she said. "Juan never threatened you. He didn't make you recruit me. You just did it to please them."

Pauline's wet face was blotched a raw color. "And it did please them, didn't you see?" she choked forth raggedly. "They were so pleased with me . . . "

When night fell Jenny found a truck stop and called Frazer, for the last time, from a pay phone. "They're all done with their book. Come right now."

"Oh, fantastic!" said Frazer, surprised. "I'm so sorry, sweetheart, I'm so sorry we fought. See you soon."

"See you soon," she echoed.

She hung up and ran back to the Bug. Pauline was curled in the back with the duffel. The night had turned cold. Jenny sat up for hours, a knot, holding herself to keep warm, waiting for understanding, but her mind had been bombed; it was only a crater. She closed her eyes against the harsh yellow lights of the lot. The rumbling of the idling trucks around her gave off something like animal comfort. Behind her, a tight ball, Pauline slept. There were many ways, she thought, to disappear. She thought of Juan's mother, and her beloved dent-with-tree in the field. There would be an oasis.

Part Three

Frazer found them, not even in the house or in the barn, but in the woods, and after walking and shouting their names for almost half an hour. They had heard his car and fled, not imagining that it was him. He didn't think he would ever forget their faces, when they saw that it was. Those expressions erased many things. Right then, they confessed, and he opened his heart in return. The flight of Jenny and Pauline they would barely discuss. "I felt them slipping away . . ." Juan murmured. It wasn't clear when he had felt this. They all, back in the house again, drank a glass of whiskey each and sat a while, stilling their senses. "One thing I always say is listen to the body," said Frazer. "If it's freaked, calm it down. Give it time. We need ours to be calm." When they felt they were as calm as they could be, they discussed what to do.

It was very hard to imagine, they all agreed, that the investigation of a robbery and shooting in a town thirty miles away would arrive at this long-vacant farmstead, let alone soon, which meant two things: that they would leave here, to be as prudent as possible, but that they would take their time doing it. They would leave without leaving a trace.

Frazer went to buy gloves and they set to work, wearing them. The fire pit Frazer and Jenny had built was loaded with wood; they got a strong fire going, and then they burned everything that they could. What would not burn they packed in the car. They did not speak of the book, but Juan retrieved the small package of their efforts from the woods and repacked it carefully with his belongings. When the house was empty of everything they had brought to it, they washed every dish, pot, spoon, cup, still gloved; they washed other movable items. Then, one room at a time, with bowls of soapy water and rags, they wiped down every surface: the windows and sills, the light switches, the bed frames, the chests of drawers, toilets . . . as each room was finished, they closed it. They had to go to sleep at one point, the work took them so long.

When the house was pristine they moved on to the barn: easier, because with so many fewer smooth surfaces. They took down the targets and burned them, wiped the tools, searched with flashlights for spent shells and casings.

Doing this strange work was calming. Juan thought it helped Yvonne, appealed to her sense of order. And he liked it too. The history of touch; it was melancholy, it was moving, it was settling, to consider the things one had touched. In the woods, panting for breath during some combat drill, he had often held a smooth, water-washed rock in his palm. Squeezed its cool, ancient form. Water had carved these hills, these rocks, turned them gently out of the soil . . . is that what had happened? His own measure of this life seemed so small. He had wanted so badly to help people. And had felt that the structures and strictures were false—couldn't one, with a true heart and a strong hand, simply plunge forth, and make right by force? This was what the army had taught him, but their notion of rightness was wrong. Now the temporal struggles of man seemed, at moments, irrelevant. He thought he understood, as he carefully blotted out every trace of himself in this place, that he was going to die soon, and not as a hero. He had sacrificed that aspiration, in the course of pursuing it. And it was a welcome premonition, his death. But like many such premonitions, it was not going to prove true. Again, he was going forward into peril, and again he would live. He would live, longer than his twenty-three-year-old self—intuiting the constricting, freeing limits of adulthood for what was really the first time—could imagine now. He would have children. He and Yvonne, so bound to each other, would part. For Juan at twenty-three, having loved her for almost seven years, such a thing is unthinkable, but the day will come when his love for Yvonne is a chapter, not the last and largest portion of his life.

None of this is known to him now. He polishes the hasp on the barn door, thinks of polishing stones. Puts the crosspiece of wood through the door handles. Polishes the bottle of polish stuff he's been using, lathers it in its own sharp, fake-lemony, naive American smell. Joins Frazer and Yvonne at the car. They feel good, gathered next to the car—or as good as they can. Yvonne has not eaten a crumb since the shooting. She is pale, empty-eyed, silent. Juan thinks of avocados; she loves those. They're going back to California, and there are lots of avocados there, and he'll get her to eat them.

Ready? Frazer says. They nod, and get into the car.

LATE THAT NIGHT Jenny retraced the route she'd first traveled to get to the farmhouse. It took less than an hour, although when she arrived she overshot the driveway, even by the light of a nearly full moon. She had to double back, losing a couple of minutes. Then she saw the chain slung as usual between its two posts. Unhooking the chain and moving it aside her palms took on powdery rust. She noticed the small sign she'd painted was gone. In its place was a mass-produced one that said PRIVATE, of about the same size.

Pauline woke as they were moving down the long unlit drive.

Jenny wished she could turn off the headlights but was afraid she'd run into a tree. The faint cones of light only deepened the darkness beyond them. When Pauline spoke Jenny started. "Where are we?" Pauline said.

"Somewhere to get rid of this car." The trees had thinned out to one side, and she saw the outline of the house, standing bravely and absurdly in its clearing like a child's play-castle, its conical tower distinct against the dimly lit sky. All its windows were dark. She continued on, down the slight dip past the pit where the ice house had been, toward the huge listing stables. The car would be there, if the car still existed. The keys would be tossed on the seat. She had embarked on this plan telling herself that if the car were there she would swap the Bug for it and go. Dolly maintained a state of cold war with the various branches of local government as her ancestors had, since the time the region's other humans had ceased to be tenants on family land. She failed to pay taxes and was condescending to the police. She hadn't driven in years. She wasn't likely to notice the disappearance of one car and its replacement by another for a while, and even then she wasn't likely to report it. And yet, despite these rationales, Jenny had already known as she crossed the bridge over the river, the Bug all alone on the road, her hands sweating so much she was wiping them off constantly, that she wouldn't be able to take Dolly's car and just go. She'd pretended she could, but she couldn't.

"Where are we?" Pauline repeated.

The wooden planks of the door to the stables moaned with age but the metal hardware glided in its tracks; that was her handiwork, accomplished as much as a year ago. She was glad for it now. Like most old people Dolly slept shallowly. The sound of a car on her road might have roused her already, but now that the engine was silent all other noise made Jenny cringe. The moonlight sifted into the vast space and she saw Dolly's car. Inside it still smelled of the cool plastic showrooms of 1961. The odometer still stood at less than halfway to ten thousand. The ashtrays were all still pristine, though there might have been invisible motes in the rugs from Jenny's own cigarettes, blown back by the wind as she'd smoked out the window. The keys were on the seat and picking them up she remembered the opposite gesture of casting them down, the night she had left here with Frazer, and then she felt sure the keys hadn't been touched in the three months since then. Turning the keys the lights came on dimly, but the car only coughed. They would have to jump-start it. "Help me push the Bug in here," she said. Pauline still sat as if glued to the passenger seat, staring at their new surroundings with something like suspicion, or dire realization; she belatedly stared at Jenny. "Goddammit, come on," Jenny said.

"He might not be dead," Pauline suddenly said, as if this were a plausible option they hadn't considered. "And even if he is, he's still just—an establishment pig."

Jenny felt her scalp glowing with heat.

"Help me push this car," she said, releasing each word with great care, as if each involved lifting a valve on a pressurized tank that might spew its contents everywhere.

They pushed the Bug onto the smooth packed-dirt floor of the stables. Brusquely removing Pauline from her path, Jenny felt her way to a work table against the back wall. There was an oily rag here, and a flashlight. Outside was the standpipe. Once there she took great gulps of air as if drinking; she knew Pauline was just inside the door, watching her from that darkness. The water from the standpipe ran clear and she wondered if Dolly had somebody new working for her. The possibility had never crossed her mind until now. She held the rag under the water, letting it soak full and wringing it out, until she realized the water had made her hands numb and the rag had been wet a long time. Her gaze seemed to have drifted away like a ghost, but it was mute and sent nothing back to her. She didn't see, again and for a last time, the steep drop of the hill toward the river, which was trench-deep and black like a fjord. She didn't see the particular things of this place, which meant nothing to her; this was just a way station she'd known for a while. She wrung out the rag lightly the last time, so that it stayed sodden. Then she went back in the stable and thrust the wet rag and flashlight at Pauline. "Put our things in this car. Then get in the Bug and clean off every trace of the blood of your so-called establishment pig. Use the flashlight. If I'm not back when you're done wait here for me. Don't move from this spot."

"Where are you going?" Pauline grabbed at her jacket.

Jenny shrugged her off. "Up to the house."

"What if somebody finds me?"

"They won't, if you stay in this spot."

The house was still dark when she left the trees and crossed into the clearing. Her shadow followed her along the twilit grass, only visible in movement; when she stood still, it melted away. Across the lawn she could see the black form of the pergola, like a miniature twin of the house. Stepping onto the dark porch she reached easily for the doorknob, not needing to feel her way to it. She opened the door and heard Dolly say, "You get out, mister. I've called the police."

"It's me, Miss Dolly."

"What?" Dolly cried.

"It's Iris."

Once Dolly had managed to turn on a lamp they regarded each other a long time without speaking, whether in astonishment, or resignation, or suspicion she couldn't quite tell. Dolly seemed smaller, as if her aging had accelerated, and constricted her bones. But her gaze was still keen. Jenny saw myriad things flicker through it: apprehension undone by impatience; dark speculation; instinctive imperiousness. "Well, Iris," she finally said. "You must be back to rob me. I thought that you had when you ran off before, but I see you decided to wait."

"I'm sorry to come here so late."

"Oh, please. It's a bit farcical to apologize, isn't it? I suppose your young man is outside in the bushes. That day that he came looking for you I was sure you must be in cahoots. I've been through this house with a comb to see what might be missing."

"If I had meant to rob you I would have done it then, as you said. Your logic is perfectly right. So you have to admit, logically, that I never intended to rob you at all."

"Don't appeal to logic, Iris. There's nothing logical about your behavior. I was very disappointed at the way you left me."

"I'm sure you've found someone better by now."

"I have not. I have not had the time to do interviews. I've had very bad health this whole summer."

"I'm sorry."

"Very sorry, I'm sure. You left all my most important projects in the lurch, Iris. If you'd had the sense to speak with me before you went we might have arranged for your wages, but I'm afraid as it is you must forfeit. I don't want to imagine what fresh difficulty has brought you back here."

"I'm not here for the wages." She hesitated, then rushed on. "I'd like your car. I can offer you three hundred dollars."

"It's a quarter past four in the morning. You can't expect me to believe that you've come here to purchase my car." Jenny kept silent and Dolly added, "My car is worth much more than that," but Jenny sensed that she'd spoken to gain time to think. "You're here in a car," Dolly pointed out.

"I'd leave that car in the stable. It would work all right as a runabout if you hire someone new, but it's no good for distance, and that's what I need now. I need to get home to my family. It's a sort of emergency."

"That's what your note said yon three months ago. 'Emergency. Must travel home to see family.' You don't seem to have got very far."

"I ran into delays."

"As I said, I'd prefer not to know what fresh difficulty brings you back here." Dolly lowered herself into her favorite armchair and pulled her robe around her shoulders. When she trained her skeptical gaze onto Jenny again it was scaled back to the usual version, as if they were bickering over their tea. "I suppose you thought of my car because you assume I'd take anything for it. Three hundred dollars! I bought that car new."

"Thirteen years ago, and you never drive it. You once told me you hadn't driven that car in a decade."

"It would still be a great handicap not to have it. Five hundred's the least I could think of, and that's robbery."

"You owe me eight months of back wages."

"I've made clear what I think of your wages. A few weeks' notice of departure is the norm, Iris, let alone a 'good-bye' to my face."

Dolly drew herself up and Jenny thought, with sudden pain, of the little tin cash box into which Mrs. Fowler had carefully counted the limp dollar bills from the house tours. Dolly must never have known how she'd pay Jenny's wages. She must have trembled with relief, perhaps very slight shame, when she found Jenny gone.

"Three hundred fifty," Jenny said. "I can't do any better. If that's not enough I guess I'll wait until morning and look in the classified ads." She sat back in her own chair, heart pounding. She felt sure Dolly saw through her bluff, but she saw through Dolly as well. She saw the three hundred fifty dollars taking hold in Dolly's mind as a sum she already possessed.

"I'll consider it a favor to you," Dolly finally said. "I was sorry you left."

"I was, too." And in some sense, she meant it.

It would have taken just a little while longer to finish. An alteration in the bluish gray night told her dawn was coming. They would drive to the state park and wait until night fell again, sheltered in the new car. Dolly was counting out each bill with awful care onto the kitchen table and Jenny wanted to shake her. But in a minute they'd be free, in this one small respect. This was how it was now, an obstacle cleared, then another, a course without end . . . "Who's there?" Dolly barked. The front door had creaked open. Jenny looked up in shock. Pauline stood trembling in the center of the parlor, just beyond the kitchen door.

"I thought you were selling me out," Pauline miserably whispered.

THE SUN had risen by the time they were moving again. It lit up the mist lying over the river; but the air was still cold, and the mist glowed like silvery fleece without burning away. It beamed bright yellow light through the trees and poured into the passenger window as they raced north between yellowing fields and along broken stone walls toward the bridge. Against it Pauline was a blurred silhouette. The scene at Dolly's seemed to press like a brick on the gas, so that the need for prudence at the moment was shoved aside by the thought of prudence's recent failure. Dolly had stared at Pauline in a stunned, transfixed way—Dolly, whose only companion in the long hours between teatime visits was the television in her bedroom. Dolly who pretended repulsed noninterest in the world at large, but was as alert as anyone to the vagaries and deviations of celebrity persons, whether they'd grown prominent for quality or crime. Dolly who watched Walter Cronkite each night as if keeping a private appointment. Dolly had accepted Jenny's stammering false introduction without asking why an old friend named Ann from New Jersey had never been mentioned before. She hadn't seemed to hear the unfamiliar phrase "selling me out." She had squared the money into a pile without completing her count, and folded it protectively into one hand. "You must be wanting to be on your way," she had murmured, and Jenny thought she saw a flush in her face—of excitement? Anxiety? Pauline had fled out to the porch, and Jenny stood waiting a final time for Dolly to make her laborious, stubbornly unaided way from the kitchen back into the parlor. "If you foul up your travels again," Dolly said between breaths, "please don't come here at an ungodly hour. Have the sense to come during the day." Jenny had thought that Dolly must be playing dumb out of fear they would kill her. Outside she had grabbed Pauline's arm and pulled her, stumble-running through the trees; Pauline had tried to talk and Jenny snapped, "Don't talk!" The jumper cables slipped out of her hands and the car's hood bit down on her finger before the car came to life and they were bumping down the drive and back over the chain that still lay in zigzags in the dust.

They turned west to cross the river at Kingston and the dark humped-up mountains faced them. They'd once made her think of those great shiplike forms of the West, the mountains that rise from the desert and grow no more near for the hours spent driving toward them. Those mountains gave off an illusion of nearness, but these did the opposite thing; up to their threshold they looked vast and wild, and then were revealed as bright sunny hills. The East had once promised refuge to her, because she'd never been to it. Now she felt smothered by intimacy. A miniature town sat at the gate of the miniature mountains, quaint and forgotten, shuttered churches and a rusted gas station, a dairy store with its pay telephone. The same kind of sad shrinking pond she had swum in for over two years. She pulled into the store parking lot. It wasn't yet open at six in the morning and it might not have opened in years. She had to turn off the engine to unlock the trunk, but then she realized that Pauline had nothing but the clothes she was wearing. No bag, not even a coat. "I don't suppose that you can understand," Jenny said quickly, before the shake in her voice broke her words, "because to you it's a *pig* that has died, but you and I are now guilty of murder. And so if I was ever stupid enough to think that staying with you and Juan and Yvonne was good for me, I know better now."

"You *are* selling me out!"

"No, I'm saying good-bye! You might have gotten into all this so that you could kill *pigs* but that's not what I'm in it for, that's never what I was in it for. I was bad enough off when I met you and now it's just worse!" She dug in her pockets, where the rest of their money was stored in disorderly wads, and thrust more than half at Pauline. "Get out of the car."

"No!"

"Get out of the car! This car is all I have left from two years of hard work and I don't owe you for it. I don't owe you at all. There's a pay phone right there—call your parents. You can call them collect."

"No!" Pauline said wildly, holding fast to the door handle. For a moment Jenny thought she was going to go around to Pauline's side of the car and drag her kicking onto the pavement. Then she yanked the keys from the ignition and got out of the car. In the trunk were her duffel and accordion file. After a paralyzed second she pulled the books and tools and half her clothes out of the duffel and stuffed the accordion file inside; she left everything else. She thought by now Pauline might have locked the car doors, but Pauline was only gaping as if she'd gone mad.

"Then it's yours," she said, throwing the keys in. "Good luck," she added, and then she marched off with the huge duffel bag on her shoulder.

The duffel was still awkward and heavy and it would be at least five miles back to the bridge and over and then another few up- or downriver for a train, but once on the train she could go all the way. All the way north as far as the border. There must be some way to get into Canada. She would hike through the woods, then cross into Quebec. She wasn't so far from safety. She had stayed for too long with those people, had let them leach into her system as if they were water and she had been parched, and their troubles had somehow been hers and their pathway hers, too, but now all that wafted away. She had not, she reasoned, even been at the scene of the murder. She had been left in the switch car, but there was no one to say she had known what her purpose would be. Would a court believe Juan or Yvonne or Pauline? Her vision had cleared, a weight lifted . . . she hardly saw the road she was stumbling on. She was hardly aware that the morning was opening, really, that the sun wasn't a cool glow in silver fleece anymore but a hot white blaze square in her vision. She didn't have a free hand to wipe at her eyes and so she kept going, nearly jogging from angry adrenaline, everything smeared in her vision, but when the car came she didn't have to confirm it by sight. She knew what that car sounded like.

The car pulled alongside and Pauline leaped from it, nearly pitching them both in the gully. The duffel bag fell to the road. "*Wait!*" Pauline screamed, as if she were the one stumbling on foot while Jenny drove away. "*Wait . . .*" she cried. "*Wait . . .*" Pauline sank down onto the duffel. Between her hoarse sobs Jenny heard insects droning, and birdsong. Otherwise the hot morning was silent. Jenny's eyes seemed to parch and now she really did see, east for miles down the flat empty road toward the bridge and the river. At her touch Pauline flinched away sharply. But Pauline had vanished in terrible wails, and when Jenny dared touch her again she gave way heedlessly, the way sleepwalkers give way to guidance without waking up.

IN A MOTEL outside Kingston she bleached Pauline's hair blond, watching the old beet-red dye job and even the new growth of natural brown slowly give up their tints and turn orange, and then yellow, and then a pale yellow closer to white. Although she'd worn the thin gloves that had come in the box, her fingertips still itched and stung. Her eyes were still weeping from fumes. Pauline had twitched slightly with pain as the bleach began burning her scalp, and now her scalp was erupting with blisters. Pauline was bent over in the chair they'd brought into the bathroom, a dry towel around her thin shoulders and a damp towel pressed to her face. Jenny looked down at the bowed head, transforming again; then looked up at herself. The same self, though the longer she looked the less sure that she was. Pauline raised her head, dropping the towel, and their eyes briefly met in the mirror. Pauline's were swollen and red, from her earlier tears, or the fumes, or the pain, or all three.

"We can wash it out now," Jenny said.

Afterward Pauline sat on the bed, her feet pushed in the sheets, her hands idly turning the comb. Her hair was yellow as straw and as squeaky and dry as a doll's. They'd given up trying to get the comb through it. Jenny sat at the cigarette-burn-covered table. The table was almost a Rosetta stone of cigarette burns, though the only thing on it was a thick-sided ashtray. The bright daytime sun was blocked out by the room's musty curtains, but the curtains were thin, and enough light leaked through to make dusk in the room. The lamps were all off. She knew it was irrational to feel safer like this, in the gloom. But she did, and she knew that Pauline did, and perhaps they both also felt shielded somewhat from each other.

After a while Pauline said, "Did Juan ever explain ego reconstruction to you? It's a game, but a serious game. It's a trust exercise."

"I can't even guess what that means. It builds trust? It can only be played with the people you trust?"

"It builds trust."

"Sounds useful in our situation." She knew her voice was sarcastic.

Pauline looked away, fiddling the comb. "I'll tell you the rules. If it's only two people, we each time the other. When I tell you to go, you say just what you're thinking of me, without stopping yourself, like you're lifting the lid on your mind. When a minute is up I say stop."

Jenny lit herself a cigarette; she pushed the ashtray aside and set the cigarette down on the table. A mark started to form underneath the hot ash. "A whole minute?" she said. "A minute can last a long time."

"We could each say the one thing that comes to our mind, when the other calls time. So instead of one minute, one thing."

She could see that Pauline had a thing that she wanted to say; the game was only a shield, like the dusk in the room. "All right," Jenny said. "I'll go first."

"So you get it?"

"There's not much to get."

"Then you're ready."

"I'm ready."

Pauline took a breath and said, "Time." Jenny thought that she saw Pauline wince.

"I wish you'd say anything to me, as long as it's true."

Pauline hesitated. "Is that all?" she said.

"Yes, it is. Okay, *time*," Jenny said.

• • •

IN THE BEGINNING, Pauline said—not the very beginning, but after she'd been with the cadre a while—the leader raised the question of whether or not they should ask her to join, and asked all the members to vote. The cadre then numbered eleven, including the leader, and Pauline knew there was already talk of how good it would be to have twelve. Twelve could be nicely divided into four groups of three. It was better for combat. Its symmetry seemed powerful. Including the leader nine voted Yes for her, but two—Juan and Yvonne—voted No.

It wasn't as if making Pauline a comrade didn't represent a huge leap of faith. It had been difficult enough to win their trust to the extent that she had—to persuade them to trust her to see all their faces, so they'd take off her blindfold; then to trust her to go to the toilet and take baths alone; then to move around freely, so her atrophied muscles could heal; and finally to sit in on meetings and offer advice, because the month-old ransom talks with her parents were rapidly crumbling. All that trust had been gained only slowly and with great difficulty, and it was nothing compared to the trust she would need to be made a comrade. But Juan and Yvonne were their own unique problem, and their "no" vote was more complicated. Although they'd renounced their marriage vows as bourgeois, within the cadre they still showed a bond that would frequently cause them to clash with the others. Monogamy was disallowed in the cadre, but only Juan and Yvonne constantly pursued sex with their comrades, as if trying to prove something; and when one of them did sleep with someone, inevitably there were terrible fights. They voted with each other no matter the subject; they teamed with each other unless forced apart. They shared secrets; they gave off a conspiring air. Their loyalty to each other clearly trumped their loyalty to their comrades and even their leader, and although they denied this, the way that they did—standing shoulder to shoulder and seeming to yell with one voice—undermined what they said. They had been Pauline's most scornful captors and had fought every privilege she'd won, but they were themselves constantly on probation. Though the leader had said that Pauline needed everyone's vote, in the end Juan and Yvonne were overruled, and Pauline was admitted.

She had hoped this would make it all easier for her, but instead things got worse. It had been her captivity that had left her so weak, but Juan and Yvonne still complained that she couldn't keep up. They nicknamed her Princess, and Publicity Princess, and they ridiculed the way that she talked. In a more serious vein, they raised the subject of whether, if the cadre were ambushed by pigs, she would fight to the death or surrender in terror; or if God forbid they were taken alive, she would probably rat them all out just to save her own skin. But meanwhile, they were making the tape on which Pauline declared, "I will stay with these comrades forever, because theirs is the only just battle there is." The tape had gone off like a bomb—the whole world had noticed. Graffiti on the streets, full-text reprints in major newspapers, establishmentarian shock. If the cadre had begun to look like a hapless and self-absorbed group of young people who had badly misplayed their first hand, and who had somehow wound up with less sympathy—even from the far Left—than the pigs they'd declared battle on, with the tape all that suddenly changed. Though Juan and Yvonne couldn't stand it, Pauline was their Sister, the ultimate prize.

After they'd robbed the bank, and then fled to Los Angeles, the long-deferred plan to divide the cadre into four groups of three—combat cells, that could act on their own or in concert with others—was finally implemented. Juan and Yvonne and Pauline learned that they'd be a cell. Pauline wanted to cry, but there was no private place where she could. Juan and Yvonne wouldn't even look at her. They argued with the leader as if she were not in the room, but he wouldn't be moved. The discord the three of them caused was a danger to everyone, and so the cell was a punishment for them, as well as a test.

Their first operation together was a basic supply run. A freak cold front had come in off the ocean, and several of their number had caught colds and wanted aspirin, and long-sleeved shirts, and socks. And the cadre had decided that they needed to be ready to leave the city, perhaps take to the woods, to a campground, and so the operation would also involve pricing camping equipment. Juan was given a couple hundred dollars in funds, in case the equipment seemed like a good buy. The house they had rented was in a run-down, mostly Black neighborhood, and the van they had bought and parked out at the curb looked like junk. So they were surprised, emerging gingerly from the house and moving quickly to the van, that they'd gotten a ticket. Juan snatched the ticket off the windshield, crumpled it up, and made to throw it onto the ground. "Don't," Yvonne said. He threw it onto the dashboard.

Juan drove carefully, Yvonne in the passenger seat, Pauline sitting in back, on the floor. All three of them were wearing "straight" clothes: Juan wore a button-up shirt and beige jacket and slacks and loafers, and his beard and moustache had been trimmed. His handgun was tucked in his waistband, concealed by the jacket. Yvonne wore a peasant blouse with pretty stitching at the neck, a full skirt, a small revolver in the pocket of her skirt. Pauline wore culottes and a sleeveless blouse with a Peter Pan collar, cat's-eye glasses, her thin brown hair, not yet cut and dyed, pulled into a braid. Her converted .30-caliber carbine lay on a doubled-up blanket in the back of the van, alongside a Browning semiautomatic rifle, a Colt .45 pistol, and a sawed-off 12-gauge Ithaca shotgun. If someone approached the van, Pauline would flip the end of the blanket over the weapons, to conceal them. If someone continued to approach the van, perhaps the weapons would be used. Juan and Yvonne wore sunglasses, which did not look strange; it was a bright L.A. day, flat blue sky overhead, although cool. A larger arsenal was stored out of sight in a duffel bag, should they, while out on their mission, be somehow cut off from their comrades and left on their own for a long interval. It was all precaution, but it was also a series of actions drummed into the body, a dance, rehearsed numerous times. If the music began this whole dance would unfold without effort. So far, this hadn't happened, but Pauline could envision it somehow, like tennis, like driving a car. Movement unspooling, instinctively. She'd been training a lot, though indoors, and with unloaded weapons, and always aware, though she tried not to be, that sooner or later a voice would say "ambush!" In life such surprises were real.

Juan stopped at a drugstore for the aspirin while Yvonne sat in the driver's seat with the engine running, and Pauline remained in back on the floor. Juan had already bought that day's *Los Angeles Times* and Pauline was reading. There was a bulletin about themselves in the A section. Also a long article on the candidates in an upcoming local election, and their efforts to court the Black vote. Juan came back and resumed the driver's seat and they tooled around for a while in search of a sporting-goods store where they could buy the sweatshirts and socks and maybe the camping equipment. The van swayed back and forth around curves, its floor rattled and jumped. She kept reading. The Vietnam War was over, but it would never be over. So long as . . . "Hey," Juan said. The van had stopped, though the engine still ran, humming and grumbling to itself. "Look alive, Sister. Yvonne's coming in with me to check out the equipment. Wait here."

"Okay," Pauline said. They were both being decent to her, and she felt gratified. But when they had gone she felt suddenly dizzy. She put the newspaper down and was struck by the sight of her hand. It wasn't visibly trembling, except for what the trembling of the van conveyed to it, but looking at it a wave of alarm passed through her. She broke out in a sweat. Crawling carefully to the front of the van, into the light shining down through the windshield, she peered out the driver's-side window. PACIFIC SPORTS—YOUR OUTDOOR STORE (SURFING-JOGGING-BIKING-HIKING-HUNTING-FISHING-CAMPING-SKIING . . . SKATEBOARDS). She had not remembered to look at her watch when Juan and Yvonne went inside. It was good to know how long things took, she was supposed to make this a habit. She knelt between the two bucket seats. Just a moment ago the back of the van had felt comforting to her, but now she was cringing from it. She rested her head on her arms, on the driver's seat, keeping out of the window but feeling its breeze. She wasn't thinking of anything that she could remember later, and that was the strange part—that her mind, so agitated for so long, was at that moment still.

She must have heard the shouting well before she recognized it had to do with her. If recognition ever came: She remembered terrible slowness and panic, like rising through water, at the end of her breath, toward the faraway surface. She looked out the window again and saw in front of the store Juan grappling with a man in a uniform, and Yvonne struggling to free herself from a second man, not uniformed. Juan, they later explained, had seen an ammunition bandolier in the hunting department he'd felt they should have, but had worried that purchasing it would raise eyebrows. He'd put the bandolier up his sleeve, but someone must have seen. Juan was shouting Pauline's name—not her real name, but her code name of that time, and then she understood that he had been shouting and shouting it. She threw herself bodily toward the blanket of guns, so that she badly scraped her knee on the floor of the van, and then, in a much less awkward movement that she remembered as a single arc, she swung her gun out the driver's-side window and sprayed a round in the direction of the store, not remembering to aim, extensively perforating SURFING-JOGGING-BIKING-HIKING-HUNTING-FISHING-CAMPING-SKIING . . . SKATEBOARDS. The uniformed man and the nonuniformed man shrieked, threw their hands up, belatedly threw themselves down. Pauline realized, perhaps from this display, that the uniformed man was not a cop but a security guard. This information emboldened her and she fired again, but the effort of the first time had already exhausted her shoulder; the gun kicked her painfully and its bullets flew wide, she could not have said where. Juan and Yvonne were running toward her and she felt overjoyed; perhaps she was merely relieved they were coming back to her, but against the landscape of her feelings at that time relief had the stature of ecstasy. This was when they lost Juan's handgun, seized by the security guard in the course of the struggle. The gun had been bought several years earlier, in Juan's actual name. Juan tore the door open and Pauline flew backwards, slid on her rump through the back of the van and almost hit the rear doors, as they sped from the lot.

"What took you so long!" Juan was screaming. "What took you so long!"

At an intersection a few blocks away they leaped from the van with their weapons, leaving the van running in the middle of the street, and commandeered a sedan from a terrified man at the stoplight. This was where they lost the parking ticket, which noted the address of the house at which the van had been parked—the address of their safe house. The ticket was forgotten on the dashboard. A few blocks farther and they left the sedan the same way, commandeered a second car from an equally terrified person Pauline couldn't even recall as a man or a woman. Procedure dictated that, if jammed up, they lie low and not try to return to the safe house for fear they might lead someone there. They didn't realize that they already had. Already, the handgun was on its way to the LAPD and very quickly its ownership would be traced and the city would realize that the cadre was there, and not in San Francisco. And the van that they'd left in the road was being combed through by cops, and the ticket uncrumpled.

They swiped a third car, left its owner in the shade of an overpass. By now they were a long way from where they had started. They got another newspaper, scanned its car ads, bought within the hour and with two hundred fifty dollars cash another old van from a genial teenager. Now several hours had passed since the sporting-goods store. They drove in their new old van farther and farther, looking for a safe-seeming motel, and it was the experience of sitting in this van, so much like the other one, that reminded Juan of the ticket. "Fuck," he said. "Where's that ticket?"

"You threw it away," Yvonne said, and in all the confusion she might have believed this. Pauline hadn't seen the transaction, had never even seen the ticket, having stayed inside the house that morning until the van was all ready to go. She didn't yet understand the debate.

"You told me not to," Juan said. "I put it up on the dashboard."

"You did not," Yvonne said. "I don't think so."

"Even if I did, it wouldn't have the address on it, would it? Do the pigs put addresses on tickets?"

"Maybe we should go back to the house."

"Absolute no, the Code says—"

It was too late by then, anyway.

The sun sank, spread the shadows of the billboards and the buildings and the telephone poles and their van across miles of pavement, diffused through the particled air and turned everything orange. They chose a motel near the roar of the freeway. Inside they turned on the TV, and there, on TV, saw their safe house: encircled by barricades, flashing police cars, helmeted armed policemen, crawling snipers, a mob of reporters with hair whipped upright by the wind from the low helicopters. The broadcast was live. Outside their windows, the sun set. Over their safe house, the sun set, and klieg lights came on to illumine the scene for the cameras. How could she describe what they'd felt? Gasping and weeping in that room, pillows held to their faces? They couldn't make telltale noise. Through the thin walls to their right, they were sure, they heard their comrades' deaths doubled by the next room's TV. Pauline locked herself in the bathroom and vomited so violently that she brought up blood. There wasn't anything else in her stomach.

Late that night they agreed to make Juan their new leader. There hadn't been dispute, or even thoughts of dispute. Pauline had only been grateful, to Juan for sifting ashes of disaster in search of some relic of how life had been. To Yvonne, for having banged on the door of the bathroom until Pauline let her in, and let her hold her in her arms. Beneath their stunned grief a purpose had begun to take form, and though it was only to preserve themselves and each other, it had a hardness to it against which all their previous purposes, so multiple and complicated and subject to argument, crumbled. At last they tried to sleep, on the sour-smelling mattress that filled up their room like a huge slice of moldering bread. Curled on her side with eyes open, Pauline saw the imperfect darkness, dyed pink by the light leaking in through the drapes. Eyes closed, she saw fire, and death. Behind her in the bed there was movement. With underwater slowness, Yvonne and Juan tried to make love. Then Yvonne reached an arm out, across the wide bed. "Sister," she whispered. "You can make love with us if you want to." They were solemnly bound—by having survived, by being pursued, and by something that might be called blood. They were a family now.

It was a feeling that sustained them through days of crisis—or perhaps crisis had sustained the feeling. The night they'd arrived at the farmhouse with Carol, before Jenny was there, they had done their security tour of the house, and then they'd carried the second twin bed from the upstairs bedroom to the downstairs, which had a double. Pauline had been relieved that it went without saying that they'd all share a room, because by now weeks had passed, an eon, since that night. There had been so many different disruptions, first having to sleep in a car, and then vagabond life in a park, then their tense time with Sandy and Tom. Separate trips crossing the country, to Frazer and Carol's Manhattan apartment. And Pauline supposed it was all disruption, except for that long night when grief married them—yet that night was the island. She'd found solace there that now seemed to be lying in wait, and they all only needed the chance to reach for it again.

It lasted a little while longer, but it was already ebbing. That first night at the farm their anxiety and anticipation had left them exhausted, and Juan and Yvonne fell asleep on the high double bed before Frazer arrived. Pauline had been left in the lumpy twin bed, wide awake, feeling suddenly hollow. A few times in those first early days, especially while they were writing the eulogy tape, it had happened again. Never promised or planned; but once they were all in the bedroom alone, Juan might hug her a long time, then slowly undress her. Or Yvonne would smile sleepily up from the covers and say, "Help us warm up this bed." She'd done things she'd never done in her life, never known you could do. With Yvonne, while Juan watched them or held them, or with Juan inside her while she hungrily sucked Yvonne's breast. Something in her, whether it had been born during her captivity, or had resided in her all along, seemed to have been waiting for this, for the mute urgent pleasure that wasn't part of any story she knew, and by day left no traces. And then day extended to night, and the chapter was over. No one ever spoke about it. Juan and Yvonne were as always, conjoined, although no longer cruel to her. Their triumvirate, having begun from the blackest hostilities and passed all the way to the opposite thing, was now just an everyday union with quarrels, and an every night sleeping arrangement of three persons, one room, and two beds. Some nights Pauline woke in her bed and heard them trying to make love, without making noise.

Jenny had arrived in the midst of these embers—absurdly built up beforehand, she now learned, because Frazer told grandiose tales about her. And threatening, with her history of exploits that Juan found impressive. And so self-sufficient, with her faraway world that she wrote to, and her lover in prison, her journal. She'd drive off in the loud little car, her neat cap of black hair flying back, her huge sunglasses on—she was always departing. You sensed any time she might just leave for good, an idea Pauline hated, and brooded upon. There was, Pauline supposed, a submerged recognition: once Pauline had had her own car, and she'd driven around with her long clean hair flying behind and her sunglasses on. But mostly she tried not to think of the past. Mostly she thought of how Jenny had altered the present. Pauline's island existence with Juan and Yvonne had become sharply lonely for her. At first Jenny just made it worse, but soon Pauline realized, with confusion and uncertain pleasure, that Jenny liked her, perhaps even preferred her. And when Jenny resisted their robbery plan, Pauline suddenly saw how a very small lie could be good for them all, in the end. Juan would be happy, which would make Yvonne happy, and they'd both be surprised and impressed with Pauline. And once the robbery proved the resounding success Juan had said it would be, even Jenny would see it was better to stay with the cadre, than be cast out alone.

IN INDIANA the thick Eastern carpet of cities and roadways and towns had at last grown threadbare. The shorn rows of harvested corn turned past them like great spokes. After the sun set they drove through profound country darkness for hours, afraid they'd be driving all night, when they finally found a motel, spied its lone neon twinkle far off like a bead lost from some cosmic necklace.

The next day at dawn that distinction was lost. Jenny eased their door open a crack and saw they were camped at a handful of weatherworn boxes the same shade as the gray country road, the gray dirt and the lightless gray sky. In the lot there was one other car that was still misted over with night condensation. Outside the office the neon sign buzzed. She slipped out and loaded the file and duffel back into the trunk, finally started the car after giving herself courage with the thought that in the dreary Indiana dawn it would sound no more foreign than rainfall or crows. A few minutes later, when the car was warmed up, Pauline cracked the door and through the mist-streaked windshield Jenny nodded to her. Pauline pulled the door shut and with rapid steps came to the car and got in and they drove away swiftly, two temperate travelers resuming their journey at dawn.

They were driving a desolate stretch in Missouri in a blinding rainstorm when the car died on them. They'd pulled onto the shoulder to study their atlas, afraid they were lost, and then the engine wouldn't restart. "Okay," Pauline said, lighting a cigarette with a trembling hand. "Okay, let's just think. Try to think." She cracked her window to let the smoke out and a slice of hard rain shot sideways through the crack and got them both instantly wet, and snuffed the cigarette out. Pauline quickly rolled up the window again. They turned on the hazards, afraid they'd be hit from behind; and then saw no one for half an hour, in either direction, until a huge truck went rumbling past, smacking their car with a wall of water. Water was standing on the road now, perhaps as much as a foot deep, and they both screamed when the truck's force struck them; they felt that all that mattered was the integrity of their car, that it remain watertight and protective. Pauline's newly yellow hair stuck like paint to her cheek. "We're going to be okay," she said. "Aren't we?" "Yes," Jenny kept repeating. The bright red taillights of the truck, the only parts of it they'd clearly seen, had continued away, but had not disappeared. Jenny squinted through the swift ropes of water; tried the ignition again; tried the wipers. The lights seemed to be frozen just short of the point at which they should have vanished. She couldn't judge motion or distance; perhaps the truck had slowed down to a crawl, so that its receding was strangely prolonged. Now Pauline saw what she saw, and they both grew silent, their silence outlined by the deafening noise of the rain. The lights winked at them, like twin planets above the horizon. And then from out of the deluge a lone figure came toward them, one arm up to shield his face. "Oh my God," Pauline said.

Jenny met the truck driver halfway and stood shouting with him, immediately as wet as if she'd been submerged. She felt her T-shirt sucking against her flesh, knew her bra and breasts clearly showed through it. Her blue jeans were so heavy with water they were pulling themselves off her hips. None of this seemed to matter at all. Her identity, Pauline's, the consequences if they were discovered; these had seemed to be crises, but the elements swept them away. She felt simplified. They were alive, after all! She shouted to the man that she thought it was the battery, he gestured for her to follow him to his truck. He would back up, and give her a jump. But when they came near the truck they stopped short, while the rain lashed their bodies. Everything seemed illusory—the taillights remaining when they should have vanished, the man's figure resolving from out of the rain, and now the truck tilting sharply sideways, because the nine wheels on its passenger side were sunk axle-deep in the mud. The driver's-side door of the cab opened and a woman leaned out, waving frantically. "It's tipping!" she cried. She came out on the cab's booster step and jumped up and down, as if this could counter the tilt, and Jenny saw she was massively pregnant. The rain had made the driver misjudge the width of the shoulder, and though the driver's-side wheels were parked on it, the other side's had been parked on the dirt that sloped down from the grade of the road. The weight of the truck had made the wheels sink in, and now this tilt and the tilt of the slope added up were enough to tip the giant truck over.

The man gave a cry—of shock, and disappointment in himself—and without another word ran back to the cab and leaped in. She ran back to their car. "Something happened," she gasped to Pauline, while Pauline dug around for a towel. They thought that the truck would extract itself soon, and come driving back toward them, but its red taillights only wavered slightly through the downpour. Steam fogged their windows, although they didn't feel warm; drenched and clammy, Jenny hugged herself tightly. "I don't think he's coming," Pauline whispered.

"I'm sure he will when he's out of the ditch."

"What if he doesn't get out?"

"He will. He's a trucker. They know how to deal with these things."

"But what if . . . ?" Pauline said.

Then they were silent, adding cigarette smoke to the steam, as the rain drummed on them. The panic of being confined could be a strange, lazy one. Once confinement was truly confirmed they conserved energy. They sat, feeling blank. Jenny tried to get out of her jeans but it was too difficult. Not wanting to flood her blank unfeeling core with frustration she put off retrying the engine as long as she could. Then she had to; she turned the key and stamped the gas while Pauline screwed her eyes shut and balled up her fists. Nothing. "Dammit!" yelled Jenny. Out of nowhere a siren screamed, drowning her voice, and then they saw red lights trailing like comets through their sluicing windshield, as a police car sped by.

"Jenny!" Pauline said. Another siren screamed past; the rain was so loud they weren't hearing the sirens until they were practically just alongside. They turned around to look through the rear windshield and saw the procession of lights streaming forth from the gloom. Each siren screamed as it passed them, so that they could not even hear what they screamed at each other; Pauline seemed to be saying, "Oh God no! Oh God!" while Jenny thought she heard herself say, "It's okay!" They seized frantic hold of each other. Jenny thought, Where would we go? Bursting out of the car to be mired in the flooded green fields? Shots would catch them a last time and lift them up strangely, like hooks, before knocking them down. The last car streaked past and they saw all the cars congregating on the stretch of roadway near the truck, which now seemed incidental, like a piece of wreckage that had been abandoned a long time ago. "Jenny," Pauline said, and her voice now was somber and urgent. "If they don't kill us I swear I won't tell them a thing about you."

"They won't kill us!"

"No, listen to me!" Pauline didn't want reassurance; she squeezed Jenny's hand furiously. She was seized by a moment of courage and she meant to use it, before it dwindled away. "I'll never tell *anyone* you were with us. I'll never tell that you drove the switch car. I'll tell them I met you this morning, I was hitching and you picked me up—"

"I know that. I know you wouldn't sell me out, I *know* that—"

"You didn't have to," Pauline said, and now courage left her and she started to cry. "You didn't have to stay with me . . ."

One of the cars freed itself from the group and began moving toward them. It was driving backward. It rolled a short distance and then the driver's door opened and an orange cone emerged and was planted at the center of the road. The door shut and the car rolled backwards perhaps another twenty yards and then the door opened again and another orange cone was expelled. She and Pauline clung to each other in silence, and without pause the car rolled past their car and left another orange cone in the road.

When orange cones stretched a fairly long way, cutting off the right lane from the left, the car resumed forward movement and passed them again with no more interest than it had shown the first time. A few minutes later they heard a new siren, and when they looked back a gigantic machine was approaching, yellow and urgent with lights and somewhat like a crane grafted onto a train car. It rumbled past, trailed by one more police car, and they felt the road tremble beneath them.

A strange calm had begun to descend, although it had little to do with their understanding, finally, that the commotion was not about them. Their capture, if it occurred, would be incidental to the rescue of the truck, but that made it no less catastrophic. And yet Jenny felt something like certainty—not certainty born of the moment, but certainty that came from without and gave the moment its meaning. Finally the rain had begun to subside; it was simply rain now, not an opaque gray torrent. The scene ahead of them came into focus, the police cruisers at angles all over the road, the huge crane, and the truck, the list of which had gotten worse. Men were standing around in long ponchos and wide-brimmed black hats. Jenny thought she caught a glimpse of the trucker, in his heavy plaid workshirt.

One of the troopers was walking toward them, and their calm, as if it consisted of a cloud of very sensitive insects, rose away slightly but still hovered nearby. The trooper came straight to the driver's-side window and rapped sharply on it. Jenny rolled down the window.

"You the girls who caused all this trouble?" Water streamed off the edge of his hat.

"Yes, sir," Jenny said.

"Leave your names and addresses, we'll send you the bill." He straightened again and peered off at the roil of lights. There had been nothing gallant about the remark; he was clearly disgusted. The huge crane had started its effort: It strained forward with the shrieking noise of a very large unoiled hinge. The towline caught and the truck seemed to rise very slightly and tremble before falling back. Mud flew up at the impact. "For Christ's sake," said the trooper, glancing with distaste at Jenny again. "Tow truck's coming for you. It'll take you to town." With that he strode back toward the action.

The truck was finally pulled from the mud and discovered to have two bent axles. The crane hauled it away. Then the tow truck came for them like a little tugboat through chaotic waters, and they sailed along with their heads tilted back and their knees in the air, as if Dolly's car were being launched into space. At the gas station Pauline hid in the bathroom. The station had a combination diner and convenience store attached, and walking inside Jenny heard the trucker before she saw him, hanging on to the corner pay phone as if to a strap on a lurching subway. "Please!" he said. "I can't pay for it out of my pay, you can't make me do that!" The pregnant woman was sitting in a booth nearby, crying. When she saw Jenny she sat up suddenly.

"You," the woman said, her eyes narrowing. "You!"

Back outside the car had been jumped. "How much?" Jenny said breathlessly.

The mechanics were all overcome by the hilariousness of events. "Oh, we ought to pay *you*. That's some show. 'What's a nine-wheeler, boss?' 'An eighteen-wheeler driven by somebody stupid.' Hey, let it charge," they scolded, when she slammed the hood shut.

"I'll charge it while driving. I'm late."

"Late for what? Come on, China doll. Where'd the blond go?"

She pulled around to the side of the building where the bathroom door was, and banged on it. "Pauline," she hissed. No one answered. "It's *me*," Jenny said. The door opened a crack and one eye, large and hazel, peered out.

"Are we okay?" Pauline asked.

The rain had finally stopped and she realized how loud it had been. In the quiet she thought she could hear, from the far side of the wall, the mechanics still laughing, from yet farther within the truck driver still pleading his case, the pregnant woman still crying. A flock of crows cawed overhead. "We're okay," she said.

• • •

SOMETIMES fear of capture, like fear of death, seems less and less possible to maintain the more real it becomes. A low-grade fear will weigh on the heart constantly. But sublime, speechless fear—it can bear down so hard you go bouncing away like a small rubber ball. For Pauline it had been that way, after her kidnapping. Her fear of death had been so huge, she told Jenny, her brain just gave up on the job. They'd advised that she not try to struggle, or talk, or do anything "stupid," and this advice, once she surrendered to it, had revealed itself as applying to everything. There had been something comforting in the idea that the best thing she might do for herself was to opt out completely. Give up the pain of pride injured, the torment of thwarted desires. Give up all the worries of what one should do and not do to be decent in life. She felt that for her, heedless childhood had lasted somewhat longer than it did for most people, and she recognized that this had to do with her family's wealth. Perhaps that was the reason her young adult life had been so overwhelming and painful. She didn't want Jenny to think she was saying it mattered, but there had been some conflicts involving her parents and her. Conflicts that seemed life-destroying, because back then the scope of her life had been small. She had disappointed them, and this failure had inspired her to further disappoint them. She had painted herself into corners. There had been inappropriate men. The boarding-school expulsions. And always, warfare over money. Then the kidnapping came, and that world, which had seemed to enclose her, shrank down to a globe that she couldn't be bothered to grasp. Her hand was too weak; she let go; it rolled off and was lost. Captivity in a way had released her, into an elemental world in which recollection of a few basic facts, like her name and birthday, were great triumphs. The old code of misstep and blame was wiped out, made absurd. It would not be her fault if she'd chosen the wrong boy to love or the wrong college subject to study. It would not be her fault if she died. It was a frame of mind needing extreme disconnection, but this she achieved, as if sinking through fathoms of ocean and at last touching down on the silty black floor.

But that extreme, like extreme fear, was also short-lived. Perhaps she only touched down before rising again. Although she was tied up alone in a closet, it took hands to tie her, and she started to notice these stringent inspections. Several would come and look in on her; someone would adjust her blindfold, maybe yank a few times on her ropes. Not even the notion of imminent murder can leach contact of all of its charge. She could hear them, as well. Increasingly, they argued over how they might salvage her soul for their cause. It wasn't in their nature, they felt, to commit a kidnapping purely for money. Wasn't it ironic that their captive, while living among revolutionaries, enjoyed none of the obvious benefits? She was as ignorant of the ills of capitalism and racism as she'd been on the day they kidnapped her. That she might depart from them as much a bourgeois as when she had arrived seemed to make them feel, in the sameness of results, an unwelcome kinship to the social order they opposed, and soon the negative reluctance to resemble the enemy was the positive yen to affect a conversion. They had not anticipated the proselytizing fervor that would overtake them, but it simply felt right—to expound things to her through the locked closet door, when the day's work was done. She would surface from unconsciousness to the sound of someone dropping down on the floor just outside, striking a match and inhaling, leaning back comfortably on the door frame. Some read aloud, from Fanon or Debray. "Hi, I'm gonna finish that chapter I started last time. I hope you're awake, because this is the really good part." Some just rambled about their own lives, about parents they hated or longed to explain themselves to, about things they had done. All spoke of joy at embracing a cause that was just and that made it all clear. She would sniff at the smoke eagerly as it leaked to her under the door. She would try to link voices with names. It was inevitable she'd come to know them, far better than they would know her. At the start she had listened as corpses might listen, without interest or feeling, but inevitably this had changed.

And she could hear them doing ego reconstruction, though she hadn't yet known what it was, let alone known all the things she would learn when she did it herself: that it was a game for a group and a discipline testing the self; that it was combat with words and also destructive and passionate love. (Though they never said this; they would say "kill the ego" or "unified well-oiled machine.") The game drew on reservoirs of inner strength and self-knowledge but didn't deplete them: it filled them as nothing else will. It wasn't something you did on your own. In principle, it should have been possible with any group of two or larger, but two seemed like a fight and even three was still awkward and small. Large groups worked the best, to absorb the shockwaves and at the same time to startle with their own innate smallness. The knot tightened, things shrank and grew sweaty and frightening. Even discord, in the large-group context, increased intimacy. Everyone rose together to cure it, or else they took sides and waged civil wars. But alliances constantly shifted, and so you were whispering rekindled love even as your heart broke due to somebody else. There was a sense of singularity, of experiencing something courageous and rare that most people would seek to avoid. It was painful. It was like drugs—no matter how awful an episode was, you still wanted to do it again. You didn't count up the few times you'd felt loved with the numerous times you'd felt hated. There were eleven of them; not a huge number, but not at all small. Eleven meant no one was ever alone; there were always three or four people asleep in the same room, so near that to snore was to lay yourself bare to them all, and to make love with one was to make love with all in a way. Desire might take root in the uninvolved comrade who acted as if she were sleeping. Eleven also meant that your turn at the game didn't come every session and might not even come once a week. Sessions were sporadic, of varying lengths, ended peacefully and formally according to some preordained schedule or erupted into shouting disarray. The person whose turn that it was—and there was always dispute about this—stood at the center of a circle of everyone else, except for the person who'd most recently gone, who would serve as the "clock." The clock would hold the cadre's alarm clock and watch the second hand closely, and like a sports referee point somewhere in the circle at random, to show the speaker the person with whom they should start. The speaker would turn to that person. Not yet having seen any of this, Pauline then would hear something like:

"*Go.*"

"I still feel you're judgmental of me. The other day, when I told you about how I used to put broken glass into our neighbor's yard? Because my parents didn't like them, and I was just a little kid. I just wanted to help. But you acted like that was a sign I was some sort of Nazi—"

"*Switch.*"

". . . I'm glad you told me what's wrong with my stance when I hold a shotgun. A lot of the other comrades think you just like to strut your stuff all the time and show off, but I—"

"*Who* thinks I like to show off?"

"No interrupting: Juan loses a turn. Speaker, *switch.*"

She learned that for some reason, they always went clockwise. That most everyone fidgeted badly—sat with legs crossed, then leaned on something, then pulled knees up to chin, then did not. Tried to assume the blank face of judgment even while being judged. Some couldn't make eye contact, some glared confrontationally, some blushed beet-red—for her all the silent aspects of the drama, when she finally saw them, had been such a surprise, an unveiling. She had had trouble enough visualizing the large-scale arrangement. She knew there were swift recitations of words, most of which she could never make out, though she felt their emotional freight. She had known there were orders from what even she understood were the sidelines. She had not known that these were the times that they truly forgot her—she believed she was always forgotten, longed for a voice at the door even if it was cruel. But at these times, she forgot herself too. She'd inch a little more against the door, feel the outside air touch her slightly through the crack if the thing that they used to block it—just a towel, it turned out—wasn't perfectly pushed into place. Her cheek pressed flat to the gritty wood floor by what felt like a great weight, her skull. Her heart would sound less laboriously, less as if it were going to stop. Its noise might even fade for a while. She sensed the charge in the air at those times. One day, when the ritual ended in shouts and commotion, a door slammed open and shut, and then open and shut again, and suddenly there were two people in the space outside her door, the space that separated the box where she lay from the void where the rest of them were. "I *miss* you," a girl wept, whispering. And in the closet the captive had listened, cheek studded with grit, her hands bound at her back, her closed eyes underneath their blindfold leaking tears of some larger emotion, some transcending form of deliverance.

Sometimes in their motel rooms at night—in South Bend, or Cheyenne, all the places they were—Jenny thought of the girl in the closet, curled up in the dark. On her side? Sitting up, with arms hugging her knees? She would open the door to the closet, stare at the small square of dirty shag carpet, the handful of wire coathangers. A string leading up to a bulb; they would have looped the string out of reach, perhaps cut it off for good measure; or maybe they just took out the bulb and left the string hanging there in the dark, to brush the girl's cheek if she managed to get on her feet. If, pouring sweat from the effort, she braced herself on the wall and inched up like a plant seeking light, though her limbs were all bound, and tilted her blindfolded head and with shock felt the string's whispered touch to her cheek.

What are you looking at? Pauline would say, glancing over her shoulder.

She would think of the girl, as if the girl wasn't Pauline at all but a ghost who eavesdropped while they talked. Curled up on her side; passing in and out of a black dreamless sleep. Waking to hear a boy's voice reading to her, the boy sitting outside on the carpet, cross-legged, intent, leaning close to ensure she could hear. Like her he's a little bit younger than everyone else. He has a clear boyish voice, almost piping; perhaps a slight rising inflection, as if sometimes unsure. The kind of voice she could fall in love with. She clings to that voice, discards the words, doesn't even attempt to perceive them. They're words that she might have once easily grasped, words she very possibly skimmed at some point in high school, neatly responded to in Comprehension Questions, then forgot. Now she lies on her side though it hurts for some reason; her hip seems to jab at her flesh like a blade. Her knees fail when they come to take her to the toilet, so they're practically carrying her; they say, "Try to stiffen your arms by your sides so we can lift by your elbows. It's less hard on your shoulder." She tries to comply. The other day, doing this trip to the toilet, they had dislocated her shoulder by accident. It had clearly frightened them, to have her right arm pop out of its socket and hang loose in its thin sack of skin. Their hands had flown away from her; her own screams of pain were almost drowned out by their cries of alarm. She had slammed the shoulder back together herself, a surge of pure instinct and adrenaline after which she'd passed out. She'd done it once before; she had dislocated that shoulder when she was fifteen, climbing on the rocks of a small waterfall with her sisters at their mountain estate in McCloud. She'd lost her footing on the slick rocks, grabbed the rock face in front of her, slipped anyway, and not let go of the rock face in time. As she'd fallen her weight yanked the arm from its socket. Splashing into the water she'd wrenched it back in with her good hand, the right response, born of sheer panic. Downstream her sisters had laughed, not realizing. She'd floated, staring sightlessly up at the pines, the chill water dulling the intense yet now manageable pain. Her heart racing. When her sisters came swimming back toward her she'd smiled and said nothing. She'd never said a word to her parents. Even when she couldn't serve at tennis for months, when her arm froze while raising the racquet, she'd keep silent, streams of sweat rolling down her sides, beneath her outfit, from the pain. Each time she tried the arm rose perhaps a centimeter higher than the previous time before ceasing in spite of all effort, but this incremental progress wasn't noticeable to an onlooker. Her father would yell with impatience. "What's the matter with you? What'd you do with that good serve I taught you?"

Why had she stubbornly kept it a private ordeal? Perhaps because it had been her first real encounter with the limits of her body, and so with the notion of death. This wasn't to inflate its importance. But it had shaken her, and confirmed her strong sense of aloneness; and when her captors, her comrades, accidentally did it again, she hadn't told them about the old injury. Not to gain advantage with them, although it had done that, she realized later; they had held council and decided it was imperative she regain her strength. And with that decision, soon enough, had come the decision to take off her blindfold. "Now you've seen us," the one named Evan said, and she'd wondered if this was a warning, *Now you've seen us, and there's no turning back*, but she hadn't seen them. All of them had been shimmery blotches of color. Her eyes had been so compromised from disuse that she'd feared she was blind. She hadn't told them that, either. Like the shoulder, it was a terror too huge to describe. Instead she stared hard, making out individual figures, growing nauseous from effort, and then she named them—she asked that they not tell their names, just say something to her. "Hi," began a blur, and then giggled uneasily. "You're A______," she'd said, and they'd all been amazed. She'd named every one of them from just a word or two spoken, and as she had little lights of kinship had sprung up. She knew it sounded strange, but that was how it had been. In her time in the closet she'd learned all their voices.

And possibly fallen a little in love. Not because they were the comrades she'd sought before knowing quite what she was seeking. Not because they had words for the frightening world, lists of reasons and crucial solutions, *power disjunctions* and *racial disease* and *the cure for materialism*. Not because they were her yet *not* her, had transcended and so gave her hope. Just because she was nineteen years old, and might have fallen in love with any collection of beings devoted to lofty ideals. She might have fallen in love harvesting sugarcane in Cuba, or registering voters in Mississippi, or just handing out flyers on the safety of her school's Great Lawn, but she hadn't even done that—it had never come naturally to her. Like almost anyone of her age living in the place and the time that she did, and lacking strident beliefs of some kind, she felt called upon vaguely to Do Something; but whether she felt more called upon, or less able to answer, by virtue of whose daughter she was, she couldn't have said. She only knew that her name was a problem to her. She had never been buoyed by it, like her sisters. She had never had the audacity to define herself against it. She'd felt too conspicuous, too obscurely guilty. When one night she had opened the door to her off-campus college apartment—a modest affair by her mother's standards, although still very large and well-appointed and tasteful for the average freshman—and been seized by masked gunmen, beneath her unspeakable terror she had felt in some way that her debt had come due.

The day the blindfold came off was humid and warm, perhaps the middle of March. For the first time in more than a month she heard street noise, and smelled the damp earth. They'd opened a window to air the place out and secured the curtain with thumbtacks at the edges so it wouldn't blow open. Though she'd been in no condition to walk, let alone try to climb out a window, they still cuffed her wrist to a couch. "Am I in America?" she asked. They said yes. "Am I in California?" This they wouldn't confirm. It was several more weeks before she learned with amazement that she was still in San Francisco, just a few miles from her childhood home, where her parents were making their daily statements to reporters. She was in an apartment that faced the Panhandle—that was the wonderful scent of damp earth.

AFTER THEY HAVE made a spectacle of themselves before the full force of the Missouri state troopers they drive east again on new roads, because they'd been driving west; they imagine the realization dawning on those men in the big hats and ponchos. Perhaps their faces have developed in those men's minds like photographs in a darkroom—and not stopping there bloomed from their hats. They imagine the belated all-points bulletin. Before this, they've imagined it sprouting from Dolly: Dolly's brain is somewhat dry from age, but still fertile. Perhaps Dolly hadn't recognized Pauline immediately, but the seed had been dropped. Later that week, or that very same day, Dolly would have settled herself in her chair for the night's date with Walter Cronkite. Walter shows her a picture, her brain blooms, she picks up the phone. The reward for Pauline is a good deal more than the money she got for the car. And so Jenny and Pauline drive west, as the tendrils unfurl behind them; then they drive east, as the state troopers come to awareness; then they turn north, because they've gone too far east—all this time, nothing happens. They make a big, gradual circle, and start traveling west once again.

Somewhere west of the Mississippi the whole continent seems to tilt slightly; they feel themselves climbing gently to a vague culmination. Dolly's car starts overheating but Jenny knows how to deal with this. "It just has to cool down. We'll be fine," she says. Pauline smokes enough cigarettes to encircle the spot where they're parked. On one of these days they see four-foot-tall sandhill cranes rising droopingly out of a field. On another—in Colorado? Wyoming?—they see pelicans turning and turning above them with unlikely grace, as if performing a water ballet. What are those birds *doing* here? They're nowhere near the ocean! Later in her life Jenny will accidentally come across, in some oddment of casual reading, the information that white pelicans migrate from the far North to the Mexican coast through the corridor of the Great Plains. She won't understand, for a moment, why this trivia startles her so, makes her heart hurt. Now the pelicans simply are magic. It makes her and Pauline strangely happy to see them out here, ocean birds in the great landlocked vastness. They wait for the car to cool off. All they hear is its light *tick tick tick* and the wind.

One day, the radiator cap bursts off completely, releasing white billows of steam. Later, at a junkyard that seems to extend halfway up the damp slope of a boulder-strewn mountain, Jenny picks her way between corpses of cars with a taciturn man. He says he can find a new cap. The ragged gray clouds seem just out of their reach; then the miles of dead cars. Nothing else, not a house or a power line on the horizon, not a lone working car on the road. They might be in Wales at the beginning of time. The man harvests a few caps he thinks ought to fit and they turn and head back toward the car. Pauline is there, with her arms crossed against the damp cold, her bright, brittle hair like a blown dandelion. The man props up the hood and asks where Jenny's from. She says, randomly, "Massachusetts."

"I meant originally."

She knows it's no use to tell him she was born in this country. "Japan," she says. This satisfies him.

"How about you," he says to Pauline. Pauline's hair is whipped off her face by the wind. She's not wearing a hat. It's too gray for sunglasses.

Pauline says, "Massachusetts."

The man doesn't seem very interested in these answers. He's testing the caps, one by one, to see which is most snug. "Heading out to the Coast," he infers, though they haven't said this. "All the kids want to live there. Ah—that's the one." He gives the cap a last tightening turn and straightens, stretching his back. "You remind me of someone," he tells Pauline abruptly.

Pauline looks at him, startled.

"I don't suppose you were ever in Laramie."

"No," she says.

"Never went to the school there?"

"No."

"You an actress or something?"

"No."

"It's funny. I feel like I've seen you on TV."

Here we are, Jenny thinks, all alone in a graveyard of cars, at the top of the world. The dark sky scuds over their heads. The damp wind smells like rain. In this light Pauline's eyes aren't at all green but gray. Pauline looks at her. Jenny looks back. They hang there, on a thread. "You must look like some actress," the man decides, shrugging. "Just give me a buck," he tells Jenny.

And then they try to get over the Rockies and the car overheats once again. They're transfixed by the glowing orange light on the dashboard, the sign of the car's great distress. Pauline manages to tear her eyes off it, examines their atlas. "There's a little town a few miles away. Do you think we can make it?" They crawl, twenty miles an hour, trailing a plume like a steam locomotive, and reach a shuttered gas station on one side and a roadhouse on the other, perhaps the first hint of the town. But the car gives out here. They come to rest by the gas station's pump in the gathering dusk. Their effusion of white steam takes on an unearthly blue tint. The roadhouse is a low, sagging, tar-papered building, barely distinct from the dark foothills rising behind and the darkening sky, but it has a few neon beer signs for BUDWEISER and COORS and these make it seem studded with jewels. They've turned off the engine, extinguished their own baleful orange light and the rest of the lights on the dashboard. They gaze across the road at the red and blue letters, the warm amber mug with its glowing white foam. They can faintly hear music. Five trucks and a car are pulled up. Now Jenny knows that there isn't a town. Only this: a named gathering point, equidistant from lone habitations.

She looks at Pauline. Pauline looks at her. Neither of them seems to put forth the idea; consensus is already there. Pauline fluffs her blond curls—they've bought plastic curlers, and they set Pauline's hair every night. "Are my freckles smeared?" Pauline asks her. Jenny turns on the dome light and checks.

"No," she says.

They get out of the car, lock the doors, cross the dark silent road.

Later she remembered the sensation of the room's attention swinging toward them as a physical thing on her skin: a wave striking, cresting, retreating to watch from afar. There had been a pool table lit up by a low-hanging lamp and together they'd comprised a distinct bell-shaped region of light, into which people dipped with pool cues, out of which they receded again. Beyond, a few neglected tables and a long bar holding up several men who had turned to look toward them. There could not have been more than twelve people in that dim little room, the ceiling of which was so low she could have stood on tiptoes and put her palm flat against it, but there was still the sense of entering a space that had been completely colonized long ago, and in which they were glaring intruders. Without seeing anyone clearly—her vision seemed shrunk to a point—she somehow sensed, in a way she was starting to think was specific to women, the presence of a few other women. In this sort of situation other women always radiated their own distinct coldness, and yet even in very small numbers they could alter the charge of a mostly male room. Perhaps she was only reflecting on how much her concerns in these settings had changed. Perhaps she wasn't having these reflections at all. The jukebox was loud, and though the room's attention had swung palpably—curiously, coldly, assessingly, all these ways intermixed—toward them as they opened the door, still no one had given up their competition with the music to be heard by each other, and so the two forms of human expression, attention and speech, had seemed to come unhooked from each other a moment, as everyone stared as one person and yet with their voices maintained their indifference. She and Pauline must have been visibly intimidated as they slowly approached the long bar, but they got there, and Jenny felt immediately better as she climbed on a stool, as if she'd pulled a door shut at her back. Pauline climbed on a stool beside her. They didn't look at each other; they wouldn't want to appear to be so cowed as to need to hold council. The bartender—barrel-shaped, middle-aged, in a plaid workshirt—came toward them with the bartender's expression of explicitly withholding his judgment, and asked what they wanted. Jenny asked for a beer and Pauline echoed her, though she knew now that Pauline didn't really like beer—she found it too bitter and fizzy. But Pauline accepted the beer very coolly, as if she'd accepted beers all up and down the great country and thought this one was handed to her in an average way. Jenny paid the man and when he'd turned away to the cash register she unostentatiously laid down an extra dollar. "Thanks," the man said when he noticed it. He picked it up and tucked it into a large glass carafe that held a loose filling of bills and spare change.

Going into tough bars with William had been a part of what she thought of as the testing period of their love affair, though she supposed you could also have termed it a hazing. He hadn't begun to include her in his political activities until she'd proved she was really *the* woman—the woman who could swagger down barrio streets at his side, as if they'd been born there. The woman who could drink beer, as he did, in bars where students were met with contempt, if not violence. William had possessed a sort of reverse entitlement, it occurred to her now—he had seemed to assume that because he dignified them with his efforts, he deserved a particularly hearty reception in the realms of the poor and the marginalized. Not that this bar was anything like those had been. Two thirds of the way through her beer she knew her senses had calmed and her perceptions were more accurate. The bar was not a small dark arena in which people would joust with each other. She and Pauline had been given the label of traveler by all of these people; their appearance was something infrequent, but far from amazingly rare. The bartender was at the far end of the bar, one foot propped up, talking to people. "Why'd you get beer?" she asked Pauline.

"I like it," Pauline said. She was drinking the beer in quick grimacing sips, as if it were medicine.

"You do not," Jenny said.

The bartender came down to them. "Another?" he asked.

"I'll take a whiskey," Pauline said.

"Rocks?"

"Neat. With a little splash of water." She straightened up, watching. "No, a little more. That's good."

"Fancy," said Jenny when the bartender had left them again.

"Shut up," said Pauline.

"I'm just glad you're not driving. Did I ever tell you what Frazer would say?" They edged their stools a little closer together. "He'd say, The handbook for fugitives has just three simple rules. Don't drive."

"Uh oh," Pauline said.

"Don't get drunk."

"Well, we barely do that."

"And don't sleep with people who don't know who you are. In case you tell them, in a moment of passion."

"Oh." Pauline widened her eyes. She covertly examined the room. "At least we won't break number three," she concluded. They broke into hilarious giggles.

With their third drink their probationary term seemed to end. "This one's on me," said the bartender, rapping the bar with his knuckles. A man had come up from the pool table to stand right beside them.

"So what are you?" the man demanded of Jenny, leaning hard on his cue. "If you don't mind my asking."

"She's a *person*," Pauline said.

"You guess," Jenny said.

"Crow Indian. No, Eskimo."

"Wrong, wrong," Jenny said.

"She's *Californian*," Pauline said, frowning when Jenny kicked her. "How come you don't ask what I am? Just because—" Jenny kicked her again.

"I know what you are. You're the girl called Trouble with a capital T," the man said, with nostalgia.

Later the bartender came to talk to them. "To New York, huh?" he said when Jenny named this as their destination. For a moment she wanted to stand up and dance, she was so thrilled by the impulse she'd had to tell him they were headed back east. It was like having erased all their tracks! When he asked where they planned to stay that night she said Casper, remembering the last big town they'd seen.

"Not a hell of a lot in between here and there, that's for sure. I don't care for Casper, I guess I'm just a country boy at heart. Now New York, you'd have to bound me and gag me and carry me, to get me out there. I don't know how they live in that way."

"You can't do it if you're used to a wide-open space," Pauline told him intensely. "When I was little my family had this big place, but not ranch land like this. It was in the—mountains—"

"I live for the fishing myself. If you asked me I'd say turn back, take a good look at Jackson. Let me guess—you don't fish—"

"We were coming from, um, Seattle. Which road? Little ones . . . not the interstate highways . . ."

"We like the back roads."

"I do, too: you find interesting things on the way. You found the Outlaw Inn, didn't you? Pardon me, ladies." A thirsty group at the bar's other end had been waving to him.

After he'd left them alone Pauline said, "Did he say that's the name of this place?"

For the first time they noticed, like a frieze above the bar, a wallpaper stripe of posters: edge to edge, taped or tacked up, spanning the bar and then spreading out over the walls. Twisting on her stool Jenny saw, through striated layers of cigarette smoke, posters papering the bar's farther walls; posters on top of posters, a few posters defaced with moustaches or dialogue bubbles or corners torn off. Some were novelty reproductions, in old-fashioned sepia tones, with unlikely pictures of their subjects in defiant postures, waving guns. WANTED: THE OUTLAW JESSE JAMES. WANTED: BILLY THE KID. WANTED: FOR CATTLE RUSTLING IN THE COUNTY OF JOHNSON. But most of the posters were real. They seemed to span decades, and Jenny wondered if they represented the length of time that the Inn had been open, or the length of time since the owner—the man tending bar?—had been inspired to begin his collection.

"There I am," Pauline whispered.

There she was, above the bar and the bartender's head, just below the low ceiling. It was the familiar three-quarters view portrait, with the set brunette hair, and the pearls. The poster had been hung with four tacks, over somebody else, and it was crisp at its edges, unfaded, and free of graffiti. She gazed at the picture a long time, and then looked at Pauline. Pauline was more precisely drawn, somehow. Her eyewells deeper, cheekbones more prominent. And her pale yellow hair, obviously bleached, tinged her whole being. It repositioned her slightly. It made her look cheap, Jenny realized. A little bit hungry, and hard.

Pauline slid her free hand into Jenny's, and threw back the rest of her drink.

"Well, we're headed to Casper," Jenny called, as they slid off their stools. "Thanks a lot for the drink."

"So long, girls. They're off to New York," he announced to the bar.

"Youth is for big mistakes," someone said.

ONE NIGHT in a roadside motel Pauline asks, "Did you ever do that?—go to bed, with a woman." Jenny's not sure where they are: if there are mountains out the window or salt flats, if it's the piney chasm of the Sierras, or the Valley, with its sticky airborne floss, and its turning windmills, and its heat. They've driven all night. Now it's day, and the sun is blocked out by the drapes. They're in bed, on their separate pillows. The TV is flickering in perpetual unrest. Neither of them can sleep.

" . . . no," she says, after a while.

"Did you ever want to?"

"I don't know. If I did, I might not have realized."

"Your conditioning might have repressed it. You might have had the feeling, but it was somehow disguised."

In sleep their bodies twine together at the center of the bed. There have already been nights with frost but even when it's not cold they still wake up touching, sometimes tightly spooned. Pauline's small breasts crushed to her back, Pauline's arm on her waist, their bare thighs front to back, their cold feet, their old T-shirts and panties. A scent like warm bread from their groins. That's all there is: in spite of the one conversation, or perhaps because of it, there is only this edging against the idea, in the same way their bodies edge up to each other in the guise of blind sleep. Later, when they have an apartment, they will assume a conventional distance apart—one room but two beds, one bathroom but no rush to get back on the road, so they will no longer shower together. Then it will only be late nights when they've possibly drunk too much wine, the kinds of nights that they fight, and Pauline almost phones up her mother, and Jenny her father, and each hates the other for seeing her armor break down—it will only be then that they'll crave some explicitly sexual battle. Possession of the other and erasure of the self. They'll want to fuck, a slick tangle of limbs, and come pressed to each other. They'll dream back to the floating motel rooms, the one mushy bed, and yet while they are there they do nothing. They wake up, feeling drugged from the long-deferred sleep. For a long moment they don't remember their childhood homes, what their parents look like. Prior history all seems unreal. They don't remember that they are two girls, fabulous prey, on the run from the law everywhere. In this sticky cocoon it's surprising, perhaps, that they never make love to each other. It isn't a secret they have to discover. Pauline has descended, under cover of dark, felt her heart race with confusion and dread. She's slid her tongue cautiously into a woman, recoiled, pushed forward again. She's done it, at the outset always more obediently than with desire, then abruptly overshooting desire for something narcotic and unprecedented. Yet now it is barely remembered; it is the way, though they don't realize yet, this time also will be. In the near future this will be the half-grasped fever dream. Perhaps that they don't make love isn't surprising; their haze is too dense to be roused into lust. At seven P.M. it's almost time for Jenny to creep forth and look for their dinner. She waits for the last of the sunshine to fade. There's a bright thread of light where the curtain falls short of the sill. Pauline shifts, stares at the TV, starts when she sees her own face. "Turn it up," she tells Jenny. But though Jenny imagines herself getting up she does not.

They are somehow no longer so moved by the sight of Pauline, floating over the news anchor's shoulder like an oversized cameo brooch. That portrait again, from the three-quarters angle, the brown lustrous hair carefully set. The usual thick rope of pearls. Below this arbitrary demarcation the image fades out before fully defining her shoulders. The short update, whatever it consisted of, ends, and Pauline is replaced by a map of some faraway part of the world.

All this time, she thinks later, perhaps they actually courted the fatal encounter: at Dolly's, and in the rainstorm with the truck and the troopers, and at the auto junkyard, at the bar. They could only be careful so long before taking some idiot risk. They drove at night and then went into bars. They changed their disguises but kept the same car. They behaved as if they meant to be prudent but in truth there was some awful impulse to endanger themselves. They feared capture completely, and at the same time they longed to be caught through no fault of their own. Perhaps it wasn't paradoxical at all: they just wanted a verdict. They knew they were failing to fully face up to their crime. They tried; but all their feelings were too full of self-regard. They were afraid for themselves, horrified at themselves. Of course their bids for innocence were concerned with themselves. Their feelings piled up like strata; at the outermost, fear and remorse; beneath this, the sinful suspicion that perhaps they were less culpable. Perhaps they were victims of Juan and Yvonne. Thinking this made them ashamed. Of just Juan, then; Yvonne was a victim as well. Perhaps they were all, even Juan, victims of bad circumstances: they were all four of them victims of Frazer. But in a larger, "truer" sense, Frazer along with the four of them was a victim of unjust government. Frazer only had wanted to help them, and why had they needed help? Government persecution. They took it to a higher, a deeper, a broader level again. Frazer, they mused, framed salvation in terms of more money, and then they did as well. In the end, it was capitalism that caused all these problems. Their lives had been compromised from the start by a legacy of imperial violence they could either have condoned through inaction, thus enabling violence itself, or resisted, thus consigning themselves to a marginal place with regard to the sullied mainstream. This marginality, morally right as it was, had bred moral wrong. But why should they be marginal? It was their duty, now more than ever, to devote themselves to revolution. But who were they to lead the good fight, compromised as they were? (Though not quite . . . they had not pulled the trigger.)

At the hot core, beneath all these strata, was a feeling they didn't yet know how to name. They might never name it while they were together. So long as each remained within view of the other a reality pertained between them, and the core feeling didn't intrude. It was amazing, Jenny thought, how a death could remain so abstract, but it was also not surprising at all. She had first known Pauline in the shadow of nine unjust deaths, but Pauline had never known those deaths truly. She couldn't bear to. And this death, number ten, they would also not bear. Mr. Morton: an honorific and a pallid last name. They came to feel they knew him well, but some day they would have to admit that they only did so in the service of their own punishment and redemption. It would take a long time for Mr. Morton to make himself heard above that.

And so they might have longed to be caught through no fault of their own, but at the same time they hoped to be spared, as a sign from the gods. (Surrender wasn't an option. Radicalism, Jenny thought sometimes, was like Catholicism, with its extreme self-referentiality, its strict liturgy, its all-explaining view of the world, its absolute Satan, and its deadly sins, of which surrender was one—the very worst, arguably.) It wouldn't just mean they were lucky—or rather, luck wasn't without deeper meaning. She knew that sheer, dumb luck shouldn't have been of the slightest significance. It wasn't embraced by a reasoned and just worldview. It failed to jibe with all humans created equal. It had no place in a liberation movement nor in a radical's ethical code, yet anyone who had committed the magical act of "going underground," of dropping into a rabbits' warren of the imagination where reinvention of the self was possible, believed in it. Anyone who had ever acted on the premise that she could escape the clutches of an unjust law indefinitely was likely to be a subscriber to the doctrine of luck just as much as the doctrine of racial equality. Outlaws live on luck, and they were outlaws as well as soldiers. In the end the verdict seemed very clear; they made it to the other side not merely unscathed but anointed by one enemy after another, who had looked them in the eye and not seen them, and so added more force to their state of enchantment.

They might have driven for almost two weeks; later on, Jenny couldn't remember how long the trip was. It wasn't possible to judge by dividing the most efficient route by the most comfortable number of hours to drive every day. They hadn't taken the efficient route, or driven the comfortable hours. They hadn't even maintained one direction; they would wend north, then south, pursuing and fleeing vague instincts of where they felt safe, where they felt vulnerable. If she had to put a shape on the journey, she would say that in the end they'd been struggling west all along. But no journey can fit in the mind as it happens through distance and time. There's no way to record it as you might the repetitions of your heart with a vibration-sensitive needlelike pen on a very long roll of paper. Looking back it does not unscroll smoothly. Moments stood out because something had happened, others because nothing had happened but sublime coexistence between the whipped hair of the woman beside her, and the glimpse of her own eyes in the rear view staring back like a critical stranger's. The lurid sunset, the wind suddenly cold though the day had been hot. An emblematic moment, neither resolved nor contented nor perhaps even hers. Perhaps the persnickety car, bought from a little old lady who kept it garaged since 1961—perhaps this car has carried them across an invisible border into somebody's movie. That would be why the wind and the hair and the critical eyes seem so strangely familiar. Other moments stood out for no reason, they were neither eventful nor emblematic, they were as randomly snatched as the insects that stuck to the grill.

As they crossed the Great Plains Pauline told her, "I can't

believe all this space. It's so huge. God, I've never seen anything like this." Propping her head on the window frame, gazing; but Jenny knew Pauline had been here before. She'd been one of those girls in a calico dress, lace-up shoes, sun-strain pinching her eyes, thin long hair always tangled and wild and not in proper braids. One day, the Crow Indians come along and attack her parents' farmstead, scalp her parents, burn the house to the ground, abduct her thrown over their shoulders, her lace-up boots kicking. And the next thing you know, she's tearing around on a horse, wearing paint, giving the Crows who've adopted her hell . . . Jenny could see it in Pauline's deep eyes, if not in her time-refined features. She might have grown up rich, but where had that money come from? From people who'd gotten here first, that was all, when this land was lawless and even more vast. People who'd stuck it out. Killed enough, grabbed enough. Never looked back.

The farther west they got, the more they traveled by day. They had long ago spent Jenny's money; now they sowed the stolen bills, one at a time, at great intervals. Each one they spent was a great burden lifted; they grew lighter and lighter. They weren't in a particular hurry; they zigged north, zagged south. In a motel in Winnemucca, Nevada, Pauline said, "I meant it that day in the rainstorm. If they caught me, I'd never tell them about you. But you, you didn't have to stay with me. I'd understand if you told about me." "But I won't," Jenny said. "I know that," Pauline said. "That's the way that you are. I know that." Before leaving Nevada they paused again in a town called Stateline, just short of the mountains. "We could try Oregon," Jenny said. They had also said, "We could try somewhere inland; a small town," but as they talked about where to touch down, about what would be safest, they sailed closer and closer each minute, so that when the flat green and yellow land of the Valley—with its sprinklers and its rows swinging by in great arcs, and its dusty, tired workers lagging home in the late afternoon down the dusty, tired roads—so that when all this began to thin out, and fall into deep golden folds, and when the road began rising again, for the last time, for its last hurdle, into the coast range, they were thrumming with anticipation, and when they first saw the water, the blue gleam of San Pablo Bay, they shouted. It seemed their decision had been made, long before. There was no question but that they'd go home.

SANDY, POOR SANDY, only recently back from her frightened self-exile to live with her sister in Tucson, opened the door to the place in North Berkeley she shared with Tom Milner and found Jenny there on her porch. Jenny, her shoulder-length hair in a small ponytail and her bangs smoothly combed to her eyebrows. Jenny was wearing a churchgoing white cotton blouse, slightly large, and a pleated blue skirt, also large, looking very much like a teenager from neighboring Virgen de Guadaloupe High School. She even had a Bible in the crook of one arm. She asked, "Have you heard the Good News?" It took Sandy a moment to know who she was.

"Oh, no," Sandy said. "Oh, don't tell me, oh *no*, oh my *God*!"

They'd gotten their first Bible from a motel room somewhere in Nebraska; they'd just driven off in the morning when Pauline produced it from under her shirt. "I can't believe you did that," Jenny said. "Motels *always* report stolen Bibles. Now we're transporting it over state lines." When she'd seen Pauline's face she said, "Oh, I'm just joking with you."

"Don't *do* that."

"I'm sorry."

"Don't *do* that!"

Jenny had taken the next Bible herself and by now they had ten piled up in the car. It marked where they'd been in some way, by subtraction, but it also made good camouflage. "Who can prove that we're not Gideons?" Pauline said. "No one knows what the Gideons look like."

Now Pauline had stepped onto the porch, in her flowered sundress and flat sandals and straw-colored hair, with her Bible as well.

Sandy yanked them inside and Pauline said, "Hi! You and I met, maybe you don't remember—"

"I remember you," Sandy said coldly.

TOM MILNER didn't paint houses full time anymore. He'd tried a succession of other jobs that accommodated his need for freedom and, to a lesser extent, his creativity, and was currently working as a tour manager for a band. But he still pitched in sometimes on large jobs, and the crew, though it had evolved and evolved again over the past two and a half years, taking on and shedding participants, growing and shrinking, had retained the same core: Mike Sorsa, and the truck on which Jenny had once lettered MIKE AND BROS. HOUSEPAINTING on each of the doors. The brothers then had been Mike and Tom Milner and William. It made Jenny feel a weird forsaken joy, to learn that the dilapidated huge-fendered truck with its ding-covered body and cheerful orange sign still went rattling across the Bay Bridge, sprinkling fine motes of rust, cans of turquoise and fuchsia and cream-colored paint hopping wildly around in the back. Forsaken that she and William had been snatched from their lives while that truck trundled on, and yet joyful for the same reason, as if she were a refugee coming back home and someone told her, "Your people are here!" The truck, with its trail of fresh oil left behind on the pavement. Against all odds it still carried its freight of paint cans and young men, and the young men were still rubbing the sleep from their eyes, lying flat in the bed to light cigarettes under the wind. They were still plying their small craft on the surface of the imperfect world to fund plans carried out in its depths. Tom had just done a job on a three-story building in a mostly Mexican neighborhood owned by a man Tom diagnosed as a very nice cheapskate who disliked the work of landlording. The third floor of the building was empty, and Mr. Minski, the landlord, had asked all the painters to pass on the word to nice friends. A few days after Jenny and Pauline arrived Tom rented the place on behalf of his "sister, and a girlfriend of hers, who were moving out from the East Coast," and after a reasonable interval

Jenny and Pauline moved in, Pauline wearing a vast floppy hat and sunglasses. Tom explained she was extremely sensitive to the sun.

They loved that apartment right away, for its hideous brand-new shag carpet upon which they could leap without sound, for its blazing linoleum kitchen—for all its internal brand-newness and cheapness, which made them feel no one had lived there before, but equally for the true oldness that lay just beneath. They were so glad to be back in a city, which they had agreed was not merely what suited their temperaments, but what suited a fugitive most: to be paradoxically sheltered by the nearness of people, and alone without feeling so lonely. The building rode a crest of San Francisco's ceaseless waves, and although in the front it had a stack of bay windows, one per apartment, it really faced back; in back there were old wooden stairs that went up the outside and each landing was as large as a porch. From theirs, at the top, where no one ever passed them, they looked onto the rising and falling rooftops, by day white and dense as a hill town in Spain, by night rolling away like a blanket of stars; or they'd watch the fog come, flat and eerie and luminous gray from the lights it had muffled. A Dutch door led from there to the kitchen, so that with the top half of this door always open they could spend all their waking hours here and yet never feel cramped. The front room they neglected; the blinds on the bay window were always pulled down. The bedroom was plain, the light from its one window shadowed by the nearness of the neighboring house. Because of that nearness they also kept the shades drawn in here. Brand-new royal blue shag carpeting, which Mr. Minski had laid just before they'd moved in, lined the floor perfectly and even extended beneath the closet door to line the floor of the closet. In the closet were Jenny's accordion file, and under the carpet the rest of the bills from the grocery store. Outside, two cot-size mattresses bought from the thrift store and laid directly on the floor with their clothes neatly folded beside them; when they moved in they didn't have hangers, and then the transformation of the closet into a vault made them not want to use it for anything else. But after all these transient years Jenny oddly enjoyed, in the context of rootedness, the compactness of her personal effects, the square heap on the royal-blue shag of her folded-up jeans and T-shirts, her paired socks, her sneakers, her hat. She was glad there was no ancient maple outside sighing at the slightest touch of wind; that there were no worn, creaking floorboards or tumbling mice. Even the rain, when it fell, sounded different. No trace of life as it had been. There already seemed to be so many intervening eras, so many layers of sediment. Their journey across the country, not one stratum but many, Indiana and Missouri, Wyoming and Nevada, and all the fine striations in between. Their first spooked and euphoric nights here. First contact with Sandy and Tom. Though at night, when the usual dimness of the room—they didn't mind it; it was cool and cavelike—was transformed into darkness, for Jenny their farmhouse life sometimes rose up. She would startle awake in the night thinking she was still there, and the inarticulate melancholy of that time, her own loneliness at a depth she hadn't known how to sound, would yawn in her again. When she heard Pauline's breathing she would not understand who it was. Then the clock they had bought and that sat on the carpet nearby would tick tick very softly and she would remember, and flood with relief.

They had been living in the apartment for almost a month when Tom came by very early on a Saturday morning with a long duffel bag that had the faded word "Milner" stenciled on in black ink. "From my dad's army days," Tom explained. The bag's canvas was soft and its contents were falling around inside and poking against the fabric in a way that seemed previolent, like the tip of a knife against skin. The drawstring closure wasn't even closed; Tom was clutching the freight to his chest like a difficult sack of groceries. "Here," he said hastily, dumping the bag in the kitchen, with a sound like a full set of golf clubs—or a full set of shotguns—coming down on a hard tile floor. He was sweating, though the day was quite cool.

"Careful!" Jenny cried. "Jesus, Tom, what have you brought us?"

But Pauline was already on her knees in front of the bag, drawing forth its contents carefully. Connoisseurially. Her touch denoted recognition and pleasure, not fear. She was like a dealer of precious exotica, welcoming home from a long expedition her own Marco Polo.

"Oh, Tom," Pauline finally said. "This is great."

"Yeah?"

"Here's the M1—it's the one that I learned on. I can field-strip it. This one is good, too. It's good for women. It has less recoil, it won't bruise your shoulder so much. This one they never let me handle. I'll look it up in that book that you brought." Pauline turned her face up to him, and it was as if he had finally delivered to her the one thing that would make her complete. That, Jenny thought, was her wonderful, terrible, undiminished, inbred social grace: that her face could say such ringing things—even mean them, short-lived as they were. "Thanks," Pauline said.

Tom glowed, all the dangers forgotten. "Sure thing," he said, grinning.

After Tom was gone she watched Pauline a long time without speaking, while Pauline sat cross-legged on the kitchen floor handling the weapons spread out around her. Finally Pauline looked at her. "They're the guns that we had to leave here, when we went with Frazer."

"I figured," she said.

Her cool reaction only made Pauline grin; Pauline had known she'd object if they'd talked about this in advance. "I know you hate guns, but I had an idea: I want to teach other women the things that I learned with the cadre. Not so that we can hurt or kill people, so that we can understand what these things really *are*. When I learned I felt so—powerful, but that's beside the point, maybe. The point is, it would be a woman's approach to firearms. To understanding why men use them, and misuse them. And if you really hate guns, don't you think you should *know* about them? Know thy enemy: isn't that what you say?" Now Pauline was even more cheerful: she knew she was winning. "And: ignorance is the most inexcusable weakness. Don't you say that too, Jenny?" They both knew that she did.

It helped that they started out with activities that weren't directly related to shooting the guns: names of parts, principles of ballistics, categories of gun and the job each is most suited for. Jenny had to admit there was pleasure in sitting on the deep pile carpet of the living room floor with Sandy, and Sandy's younger sister Joanne, and Joanne's housemate Lena, the five of them dismantling a 12-gauge shotgun, cleaning it with pipe cleaners and household rags, using their hands. A pleasure in framing questions and absorbing the answers, in making lists upon lists of ideas. A pleasure in wonderment, she realized. Learning to learn without being embarrassed. One thing they all agreed on, one thing they realized was true across contexts and even in the best of situations, was that in their relations with men they had subtly but constantly presented themselves as more knowledgeable than they were; all the time, in the wings, playing catch-up. She knew that for her that tension, between the girl she was and the bold, brilliant woman she'd pretended to be, had been central to falling in love—had *been* love, the thrill of transforming, in secret, into the lover her lover desired. She and the others didn't think men had known more than them. But, they agreed, men had a culture of already-knowing, so that you could never read Marx, you had already read him. You could never have an orgasm for the first time because you already had one each time you had sex. You could never ask directions when driving—you knew where you were, even if you were lost. With men it was a confidence game, and there was nothing about this that wasn't seductive, that didn't make a woman want to play along. But being just among women was something more sweet, the fresh pleasure of coming to things the first time, and of showing their wonder—of not having known, and then knowing.

Of course, Pauline said, there was no substitute for the shooting of guns—for the punch in the shoulder, the noise, for the fleet, pungent curl of smoke—Jenny shot her a stern look of warning, and Pauline concluded it was still valuable just to hold the guns up and pretend. Even that had its dangers, because someone outside might see them, so before they began she and Pauline made drapes for the windows. They hadn't minded the cheap window shades that came with the apartment, but when the shades were pulled down a thin band of light showed at their edges where they didn't quite cover the windows. Now they felt their group wouldn't be safe until this was corrected. All they did was cut long rectangles of fabric and sew deep hems at one end for a dowel to run through, but when they were finished it was another improvement the pleasure of which exceeded the purpose it served. "Our beautiful feminist curtains," Pauline said. "They might *look* bourgeois, but they're not."

IT WAS ONLY a matter of time before they would have to appeal to fresh resources. They couldn't rely on Tom and Sandy indefinitely, and now the grocery store money was gone. Jenny asked Tom to contact Mike for her, and one afternoon left Pauline alone and took the bus to Golden Gate Park to meet him. In spite of her hat and her glasses he recognized her immediately; he strode across the grass toward her and without speaking pulled her into his arms. When they stepped apart to look at each other he pressed something into her hand, a doubled-up envelope full of money. It turned out to be five hundred dollars, in twenties and fifties. "Don't object," he warned her. "I'm pissed off already you didn't call me right away. I knew something was up—Milner's been looking like the cat who just ate the canary. I never dreamed it was you, though. Christ, Jenny. And I hear you've made interesting friends."

They stayed in the park talking for as long as she felt comfortable, and then Mike offered to drive her back home in the truck. "Oh, my God," she said when she saw it. "Oh God!" She hugged him again, and now she was laughing and crying. "Tom said it still ran but I couldn't believe it."

"Believe it, baby. This little truck's gonna keep you afloat.

Brothers' business is booming. I think it must be the pretty orange sign."

They drove a few moments in silence. "I don't know why you'd do this," she said finally.

"William's my friend."

"And so you'd go broke—and risk your neck, by the way—for the girlfriend who should have been locked up with him."

"You're having a really hard time seeing me as a noble kind of guy. Would it help if I said that I promised? A long time ago. He once said, if anything happened to him, would I make it my sworn fucking duty to keep you okay. Those were his words. My sworn fucking duty."

"As if I couldn't survive without him," she said irritably.

"No. As if you might one day have legal hassles, which you do, and so need help you wouldn't need otherwise. Even so you've made me wait all this time to keep my promise. Frazer got to be the hero instead. The hotshot beat me to the punch."

"You never liked him, did you?" she said, smiling.

"I guess I was jealous," he said, smiling too.

It was only after he'd driven her back that she asked what he'd meant. She had let it drop at the moment, and not felt she would ever retrieve it. That had taken her so long to learn: that you could end awkward moments by holding your tongue. Oh, the tongue!—which she so often thought of now that she'd returned. The tongue that had been so shy when it met William Weeks and then so voracious once he'd finished with it. Not just voracious to prosecute wrongs but to change standard vision, to challenge as William would challenge, to hammer on innocent comments, make people think twice, knock away their complacence. And then also voracious for sex. All the regions of flesh he had driven her tongue to make love to. That was a liberation that felt like a discipline. Finding silence at moments like the strange one with Mike was a discipline that felt very much like liberation. And yet as they sat in the truck she couldn't resist going back to it. This was part of homecoming, she knew; this picking away at old scabs. In the window she saw the drape twitch. Pauline must hear the truck. Pauline would be trying to line up her eye with the fissure between drape and wall. That reeling desire for aloneness to end and the bottomless fear that goes with it. Pauline would know that the truck was Mike bringing her back, but clutched in the animal heart of her mind was the fear that the truck was an agent, the start of an ambush, The End. "I should go in," Jenny said, but then added, "What did you mean by you guessed you were jealous?"

"I always had the sense," he said, and then paused to feel for words. "I always had the sense that there was a kind of what-if drama going between Frazer and Carol, and William and you. Maybe Frazer just wished that was true, and made everyone think so."

Of course she knew what he meant. But she still said, "What-if?"

"What if you weren't hooked up with William, and Frazer wasn't with Carol. What would happen with Frazer, and you."

"That's absurd," she said. "I love William. And you know how Rob is."

"I know," Mike said, smiling.

"What?" she demanded.

"Nothing. I just think it's funny. We spend so much time hashing out the big forces that control our lives. Capitalism, the class system. Private ownership of the land. Like, I'm always wondering how come I can't grow my own food and just live in a hut and be happy. Instead I paint rich people's houses. Now I'm learning to paint fake marble surfaces so that not-so-rich people can feel like they are. Have a little touch of class on your fake fireplace. Isn't that crazy? People like William and you understand, but then sometimes I think you don't notice the personal things. All the messy emotional things. Those control our lives, too."

"For example?"

"God, I don't know. For example, Frazer rushed to the rescue. I won't comment further on why. All I know is I never got to fulfill my old promise, so let me do it now, right? Let me think about how you could earn money. Let me meanwhile keep you afloat. Let me help you survive. And your new roommate, too."

She leaned back in the truck when she'd finally got out, wanting to say something else. But she couldn't.

"You should have come home sooner," he scolded, ignoring her tears.

"WHY DOES EVERYONE love him so much?" That was Pauline's response when Jenny showed her the money from Mike, and Jenny knew "him" meant not Mike, but William. "As if it's not bad enough that we're dependent on men," Pauline added. She and Jenny should take out an ad like the ones that you saw for the Third World orphans. For a dollar a day you can feed and clothe two fugitives! Help them live on to fight for your rights! What kind of feminists lived as kept women?—but it wasn't Mike's money that bothered Pauline. The complaints were all code for Pauline's first demand: Why does everyone love him so much? And that was code for the actual question: Why do *you* love him, Jenny?

Pauline had decided that Jenny, in her years underground, had changed too much to reunite with William once he got out of prison. For one thing, Pauline pointed out, Jenny herself had begun to feel that the actions she and William had done had been flawed and perhaps even wrong. It was true that when Mike Sorsa had asked Jenny if she was interested in meeting with new comrades of his, though she hadn't shown it, within she'd recoiled. She knew that to him she looked even more hardened, impatient to get off the sidelines. Though from the inside out their weapons group had transformed her, made her feel braver and more capable, and though she could see the way in which it had emboldened Joanne and Sandy and Lena, and no one more than Pauline, there was also an outside-in view that she'd glimpsed while with Mike. She could see them as outsiders would: violent, courting destruction. It frightened her badly. More and more she thought of revolution not as mustered force that might topple The System, but as a delicate process of changing individual minds, or as the rare chance to try.

When she talked about this with Pauline, and especially when they discussed her past actions with William, Pauline took a narrower view. "It's no wonder he used methods we now see weren't the most effective," Pauline said. "He's a man, after all." In their group they had been discussing the problem of women's role in the revolution, and had finally opened their eyes to the fact that everywhere in the world, women followed. Even history's most notable women revolutionaries were the helpmeets to more-worshipped men. They'd been dismayed but also electrified to have seen it so clearly; *resolved*, Pauline wrote (she kept minutes because she had the best handwriting): *Women must assume leadership roles in the revolution.* But after this they began arguing. Pauline talked about her kidnapping: her old comrades grabbing her in her bathrobe, at gunpoint, was so typically masculine, rapacious and violent. It was as if men, even when trying to effect positive change, could only do so in the most backward, masculine way. It was the same thing with William—

"Wait a minute," said Jenny. "You can't say men are doomed to do things certain ways, just because they're born men. That's like saying that women do housework because it's their nature."

Pauline, flushing, disregarded the actual point. "Why do you always defend him?" she said. "Why does everyone love him so much?"

But their worst argument came when she suggested Pauline try to contact her parents—just to send them a small sign that she was alive. They would make sure it couldn't be traced. Pauline screamed, "How could you say that? Just when everything's finally fine!" Jenny was a traitor, a turncoat, no better than Juan and Yvonne; now that Jenny had reunited with all her old friends she just wanted to get rid of Pauline. Perhaps the years separating their ages made Jenny less like Pauline than like Pauline's parents! An illogical, terrible insult, considering the amount of time they had spent puzzling over the enormous abyss that seemed to separate them from their parents. Yet Jenny feared that there *were* differences. Pauline was not quite twenty-one while Jenny had just turned twenty-six. Jenny had always thought that age brought greater focus on the past, while youth looked to the future, but she found that her own aging fixed her on the future in unprecedented ways. Concerns she would have shrugged off as recently as one year before, like the peace of mind of her father, and her own future relationship to him, were gaining legitimacy. Her appeal to Pauline was really a selfish appeal, that they protect their future selves from present behavior those selves might regret. But Pauline saw Jenny equating a slight advantage in age with broad advantages in understanding, and perhaps that was the real betrayal—not Jenny's suggestion that they breach their closed circle, but Jenny's breaching of it herself in suggesting their minds were different. "If you want to leave you can leave!" said Pauline. "You're a self-centered child!" said Jenny. Pauline hurled a heavy glass ashtray that might have killed Jenny if it had connected. Instead it sailed through the closed kitchen window, showering shards of glass onto the ground. The next day was one of the few occasions in their entire time in San Francisco when the debilitating anxiety of their previous life, which they'd almost conquered, rose with all its old force. Jenny called Mr. Minski about the window. She'd known that she had to tell him, before he possibly heard it from one of the neighbors. The long respite she'd had from her vigilance had left her out of practice in managing people. She was overwhelmed by the consciousness of her and Pauline's mistake, and she stammered when she spoke to Mr. Minski, and could feel herself trembling as if it were cold. "Of course we'll pay for it," she told him. "We were having this dumb argument." Mr. Minski said, "Girls fight! My two daughters are close like you girls, but when those two fight," and he'd trailed off, impressed. How sexist, Pauline would have said. As if it's surprising that women would fight. But Jenny was satisfied that their mystical luck seemed intact, and that because there was no danger she did not have to share the conversation with Pauline and so destroy, with needless retrospection, the moment at which they'd reforged their link whole. Pauline coming into their room; it was hard for her, Jenny realized. It was possible she was too proud: she would sooner recite all her wrongs, head tossed back, than admit the least wrongness of one of them. But Pauline had come in and apologized, and then they'd both cried. And been fine.

One afternoon they smelled the sweet heavy perfume of wood smoke in the air. It was scattered too thinly on the hot breeze, was too much like a memory—they sniffed intently, and it faded; they relaxed, and it surged up again—for them to be frightened of actual fire. They were only vaguely aware of a strange overcast, the light falling through their repaired kitchen window as if out of clouds of fine dust, the strength of the sweltering breeze, like the gusts from an oven. They had a container of yogurt in the fridge, a jar of cold coffee from yesterday that they poured over ice; they padded about the warm kitchen in cutoffs and tank tops, self-sufficient, serene, with a music tape playing instead of the news. They would have gone out eventually, would have finally seen an unobstructed patch of sky above them and their flesh would have crawled in alarm, because the sky would have looked like apocalypse. But instead it was Mr. Minski who came red-faced and excited up the outside back stairs and put his head in the door—it was open, as always. "You girls okay?" he demanded. "You think I should spray on the house with a hose?" There was a drought on, as everyone knew; lawn watering was forbidden, the few owners of private swimming pools in this crowded city representing the height of bourgeois self-indulgence. "Spray the house with a hose?" said Pauline rather sternly. "Why would you? There's a *drought* on, you know."

That was the day that the East Bay was burning; wildfires had sprung up overnight in the Berkeley hills, perhaps from a dropped cigarette. Fire had spread in all directions with incredible speed, and now threatened the city. There were trees in the Oakland graveyard that had gone up in flames, like the Biblical bush. Mr. Minski went off down the street to talk the situation over with other home owners; they took their radio and went up to the roof, and there, beneath a strangely red sun, awash in the ovenlike wind with the scent of wood smoke twined within it—and stronger, it seemed, every minute—they watched a shelf of black smoke coming toward them. Great heat trapped beneath it. They saw the orange sparkings of fire on the smoke-shrouded hills. The radio said that the Bay might not stop the advance; wind-borne embers were traveling miles, and the city was tinder. The smell of fire filled their nostrils; they sat close by each other, wordless, as the frantic dispatches came in from reporters in Berkeley, and the vista of hills seethed black smoke and the sparks flared and faded. And although they knew that they ought to be frightened, as if God Himself had arrived to destroy them, they still felt strangely far from the world. Its pulse beat just under their fingers, and yet it was distant and miniaturized. It could never touch them.

THE FARMHOUSE had been empty and quiet through the rest of the fall and deep into the winter. One morning, tiny brown pellets of mouse shit must have begun to reappear near the edges of things, where the mice like to leave them. A cluster were dropped on the rear of the stove. Nearby a box of McCormick's black pepper was upended and marked by small teeth. The seedlike shits lined up at the back of the sink, in the damp place behind faucet and taps. The teeth marks appeared on a round cake of soap, and the toilet paper roll was shredded. A week after Labor Day 1974 the owner still had not gotten the key in the mail and so he drove out there, expecting the worst, but he found a clean house, not including the work of the mice. His tenants must have moved out early and forgotten to send back the key. He secured the house for winter and left again, pretending he'd change all the locks, though he knew that he wouldn't.

The house was empty and quiet again, as the hills that it lived in flamed red and then faded away and the scalp of the land started showing through denuded trees. Mice did their work, with energy and puzzling inconsistency. Why eat soap and not curtains? Why ravage one spot with passion, while leaving a similar spot barely touched? Those fingerprints that might have survived the housecleaning would now be deteriorating. They did deteriorate; fine impressions of bodily sweat, there's no reason they wouldn't. No one knew how long they stayed intact, or what factors affected their breakdown. It was the kind of thing you'd think someone would know, but they'd never done studies. The man, the first person to enter the house since its owner had left it, contemplated the rational bases for ghosts. Delicate whorls of sweat, the fine snow from a scalp, orphan hairs, crusts from nostrils and eyes. All discarded by the body in the nonviolent course of a day, to no purpose apart from provoking the sense that the body lives on after death. Only fingerprints served the additional purpose from which his profession derived. He moved slowly through the house, thinking of ghosts. The house was cold, and he could see his breath in the air before him, an ephemeral ghost of his own. His team was waiting outside in the ankle-deep snow. He divided the house in his mind, and then brought them inside. The rest of the agents would wait until his team was done.

Oh, for the ballpoint clutched tight by the scrivener, the glass grasped by the drinker, the window or counter or table against which a weary one leaned with a palm! They didn't find any of that, but they did find a clear partial that matched the man's left index finger. This brought them onto the trail, though the trail was, as usual, cold. The man had been here, perhaps with the girls, perhaps on his own, at least six months prior to this. The house had been empty at least since September. The fingerprint expert stepped out and accepted a thermos of coffee. After a while he went in again and oversaw the gentle disembowelment of the couch. No pens hidden in the couch cushions; not even loose change. This absence of standard detritus was its own kind of presence; the house wasn't this clean by accident. The young fugitives had learned something these past thirteen months. When this had begun they'd left great bratty messes behind, heaps of spiral-bound notebooks of nonsense, filthy clothing, spoiled food, cigarette butts all over the floors like confetti, graffiti on all of the walls. A bathtub filled with water, piss, rancid red wine and whatever they'd had in their fridge, within which they'd submerged "evidence." DIVE RIGHT IN, PIGS! they'd scrawled cheerfully on the mirror. A fearless exuberance that he'd admired, in secret. Now this was replaced by resigned apprehension. There was something paradoxically doomed about the effort with which they'd protected themselves, through erasure.

He went around door and window frames and into the backs of the cupboards and along the floorboards with a flashlight, looking for telltale niches, loose boards, too-wide cracks, anywhere they might have concealed and forgotten something. He had the kitchen dismantled and dusted each plate, fork, spoon, mug, rusty pan, knowing he was echoing them in a sort of reverse. The partial had come off a metal cot frame, and after a while they circled back to the beds superstitiously. Then one of his team said, "Here's something." One of the mattresses, turned over, revealed a thick patch of tape. The tape adhered badly to the cloth mattress ticking and came away easily, with a fat plug of newspaper attached. A filled hole in an old rotting mattress. As if unfurling another cache of the Dead Sea scrolls they flattened one sheet of the newspaper and regarded its primitive date. June 12, 1974, almost ten months before. The temperature in the room seemed to have dropped ten degrees. Someone tried dusting the newspaper but it was ink dust to start with. "Take a look at the tape," the man said. A few moments later he said, "Oh my goodness," with gratification. In spite of the coldness of the room and the trail he broke into a grin. "We've got both thumbs here. I think we've got a right index finger, I've got a middle finger, a very clear partial . . . " They were all piled up like a spill of coins sliced from a tiny tree trunk, but as he squinted into his eye piece they resolved from each other. Each print preserved between layers of tape in a beautiful concatenation. Ghostly hands playing as if on a keyboard; a summer thunderstorm of evidence in the middle of winter. It was a letter to him from this person, in fingerprint-newsprint, a language. What it wasn't was any of the three fugitives, or the house's owner. "Some random person who plugged up that mattress a long time ago," someone said.

"There's a date on the paper! June 12, 1974."

"Some person who sold them the mattress?"

"The mattress was here when they got here. The house came fully furnished."

"So we see if the lab can get a hit? I guess search by known radicals. East Coast, to narrow it down."

"Ought to at least do east of the Mississippi. That gets in Wisconsin. That East?"

"That's Midwest."

The man interrupted. "Look at how many fingers we have! Tell them to search the whole country."

APRIL WAS MILD. They planted a garden in a corner of the neglected backyard of their building, hacking the earth with a hoe: lettuce, zucchini, tomatoes, and carrots. In their group they spent less time on guns than on feminist books, so that when they met they could all sit outside and enjoy the good weather. They got drunk and discussed their orgasms; "No, stop!" Pauline shrieked, as a flushed Sandy regaled them with pornographic descriptions of her and Tom Milner's sex life. In oddly formal, intellectual terms, they discussed sexual love between women. It was just as profound and legitimate, they agreed, as was sex between women and men.

In May, whether because of her heightening consciousness, or lessening orgasms, or some other distress, Sandy broke up with Tom Milner and moved in with them. She stayed up all night and slept during the day, so that they had to tiptoe and whisper to avoid waking her. She scattered her things everywhere and then, although they hadn't asked her to, heaped them on top of her suitcase again angrily. She locked herself in the bathroom for hours to cry. One night, when they were sharing a bottle of wine, she announced guiltily, "Frazer was here looking for you. I mean, not here. Not at this apartment. He was here in the city, last week. I told him I didn't know where you were, but he didn't believe me. He said so to my face. And then he told me not to tell you I'd seen him, if I 'happened' to see you. He said he thought if you knew he was here you'd leave town and he'd have to start looking all over again."

"How did he know we were here?" Jenny asked. Pauline said nothing, but she lifted the bottle of wine from the carpet and emptied it, completely, into her glass; they were drinking from tumblers, so that this was possible even though the bottle had been almost half full.

"I don't know if he *knew* you were here. He just thought you might be. He was really freaked out about finding you. He kept saying it was really, really urgent and he totally lost his temper with me and accused me of lying but I held out, I just gave him a stone wall." Now Sandy launched into a diversionary account of the heroic effort with which she'd withstood Frazer's queries. "I wanted to tell you right away," she added, "but Tom really thought that I shouldn't, he kept saying we could keep our word to you and Frazer both, but I thought he was wrong. We fought hard about it."

"So that's why you broke up?" Pauline asked, rather coldly.

"God no," Sandy moaned, seeming not to have caught Pauline's tone. "It was so much else. Things between us are just so fucked up."

Jenny didn't sleep well the next several nights. Then Sandy and Tom joyfully reconciled and Tom came by to get Sandy's things. Frazer was mentioned again, but this time it was clear that the ominous note had arisen from Sandy's unhappiness more than the facts. "He was here," Tom admitted when Jenny asked him. "But, frankly, I didn't think it was worth upsetting you two just to satisfy him. I think he was desperate for money, and wanted to get that book project going again with Pauline."

"Fat chance," Pauline said.

Jenny said, "Sandy told us he told you *not* to tell us he'd talked to you."

"No, no. She's confused. He said not to tell you he'd *been* here. He thought it would make you take off. It was fine if we told you we'd spoken to him. I mean, he asked us to give you a message. Obviously that would mean that we'd spoken to him."

"What's the message?"

"I don't know. We told him we'd never been in touch with you at all, like you wanted us to. So we couldn't pass on any message. But he gave me a contact number if I 'happened' to see you. That's another reason I think that it's money. The number is his parents in Vegas, as if he's had to move in there or something. I bet he lost that Manhattan apartment, and he's all out of money. He acted like an absolute asshole to Sandy and me. He kept saying stuff like, 'Tell the truth, quit the games! This is life or death! Don't be so stupid!'"

"Oh, *God*," Pauline said.

"Thanks for covering for us," Jenny told him.

In June Tom retired from band management and went to work for a car customizer. Although at first he claimed to find the entire culture of car customizing laughable, he was swiftly infected by it. When he'd started his employment he hadn't even owned a car; then a sporty brown Gremlin had been advertised on the company bulletin board. Tom bought it and tinted its windows, an investment of almost a month's salary even after his ten percent discount. He drove the car over to show them, and as they all went downstairs together declared gallantly that Jenny and Pauline looked like a commercial for something, with their hats and sunglasses and hair, which was getting so long. Nair hair stuff? Coppertone? Jenny and Pauline were both wearing blue jeans and T-shirts. From the garden they'd both gotten suddenly tan. Jenny was so dark she looked like an Indian, but Pauline was tan also, in a pale-gold way. Tom said he could hardly believe this was the girl he first saw in the barricaded back room of his long-ago coworker's apartment, the girl with the lank lusterless hair and the green circles under her eyes and the skin like the belly of something, death-white and unhealthily damp. The girl who wanted a *dry* burger with absolutely nothing wet or mushy involved, and who smoked constantly. Tom had been terrified for her; now he was the slightest bit terrified *of* her. Pauline laughed merrily and when they got to the car she kept laughing. "This is what you spent your month's salary on?" Pauline teased him. "So people will think you're a pimp?"

"I think it's terrific," Jenny said, seeing Tom blush at Pauline's reaction. "It could be really useful."

"For what?" Pauline said. "For making cops think you're a pimp?"

"What do you know about pimps? It looks like a car that a surfer would have. And you really can't see in at all. Doesn't that seem appealing? To drive around knowing no one can see you?"

And so after forming the idle idea that they might drive around unseen in Tom's car, one day the impulse seizes them and without pausing to reconsider they borrow the car and just go—Jenny driving, Pauline navigating—to the house that Pauline grew up in. More than a year has passed since Pauline was kidnapped. Now it's even been more than a year since the tape was broadcast on which Pauline declared she would stay with her captors. And more than a year since all but two of those captors were killed. In the heyday of the case, before the eerie lull after the last tape, the eulogy tape, the house had been a round-the-clock circus; for months without pause television vans lined the street until the neighbors complained and the trucks had to pile up in the long arc-shaped driveway, and the drivers of the trucks had to post their names on the windshields and wear name tags themselves so their colleagues, both brothers-in-arms and combatants in the ongoing battle for news, could locate them if they needed to move; then the maddening Chinese puzzle of inching out, one after the other, to idle in the street until the one van had pulled itself free; and then the reassemblage of the van parking lot and return to the business at hand. In the heyday, there had been a bank of telephone booths near the curb on the lawn, their cables snaking away through the lush shrubbery to the nearest phone pole; a courtesy from Pacific

Bell to spare the family from opening their home and their phone to hundreds of reporters. Klieg lights standing at the ready on their mantislike legs, near the podium bristling with microphones that had come to seem like a permanent part of the portico. The grass had been trampled flat and gouged full of holes until the family, with greatest respect and gratitude for the media's efforts, issued a gentle request that the walkway be used, and then had the whole lawn resodded. It looks resodded now. A light fuzz of new growth mars the level blade surface. The box hedges have grown just the slightest bit shaggy. The portico is swept clean but there's a telltale barrenness to it that isn't just the absence of klieg lights and podium. When they first came home to San Francisco they never dreamed of coming here. FBI agents had been camped on the lawn with the news trucks, maybe even tucked away in the house. A chosen few given the children's old bedrooms and the old playroom for all their equipment. Jenny and Pauline don't know what the equipment would have been exactly, but it isn't hard to imagine the wire-sprouting boxes and punchcards and printouts, the twin wheels of the huge tape recorders like a grim caravan rolling into the night. Agents padding up and down the halls in their bathrobes and slippers, clutching big mugs of acrid black coffee. Her parents had declined to let the press into the house, asking not just for its cooperation but for its proud participation: The press ought to proudly assist this defense of the family's last shred of privacy. While all the while, in the shadow of such grand pronouncements, they were harboring FBI agents. Feeling, perhaps, that unlike capitulation to the press this was a worthy crown to their martyrdom, because so elitist. Only the innermost circle of agents, the chiefs of their tribe. Cook told to be on her toes day and night, brewing coffee and making nice sandwiches. Driver with careful instructions on smuggling the men in the family limo, with its black-tinted windows. At least, this is Pauline's vision of the exigencies of that time, as she and Jenny sit in the friendlier darkness of Tom's Gremlin, the windows of which are a sepia shade sort of like Coca-Cola, to go with the burnt-orange pinstripes. Now even the house's hidden encampments have been dismantled. Drapery hangs in the windows, and if they were to go inside they would find the house furnished luxuriously, but devoid of inhabitants. Pauline's parents have moved into their pied-à-terre on Russian Hill, and the house is discreetly for sale. The luxurious furniture has been provided by the real estate agency, because a house can be sold for more money if shown nicely furnished, and at this level the difference might be in the hundreds of thousands of dollars. This is the kind of thing Pauline knows about, the brand of arcana that weaves itself into her musings as she and Jenny dare themselves to sit idling at the curb opposite the house one full minute, then one minute more, each of them having mastered the art of keeping excruciating track of the time even while feeling lost in the scene before her. Pauline's parents' departure from the house has been portrayed by the press as a grief-stricken retreat from a nest that was emptied by violence, although Pauline lived away from home for a year before she was kidnapped. In this way things haven't changed much from the first few days after the kidnapping, all those eons ago, when Pauline's parents tried to imply that she'd been seized from their home like a child, when she'd really been seized—no less terrifyingly, but still, *differently*—at her own apartment, where she'd lived with a boyfriend. "Now they say that they can't bear to live there alone, but they lived in that house for a year after I went to college, and it wasn't too big for them then," Pauline says, gazing at the irregular lawn, at the bare portico. She lights a cigarette and cracks the dark window to let the smoke out.

After a while she adds, "The first time the cadre let me watch TV with them, it was right after they'd made the demand that my mother resign from that board, as a gesture of good faith to them. My parents had said there was no way they could meet the ransom, because of the structure of the family trust. Well, I'd told the cadre that might really be true. I wasn't sure, but it seemed like it might be. So they went back and said the ransom could maybe come down, but my parents had to make a real gesture to show their good faith. And the gesture was, that my mother resign from that board. The board of a company that sponsors military coups in South America. That uses child labor. That does terrible stuff. And, not that this matters compared to those issues, but a company my mother doesn't even—you know, it wasn't *hers*. She just sat on the board. Like she sat on the board of the opera. And my mother came on the TV, she was standing right there, and she said, "I don't tell *these people* how they should live, and they will not dictate how *we* will live," and she stayed on that board. Because she said if she resigned it would send me a signal, that she wasn't fighting as hard as she could! And I thought at that moment, I'm finished with them. I was so terrified. I felt dead."

"But now you're finished with the cadre, also."

"It doesn't mean I'll go back." Pauline stares out the window. "I am finished with the cadre. They used me just like my parents used me. I hate them." Her cigarette hand shakes and she reaches for the ashtray and misses. The ash falls on her jeans and when she swipes it away leaves a long messy smear of gray ash. She glares at Jenny, lip trembling. "Let's *go*," she says impatiently.

Jenny writes more and more often to William, neglecting her journal and instead directing all chroniclings and debates, all notations and outpourings, into letters to him; like the philandering husband who brings his wife flowers, she knows she is prompted by guilt. She isn't sure she can see him again. He has become a magnetic pole, a singular point by which to navigate, a confessor, but she doesn't think she can see him and still retain hold of her delicate sense of herself. She might not love him anymore. She'll be jarred by the thought on the nights she and Pauline stay up so late on the porch talking, in the dark, that their faces slowly evolve out of the void like dim moons. If they go to bed at all on these nights they pretend that they've fallen asleep right away, or sleep never will come. That's their ritual of separation: giving each other silence as a prelude to sleep, and then hearing the other one's breath in the compromised darkness. Their room, sad with forms in the dawn. She chalks up the sadness she feels to the light, to its eerie betweenness, not thinking of the fact that this time is the only time they spend apart. They're in the same room, but they've opened a silence between them. She knows they talk themselves exhausted each night because they're both afraid not to fall asleep first, and be left lying there all alone. They're both aware of their losses—not of the lives they once had, or the people they knew, but of all the attachments they felt.

By August their garden has been so productive they've given grocery bags of vegetables away, to Tom and Sandy and Mike, and Mr. Minski and Joanne and Lena. Something about those vegetables, how quickly and how huge they grow, seems to them like a sign. They sit in the kitchen, the Dutch door standing open, the warm breeze pussyfooting around them. Birds are rioting out in the yard, a tape's playing low in the front room. The tape recorder was donated by Joanne's friend Julie, who's also interested in feminist issues. They're considering letting her into their group. Their life, now, is so hushed—not furtive, but serene. It's so still they discern subtleties they've never noticed before. Things that might have once seemed self-indulgent to them are important, and they've made their peace with them: flowers in a vase on the table, a pretty cloth Jenny found at the thrift store. When their first zucchini had been big enough to harvest they'd spent the whole day making dinner: ratatouille of mostly zucchini, and a salad and homemade bread, and a cake, just for them—how absurd! And a bottle of wine . . . bourgeois things, but are they? Aren't they beautiful things? Jenny isn't so sure anymore; part of the letter to William addresses these issues. Pauline reads a passage and chews on her pen thoughtfully. Lately Jenny gives her letters to Pauline to read over and edit and Pauline pores over them, spreads them on the kitchen table and ponders them, a pen in her mouth. The two of them have been laboriously co-composing this particular letter for so long it's become a long letter between them, and they still haven't mailed it. "'We feel bad if we want to be happy,'" Pauline reads, and then says, "But it can't be so selfish. I used to think so, I used to think I was rotten. But is it really so wrong?"

And yet, as quiet as their life is, their ears have not become hyper-tuned. This might have been the case, once. On the farm, when quietness bred sensitivity, to an exquisite degree. Now their senses are softened a little, as with wine; they're just a touch intoxicated, not stupid. Serene. Sometimes you see serene people on the sidewalk, and they don't see or hear, but those people aren't stupid. If their thoughts are elsewhere, it's a good elsewhere. They don't hear the make and model of the car sliding past in the street. Or perhaps they're inside, in the kitchen; they don't hear the soft tread, on the outside stairs, though the Dutch door is open. They don't sense the man's approach until he's there, as surprised as they are, his weapon gripped tight in both hands. He points it at them. Pauline drops the pen with which she's been sketching out her idea of when it's all right to be happy. Jenny's body, still hoping, leaps up from the table, but her mind knows, and her inner voice echoes the man's: "Freeze! Put your hands up!"

So it happens, at last.

Part Four

1.

Anne Casey is packing her books. They're books she won't need—now that something has finally happened she won't need books at all—but in the past year of inaction and boredom covering Pauline's story she's grown attached to them. All are startlingly overdue from the Mid-Manhattan Library. Most are picture books, of the estates Pauline's grandfather built. Pauline's grandfather, the family patriarch: the subject of those huge oil paintings in the Gilded Age style that he sought to apply to every part of his post–Gilded Age life. Like those earlier American titans on whom he patterned himself, he grew up poor, early-hardened, and shrewd, and made his fortune and name very young—in his case, in the newspaper business. Anne's business, and the business of all of her colleagues now packing their bags just like her, streaming toward California as if part of a latter-day gold rush.

And oh, those incredible homes—not mere homes, but kingdoms. There's Casa Mare, the coyly plain name for the tile-by-tile copy of Alhambra, a folly the size of a town that sprawls miles atop cliffs overlooking the sea. And Big Red, the faux cattle ranch at the confluence of three rare rivers whose huge weeping willows, an arboreal trophy of wealth, can be seen miles off on the almost-bald plains; imagine, sitting on all that water in the water-starved land just to pretend that you ranched. But McCloud is Anne's favorite, the Swiss village of delicate cottages and a huge-timbered lodge, somewhere in the wild Cascades. No one apart from its servants has ever known the location. In Pauline's grandfather's day, visitors were blindfolded on the last leg of the journey, setting out from beneath great, white, terrible, mystic Mount Shasta, which must have seemed like a Cerberus guarding the gates. McCloud is the one that stirs Anne, that gives rise to real envy. Not the secrecy of it, or the power it stands for—rumor has it that even the military is barred from its airspace. Not its comic-book unlikeliness, but its actual beauty. The vines tendriling around gingerbread shutters; the cold river speeding, caught at the edge of the frame. The few photographs of McCloud that Anne has are ancient, black-and-white, badly focused; McCloud isn't in the big picture books. Unlike Casa Mare and Big Red, which were family houses, McCloud was Pauline's grandfather's sacred retreat, where he lived with his mistress. It had been hers to rule like a queen, an open secret from the wife and the children. It must have been she who took the bad pictures; it was definitely she who pounced, exuberantly, on the friends who arrived in blindfolds; squealing, she thrust flutes of champagne in their hands before letting them regain their sight.

If any of those things is true. All Anne has been able to learn about life at McCloud comes from this girl's memoirs, and the memoirs were picked almost clean by the family's attorneys. The memoirs are silly; they make Pauline's grandfather out as a harmless old coot. References to the wife and the children are entirely absent. Also absent is any reference to the man's death and the girl's subsequent ejection from the house by the children, finally defying their father now that he is safely six feet underground.

Perhaps McCloud is exterminated, or exorcised, before Pauline is taken there, as a very young girl. McCloud was apparently Pauline's favorite place too, in her childhood. Anne guesses Pauline doesn't know about her grandfather's mistress, let alone the memoirs. Though the memoirs were finally published, they still seem to have been sabotaged. In spite of its subject the book was ignored, was conspicuously not reviewed. The vivid authoress has since died, barely fifty, forgotten, from alcoholism.

Anne has dug the book up from her closet; Little Man, the small parrot she impulsively bought when her husband left her, gouges her books with his beak and splatters them with his odorless yet ubiquitous shit, and so she locks up the ones from the library to try to preserve them, and then forgets all about them for months. The memoir she checked out purely as a distraction, a queer novelty, but then she'd been mesmerized by the mistress's robust vulgarity and her casual racism. There are constant blithe mentions of "coloreds" and "cute pickaninnies" and "little Jew lawyers," and daffy tirades about "Japs" while recalling the years of the war. "We had to make sure to black out the windows, even up at McCloud, so the Japs wouldn't come bomb the house! Oh, those dirty Japs hated the Boss. Back in his newspaper days, Boss was one of the first telling it like it was. California had gotten so careless, and let in all those Japs. Japs are like rats—now, they *are*: they eat garbage, and there's no way to kill them! Boss and I were so relieved when we heard from the President that he would put all the Japs into camps. Boss called to tell FDR it was high time already!"

BUT THE MISTRESS isn't part of the story; the stunning kingdoms aren't, either, although Anne keeps thinking, as she tries to scrape away all the trivial matter that sticks to this story like lint, that nothing much ever remains when you get to the bottom. There is only the girl, Pauline, who has always been a story, from the time of her birth, no matter what she has done. Pauline, snatched by the cadre for her totemic power; she's ended up looming over them all. They will all be forgotten, the dead and the two who've survived. No one will ever wonder what they were so angry about, what they hoped to achieve. Those things are too easily known, while Pauline is unknowable, although the promise of her upcoming trial has obscured that dull truth. Her trial will reveal everything, or so everyone hopes; the story will finally write itself. Anne, plying her beige rental car across the Great Plains with her parrot and her pile of books, is just another small striver in a great wagon train, hopeful and facing long odds.

Joe Smith isn't part of the story, either. But as with the mistress, Anne attached great hopes to him at the time—until she actually met him. It had been at the start of the summer that an old friend of hers from her very first job in New York called her out of the blue. "Is it true that you're doing a piece on Pauline?" her friend Michael asked. "I might have something for you, or at least someone to fob off on you. He may be completely insane, or he may be your Deep Throat."

Michael told her that the previous summer, long before he had heard from the current "Joe Smith," another man who declined even to provide an unconvincing pseudonym had phoned to claim that he "might have a way" to get a tell-all book penned by Pauline. "I told him, give it to me," Michael said, "and don't you breathe a word to anybody else! I promised him all kinds of money our press doesn't have. I begged for a meeting but he wouldn't even give me a phone number. We'd meet once, he'd hand it over, I'd pay. I said sure; I figured I'd work out the details later, if it turned out to be even a little bit true. After the phone call, I thought I might have met him before. I mean, why me? His voice rang a bell, as if we'd met at a party a long time ago. A few weeks or a month after that he called again to ask was I still interested. I said I was, he said that he'd meet with me 'soon,' and that's the last time I heard from the guy. I think."

"What do you mean?"

"This 'Joe Smith' guy rings a bell, too."

"The same bell?"

"Honestly? Who the fuck knows. The phone calls were a whole year apart. I can't be sure that the voice was the same. I just can't believe it was two separate guys and their both calling me was a total coincidence. Sure, nowadays two hundred people a day claim Pauline's come and shopped at their store, that she ate at their diner, she played pool in their bar, she pumped gas at their station, she's pregnant, she's a lesbian, she's with the Black Panthers, whatever. Those two hundred people a day call the cops, they don't call Michael Levitz, Book Editor."

"So this 'Joe Smith' was a book agent, before he turned into Deep Throat?"

"It doesn't help his credibility much," Michael joked.

"It sure doesn't," she said.

"Joe Smith" had her meet him on the pigeon shit–spattered, exhaust-hazed, deafeningly loud traffic island park a few blocks south of Macy's. "Can we talk somewhere else?" she asked when he arrived, but he insisted on telling her everything there; he wouldn't even sit down on a bench. He was her age, early thirties; athletic and restless; he made her walk up and down on the cramped little island with him, as the midday traffic coursed around them. At some point within the past months, he told her, the FBI had discovered a farmhouse where Pauline had been hiding. They'd also linked Pauline to someone named Jenny Shimada. Joe had happened to drop by the farmhouse, because he'd once had a friend who lived there, and who he always hoped to track down again. Instead, FBI men ambushed him. They hadn't been able to keep him—he'd done nothing wrong—but they'd asked lots of questions, revealing much more of what they knew to Joe, than Joe revealed to them, in the end. This boastful remark oddly clashed with the tic Joe had going in one eyelid, like an insect trapped under his skin. "You write for *Time*," he broke off suddenly.

"Well—not anymore." She tried to explain the difference between freelancers and staff writers; she had worked for *Time*, but she'd been just a so-so reporter, she hadn't had the gene for it. She was better at features. Now she contributed to a few different general-interest weeklies—this was too esoteric for Joe. He convulsed with impatience.

"I've seen your byline in *Time*," he insisted. "Listen: this is what you need to print. The FBI knows that Pauline is with Jenny Shimada. They never knew Jenny Shimada had ties to the cadre. But now they've found out, and they're not telling anyone else. You've been on this story a while. You've never heard Jenny's name, right?" When she agreed this was true he said, "See! You don't rustle the bushes when you've got the deer right in your sights!"

"Joe, the fact that no one at FBI headquarters has mentioned Jenny Shimada isn't *proof* that they're interested in her. Don't you think that's a little bit paranoid?"

He paused to let her know that he'd taken offense. "If you knew what I know, you would never have said that," he said.

"I'm just trying to explain that I need more than you've told me so far. Please. I need a way to substantiate this."

"Don't call the Feds with the stuff I've just told you," he cried. "Then they'll move, right away! Michael said I could trust you."

"You *can* trust me—"

"And you can trust me," Joe cut in. He'd grabbed her notebook and written *SHIMADA* in an almost illegible scrawl. Then the light had changed on Broadway, and before she could stop him he was instantly gone in the crowd.

IN SAN FRANCISCO after five days of driving—she's traced the route the girls took, another bit of lint that won't be in the story; already this long past year of Pauline's invisibility and Anne's questing confusion has been termed by the fast-thinking TV newsmen as "the lost year," which means no one need find it—Anne knows Jenny Shimada isn't part of the story, either. Even now that she knows that Joe Smith told the truth. She thinks of what her friend Michael had said: that two hundred people a day claim Pauline's in Tibet, that she's riding a Harley. That she's with someone named

Jenny Shimada. The whole year before the arrests that was how it had been: the static so constant and loud, the sightings so scattered and varied. The FBI couldn't know if Juan really had broken a tooth and was likely to visit a dentist; if Pauline really had materialized on an old woman's crumbling estate outside Rhinebeck, New York. So that the FBI had, on the one hand, gone with the broken-tooth tip and wasted countless man hours briefing dentists all over the country. So that Anne had, on the other hand, checked that Jenny Shimada was a known fugitive, and left it at that. Now she knows the truth, but Jenny still isn't the story. Jenny's nobody's story. Although this might be why Anne pursues her, if only in her spare time. Because she knows no one else will; and that even she, in the end, will stash Jenny away with the mistress and the wonderful homes, and with whatever new lint—good, unusable stuff—she picks up.

The State of California turns out to have far more extensive records on J. Shimada, b. 1924—Jenny's father—than on Jenny herself, b. 1949. Anne feels the lint settling again. James Shimada is the only child of immigrants from Japan, a farmer and his wife who by the late 1930s have saved enough money after years of truck farming to open a small produce stand in L.A. James Shimada excels at baseball, is called "Jim" by his friends, wins a scholarship to UCLA; he professes an intention to go to film school and make Westerns. But in the fall of 1942, instead of entering UCLA on his scholarship, Jim, like all other Japanese and Japanese-Americans who live in California, is interned in a "War Relocation Center" by the federal government. After Pearl Harbor, the previous winter, Jim had gone to enlist, as had some of his friends. He had not been allowed to, not because of his age—he'd been just seventeen—but because of his Japanese blood.

Jim and his parents are sent to Manzanar, in the Owens Valley desert northeast of L.A. Nothing in particular seems to happen to Jim in the first six months or so of his internment to set him apart from the rest of the camp. But in the spring of 1943, the government drafts a loyalty oath to administer to internees that consists of two questions. 1) Will you serve the U.S. in the army—if you are allowed? 2) Will you renounce loyalty to Japan? By the spring of 1943, a pro-Japan movement—very small and very violent, made up mostly of boys who were once sent to Japan by their parents for a few years of school—has given rise to gang violence throughout Manzanar. The loyalty oath causes panic. The second question particularly, about renouncing loyalty to Japan, is rumored to be a trick: if you answer yes, it will be used against you, as an admission you've *had* loyalty to Japan. The panic is exploited by the pro-Japan gangsters, and both the panic and the gangsters are exploited in turn by anti-Japanese opinion makers in the press, who point out that the Japanese in the U.S. are clearly a threat, their prior Americanness just a cunning façade. Pauline's grandfather, in a series of loud editorials, propagates this view in his newspapers.

Inside camp, Jim Shimada is beaten by the pro-Japan gang over whether he'll say yes or no to the loyalty questions. Jim Shimada, before this, had not been a political person. There were ways in which camp, in the beginning, had almost seemed tailor-made for the restless teenager, before his parents lost their home and their just-purchased fruit stand because they'd failed to make mortgage payments while interned and unable to work; before he'd heard his mother sobbing one night on her cot. Before the Rubicon of the loyalty oath, when camp just seemed strangely—like camp. Unsworn, as-yet-uninquisited, neither a yes/yes, no/no, yes/no, or no/yes, Jim is picked up by one of the administrative security details in the midst of his bloody beating, which he is fiercely resisting, and transferred, away from his parents, to a new camp for "incorrigible" Japanese, which has just been established at the northernmost edge of the state, in the wild Cascades.

The Camp for Incorrigibles, unlike Manzanar, has no ameliorating aspects. There are no old people or children, no family groups whatsoever. None of the "amenities" that have been slowly established at Manzanar—the weekend dances for the young people, the permission to grow vegetables, the earnest white lady librarians who come from the cities with donated books. The Camp for Incorrigibles is an actual prison, even if none of its prisoners have been confined with due process. The cellblocks are horse-stable construction, with no heat or hot water to bathe. Jim has bronchitis almost from the time he arrives to the time he leaves, fifteen months later. He is also given, and gives in return, broken bones, concussions, knife wounds, purple bruises, split skulls, and continual torrents of verbal abuse. By now the war is an abstraction to them, the reviled "Japs," half of them just teenage boys, who eat their often spoiled food, cast-off rations from everywhere else, beneath the poised muzzles of guns of white boys their same age, sometimes from their same towns. With overseas casualties climbing, Roosevelt reverses himself on Japs in uniform, and Japanese-American boys are invited to get out of camp by enlisting in segregated battalions. This is a moot point for Jim, not even thought of, but then the policy is liberalized further, and all boys in all camps over eighteen are drafted. Jim refuses; he suggests the government give back his parents' house and fruit stand, reimburse them for the years of lost income, and let them go home, and he'll think about it. He's tried and convicted of draft evasion, and transferred to a federal prison.

Before that, though; before the draft, the refusal, the trial, the words spoken in court and transcribed and ensconced in the great vault of criminal annals; before Jim Shimada's release under President Truman, who quietly pardons all the Jap draft resisters in 1947; before Jim briefly marries a young woman who is probably already unhappy to be attracted to him, who is made more unhappy by him, who bears him a daughter and then blessedly dies; before Jim renounces his country and takes his daughter to the land of his parents, Japan, and renounces it, too, and moves back, penniless and defeated; before the daughter embarks on her own catastrophic adventure; one night at the Camp for Incorrigibles, there's a riot, and then a jailbreak. As is often the case, the cause later can't be determined, but it seems trivial; it has something to do with the dinner. Dinner is rotten again, or there isn't enough. Chaos breaks out in the kitchen and spreads through the mess; boiling water is thrown on a man. Guards come running with guns, there's a general stampede. One of the incorrigibles runs outside and steals a truck and drives off wildly; others cling to the side doors or jump in the back, catching the outstretched hands of comrades. The truck careers wildly left and right, the boys and men bang back and forth, armed guards dive out of the way and then suddenly there is a breach, the front gate has been flattened, and those who've rushed out of the mess, which is smoky with tear gas and awful with shrieks, breaking glass, firing guns, without thinking rush into the night. Jim Shimada, just eighteen years old, always thin as a whip but now skinny, hacking from bronchitis, limping from a fresh fight, his cheek purple, his lip split, his thin shirt in shreds, runs also, awkwardly, in his camp-issue sneakers, which are splitting away from their soles. Like the runners of a marathon the escapees surge out as a mass, but then thin out, slow down, break into little groups. They are suddenly silent with terror. It is a winter night, well below freezing. Jim is inured to the cold now but sees his breath clouding the air, feels the burn in his throat. Above him he might see the distant pristine Cascade moon. The next morning the news of the "jailbreak" is sensational all over the land, is particularly trumpeted in Pauline's grandfather's chain of newspapers under such headlines as JAPS BUTCHER COOK, OVERWHELM PRISON GUARDS, ATTEMPT FURTHER MURDEROUS RAMPAGE, but it isn't a rampage at all. They jog wordlessly down the dirt road, by the delicate light of the moon. Soon they'll be picked up by soldiers with guns, soldiers of their own army, but for now they just slowly lose steam. They would die in these mountains, they know; there is nowhere to go. Anne unfolds her map of California and traces the McCloud River's route. She finds the long-ago site of the Camp for Incorrigibles by the small lake it once sat beside. No, Jim Shimada could never have made it. Even at their closest proximity the two places are almost fifty miles apart. Fifty miles of twelve-thousand-foot peaks and untamed wilderness. Still, for the mistress ensconced at McCloud the putative threat was delicious; perhaps those hysterical headlines had all been for her. Anne still remembers the passage, but she's glad that she brought the book with her. "One night we had the awfullest scare. The Japs at the camp had a riot—who knows what they all got so angry about? There the President was, letting them live without lifting a finger on your taxpayer dollars, but they still had to make a big fuss. They broke out and we *knew* they were coming to murder us all!"

THAT NIGHT in her hotel room Anne lies in bed and treats herself to a bottle of wine. She has to be careful; on some nights like tonight, strangely stirred up and sad, she's gotten in bed with a drink, because it's fun to play with Little Man that way, and let him march up and down on her chest. She usually wakes up the next day with a throbbing hangover, Little Man looking down from the headboard at her with reproach. You're not supposed to fall asleep with your parrot, lest you roll over abruptly, and crush him.

But this night she lets herself drink, and thinks about the strange contacts that make up the world. "Joe Smith"—she knows now his name is Rob Frazer—and Jenny Shimada. The other Shimada, jogging down a dirt road on a subzero night by the light of the moon. Jim Shimada's not part of the story. Pauline's grandfather fifty miles off, his excitable mistress. None of this is the story. There's no room, there's no good place to put it; in the end it's just static and lint. The two girls who thought they could make history, while all the while *it* had made *them*: that's not even the story. Although Anne thinks she sees that part clearly, sees the actors hemmed into their stage, the stock costumes they wear, the old backdrop hanging in wait.

2.

Months before learning that Jenny had been arrested Jim Shimada felt a heightening of sensitivity, or maybe just of irritability. He hated to call it paranoia, but it *was* paranoia. If it wasn't that, it was something worse: guilt. A habit of guilt it repulsed him to find in himself. He had felt a tinge of guiltiness his whole life after being interned; the same blameless guilt that had made him feel disgust for his parents, and for everyone else who'd been wrongly accused. Jenny once had asked him why they knew no Japanese in California. "Do you *want* to?" he'd said. "They're all sheep!" But he'd been the same way and still was; so that he sweated when he saw a policeman; and though he even filed his taxes on time, he still expected the dark suits of the FBI men to appear on his doorstep again.

He'd been working in the greenhouse, sorting through and getting rid of the bulbs—he did it every year in June; if they hadn't been bought by now, no one was going to buy them, so they'd rot, unless he planted them himself—when his eye was caught by a movement outside on the road. The movement was irregular and slow, not simply swift movement, the cars that streaked past his outpost on the two-lane highway outside town. He thought it might be a customer, idling on the shoulder on the far side of the road while awaiting a chance to turn into his lot, but the crunch of gravel beneath tires didn't come, and so he peered out between tangles of leaves. To his left, a panel of black plastic in place of a pane sucked in and out like a lung with the slow wind outside. He didn't usually peer out like a suspicious old woman at the least sound of traffic, but something stirred in him and he remembered, as if under hypnosis, the same utterly mundane occurrence a few days before. A car, seeming to idle a while on the shoulder opposite his house. When he peered out he saw, briefly, a dark nondescript sedan with two men in the front seat, just pulling away. He dropped the bulbs and strode outside, but the car was receding now into the sun.

The black plastic patch had been on the greenhouse almost precisely the length of time Jenny had been gone. On this bulb-sorting day in June 1975, the length of time was three years and three months. Three years and three months since her boyfriend had been arrested, and she had disappeared, and several shrill articles about her—local girl, only daughter of Shimada of Shimada's Nursery—had appeared in the Stockton newspaper. He had been in the house at the time, sitting inside with the drapes drawn, the phone cord yanked out of the wall, the CLOSED sign on the door, when he heard the explosion of glass; the margin of the great pane had held on for an infinite instant after the hole was punched in the center before falling away in a second, more delicate crash. When he had finally ventured into the greenhouse he'd seen his plants and trees rippling in the unfamiliar breeze. Great sickle-shaped shards of the glass, and then the tiniest flakes, and every size in between had been everywhere. For years to come, repotting a jasmine, or rearranging his shelves, he would keep finding more. The brick had lain on the floor with a note wrapped around it: a hackneyed, almost quaint vandalism except for how much it scared him. *Jap commies go home!*

For the next several months he had been under matter-of-fact surveillance, and although the brick and the surveillance weren't connected, except insofar as they were both linked to Jenny, they felt like two sides of a coin. He had suddenly acquired a new customer, a man from nowhere in the area whose gardening needs, in spite of total gardening ignorance, brought him by the greenhouse every couple of days. But Jenny's trail had been cold from the start, and soon the fraudulent gardener had stopped coming in. Jim knew of nothing that would have made her trail less cold this summer than it had been for the past thirty-nine months. He decided that the slow-moving car might as easily be his brick-thrower, still frothing after all of these years. When paranoia was a habit, indifference felt fun. He told himself not to worry about it.

A few days later, he shaved. He was fifty years old and he could still go for days without shaving. His face still only produced sparse patches of hair that never spread into a beard; he still felt, as he had at eighteen, a little foolish and theatrical spreading shaving cream onto his face. Although at that age the lack of facial hair had grieved him, and now he liked it. One less thing to do every day. In every other way the face of himself as a young man was gone. Himself at eighteen: just a kid. He remembered dancing with the girl he liked, flipping her and sliding her between his legs. Though he rarely thought of it in benign terms, Manzanar had been a girl heaven; he'd never before or since had so many girls concentrated around him. Of course he wasn't thinking of the very beginning, when no one even had solid walls. He was thinking of the brief period of time further in, when camp life had been "ameliorated" to a surreal degree. The girl's name he needed a long moment, a squinting moment as he shaved, to remember. He'd thought he might marry her then. Camp life had been a strange shot of adrenaline that way: it yanked you out of the world, removed everything, hung you up in a void but for some reason instilled this unbearable urgent desire to grow up as quickly as possible, there where parental authority had been snuffed into nothing. Where parents had been made irrelevant, and children able to govern themselves—though what he hadn't yet seen was that the disempowerment of his parents had not brought adulthood to him, but childhood to all of them.

There he was at the dance. It was the same night this particular week as a "family workshop" being held by the absurd, self-important, bespectacled "camp psychologist," who was really only another kid like Jim but with three years of college and so most of a bachelor's degree before being interned. In the camp context the kid had translated his aborted education into professional credentials; he was not just psychologist but prophet, explicator, architect of the new and improved Japanese-born American people. Another side to the seeming pan-adulthood the camp's real pan-childhood promoted: by now, they had all been good enough to have been awarded the privilege of self-amusement by their captors. In part this had meant the frantic, overheated mixers; bands competing for fans; foolish hand-painted placards for JOE IKEDA AND HIS SWINGING ALL-STARS; everyone getting the sheet music to the current hits by mail order, seeing no real contradiction in their fervid pursuit of the latest in American wartime fashion from the inside of a jerry-rigged American prison. And, in part, it had meant a self-serious explosion of expertise, the high-mindedness of the "psychologist" masquerading as concern about the future. Jim had very honestly not given a shit for the future. He had been very interested in the girl who could dance, and she had been interested in him, and because they had thought they were instant adults they had embarked on a program of sex and amusement and had ignored the program for self-improvement.

And because Jim's peers felt the same way, the psychologist's patients that Saturday night were as always the camp's oldest people, who had nowhere better to go. Jim's mother and father were there, having filed into Mess Hall 16 to get out of their room. They filed in, took their seats sleepily, and were soon being told that he, Jim, was a stranger to them. Jim—who'd turned eighteen in a prison, who wasn't getting to UCLA after all. Jim, with whom they had never sat shooting the breeze, because they spoke one language, and he spoke another. Jim was a stranger, and this was their fault—they had startled awake with their neighbors and friends, and denounced the young man for his rudeness. And then they'd streamed out of Mess Hall 16, not a fraction as angry as they had behaved. They were enlivened, to have vented frustration and defended themselves. They had gone to the workshop to get out of their rooms, and now it felt just as good to get out of the workshop. They excitedly voiced indignation, they noticed the wonderful breeze. It was warm. It was spring—their first spring in this place. There was an almost-full moon and they could see the ghostly wall of the Sierras standing right above them, glowing as if from within. They could hear insects—that had just happened, they realized. Insects had just, in the past night or two, come to life around them, as if squeezed from the newly warm air.

Walking unhurriedly away from Mess Hall 16, they splintered as successive blocks were reached, some going left, some right, down the barely distinguishable rows. Gardens were just being planted, rocks arranged near a couple of doorways, but it was more the deep instinct resulting from endless mindless repetition that told each increasingly smaller clutch of old men and women when they had to turn left, turn right, and continue until a next turn or a next. The barracks stretched out for a mile in every direction, black oblong boxes, level beneath the black night. Those who remained had grown quiet. They walked together in increasing distraction. Camp was so large that it was a while before they came within hearing range of the mess hall where the Saturday night dance was held, and they were only a few now whose barrack number had required that they come this way at all. Those who had already turned away into the night might have seen their sons and daughters setting off in this direction earlier that evening, or they might not have; most of them no longer even had dinner together. Their sons and daughters came home to sleep, hopefully. That's the most they saw of them.

At least, this was how Jim Shimada imagined it. This was how he imagined his parents, fifteen years after their near-simultaneous deaths and decades after camp, with the facility of empathy he hoped came of being a parent himself. He knew this idea was false; he knew that the fact of his fatherhood didn't make him any more able to understand his mother or father than Jenny, if she ever had children, if she even emerged from her own fiery youth, would be able to understand him. He knew no more of his parents now than he had at the age of eighteen, but he could imagine. They heard the gay, stubborn music from Mess Hall Number 4, and the music twined itself with the uncomfortable meditations that had been sparked by their long walk through camp. They knew they appeared, to their children and to many outsiders, without thought and perhaps even stupid. This was because, unlike their children, they'd perfected the dissimulating arts. They could even fool themselves into thinking they were without thought, but they were never without it. Every moment of their lives had been the product of pained calculation, of doubt and its opposite, the wild urge to gamble; they thought ceaselessly. The psychologist, of course, had hit home. The truth he'd spoken was one they lived close to but tried to ignore. Yes, their children were strangers. In certain ways they were even unlikable. They loved them, of course. But like them? It wasn't easy to like their rudeness, their self-certainty, their callous smugness, their astounding greed, their repulsive capacity for the American sense of entitlement. Even so they still longed for their children, especially now, on the year's first warm night.

Standing before Mess Hall 4 they hesitated, then opened the door. They were met by a wall of cacophonous noise and by unpeaceful darkness; the dark seemed to roil and billow like smoke. Within it lights flickered and faded, illuminating their children, who were flipping and swinging each other. Their children were wearing flared skirts and slim loafers and garish sport shirts that they'd ordered from the Sears, Roebuck catalogue. Where had the money come from? It was their parents' life savings, withdrawn from the banks and sewn into their coats before leaving for camp. They'd feared the government somehow would tap their accounts, that the same force that had unsurprisingly breached storage units and misdirected mortgage payments would also remove their last hope and so assets were made cash and carried, and now the kids had breached the citadel themselves. They'd ordered ankle socks and twin sets and trombones from Sears, Roebuck, which delivered great heaps of American goods to the camp constantly, as if camp were like any small town.

Jim's parents, for all their superiority to him in age, in experience, in suffering and forbearance and prudence and cash management, were frightened. They entered the mess hall like the citizens of a subjugated city entering the bonfire-lit camp of the conqueror. They entered like supplicants, and instinctively ranged themselves close to the wall. They blinked in the spangled darkness. Party lights from Sears, Roebuck had completely transformed the dank, unpleasant space, so that now it felt stirringly vast. Their children handled each other with an intimacy and dexterity that were stirring as well, if disturbingly so. They strained their eyes scanning the crowd, seeking their own, only children. Jim's parents were so static and shadowed and old that they were sure they themselves were not seen, but Jim had seen them instantly from the far side of the hall as he unfurled his girl almost cruelly, felt the joint of her shoulder pull and catch, yanked her back. He had seen his parents and let his own face go stiff like a mask, imagined himself invisible as they imagined themselves invisible, though they were more than visible; they were small weighted shapes, like hanged men. His parents seemed to dangle in death even when they were moving, while he, Jim, was wildly alive. It didn't surprise him at all they could not recognize him.

Finished, he squared his shoulders and examined himself in the mirror. An old man, suddenly. His thoughts were interrupted by the sound of a car cruising past on the road. Another car seeming somehow furtive; for the next two and a half months, until she was arrested, this would happen a handful of times, and he would never know whether this was really the net closing in, or his old paranoia. The paranoia operating as always, but soon to retrospectively look like clairvoyance. He darted his face close to the half-open window, felt the air from outside on the traces of lather that still streaked his cheeks. The car passed at a crawl and went out of his sight to the left, but the road was quiet this morning, it wasn't hard to U-turn, and in a beat he saw the car passing slowly again, from the other direction. If this was an undercover car it was a good one, a customized surfermobile with brown-tinted windows and absurd orange pin stripes. Then it bumped onto the shoulder on the far side of the road and he stiffened, thinking of his other theory, half expecting the window to roll down and the brick to fly out. He would get the goddamn license number this time. And of course he was thinking of Jenny, and then it crossed his mind that this car could be hers. Without wiping his face he ran out of the bathroom, down the hall, out the front door and onto the step, and he could almost see the car start with alarm.

"Wait!" he shouted.

But the little car had sped away; and he'd been so stricken, so convinced suddenly it was her, that he'd only tried, futilely, to see through the dark windows. He forgot about the license plate number until the car was a speck, and then gone.

ON AN AUGUST EVENING a year and a half after Pauline was kidnapped, Jim Shimada saw Pauline's arrest on the six o'clock news, just like everyone else in the state and perhaps in the country. By the time the cameras had caught up Pauline was being pulled from a squad car in front of San Francisco's Federal Building. "Say something!" a voice called from the crowd.

"Venceremos!" Pauline yelled, and was hauled off to cheers.

It didn't take much attention to register that the yelling handcuffed girl looked nothing like the remote, wealthy girl whose pictures had dominated the news for so long. This new girl had long wild hair, a deep tan, wore a small pair of wire-rimmed glasses, striped T-shirt, and jeans. Jim barely glanced up from his dinner. It was a sweltering night, all the windows open, rush-hour traffic, such as it was in these parts, hissing past on the road. Jim's several barely functioning fans feebly stirred the hot air and made a disproportionate noise doing so. The TV volume was all but drowned out. It wasn't until the next morning, when he opened the paper, that he learned of the other arrest. The other girl rated barely a sentence: there were only the facts that she'd also been wanted, that she'd lived with Pauline, and her name. Jim dropped the paper, hands trembling. Then he closed and locked the greenhouse and the house, and caught a bus into Oakland.

By the time he arrived she had already met with her court-appointed lawyer, and it was this person Jim spoke to, not her. "She's fine," the lawyer said. "Of course, frightened. And not eager to open up to me. I think she wishes we'd all leave her alone, an understandable wish, if imposs—"

"She doesn't want to see me," Jim interrupted, guessing.

"She asked me to tell you, if you came, to please come back after she contacts you. I think that's normal in these circumstances. I think in a few days—"

"Tell her I'm waiting here," Jim said. He gave the lawyer the number of the motel a few blocks from the jail where he'd taken a room. Before they parted the lawyer asked him if Jenny had any preferences in writing materials. The lawyer was going to ask Jenny to write something for him—not a confession, or a declaration of innocence, or anything that touched on the charges she faced, but a statement of feelings, beliefs. Jim gazed back at the man with distaste. It didn't seem likely to Jim that Jenny would "open up" to this person, ever. She would find such fastidious gestures as this condescending—preferred writing materials? Jenny was hardly a fetishist when it came to that stuff. She wrote on legal pads and with disposable pens, a certain brand that she bought by the box. She hated ballpoints, fat felt-tips, and overpriced fountain pens that needed cartridges. The pens she liked achieved a perfect balance between quality and accessibility. They weren't high-class—you could get them in a drugstore—but they made a fine line. As for paper, Jim would never have said she thought much about it. She liked legal pads or spiral-bound notebooks, didn't like fussy notebooks that tried to be pretty, or fancy paper that didn't have lines. Preferred writing materials? How on earth would he know? And yet he found himself answering, "Yes. Yes, she certainly does."

Every day he called the lawyer from his motel room. He learned that Jenny had been pleased with the legal pads and the box of disposable pens. He learned she'd been willing to work on a statement that detailed her feelings and beliefs about things. He learned that she still wasn't willing to see him, but that she might feel more able when she'd finished her statement. Her statement, though her lawyer did not say so, never seemed to progress. For the rest of that week Jim ate all of his meals at a terrible diner next door to a storefront that said BAIL BONDS. He lay in a motel-room bed, mattress lumpy, sheets scratchy, and stared at the TV. He waited—while his greenhouse stayed shuttered, while his plants gasped for water and sagged in the heat. While bricks, in his insomnial half-awake dreams, exploded through his windows. He knew there was nothing to wait for. As extraordinary as all of this was, it was also just one more stubborn face-off between himself and his daughter. He was staying to show that he'd stayed. At week's end nothing had changed as he'd known nothing would. He gave the lawyer his number in Stockton, and took the bus home.

WHEN HE stepped down from the bus to the shoulder on the far side of the highway, his gut heavy with dread, the bus driver having done him a favor and dropped him off here instead of making him ride all the way into town, the dim highway light showed him only the lopsided form of his house—yet he somehow could tell that the house had survived unmolested. Perhaps just because he'd been gone, he thought then, as he crossed the quiet highway in darkness, his backpack on his shoulder. Perhaps they were waiting for him to unlock his screen door, step inside, feel his way to his lamp. Then they'd home in on him.

Or would they? Jenny was so overshadowed, he thought the

next several days, with mingled relief and annoyance, as he read the newspapers. Column after page after section detailed Pauline's condition in the words of her lawyers and doctors and brainwashing experts and family spokespeople, while Jenny was never mentioned. Pauline's doctors were there to explain that Pauline was severely malnourished, hallucinated as if experiencing flashbacks from drugs, spoke in flat tones "like a zombie," and initially failed to recognize her own family members. Pauline's brainwashing experts were there to assert that like the prisoners of war of Red China, she had been brainwashed by her captors through deprivation and violence, and had committed no criminal acts willfully. Pauline's lawyers were there to detail her pathetic condition in a motion for bail, although the judge, just like Jim and the rest of the world, had seen the tanned Pauline yell "Venceremos!" at the TV cameras. The judge denied Pauline bail.

It was just after this that Jim had his first glimpse of his daughter. Not a glimpse that would tell him whether *she* was in any way malnourished, or drugged, or brainwashed. Not a glimpse of her hair—short or long? he wondered. He'd forgotten to ask the lawyer that. Not a glimpse of her dark severe eyebrows, the same eyebrows as his, like a double-dash chunk of Morse code. But a glimpse nonetheless. Two days after the judge had denied Pauline bail, Pauline's lawyers filed a second motion for bail, this one containing the testimony of an "unnamed person" said to be uniquely qualified to comment on Pauline's situation in the months leading up to her capture. This person had known Pauline during what was now being called "the lost year," and this person affirmed that Pauline *was* malnourished, drugged, brainwashed, an unwilling prisoner, never a willing participant in any criminal act. This person—this mysterious defender of Pauline—went not just unnamed but also uncommented-on in the paper. No one seemed to wonder who this person was, but Jim knew—"That's you, Jenny!" he said. He jerked forward over the paper, and his loose glasses fell down his nose—broken temple, reattached with a paper clip, he couldn't remember to go to a jeweler. "Goddammit, what the hell are you doing?" But he was strangely glad to see her surface amid the newsprint, above the rough waves of the other girl's story. Because it was her story, too—that was what moved him now, that in this carnival of news and headlines and nightly TV updates and interviews and op-eds she was forgotten, discarded. It was also a blessing, of course. It meant this time his windows might stay unbroken. Meant she might have some life to return to when she got out of there—it was the first time he'd let himself think about this.

That afternoon he was in the greenhouse, moving slowly down the rows with his watering can, when he heard a car slow on the road. His heart, like a warm ember beneath wind, grew immediately cold. He peered out between leaves and saw the car roll away, almost reluctantly, as if the driver for some reason had to defer, stay his hand, leave the brick on the passenger seat—but just for the moment. Jim couldn't see the driver, but he knew the slowness was no accident. This was someone for him. It was a car he'd never seen, he was sure, although there was nothing distinct about it. It was a four-door, bland beige, recent model, the kind taxi companies buy or rental agencies rent.

He was standing in the open doorway, half-full watering can at his feet, a good two thirds of his plants still unwatered—waiting—when the beige car returned. He'd known that it would. He stood his ground, although belatedly remembering he didn't have a pencil and paper for the license plate number. It was too late now. The car was bearing down as if it too had strengthened its resolve. They were finally confronting each other, Jim and this car, this car driven by some racist bastard, some hater of him and his daughter—two Shimadas, one brick. He tried to ready himself to do battle, though he was not even holding a weapon, just his battered sun-bleached baseball cap, which he'd taken off to wipe the sweat from his forehead. The day was suddenly hot, very still—so that he was squinting as the car swung decisively into his lot across the oncoming lane.

It wasn't a brick-wielding kid or a cop who got out but a

woman, petite and blond, in her mid-thirties or perhaps slightly younger—she had a plain face that made it hard to judge age. Shutting her door she glanced quickly at him before she opened a rear door to bring out a large shrouded form, which she carefully set on the hood of the car. Approaching her, Jim was considering what a sorry state his business must be in, that it hadn't even crossed his mind in the preceding tense moments the car might hold a customer. Then the woman said, "I'm a reporter." He stopped short. "But this is my day off," she added. "I just want to buy a tree for my bird."

"And maybe talk a little, too?" he said, sharply. He didn't want to seem unkind, just undeceived. A light jangling noise came from under the shroud, and the woman broke away from his hard gaze and uncovered the cage. The bird, unsedated by the blaze of daylight, gave an interested squawk. The bird was small, an iridescent bright green. When Jim touched a fingertip to the bars the bird lunged eagerly, beak open.

"He's just playing," the woman said, in apology.

"I know. The bird's got moxie. That's good."

He pulled on his cap and turned away toward the greenhouse, and after a moment he heard her pick up the birdcage and follow. When they were standing together in his small indoor forest he thought he saw her trying to avoid looking at the black patch of plastic. "I keep meaning to fix it, but somehow the day never comes," he said.

"It's been broken a while?"

"Years. Someone put a brick through it, when my daughter was first in the news."

At that she set down the birdcage. The bird began whistling provocatively. "He knows when he's been used as an icebreaker," she said. She was taking an envelope out of her purse. "It's true that I didn't just come for a tree, but I'm not here to pump you. If you want to talk to me, today or someday, I would be very glad, but that's not why I came."

"Go on," he said after a minute.

The envelope was unsealed and unaddressed. "A few months ago, I was contacted by someone who I think was a friend of your daughter's," she said. She told Jim about her encounter with the man called "Joe Smith." "I couldn't find substantiation for any part of his story. I couldn't do what he asked, and get it printed somewhere. I don't know why, but I wanted to tell you. I thought you should know there was someone out there who tried to help Jenny, though he didn't succeed."

After a long time, he didn't know how long, Jim said, "What's in the envelope?"

It was just a strange little detail she had found while reporting the story; he could have it, she said. It was a mimeographed, smeary newsletter, two sheets stapled together, small typed announcements and badly reproduced ads ranged in teetering columns. Jim stared at the earnestly drawn masthead: *Historical Society of Rhinecliff and Rhinebeck, New York*. On the second page someone, this reporter, he guessed, had loosely circled a short entry under "Restorative Tidbits."

> *Those of you who have followed the restoration at Wildmoor chronicled in these pages will be as reassured as we were to learn what a boon to the effort has arrived in the person of Iris Wong, of San Francisco. This quiet young visitor from the West Coast has made an impression on all who have met her with her patience and fine workmanship. The RRHS invites all to take a Wildmoor house tour to view Iris's magic.—Louise Fowler*

He didn't need to ask, but he said, "This was her?"

"This was her," she told him.

THAT EVENING, after the reporter was gone, Jim unfolded the newsletter again, and thought of the shock of excitement he'd felt, not just on realizing the note concerned Jenny, but on seeing the two words *New York*. Rhinecliff and Rhinebeck, New York, wherever those places were. Still the Empire State: close enough. Jenny didn't know this, but when she was a little girl he'd dreamed of moving with her to New York. He'd thought it was the place he could teach her to be a citizen of the world, a Universal Human. Neither American nor Japanese, but New Yorker—it was a romantic idea, he knew. Being San Franciscan or Los Angelean never held the same promise for him. Perhaps all California was too tainted with old disappointments. He knew he was ignoring the idea of New York as the immigrants' city, Ellis Island and the Statue and the masses and their Babel of tongues. But he was a Westerner, born with his back to the Pacific. He'd always associated the journey East with the final achievement of American belonging, sheared free of ethnicity. He saw it as something to be sheared free of, yes. Yet they never did make the trip East, or rather, they went backwards, to the wrong East, Japan. Jim remembered the day he'd come home from prison—the world, well into its postwar good times, must have flinched at the sight of him. The boys who'd left camp for the war had returned as heroes, while Jim had been the reminder that nobody wanted. And then to have been left alone with a child. He supposed he had never, through Jenny's childhood, thought of her quite as much as he had of himself. Dragging her to Japan, the captive of his anger, was an example of that. Although in spite of his failures he still thought she'd turned out very well.

The reporter hadn't been all that bad. She'd only asked him the questions he'd known he'd be asked. And she'd made it clear to him, somehow, that she was on Jenny's side. After they had talked a while longer, not even about Jenny so much as the world in general, the news, their opinions of things, the little bird making a worse and worse racket the more they ignored it, she'd said she really did want a tree for the bird, if she could find one it liked. She'd spent a small fortune on bird toys already, but the bird still preferred to shred the spines of her books, and yank the ribbon out of the typewriter while she was writing.

"Kids," Jim said jokingly.

He'd latched his flimsy screen door and then shaken it a little, to confirm that it wouldn't drift open, and then he'd given the black plastic patch a hard push with the heel of his hand. He'd done a bad job, he was forced to admit. He'd used prodigious amounts of duct tape in a haphazard way that spoke volumes, he supposed, about his mind's angry turmoil at the time that he'd made the repair, but the seam seemed secure. "The bird flies, right?" he asked.

"Yes," she said. "How did you know?"

"I saw he's got the primaries. You didn't clip them."

"I couldn't do it."

"Sentimental."

She laughed, embarrassed.

"It should be all right," he added. "If he tries to eat his way out through the plastic, we'll stop him."

When he'd lifted the cage door the bird had stepped onto his hand and looked at him expectantly. It hadn't surprised him, but the reporter had been thunderstruck. Whenever she let the bird out she had to wear a tube sock like a mitten, she said, because the bird sparred savagely with her hand.

"Do you have birds?" she asked.

"No," he said. He'd unfurled his arm in a slow, graceful arc, like a dancer, and they watched her bird launch himself into the air.

3.

They'd made the trip by brand-new DC-8 jet, not by ship, her father spending most of their savings on the two one-way tickets. San Francisco to Honolulu for new passengers and fuel, and then from Honolulu to Tokyo. But the purchase of the tickets seemed to absorb all her father's bravado as well as his money, and once they were at the airport apprehension disabled him. They somehow lost their pair of seats together and were told that they would have to sit apart. Her father had probably felt people knew he was a novice with airplanes and were taking advantage of him. She remembered a terrible scene, of the sort that featured a blond, silk-scarf-wearing woman repeating, "I'm going to call the police." Somehow the crisis had ended with the two of them reseated in First Class. This should have been a triumph, but her father's shrillness in the fight for the seats, and the defiant way he led them onto the plane afterward, had mortified her. As soon as the plane was airborne, she left her seat. Her father, white-knuckled and stiffly erect, was too frightened to stop her; and she was too young to see any reason to be afraid.

At the rear of the First Class cabin, just before the opaque curtain that hid Coach from view, she had found a metal spiral staircase, tightly twisting upward. As she started to climb a stewardess appeared and said, "Little girl! You can't go up there. Where are you sitting?" Without speaking, she pointed—forward, toward the other First Class seats. The stewardess hesitated, and she was later aware, reexamining the memory, of frustrated scorn. "Go on then," the stewardess finally said.

The spiral staircase came up into a bright, bubblelike lounge, with curved walls and ceiling and seats arrayed casually in two facing half-circles instead of lined up severely in rows. From the seats, and from the carpeted floor, a dozen or so faces looked at her with pleasant surprise. Most of the faces were children's, and most of the children were sprawled on the floor, with quantities of beautiful toys. There were also adults, at least a few, and it was one of these who said, "Come on up! What's your name, dear? Are you going to Hawaii? Are you Hawaiian, yourself? Are your mum and dad traveling with you?"

It was one of those immediate, effortless intimacies that seem only to happen in childhood, if they happen at all. And perhaps it had happened to her just this once. She remembered little else of her initiation into the world of these people; she seemed to have arrived, and then been among them. There had been girls, and boys, in what number and of what ages she had no idea. There were games and more toys and overhead a reassuring babble of cheerful adults and the sound of ice moving in glasses. Stewardesses had risen from and sunk back into the stairwell, and a meal had come, and extra sweets, and particular confidences shared between Jenny and one little girl, with a vow they would write to each other . . . At some point there was turbulence. A stewardess, pale and with hair coming loose from her bobby pins, clanked swiftly up the stairs to ask them all to please put on their seat belts. There were seats enough for everyone and, strapped in, they faced each other across the brightly colored carpet, and Jenny noticed for the first time the painfully blue ethersphere outside the round little windows. The plane bucked hard, like a horse, and one of the grown-ups—the father?—said "Oops-a-daisy!" and winked at the children, and all of them laughed. And then were quiet, but smiling and calm, as the plane jolted several more times through invisible, powerful currents. She remembered that even then she hadn't been at all frightened.

It was after the turbulence—probably shortly after, although, with the temporal dilations of childhood, it seemed like a very long time—that her father found her. His head and shoulders rose uncertainly and so strangely slowly into view, as hers must have, hours before. Hours really had passed. Soon they would land in Hawaii.

"Oh, dear," said the same mellifluous, wonderful voice that had first addressed her. "Your dad must have been worried about you. I'm sorry, we should have sent her down to make sure you knew where she was. Even if it's an airplane, it's still very large. Won't you join us for a drink, Mr.—?"

"No, thank you," her father said coldly. "Come, Jenny."

"She's such a lovely playmate, she's been a dream come true for the children, they were sure they'd be bored—"

She remembered saying good-bye, and then crossing silently to her father. As she took his hand and started down the stairs, stooping awkwardly after him because the stairs were so narrow, she heard one of the girls, the one she'd vowed penpalship with, start to cry. They hadn't traded addresses.

After the plane landed she felt sure she'd see them again, but, whether because she and her father were among the first to get off, or because there was some secret separate exit from the lounge, she did not. The plane was cleaned and refueled and reboarded, and they returned to their fraudulent seats. Her father finally managed to sleep. When she stole back to the staircase, another stewardess, from the new crew, stopped her.

"My friends—" she began.

"There's no friends up there, honey. There's businessmen up there. A meeting. You leave them alone."

And later still, she remembered having the idea that the people had been some kind of royal family. She didn't know where this idea came from. They had certainly been beautiful—incandescently gold-skinned and gold-haired. And they must have been rich. But when she tried to trace the origin of the impression, she only saw her father's head and shoulders, awfully emerging from the stairs. And the look on his face that had not been concern, as the other adults might have realized, but wounded and rewounded, vengefully bandaged-up pride.

It was a durable memory, as vivid as her most vivid memories of the five years they spent in Japan. But it tended to lie fathoms deep in her mind, untouched by consciousness, for years at a time. When she did think of it she had the sense of discovering a book, with a bookmark stuck in it, she hadn't realized she owned. There was the incident itself, the marked page, but there was also the unexplored volume of her own character. She had thought of it when William was arrested: Hadn't she found herself, without quite knowing how, among the self-confident children of the white upper class? With whom she had fought for the rights of the colored and poor. And she had thought of it again that last winter she'd been at Wildmoor, when front pages and national newscasts were carrying the story of the nineteen-year-old kidnapped heiress who'd renounced wealth and joined with her captors. Everything about that unknown girl had interested Jenny: her ancestors' legends and ancestral homes and her alleged boarding-school rebellions. The inexhaustible store of her portraits: in tennis whites and first communion whites and giggling on the beach in a T-shirt, and unsmiling in formation with her parents. Her two-seater car and her desire "to be normal," as described by her boarding-school friends. Her labyrinthine relationship to her own money. Her towering American pedigree.

• • •

THEY WERE separated when they were arrested, taken in two cars to their two destinations, Pauline to the Federal Building in downtown San Francisco, trailed by news vans with cameras and speeding cabs full of reporters, Jenny to downtown Oakland, the car she rode in alone and anonymous in the cross-Bay traffic of the late-summer day. She was alone but didn't feel alone. She was still with Pauline, as if trysting. They might be penning secret letters at night, slipping from cells clad in cloaks or with heads wrapped in scarves. Meeting in the lady's rest room in some railway station; at some landing dock; at the end of some long, lonely road. They'd be together five hours, five minutes; they'd say good-bye tightly holding each other, and then board two trains going different directions.

She hadn't been surprised when Pauline's lawyer visited her: he had seemed like a messenger she'd been awaiting. He was the youngest member of Pauline's five-attorney team, someone whose personal style had earned him, not quite accurately, a reputation for being Left-leaning. He had been retained by Pauline's parents on the advice of Pauline's trusted cousins, who had felt the family should exhibit some degree of comfort with the political climate in which Pauline had been living, whether or not willingly. The lawyer had the air of someone who felt himself to be hipper than all those around him. He told Jenny he'd been the first person to talk with Pauline. She'd seen her parents, her siblings, some cousins, but these encounters had barely connected. From the family's side had come tears and unspoken demands; from Pauline's side, a virtual silence. Pauline was a piece of statuary in the scenarios her lawyer described. Pauline: vivid, annoyed, sloppy, thin, never does the dishes, slaps the floor with her rubber flip-flops, buys ugly glasses, and flaunts her flat chest after she and Jenny finally—finally!—finish reading *The Second Sex* and yet still experiments with curling her hair, decides she likes yogurt but only after they buy every brand that exists and rank them all on a chart on the fridge. Not very much like statuary at all. Pauline seemed so near to her if she was looking indirectly at the absence, the way some very faint stars emerge when you look to one side of them. But then she looked straight at the empty chair—the empty space; there wasn't even a chair anymore. She thought of the stories of sudden explosions, the man and wife hand in hand on the roof of their townhouse while an unperceived gas leak fills up all the rooms. The gas ignites and the building collapses and buries the man instantly, but the wife rides the rubble down somehow, lands still feeling his hand on her own. Or the family in a waterfront town at the time of the First World War: a father reading the news in the parlor, a daughter playing piano a few feet away, a mother making lunch in the kitchen, a son on his way down the stairs. A munitions ship has caught fire in the harbor and when it explodes the force radiates like machetes, shears some places, skips others, obliterates half of the family's house, kills mother and daughter but somehow spares father and son. She used to collect these stories like talismans, as if their randomness could inoculate her. Against what? Against the randomness that could turn any well thought out action into a disaster? Against loss, she thought now.

The lawyer begged her to use his first name. He spoke confidentially to her, as if she and he were the immediate family and Pauline's parents and siblings and cousins some lesser contingent. "There's so much accumulated expectation and resentment, misunderstanding and disappointment, piled on from way back," he explained. "Not just from the start of this business." He waved one of his long-fingered hands, easily shrinking it all to the size of an episode. "The bonds of blood are such shackles," he mused. She hadn't liked him; of course she had not. She hadn't liked the way he flaunted his access to Pauline, or the oily smugness with which he claimed to have won Pauline's confidence. But she'd been ready to do what he wanted before he showed up; she'd been ready from the instant the cop pressed his hand on her head. Somehow it had not been the gun or the handcuffs or the neighborhood kids pedaling up frantically on their bikes, the windows and doors flying open the length of their block, the cries of "Get back!" but that firm touch to which she'd submitted, the hand on her head, that had made it all real. Across the roof of the car she had seen Pauline's head, also clamped by a hand, also next to a car. Then they'd both been pushed down and she was sitting in the backseat alone. Her response, like a policy paper, had presented itself fully formed to her mind, and she'd realized she'd always expected one day they'd be caught. For almost a year she and Pauline had never discussed it, as if superstition could strengthen their luck. But at her core she had come to decisions she'd held in reserve.

She wrote the statement for Pauline's bail motion with the lawyer's assistance, but she could as easily have written it alone. Writing, she almost forgot where she was. Almost forgot she was locked in a cell. Line after line filling the page, laying in the deep shade from which one found the sun. Legal language couldn't tell what happened to Pauline; she knew its version of a close approximation might be worse than a lie. And so she told lies herself, feeling the needle within herself pointing, unwavering. She wrote that Pauline had always been a captive, and that even she had been one of the captors. She wrote that because of this it must follow that Pauline's participation in any criminal act was against her free will.

This second motion for bail also failed. By now Juan and Yvonne had been captured, caught like Jenny and Pauline in the delicate net of acquaintances, the light contacts between Jenny and Sandy and Tom, between Sandy and Tom and Frazer, between Frazer and Juan and Yvonne, that agents had gradually knotted together beginning from Jenny's newsprint fingerprints. From the prints and her name and her outstanding charges they had gone to William in prison and his visitors' list; from there to Sandy and Tom; here the path forked, one branch leading to Jenny and Pauline, the other to Frazer, who like Sandy and Tom would escape being charged, after inadvertently leading his surveillers to the apartment in Daly City where he'd helped settle Juan and

Yvonne, as well as the loose ramblings on tape and the scrawled notebook pages that were all of the book Juan and Yvonne and Pauline had ever managed to write. On the tape and in the handwritten pages Pauline extensively told of her joy upon having been voted into the cadre, and as compromised as Jenny knew that these documents were, they must have ranged themselves in the mind of the judge alongside Pauline's shouting "Venceremos!" deeply tanned on TV. Jenny's statement was dismissed by the judge as a cynical ploy Pauline's lawyers thought up.

But even after this she still felt battle-ready: they would win the next one. Then her own lawyer, George Elson, came to see her. She'd just finished expressing her thoughts in a letter to Pauline, her first. Elson brought in a folding chair for himself, and when the matron left them alone balanced carefully on it and tented his fingertips over his knees. She was absorbed in rereading her ending: among other things she had written, of the lies she had told in the bail statement, "Once Juan said, 'There are things that are facts that in context don't help make the point.' Can you believe I am quoting *him* now? But he would never have influenced you if he hadn't said things that contained grains of truth." The letter was almost fifteen pages long. "I don't have you as my editor now," she observed. She told Pauline to try not to worry about denial of bail; in denying bail the judge had ordered a psychiatric evaluation, and Jenny thought in the end this would be advantageous. "It doesn't mean you're crazy, so don't get embarrassed and not tell them things they should know." She signed *Love.* She pressed the thick sheaf into thirds and started working it into an envelope. Elson cleared his throat. "Jenny," he said.

"Can you mail this for me?" she asked him. "She can get mail, right?"

"Jenny, I don't want you to say anything in response to what I'm going to tell you. Pauline has named you as an accessory to the murder of a grocery-store owner in Monticello, New York."

For a moment, although she'd heard all his words, they seemed to hover awaiting translation. "I don't believe that," she said.

Elson opened his battered briefcase and took out that day's paper. He leaned forward and set it gingerly on her cot, by the unsealed letter. He'd circled the part about her. Juan and Yvonne were named also, the make of the gun. Staring down at it, she could feel him watching her face. Her face seemed to be glowing, not with a blush of humiliation or shock but with plain, beating, furnace-strength heat, independent of any emotion. She became aware of the oversized letter, bursting out of its cheap envelope.

"Not another word," Elson said. "Until and unless you face charges we don't talk about this again. I will say that I don't think charges will be brought, at least not soon. They don't have anything besides Pauline's say-so, and that won't be enough. She doesn't have credibility."

After a moment she heard him closing his briefcase, and the squeak as he carefully folded his chair. "Your father's still waiting to see you," he said. "I told him what you said about wanting to wait until you'd finished your statement. Please don't make a liar of me." Elson knew, as well as she knew herself, that she hadn't been thinking of her statement any more on the day her father first had appeared than she was thinking of it now. The legal pads Elson had given her, the new box of pens, had been used for Pauline's bail motion, and now for the letter that lay on her cot. She shook her head, still not looking at Elson, and he was finally calling the guard to get out of her cell.

THIS DAY always felt like the thunderclap, although later she thought back to that other almost too-quiet day, on the hill with Pauline and the hawk, when she'd chosen to believe that Pauline was in danger—chosen to believe and not simply believed. Chosen a true leap of faith toward a putative rescue, because, she supposed, she hadn't wanted to be left behind. And had recognized, as perhaps she didn't recognize anything else, that Pauline did not want to be left behind, either. Pauline had reached for her and she'd taken the hand, knowing now that she'd felt abdication, the relief of giving up, of removing, as Pauline had said, the temptation to escape by removing the option completely; of dropping the insuperable obstacle just at her back. She'd stopped fighting and known, as Pauline must have known when she'd joined with her captors, that any bond is its own great salvation, no matter how damning in all other ways. She'd bound herself then to Pauline, and Pauline's rushing fate.

Of course, when George Elson first left her she didn't think this. When he left she was glad, because his stern, pitying air of knowing better than she did went with him, and she was free to refuse to believe. For as long as she could she simply wouldn't believe that Pauline had betrayed her, although with every day's paper Pauline betrayed someone else they had known in their time on the run. Although Juan and Yvonne, from whom Jenny had been sure the information first came, denied being in upstate New York at the time of the murder, and even denied knowing Jenny. Although nothing held up Jenny's theory that Pauline had been cornered, and left with no choice, and although Jenny's letter, which she sent anyway, never got a reply.

Left alone in a cell with her grief was a weird, weightless thing —there were no imperatives of time or of action, of get-over-it-now-and-move-on, there was nothing to do but sit balled at the end of her bed, because lying flat all her guts would fall out. She must have slept, risen, emptied her bowels. Addressed herself to her meals and her lawyer and the other constant and brusque interruptions that ensured she had no privacy. Yet her pain had seemed flawlessly private. She was finally angry, so angry at Pauline, so determined to hold her to account that she longed to see Pauline again just to hurt her, badly. Her letter's fifteen loving pages now mortified her and she tried to eclipse them with pages of harsh accusation, condemnation, they-were-*right*-about-you! But whenever she took it that far she was left horror-struck, as if after a frenzy she'd looked down at her own bloody hands. She'd be somehow reminded of Juan's vitriol on the eulogy tape, giving way to Pauline's quiet chant. Her own pen would shift in its tone. She admitted her long-ago feeling—tender, jealous, frustrated—

that Pauline might bloom under her care, but would always be rooted in some other sphere. Then the tender hiatus would break off again; none of these letters got sent.

In her dreams of revenge on Pauline, which were really heartbreak—it was possible this was the first true heartbreak of her life—she eventually sensed a kinship to another transformative anger she'd carried for years. It had been overwhelming anger that drove her when she set out to protest the war. She had been enraged by the state of the world, but perhaps even more she'd been enraged by herself, such a ridiculous, small, not-taken-seriously, average American girl. Not the president, or the chairman of the Joint Chiefs of Staff, or the CEO of Dow Chemical. If she withheld her approval, those in power wouldn't scramble to suit her. The poor wouldn't be fed, tanks withdrawn. Or apologies made. She had wanted apologies made. She had wanted the powerful men who wreaked such great destruction to feel remorse. It occurred to her now, as she stewed in a pain even worse than she'd felt after William's arrest—for he hadn't left her, he'd been taken, and she'd known that she still had his love—that her most carefully rational acts had been shot through with rage. She had always felt she would have done the same things without William as with him; that they were soulmates must mean they would have acted and thought the same way, even if they had lived separate lives. But it was also true that she'd given herself to William, feeling privileged and grateful that he could channel her fury, and transmute it into useful action. Together they'd been such a closed globe; it had been easy to disregard the vast anger that fueled them both. As much as she'd thought she was fighting for justice, perhaps what she'd wanted was less justice than vengeance—because justice wasn't an eye for an eye, an act of violence to match acts of violence. Even if the violence was planned to occur late at night, when not a janitor roamed the long halls. Even if it was staged as a symbol. She had never *believed* in violence as a provocation, as a means to incite revolution by inciting the government to repress its own people. And she had certainly never believed in assassination, like some of the comrades she'd known. But nevertheless she'd believed in violence—as the only reliable way to seize people's attention. As a means toward enlightenment. And, perhaps, as a way to wreak vengeance; she feared this about herself now, as she seethed in her cell.

She thought of the monk she had seen years ago on the news, immolating himself. It was a sight that had shocked and transformed her perhaps more than anything else in her life. She supposed now that in her time with William it had been that unparalleled shock of the real she had wanted to force onto others, the way she'd felt it forced onto herself, by the monk in his column of flame. She had wanted to force others to see, no matter what it might take, and had felt this was just what the monk had been doing. But perhaps she'd been wrong, and the monk had really meant to convey the horrifying idea that had first crossed her mind seeing him, and that afterwards she'd so urgently tried to refute: that a passion for rightness was never enough, that one's every attempt would be futile. That in the end the only way to protest was by simply removing oneself from the world.

Because what other way guaranteed you would never do harm? She and William had taken such pride in their careful actions, but they'd owed more to luck than they would ever have wished to admit. Mere dumb luck, the god she'd so slavishly served in her year with Pauline, all the while believing it was not luck, but righteousness, that preserved them. As she'd believed with William: that it could never have merely been luck that kept the buildings she bombed as empty as she'd meant them to be. Bombing a building that "ought" to be empty was not so different in type, if very different in scale, from bombing a village that "ought" to house only the enemy and not any civilians. And yet there were always civilians; and there never had been an employee returning, past midnight, to Jenny's targeted building for a left-behind coat. Was this because Jenny was righteous, or was it just her good luck? Good luck that kept her from being a killer while she was trying to save and redeem. If so, bad luck that killed Mr. Morton, not Juan's impure motives, as she'd wanted to think.

In the past, with William, she'd believed high intentions gave her the right to use violence; the same violence she abhorred in her government, and even among other comrades whose aims weren't sufficiently pure. But it wasn't intentions, however lofty or petty, that mattered, but how things turned out. When she shined that harsh light onto all of her acts, her bombings no longer seemed so exalted. Exalted intentions—never fatal results, perhaps just thanks to luck. No salvation, either. Only anger, infectious like fire: Jenny's anger at her nation's abuses; the patriotic American's anger at subversives like her. The anger of the young men who'd risked their lives fighting and come home to be spat on by peers. The anger of the Vietnamese—although it was hard to know, caught up in the rage and confusion at home, if the Vietnamese were most rightly described as "angry." Hard to know anything concrete about them, these people to whom she'd felt pledged. They had been an abstraction, the way Mr. Morton had been an abstraction, although now Jenny sees him with almost unbearable clarity. She sees him coming out of his store on a bright summer day and calling out to a favorite employee. Pushing his glasses up the bridge of his nose, squinting carefully back through the doors. The glasses' prescription is years out of date; Mr. Morton is trying to stretch things as far as they'll go. Wearing glasses that reveal a watery, imprecise world, so that when a pretty young blond calls his name and takes hold of his arm, he's a long time in grasping that what she holds out is a gun.

This is when Jenny returns to that day on the hill. With the hawk in the air, and Pauline strangely nervous beside her. A tremor far off, gaining strength. Jenny forgave Pauline's lie, because she thought it revealed a rare truth about Pauline's desires. And because, Jenny knew, the true bond with a comrade was what she herself craved most of all. It was what, even now, some submerged stubborn part of her feels she had gained, for a time. A perfect comradeship, unlike the farce that the cadre had lived. Unlike, even, Jenny's previous life with William, in which she had felt herself struggling to keep his approval, and always amazed at his interest in her. With Pauline she had never felt that, but that their mistakes they at least made together, and their remorse they'd at least get to share. Now she prepared to face all of it newly alone.

WHILE EACH of Pauline's pretrial hearings, and the results of her numerous psychiatric exams, and the fluctuations in her family's optimism about her case's outcome, continued to be news everywhere, Jenny was mentioned just a handful of times overall, and always fleetingly. Still, the bare appearance of her name registered in a few different places with a few different people, and in the first quiet hum of what became a significant murmur those few people contacted others of similar background to Jenny, if not similar frame of mind. The people who joined in the murmur were mostly those who'd eschewed politics all their lives—they didn't need the additional trouble. People whom outsiders called "Very quiet—they keep to themselves." People who never had quite enough money. These people, slowly but steadily, had begun finding their way to George Elson's small Oakland law office. There they'd sit in the waiting room, waiting to have a word with him. Unsought, unexpected: first one, then five, then a church congregation. They were all Filipino-, or Chinese-, or Korean-, or Japanese-Californian-American. Some were apolitical truck farmers or small-business owners. A very few were politically Left college students. One was a Japanese Unitarian minister. All had concerns and suggestions, in some cases complaints, all insisted on donating money, and now they were calling George Elson around the clock to put in their two cents' worth about what he should do to help Jenny, and so far Elson's secretary had received almost nine thousand dollars. Nine thousand dollars had walked in the door uninvited; imagine what was going to happen now, with the left-wing college students and the Unitarian minister organizing a fund-raising campaign! "How do you like that?" Elson asked her one day. "These people act like you're their sister or granddaughter. They glare daggers at me because I'm not an Asian, but at least they'll be glad if we win. Unlike you. Have you eaten a thing since the last time I saw you?" Elson nudged her lunch tray with his toe. "Would you mind saying something?"

"Thanks, George," she whispered.

"You look thin," he said sharply. "Your father's still waiting to see you. Enough of this, Jenny. Say yes."

She knew she ought to write her statement for Elson, and sometimes as she sat on her cot, knees drawn up to her chin, the dull ache in her gut like an illness she'd gotten used to, she would make idle schemes of her life: she'd let it fall into passages, odd-shaped blocks of years. Hearing but not really hearing the volleys of voices up and down the hard surfaces of neighboring cells. Jangling keys, heavy doors shrieking open and shut. Sometimes as the project slid out of her mind and she felt blank and empty she glimpsed the solution; for a moment she would see the whole structure, the determinations, the connections, the roads not taken, the junctures at which she'd done things that had later proved crucial. As if her life were a maze that a hand sometimes lifted her out of, but never for long; she would gasp at the vision, trying to take it all in, and be dropped down again.

She and Pauline were destined to pay different prices. How different it would take a long time for her to see clearly, because it would have so little to do with their charges, their trials, their legally meted out punishments. The prices they paid would not really be reflected by the legal system's strenuous efforts. Pauline would "get the book thrown at her," as the papers would crow. She would prove that there were no exceptions, she would be an exemplar, at last, through no acts of her own, of all-persons-created-equal, but she would still emerge somehow restored, made more interesting by her adventure, a reinforcer, in the end, of the privilege she'd once seemed to spurn. More than anything else Pauline would come to symbolize the immutableness of her class. She would seem to have gone through the muck and emerged from it clean. Even being convicted, as she would be, of the bank robbery, reinforced this; she was seen as being purely a victim, finally of her attorneys, who'd done such a bad job. She'd serve less than two years of her sentence before it was commuted, and the stigma of prison would not stick to her. It would be something else she'd endured, without being degraded.

Jenny, by contrast, would "get off easy"—easier, even, than she wanted to. She would be sentenced to the minimum for her participation in the selective service recruitment center bombings. After a year she would be transferred to a work-release program, as a reward for her good behavior. But she would feel, perhaps indelibly, a new shame, an impulse she'd never before exhibited to scrape and be thankful, an instinct toward obsequious accommodation, as if she were the lucky recipient of some benign power's unusually good graces; as if she were not simply serving her time but, as the phrase put it, "getting off easy." Being given fun tasks in the kitchen, being labeled as "good" in a tone of unending surprise. She felt like a token for the first time in her life. "The model minority," the one extended privileges as an example to the rest of her less worthy kin—she thought of Thomas again, Thomas who was honest and loyal and open and who perhaps all his life, if the world didn't embitter and ruin him, would be rewarded for being better than expected, for not being a "typical black." Prison made Jenny feel a member of a despised category, the more so for every time she was praised for behaving so remarkably well. And so the rift she had felt open up between herself and Pauline, which at first seemed entirely intimate, a rift between two individual persons, would come to seem increasingly social, inevitable and ordained. Pauline would "get the book thrown at her" yet somehow be redeemed, or rather shown to require no redemption, while Jenny would "get off easy," for somebody like her.

And she and Pauline would be tried, and convicted, and sentenced, only for the acts they had committed before they had met—so that their time together would be further obscured, or rather, never inscribed into the record at all. No one would be charged with Mr. Morton's murder, and this strange way in which punishments never seemed to coincide with their crimes, in which everything was so out of sync, in which there was such a freight of confusion and pain left hovering and unseen, would make it seem to Jenny, in the least welcome way, that infinite revisions were possible now. Although even at the height of their friendship Jenny somehow might have known she was destined to be so revised, to be described by Pauline as "nicer than most of the people I met—but still a terrorist I lived in fear of."

SOMETIMES, though, Jenny didn't believe any of it. She imagined Pauline, a true captive again, desperately tying her confessions, her namings, her pointings-of-fingers, end to end like bedsheets. Pauline could expel everything that she had, name Mike Sorsa, as she did, name Sandy, Joanne, Lena, Tom, Carol, Frazer, give up all the goods and she'll never touch ground. She'll never have made enough rope to effect her escape. Once again she'll have no choice but to make the best of it. She'll learn or relearn the harsh rules of her family's game. She'll rub the flint tirelessly until new lights of kinship spring up. Jenny had to acknowledge that even Pauline's stark betrayal of her had its element of cooperativeness, with Jenny. Jenny had lied, and called herself a captor, a cruel prison-keeper, for the sake of Pauline, and Pauline's response just conformed to that fiction. Even the ax falling, severing them, made a chime of harmonious lies. Pauline knew how to do what it took. She'd survive—she was built to do that, delicate as she seemed.

Jenny knew she'd survive, too. Of course she would, although with certain huge losses. The loss of William pained her most for her awareness that it was she who betrayed him, and not even consciously so much as with inattention. William continued to respond to her letters through her sentencing and her own entrance into prison, he assiduously advised her with the aid of his prison's law library, wrote her generous words of encouragement, exhortations to courage, admonitions to do this or that, treated her, in other words, as if she were one of his prison comrades, a worthy cause, a noble person brought low by complex circumstance, a pillar of strength who only needed reminders to hold herself up. The one thing she was not was his lover. Selflessly, rationally, always bearing in mind that the work of the struggle is more important than the trials of the heart, William offered her everything he could give from his own prison cell but his previous love. She received the same love he extended to all humankind. He never upbraided her for leaving him, and this rationality of his, whether a put-on or not, was another shocking loss, though she knew it was enormously selfish to want the man that you no longer loved to keep pining for you. He finally, quietly let her go, let three months pass before answering one of her letters. She knew then to stop writing back.

The loss of her freedom, of these years of her twenties, ended up being nothing next to the loss of her confidence in the choices she'd made. The world hadn't healed itself in the meantime. If anything she felt it was worse, now that there was no war to focus protest and discussion, no palpably identifiable evil to point fingers at. It was just the same fatal world as always, with its staggering inequities, which she realized now weren't exceptions to be excised but the rules of the game, the very engine that kept the thing running. She felt more powerless now than she ever did in the years of the war, and not just because the problem had grown so diffuse, but because no solutions remained. It was this ultimate disenchantment that disfigured the largest portion of her, that took up the most space. She'd carry this unsolved problem forward, into the rest of her life. As well as the knowledge—and here the injured party was her pride—that she was no better than Juan or Yvonne. No wiser, no less prone to dumb, selfish acts. In the months leading up to her trial she, too, was interrogated as to what else she knew, and she thought of the lawyer in Peekskill, and his warning to her. He'd said it would be hard not to tell what she knew. It was hard, but not because she was tempted to win herself points. She always knew she wouldn't be a stool pigeon. She still had her strict moral code. But her act of loyalty to Juan and Yvonne was, in the end, her acknowledgment to them that her moral code had failed her utterly, that she was not morally better than them but the same, flawed, her failure as great.

• • •

CAREFULLY, she tried writing. She wrote that maybe life waxed and waned, like the light, which she missed more than anything else. That maybe the hour before sunset, when a day's worth of the light's alterations seem exposed all at once, was the light's way of knowing itself, in the same way she was trying to know herself now, with her life in a forge. She remembered a book she'd once read, in which the narrator was only three different ages: he was first a child's age, around twelve, and then for chapters and chapters he remained twenty-two, before finally, suddenly being forty. She thought it made sense for herself; she could only sporadically seize on the course of her life. She could only await the rare glimpse of its change in direction. Decades from now she would remember this time in the most broken-up, episodic, disjointed way, but the great change taking form would be clear, like a superimposition of a cell, dividing and dividing, eventually swallowing all that lay near it. While the change was occurring she'd hang between two far-flung places, as if on a wire. Sitting in her cell, and writing, amazed she could render herself into words.

There were so many things about herself that she had never told Pauline, lost continents of her life, or simply odd moments, resonances, connections, in which she found herself most fully for the fact that she somehow retained them. Their intimacy, from the moment it really began, had seemed so complete that she supposed it would have been an aspersion, a tremor of doubt, if either had begun to bring forward such artifacts. They spoke intensely and exhaustively within the frame of their short time together, about the kidnapping and the cadre, about Juan and Yvonne and Tom Milner and Sandy and Frazer, about power for women and the rent that they owed and the news in the paper that morning—and even about William—but they never carefully tutored each other in their own histories. There'd been the sense that all that was assumed, that each knew the whole of the other one's past. To suggest otherwise would have shattered their union somehow.

And then after they were apart, for a time she had felt in the opposite way: that there was nothing she shouldn't have said, and that a failure of hers in conveying herself must explain why their friendship had ended. That had still been the tail end of longing; all the self-immolations of heartbreak are their own forms of love. Perhaps this was still why she finally filled up the notepads: for Pauline, not herself. But in the process she slowly recovered; tunneling so long she came back aboveground a vast distance from where she'd last been. She understood now that Pauline had realized her adventure was over. Pauline knew that her place in the world was assured—she need only resolve to accept it. And she had, out of fear, or resignation, or hard pragmatism, or perhaps just because, for them both, youth had come to an end. Old enough to feel rage, young enough to indulge it completely!—they hadn't had children or aged, ailing parents, none of the minor responsibilities of the heart, so insignificant when compared to the woes of the world. Even if Jenny was wrong about Pauline—even if Pauline had not become wise but had just lost her nerve—Jenny knew that her own youth was done.

Her trial began a few months after Pauline's, was short and disregarded by the press. But every day the courtroom was full of the Japanese and Filipino and Korean and Chinese faces, the tight-knit people her father had always avoided. They clustered resolutely around him, invited him to eat in their homes, brought him casseroles when he demurred. They wore buttons that simply said JENNY. It was the tireless support of these people—she did nothing to earn or retain it, she simply received it dumbstruck, as she would any miracle—which the judge cited as his reason for sentencing her to the minimum. Not any unusual worth of her own.

Toward the end of this time, though she knew it was an awful cliché, Pauline came to her in a dream. In the dream Pauline read Jenny's notepads—a pen in her mouth, one skinny leg folded beneath her. Jenny had given the notepads to Pauline as if nothing were more natural, and it was only after a long peaceful silence, Pauline reading, Jenny watching her read, that it occurred to her what she had done. She wondered urgently how she could take back the notepads, before Pauline understood that what she was reading was all about her. That Jenny's unedited thinking of her stomped and thundered across every page. Jenny's heart pounded, her palms sweated, she saw Pauline calmly reading, turning the page back, turning the next back, every once in a while deftly flipping all the turned-over pages beneath the notepad's cardboard backing the way she deftly rearranged her lengthening hair when it slipped free of her ears, as it did with a slow regularity. Jenny could just sidle over and slide the whole pile of notepads out from under Pauline, and surely Pauline wouldn't notice. It was a dream, after all. What had she said: that she loved her? Loathed her? Dreamed of her, even during this moment? That she'd surrendered her whole self somehow, the one thing she'd sworn not to do. And then, as she was expecting realization and anger, Pauline's face finally turning to her hard with accusation, Pauline looked up and said, mildly puzzled, "Jenny, why do you always say 'money'? We never called it that, don't you remember? We always called money 'bread.' That's the word that we used."

HOME AGAIN in Berkeley, two years later, she was sometimes surprised to find herself missing the East Coast: its lushness, its quiet. Though she still associated it with a degraded past self, a self that craved irresponsible freedom. She could be guilty, she knew, of victimizing herself with her own politics—her politics were all she had to justify the wrong turns and lost time, and so she cherished them, even when they made more difficult the justification of herself. Or rather, the justification of her intense, unimportant desires, like the desire to have a nice room. She was afraid to want things for herself. She didn't think she deserved them.

But in time, she answered a roommate-wanted ad for a house in Berkeley, and in the house found her room, though it wasn't yet hers, or even really a room. It was the dining room, a three-sided space off the kitchen with a giant bay window. But she fell hard for that window, with its view of the rosemary plant in the yard, and beyond it, the lime tree. The room they'd meant her to have was a real bedroom, upstairs, with four walls and a door, but it was also dark, under the eaves, and with a view of the roof of the neighboring house. Nothing green. Something in her was determined to have that bay window. Something in her, then, was ready to want things again. Humbly, but distinctly. Already she had been thinking of how she would remember this time of her life. She knew it was a temporary station; every station is, but some convey this feeling powerfully from the start. The members of the house had seen her face, her lingering in the dining room at the bay window, her cursory glance at the bedroom. They liked sitting in that dining room together, drinking tea or wine around the big wooden table. But after she left they had a house meeting and voted—they wanted her in. She had a modest aura of heroism about her she would have tried to snuff out if she'd glimpsed it herself. The members of the house were all younger than her—she was now twenty-nine, and feeling within herself an almost completed transition. She'd been thinking, with bemusement but routinely, of how much she'd like to have a child. Secretly saw herself, now, as a person accumulating the knowledge and ability to be the best of the world to a child. She never thought of romance, or marriage, or family life, only of herself as a companion to a child. Perhaps this wasn't true leaning toward motherhood—perhaps those other things, those amusingly traditional things, would turn out to be crucial. But she didn't think so. And so she had the idea, as she chose her place for the moment, that this was mere preparation. She would spend a little more time with herself, and then the child, she had the strange faith, would come. On its own, she imagined.

This calm must have shown in her face, and been attractive to the young people in the house—the twenty-one and twenty-three-year-olds, all young graduate students or searchers. All of them, she imagined, the sort of people who had they been born just a few years sooner would have met the world at a sharply different angle, done things with no hesitation that now, in their remarkably altered world, would seem wild, laborious, frightening. They were the same people, Mike Sorsas and Sandys and Toms. Even a Pauline of a sort, a beautiful, cocky girl from Maine, slumming a while in California. But theirs was a different world; living communally, buying their staples in brown paper bags, pushing the compost around with a hoe, were their forms of resistance. They called her at her father's and told her they wanted her to live with them, in the dining room nook—they'd help make a partition. "We just could see you in that space, and we couldn't really see you in the other one," their spokesperson, Jeremy, told her. "We thought we'd make the upstairs room into a sort of library. You know, a quiet reading place where we can hang out, and not be lying in our beds? Everybody liked that idea." She thanked him and said yes, she would come.

IT WAS THROUGH those housemates that she got a job at a juice bar—another collective, but one with a surprising sense of permanence. She found that she had desperately missed regular work. She liked going to a place separate from her home, with a small social order distinct from that of her home, and working, with her hands, and roving idly in her mind. Of course the work wasn't of staggering significance, but she liked the earthiness of it, the elemental connotations. Taking fruits of the earth and reducing them to bright, fragrant liquid. The juice bar was a little bit of a scene, young—even younger than her house—and ebullient, carefree, pleasantly silly. Sometimes, she could tell that the person buying juice from her knew who she was, thought of her as a minor celebrity, had come to see her. A shyness in their manner, that asked to be noticed. A certain wry or hopeful smile when they met her eye, as if to telegraph that they knew her, understood her, were with her. She neither shrugged off nor acknowledged these people—she simply smiled her usual smile, asked her usual questions, made the usual juice. Her minor celebrity had gained her, she noticed, a new and different sort of estrangement—her very conspicuousness meant that strangers were timid with her, and that she could, in playing dumb, repel them easily. She never let on that she knew that they knew. They would go away slowly, glance back quickly. She pretended she wasn't looking for anyone in particular, but she did mark certain private watersheds, and view the world differently after she had. William had finally gotten parole; even if he did not know she had been paroled too, he would have remembered her original release date. When this passed she waited, not sure if with hope or with dread, but he never came. When Pauline was released Jenny half expected her to come ducking through the door, although she never would. This didn't mean Jenny saw it less clearly. Pauline would use her slouchy walk but she wouldn't be able to hide the half-cowed, half-arrogant habit of looking all around her to ensure she hadn't—or had—been noticed. She would be wearing jeans, a sweatshirt, a sunhat, big shades. Flat, limp canvas sneakers. That remarkably alluring sloppiness of the very, very rich. Her long hair in a rubberband.

In the end it was Frazer who came, the last person she had ever imagined would walk through that door. She was in the middle of an order, and so he was greeted by her co-worker and asked for his order. He stared at the juice list a little belligerently, to convey that juice was not what he'd come for, and finally chose carrot and ginger. Because carrot took so long, she was free before his order was filled, and she came down the counter and was surprised when he leaned across it, pulled her toward him, and kissed her. "This is your unlucky day," he said. "A little bird told me I'd find you here."

"How did it know?" she asked, still feeling his kiss, like a brand, on her mouth.

Frazer shrugged. "Little birds hear these things. But it hadn't seen you. You don't want to see anybody, I guess."

"No. To be honest, I don't. But I'm happy you came."

He smiled, embarrassed. He cast about—happily, she could tell—for some good light rejoinder. Finally he seemed to give up, and instead asked, earnestly, "Are you happy, in general?"

She looked at him with her head cocked, surprised. It wasn't his kind of question.

"I am," she said. "Are you?"

"I—no, not really. Me and Carol are getting divorced. But what the fuck. I didn't come here to talk about me, if you can believe that. I just wanted to see how you were."

"Good. I really am."

"I'm glad," he said.

They looked at each other a long time, unstintingly, across the counter. Her co-worker came and gave him his carrot and ginger, and he thanked her and paid and looked at Jenny again, and then somehow their gazing tipped over the line into too great, too confusing intensity, and they both blushed at once. She didn't know why—was this one of those moments of dumb truth Frazer used to expound on? He would say, The one thing you must do, the one thing that if you do it it'll always keep you safe, is listen to your body. Know what it's saying. Follow its dictates. Hers was hot, teeming, pleased in some way. Exact message unclear.

"I'll see you," Frazer said, and across the counter they embraced again, awkwardly, the width of wood between them. And then, as she watched, he was gone.

IT WASN'T QUITE true that she never saw Pauline again. One spring evening, curled up on the couch with her dinner and watching the news, Jenny learned that Pauline had been married. The groom was a member of the around-the-clock security detail her parents had hired for her when she got out of prison. On Jenny's small, snowy TV, Pauline emerged from a great limestone church, an unrecognizable girl in a huge puff of gauze. Then she ran down the steps to a car, with her skirts in her fists. Ran, as if the girl she'd once been still lurked there, in the crowds of reporters. Or as if the girl that she had to be now still might leave her behind.

Celebrity was strange, Jenny thought. It provoked the delusion that you were near to a person, but it was not like a person at all.

It was more like a movie, diffuse streams of light briefly caught on a screen. Should the actual person have ever appeared in your life—small and solid and uneasily making her way to her seat, casting a blot on the image behind her but otherwise coinciding with it not at all—that other image could not be sustained. She was sure she remembered sitting with Pauline on their porch every evening at dusk, wondering why the birds surged from their roosts and then settled again and then surged, and then settled—were they trying to get comfortable?—but she couldn't align this real time in her life with the person whose image she saw. She was full of other ghosts, of the oval-shaped track that they wore in the pasture, and the sound of Juan's gun riding up on the wind, and the blood of the man that they killed, on the seat of the Bug. A worn patch and a noise and a trace, all alive in her mind. It was only Pauline that had long disappeared.

That was the same spring that Jenny had bought her own car. It was surprisingly wonderful, driving legitimately. Or at least, driving with her own registration and license, if not within the speed limit. One Saturday morning she drove out to Stockton, speeding, and arriving there felt the sweet, cinematic, slightly grandiose sensation of returning to her childhood home in a fast-moving car and sunglasses. Then as always the house and greenhouse made her wince when she caught sight of them. They probably hadn't been painted since she was a child. Lately she'd been telling her father he ought to retire. "Yeah right," he would say. "Because you'll take such good care of me. I can live in your commune and eat your steamed tofu. No thanks."

To her surprise he was already dressed when she got there. Sitting on the small bench outside the front door, hands in his lap, as if it weren't his own home and he were awaiting the owner. He had a knit watch cap pulled over his ears and a scarf around his neck, although it wasn't cold, and his neck was also circled by a bandanna. When she got out of the car he held another bandanna out to her, but didn't get up. She could see that the house and greenhouse were all locked. His was a state of uncharacteristic readiness. She'd told him she was coming at seven in the morning because she'd expected she wouldn't get him into the car before eight. "I don't want to do this," he announced, waving the bandanna toward her with irritation. She took it from him.

"What is this for?"

"For putting over your face when the sand blows around. It'll fill up your ears, too. You don't have a hat? This is the most miserable place in the world you're dragging me to. I don't want to do this."

"Come on," she said.

"I don't want to do this," her father repeated, standing up and getting into her car. As they headed back down to 120 he added, "There's supposed to be blizzards up in the Sierras. They might close 108. And the Yosemite road isn't open this early in the season. We won't get across."

"Calm down," she said. "It's April."

"Blizzards happen up there in July. Didn't you call the Weather Service? You should have called to make sure it's still on. It's a crazy time of year to go out there. If it's not rain it's wind. Then sand fills up your ears."

"It's on," she said. "If it's not we'll turn around and come back."

At Twain Harte they left the floor of the valley and began climbing into the mountains. The pine forest rose on either side of them like a dusky cathedral; she remembered the days at the farmhouse, lying in the cistern on the hillside with her head back, staring up at the trees. No, those trees had been nothing like these. There was no mistaking the East for the West. The air had cooled swiftly around them, as if there were water nearby, though it was only the vault of the woods. The road was narrow now, and dark gray from a recent shower, but she didn't see snow. In Dardanelle, at the foot of the pass, she stopped into a log-cabin lodge like a toy between columnar trees and asked about the weather. "All clear," the man said. They did the pass at a crawl anyway, her father staring wordlessly out the window, at the flanks of the mountains above them, and then into the spume of the fast-moving river that flowed for a while beside them. All these years, she thought, living an hour away from these almighty mountains. He had only seen them a few times, and like this, from a car. And he loved mountains; when they'd arrived in Japan he had only been comfortable there, in the dense mountains outside their town.

Descending out of the pass again they came to 395 and then it was a more regular drive through deep forest, with the knowledge of the great mass to the west but not so much of a lump in the throat from inexplicable sadness. "You hungry?" she said. "I have sandwiches."

"I thought there's food there."

"There is, there's going to be burgers on the hibachi. I just thought you might be hungry now."

"*Burgers*." His face darkened and he sat back in his seat abruptly, snapping the lever underneath to make it scoot back as far as it went, and at the same time swinging his right ankle up onto his left knee. This was a familiar expression of disgust, but she wasn't sure if she'd ever seen it in a car—it most often occurred at the table. He would push himself back and assume that remote, haughty posture. She realized that she had never seen it performed in a car because she'd never been the driver, and he the passenger, before. "They think this is some kind of cookout?" he spat. "So we'll all sit around and eat *burgers*?"

"So have a sandwich," she said rather shortly.

"*Sand*wich. It'll be a goddamn *sand*burger."

"Ha ha," she said, and got silence in reply.

South of Bishop they were suddenly driving through desert; as with all such amazing transitions, she could not understand when it happened, when the earth went from black and dark green and snow-white to this pondwater brown. The forest was gone and now the nude brown hills dotted with sagebrush rolled into the distance, to meet the white wall of the mountains, still the Sierras, exposed to their very spine now, and continuing their march to the south. The Owens River came to accompany the road on their other side and she felt that they'd left California and gone to some far-flung frontier, or perhaps to the past. "My God," said her father, uncrossing his legs. "It all looks exactly the same."

"Remember stuff?"

"Don't ask me to." But after a few minutes he said, as the endless dun hills and the endless sagebrush and the distant white wall unscrolled slowly beside them, "A landscape like this, it takes a rigorous mind to appreciate. There's a certain austerity to it. Most people find this too lonely. These ugly hills, how tall do you think they are?"

"I can't tell. They seem like they might be little humps, or big enough to be small mountains. I'm having trouble judging how far the Sierras are, too."

"They're close. Close. At night out here, you can feel the air coming off them. Like out of a freezer. You're having trouble judging the height of these hills because there's nothing on them to give you a sense of scale. That's what's so amazing. They're only a few hundred feet at the most. *But*—" He paused dramatically. "But, when you climb one of them, it's just like you're up on a mountain. Why?"

"Visibility," she answered.

"Exactly. It goes on forever."

"So you did have an all right time out here," she said, ruining it. She was sorry the minute she'd said such a facile thing.

"An *all right* time? They let us go hiking *one time*, under guard. With goddamn rifles pointed at us."

After that, he was silent the rest of the way.

Her first glimpse of it was as a strange living patch in the desert, a tattered green quilt of grasses and weeds. She knew this was because they had diverted water here to grow crops for the camp. There were supposed to be fruit trees still alive on the site. The road had swung west and now they were so near the Sierras again, to their sudden ascent from the level, to their startling cut-diamondness, she felt gripped by a weird, thrilling fear. A magnificent wall for an abandoned and overgrown prison. A dirt track led off 395 and as she turned she saw a small sign banged into the weeds that said MANZANAR REUNION, STRAIGHT AHEAD, but there was no need for the sign. Even from here they could see, perhaps one mile distant and that much closer to the upsurge of mountains, a scattering of cars parked at all kinds of angles on the scrub-covered ground, and the small forms of people moving purposefully on the floor of the desert beneath the vast peaks, setting up a crude stage, unfolding long portable tables for food, hunting big rocks to weigh everything down. They bumped slowly along the dirt track and pulled up next to an old school bus. *MANZANAR OR BUST!* had been spray-painted onto the back. When Jenny turned off the engine they heard hammers *tocking* briskly, their noise seeming to echo for miles. Besides that the wind, and the voices it snatched. The earth was the color of concrete dust; pale gray, and grainy. The wind lifted it up by the handful and rained it back down. She pulled the bandanna out of her pocket and tied it in readiness around her neck, as her father had. "Thanks for this," she said, but he was already getting out of the car and gazing around him.

A young man passed them, clutching a taiko drum like a beer keg to his chest. "Welcome!" he called. "We're just now setting up. Give a hand if you want, or just dig the cool view." But her father seemed not to have seen the young man—the young man who was about the same age he had been, she realized, when he was brought forcibly to this place.

"Hey," her father said. "I *lived* here."

"I know," she said.

"Let's go help them set up." He turned and strode off.

In a moment, she followed.